ADVENTURES OF

EOVAAI

PRINCESS OF IJAVEO

ADVENTURES OF

EOVAAI

PRINCESS OF IJAVEO

A PRE-ADAMITICAL HISTORY

Eliza Haywood

edited by Earla Wilputte

broadview literary texts

Canadian Cataloguing in Publication Data

Haywood, Eliza, 1693?-1756
    Adventures of Eovaai, princess of Ijaveo

(Broadview literary texts)
Includes bibliographical references.
ISBN 1-55111-197-7

I. Wilputte, Earla Arden, 1959-   . II. Title.   III. Series.

PR3506.H94A64 1998   823'.5   C98-932524-5

Broadview Press Ltd., is an independent, international publishing house, incorpo-
rated in 1985.

North America:
P.O. Box 1243, Peterborough, Ontario, Canada K9J 7H5
3576 California Road, Orchard Park, NY 14127
TEL: (705) 743-8990; FAX: (705) 743-8353;
E-MAIL: 75322.44@compuserve.com

United Kingdom:
Turpin Distribution Services Ltd.,
Blackhorse Rd., Letchworth, Hertfordshire SG6 1HN
TEL: (1462) 672555; FAX (1462) 480947; E-MAIL: turpin@rsc.org

Australia:
St. Clair Press, P.O. Box 287, Rozelle, NSW 2039
TEL: (02) 818-1942; FAX: (02) 418-1923

www.broadviewpress.com

Broadview Press gratefully acknowledges the financial support of the Book
Publishing Industry Development Program, Ministry of Canadian Heritage,
Government of Canada.

Broadview Press is grateful to Professor Eugene Benson for advice on
editorial matters for the Broadview Literary Texts series.

Text design and composition by George Kirkpatrick

PRINTED IN CANADA

Contents

Acknowledgements

I wish to express my gratitude to the St. Francis Xavier University Council for Research for financial assistance in preparing this edition; and to the several libraries whose materials I used: the Thomas Fisher Rare Books Library and Robarts Research Library of the University of Toronto; the Mills Memorial Library of McMaster University, Hamilton; and the D.B. Weldon Library of the University of Western Ontario, London. I would also like to thank Rachel Anderson, Marie Gillis, Monica MacKinnon, and Donna White who proved invaluable for their technical assistance. Juliette Merritt was inspirational in her dedication to Haywood, in offering encouragement and solace, as well as helping in her tireless xeroxing and tracking down of source material. I thank Barbara Conolly, Risa Kawchuk, and Don LePan at Broadview Press for all of their help and enthusiasm. As always, I would like to remind Jamie Powell how much he is loved and how his patience is appreciated. I dedicate this edition of *Adventures of Eovaai* to our daughters, Arden and Logan.

Introduction

Eliza Haywood's *Adventures of Eovaai* (pronounced EE-oh-VAH-ee) is a wild blend of genres that denies easy categorization. A political satire of Sir Robert Walpole, a woman's romance, imaginary voyage, oriental fantasy, and erotic novel, *Eovaai* is an intelligent and original investigation of eighteenth-century political philosophies, sexual politics, and Art. Chronologically situated between the amatory novels of her early career and her later domestic novels, *Eovaai* manifests Haywood's development as an author, and her awareness and employment of contemporary literary trends.

Always with an eye to the literary marketplace, Haywood utilizes scandal, slander, and sex to expose Walpole's perceived moral and political vices as so many of her contemporaries did; however, Haywood is also intrigued by the idea of how Truth is represented and manipulated by politicians, authors, and lovers to a nation, readers, and women. To this end, *Eovaai*'s structure is particularly compelling for its reflexivity and its drawing attention to its own artificiality. Readers are not permitted to forget that they are reading a story or that it has been wilfully constructed by an author with a particular agenda who must be challenged by a perceptive audience that will not unquestioningly accept the illusions or opinions of others. The argumentative intrusions by the fictional Author, Translator, Commentators, and Historian demand that readers formulate their own conclusions on the story's action, and, by extension, eighteenth-century society and politics. Haywood interweaves political and amatory storylines, presents an unstable mixture of generic forms, and employs intrusive textual machinery to help represent the chaotic activity of the political, sexual, and literary world she satirizes.

The main story of *Eovaai* is fairy-tale like in its simplicity. Princess Eovaai is a beautiful fifteen-year-old girl who naturally possesses all of the admired accomplishments of young ladies – singing, dancing, music – and who was educated in the virtues of the mind. Her father was careful that Eovaai should not become proud of her physical beauty and so "he suffer'd her to converse but little with her *own Sex*, and strictly forbad those of the *other*, to mention Beauty, or any

Endowment of the *Body*, as things deserving Praise" (53). In grooming her for the throne, Eovaai's father teaches her the values of liberty in words that echo John Locke's philosophy of a balanced government:

> The greatest Glory of a Monarch was the Liberty of the People, his most valuable Treasures in *their* crowded Coffers, and his securest Guard in their *sincere Affection*. ... Remember, you are no less bound by *Laws*, than the meanest of your Subjects; and that even *they* have a *Right* to call you to account for any Violation of them: – You must not imagine, that it is meerly for your *own Ease* you are seated on a Throne; no, it is for the *Good* of the Multitudes beneath you; and when you cease to study *that*, you cease to have any *Claim* to their *Obedience* (53).

On his deathbed, Eovaai's father gives her a jewel which will protect her person and her reign from evil. She loses it, is overthrown, and Ijaveo is embroiled in a civil war: "the crystal Rivers received another Colour tinctur'd with human Gore: The Streets were so encumber'd with the Dead, the Living had no room to pass" (60).

Eovaai is magically transported to the land of Hypotofa by the evil yet handsome magician Ochihatou (Sir Robert Walpole) who plans to seduce and marry the princess in order to gain her throne and extend his power. A protective genii gives Eovaai a magic telescope which reveals to the princess that Ochihatou is really "crooked, deformed, distorted in every Limb and Feature, but also encompassed with a thousand hideous Forms, which sat upon his Shoulders, clung round his Hands, his Legs, and seem'd to dictate all his Words and Gestures" (94). Repulsed by Ochihatou's real appearance but reluctant to give up his recent appeal to her sensuality and her attraction to absolute power, Eovaai is convinced that she must learn "to distinguish the Hypocrite from the Saint, the Betrayer of his Country from the Patriot, the Fool from the Politician, ... the Foe from the pretended Friend" (94-5). It is a lesson for women as well as a governed people.

With the aid of the genii, Eovaai escapes Ochihatou's palace and meets Hypotofan Patriots who educate her about Republicanism. Just as she was seduced to believe Ochihatou's justifications for absolute power and pleasure, Eovaai is so pleased with the arguments of the Republican "that she resolved, if she was ever happy enough to regain her Crown, she wou'd make [Republican Principles] Part of the Constitution; and to live in such a manner herself, as should render the Expences of Regal State no way oppressive to the People" (118). But her return to Ijaveo is hampered when she is kidnapped by Ochihatou's henchmen and threatened with rape by the magician. Eovaai does manage to break Ochihatou's magic wand – his phallic source of power – but he gains the advantage. Her screams bring a stranger who rescues her, and the prime minister dashes his own brains out against a tree.

The stranger is discovered to be Prince Adelhu, heir apparent of Hypotofa, whom Ochihatou had earlier plotted to have murdered. Adelhu relates his history to Eovaai, telling her that he has restored peace to Ijaveo and has been given a jewel by a genii who informed him that he must save himself for the woman who possesses its case. Eovaai presents him with the case into which the jewel fits, and when Adelhu restores the stone to it, the jewel becomes securely cemented within it. Adelhu and Eovaai fall in love and marry, uniting their hearts and their kingdoms, to live happily ever after.

Interwoven into this main plot of *Eovaai* are the histories of Yximilla, an unfortunate princess forced into an arranged marriage for political reasons, and Atamadoul, a woman transformed into a monkey for her sin of loving Ochihatou when she was past her prime. The novel is further enhanced by the footnotes of various fictional editors, translators and commentators – textual machinery that Haywood adopted for her own political and feminist purposes from the likes of Alexander Pope's *Dunciad* (1728) and Henry Fielding's *Tragedy of Tragedies; or, The Life and Death of Tom Thumb the Great* (1731).

The *Adventures of Eovaai, Princess of Ijaveo* is an exciting story of a woman who experiences political and sexual awareness and is still allowed a happy ending. Such a conclusion is unrealistic and Eliza Haywood knows that; however, she also feels that it is possible to make it real by challenging the authorities and their empty rhetoric.

Historical Background

When Eliza Haywood's *Adventures of Eovaai* appeared anonymously in 1736, it joined an ever-increasing body of popular fiction satirizing Sir Robert Walpole, the leading minister of the Whig government from 1721 to 1742. This literary upsurge, which exposed and opposed the perceived political and moral corruption of the most famous (even infamous) figure of the age, reflected a national obsession with Walpole and his policies, and made of him a monster of mythological proportion.

Britain had undergone serious political and philosophical upheavals in the half century before *Eovaai's* appearance. Precipitating many of the changes was the Glorious Revolution of 1688, when the British people exercised their constitutional right to liberty by refusing to allow King James II, a Catholic, to remain on the throne.

James Stuart came to the throne in 1685, upon the death of his brother, Charles II. During his short reign, it became evident that James would attempt to give Catholics more power in government while he became more intolerant of Church of England men. His pro-French policies and his push toward more overt Catholicism made his government nervous. When James's son was born in 1688, British anxiety over the King's papishness reached its zenith. Rumours spread that the new heir was an imposter who had been slipped into the Queen's bed in a warming pan. British subjects who had tolerated a Catholic monarch without a son, now reacted against him. Parliament invited the King's son-in-law, William of Orange, husband of Mary Stuart, to England. When William landed in Torbay in early November 1688 with an invasion force, James fled to France. Parliament, proclaiming that the King had abandoned the throne, offered the crown to William who ruled until his death in 1702.

The subsequent constitutional changes between 1688 and 1701 established a parliamentary monarchy, implemented the Triennial Act (1694) which made it necessary to hold elections at least every three years, and debarred Catholics from the British throne. The 1689 Bill of Rights ratified the principle of constitutional government by the consent of the people, and limited the power of the Crown so that it was dependent on the Parliament. It also emphasized the importance of the individual. According to the political philosophy of John Locke, the monarch held his power in trust in order to serve the interests of the people. If he grossly abused his power to the point that he endangered the liberties of his subjects, the people had the right to resist him. In a mixed government of monarchy, aristocracy, and democracy, the civil liberties of the subject were still dependent upon the King, Lords, and Commons; however, the system of checks and balances seemed to offer an equilibrium of power.

King Louis XIV of France refused to recognize William III, and war between Britain and France followed from 1689 to 1697 and again in 1702 to 1713. "Jacobites," supporters of the Catholic Stuart King James II, his son James Francis Edward, and grandson Charles Edward Stuart (Bonnie Prince Charlie) threatened uprisings in England and Scotland. In 1715 and again in 1745 there were violent Jacobite rebellions. The British government was particularly tense during the reign of Queen Anne (1702-14) as the Queen seemed sympathetic to her brother's cause, and the Tories, particularly Lord Bolingbroke, kept up communications with the French court and the exiled Pretender (as James Francis Edward came to be known). Fearing the overthrow of the House of Hanover – the successors to the British throne after the death of Queen Anne – the government spent a fortune to spy on known and suspected Jacobites, as well as to support standing armies in case of civil war in Britain or an attack by France.

Robert Walpole joined the Whig ministry in 1720, and by 1721 was the First Lord of the Treasury. He had the favour and support of the two kings under whom he served – George I (1714-27) and George II (1727-60) – and he was closely allied to Queen Caroline, consort of George II. Walpole was "sole and prime minister" for over twenty years, yet, due to the Whigs' Septennial Act of 1716, he stood for election only three times in his long career. The passing of the Septennial Act had demonstrated the Whigs' contempt for the political ideal of government by consent of the people set out in the constitution by deliberately restricting the democratic process to every seven years. The Whigs (mostly City and Court politicians) believed that "Authority" was the key to administration and that the constitution could be abused in order to maintain power.

Walpole was an astute statesman, building up Britain's economic stability and prosperity and managing peace through such foreign policies as the Treaty of Seville (1729) and the Treaty of Vienna (1731), which effectively settled Austro-Spanish relations which had threatened war in Europe for over a decade; however, a strong opposition arose against him and his ministry. His taxes (especially for maintaining the standing armies); his proposed Excise Bill of 1733; his reputation for bribery, patronage, and nepotism; his personal extravagance and proclivity for mistresses; his lack of financial support for culture and the arts – all led him to become a notorious symbol of the corruption and moral decay of Britain.

Although there was no organized opposition party, Henry St. John, Viscount Bolingbroke, and his followers, known as the Patriots, did stand up against Walpole and his ministry in Parliament and in the press. Walpole had had Bolingbroke impeached from his position as Secretary of State in 1715 on the charge of high treason for plotting James's restoration. Bolingbroke had exiled himself to France until 1723 when his conviction was revoked; however, Walpole was instrumental in barring him for life from his seat in the House of Lords. Upon his return to England, Bolingbroke joined with disaffected Whig William Pulteney to write, theorize, and plan strategies to oppose the Whigs and specifically Walpole. The *Craftsman*, a periodical which Bolingbroke and Pulteney created, repeatedly voiced the Patriots' principles of liberty and virtue as the foundations of good government, while looking to a patriot king to lead through example. The Patriots (mostly Country independents) represented the humanist tradition, "Liberty" (as opposed to the City's "Authority"), and the ancient constitution. As J.G.A. Pocock has pointed out, the Country ideology sought to defend Virtue against Change which was represented in such corruptions as "trading empire, standing armies, and credit" (1975, 458).[1] Corruption was seen "in terms of a chaos of appetites, productive of dependence and loss of personal autonomy [through the system of bribery and patronage], flourishing in a world of rapid and irrational change" (Pocock 1975, 486). Robert Walpole easily became a symbol for this corruption as the Court ideology

---

1. Parenthetical citations refer to works listed in the Bibliography.

stressed credit and personal satisfaction and ~~found no place in govern-~~ ~~ment for principles of personal virtue or civic morality.~~ The republican ideology required the individual citizen to act responsibly by "pit[ting] his virtue against fortune as a condition of his political being. Virtue was the principle of republics" (Pocock 1975, 349). ~~Self-~~ ~~interest~~ was portrayed as the guiding principle of Walpole's government.

As the 1730s began to unfold, it became apparent to those opposing Walpole and his government that the minister was intent on expanding the range of products exempted from customs duties. This practice was called ~~excise,~~ and it had been experimented with in 1724 when tea, chocolate, and cocoa were taxed only when they were bought to be sold within Britain. For Walpole, the advantages of excise were that customs procedures were simplified, products could be re-exported from London more easily, smuggling and fraud were lessened, and the yield from excise taxes increased. The public feared a general excise, and in 1732 Walpole admitted that he would excise specific luxury items, namely tobacco and wine. The press immediately opened attack. "[S]uch a tax would destroy British liberty.... [E]xcise destroys trade, destroys liberty, breeds intolerance, brutality, despotism, poverty.... The additional excise officers appointed by the King would add vastly to Crown patronage and subvert the Constitution" (Plumb 1960, 250-1). Merchants feared an army of excise officers who would have the power to search their businesses and homes for illegal goods while harassing their families and customers. The press, through essays, editorials, broadsheets, and ballads, helped to publicize these fears as well as magnify them.

Although King George II and Caroline heartily backed the Excise Bill to the point that George regarded opposition to it as almost treasonous, Walpole could not garner enough support for it in the House of Commons. Lord Hervey recorded the event of Walpole's decision on April 10, 1733 to withdraw his unpopular bill:

> After supper, when the servants were gone, Sir Robert opened his intentions with a sort of unpleased smile, and saying "This dance it will no farther go, and to-morrow I intent [sic] to sound a retreat; the turn my friends will take will be to declare

they have not altered their opinion of the proposition, but that the clamour and the spirit that has been raised makes it necessary to give way, and that what they now do is not owning what they have done to be wrong, but receding for prudential reasons from what they still think as right as ever" (cited in Plumb 1960, 269).

Walpole was not a man to back down; however, knowing that his Excise Bill would be defeated should he proceed, he chose to "postpone" the vote on it. Everyone knew, though, that it would not reappear after it was withdrawn on April 11. Celebrations in London were riotous: mobs besieged Parliament in an attempt to harass the prime minister who had to hide in coffee houses and doorways to make his escape, while his son Edward and Lord Hervey received bruises as they accompanied him; Walpole and Queen Caroline were burned in effigy in the streets of London; and crowds danced around bonfires. Lord Bolingbroke, the Patriots, and the popular press were successful in defeating what they touted as the Whig government's proposed oppression and tyranny of the British people.

But in the election of 1734 Walpole won, remaining in power for another seven years. Walpole's dance did continue. The opposition suffered fragmentation, and Bolingbroke, disillusioned with politics, left England for France in 1735, not to return until after Walpole's 1742 resignation.

Literary Background

The figure of Sir Robert Walpole appears with great regularity in the literature from the 1720s to the 1740s in a number of incarnations. Known by numerous nicknames – "Bob, the Poet's Foe," which Jonathan Swift dubbed him for his antagonism against men of letters; "Brazen Face," because it was said he was incapable of blushing over his corruptions; "the Great Man"; "Screen-Master General," for protecting or screening his friends from parliamentary enquiries; "Sir Blue-String," referring to his pride in his Garter star and ribbon – he could also be recognized variously as "magician, gamester, quack doctor, puppeteer, and stage-manager" in many works (Mack 131).

Greatly suspicious of intellectuals and authors, Walpole would not tolerate criticism of himself or his ministry and often attempted to suppress or punish explicit fault-finding and censure. The threat of prosecution for libel was a serious one, leading the opposition press to employ many inventive, witty forms such as allegory, imaginary voyages, visions, myths, and oriental fantasies to attack the prime minister and his government. Satire was their primary weapon: to diminish Walpole by making him and the court Whigs ridiculous and evoking toward them attitudes of amusement, contempt, indignation, and scorn.

In his study, *Walpole and the Wits*, Bertrand A. Goldgar points out that satire came to be identified almost exclusively with the Opposition, while panegyric was associated with the courtiers and hacks who defended the ministry (20). Indeed, satire of Walpole and the court became so rampant that the *Craftsman*, tongue-in-cheek, complained that *nothing* could be interpreted as *not* satirical of the government:

> It hath lately been asserted very roundly *that there is not a* Virtue *mentioned in one of our antient Kings with any other View than to insinuate that it hath* no Parallel at present; *nor any* Vice *mention'd, but to hint that there is* a Parallel at present.
>
> ...If you endeavour to recommend the *Virtues* of a *good Prince*, such as *Edward the third*, it may be represented that your Design was to shew that it hath *no Parallel at present*. If you think proper to expose the *Vices* of a *bad Prince*, such as *Richard the second*, by shewing the Consequences of them, it may be said that you do it with an Intention of hinting that there *is a Parallel at present*; so that whether there is a *Parallel*, or there is *no Parallel*, you may be prosecuted for a *Libeller* (quoted in Mack 136).

When Henry St. John, Viscount Bolingbroke, and William Pulteney joined forces in 1726 to oppose Walpole, they attracted a number of talented writers who had been denied patronage by the government, writers of such calibre as Jonathan Swift, Alexander Pope, John Gay, and Henry Fielding. While the Scriblerus Club — Pope, Swift, Gay, John Arbuthnot, Bolingbroke, Thomas Parnell, and the Earl of Oxford – would have made a formidable literary assault on Walpole, they did not consider themselves party writers. Though they were sympathetic to the Patriots and the Country cause, their satirical attacks were "independent expressions of their own hostility to the administration" rather than a unified Oppositional scheme (Goldgar 42). Despite the lack of an organized literary opposition to Walpole, the various works against him amounted to so great a number that Jerry Beasley suggests that "Robert Walpole... [may have actually given] direction to the development of English prose fiction during that critical early period of the novel's birth as a new and distinctive literary form of great popular appeal" ("Portraits" 408). It is ironic that Walpole, so hostile to literary culture, may have helped to develop such a powerful genre as the novel.

Whether Swift intended it or not, his *Gulliver's Travels* (1726) became a key prose fiction for the opposition to Walpole's administration. The imaginary voyage and the discovered manuscript were popular tropes to avoid legal prosecution, and Swift used both in his satire. Walpole is satirized as Lilliput's Treasurer, Flimnap the rope-dancer; the British court's viciousness and paranoia are exposed in the Lilliputians' attempts to impeach and destroy Gulliver (an allegory for the Whigs' impeachment for treason of Swift's friends, Harley and Bolingbroke in 1715), and in their petty politics of Big-Endians versus Little-Endians (a satirical reduction of the conflict between Catholics and Protestants). When Gulliver attempts to explain the ideology of the British government to the gentle giants in Brobdingnag, his country's affairs are regarded as "an Heap of Conspiracies, Rebellions, Murders, Massacres, Revolutions, Banishments; the very worst Effects that Avarice, Faction, Hypocrisy, Perfidiousness, Cruelty, Rage, Madness, Hatred, Envy, Lust, Malice, and Ambition could produce" (Part 2. Ch. 6, 125).

Such a chaotic list of moral disorder represented for the Opposition the consequences of Walpole's ministry. As Bolingbroke defined the principles of classical republicanism as virtue, liberty, and civic morality, Walpole's government of patronage and luxury was regarded as a blatant infringement on the ancient constitution. Bolingbroke's Country ideology, with its basis in virtue and history, "was perpetually threatened by corruption operating through private appetites and false consciousness" (Pocock 1975, 486), and therefore lent itself easily to the paradigms of virtue in distress and the loss of the golden age.

The *Craftsman*, the Opposition journal founded by Bolingbroke and Pulteney, hammered away at Walpole's corruptions for over a decade. "The Vision of Camilick" (see Appendix C.i), believed to be written by Bolingbroke, contrasts the hard-won peace resulting in a pastoral world of "golden harvests" with the destruction of "the sacred *Parchment*" (the Magna Carta) by a "bluff, ruffianly manner[ed]" man, whose "Face was bronz'd over with a glare of Confidence." His tossing of gold to those who murmured their disagreement represents the bribery for which Walpole had become notorious, as well as the ministry's greedy desire for luxury which Bernard Mandeville, in his poem *The Fable of the Bees* (1714; 1724), was to defend as an economically sound way to run Britain: private vices leading to public virtues.

"The Vision of Camilick" was not a particularly inspired satire; however, it helped to establish the patterns employed by the Opposition writers for the rest of Walpole's reign. For the next fifteen years, Walpole would be exposed and reviled in imagery of gold, brass, audacity, and magic, and in allegories of tyrannical power.

John Gay's *The Beggar's Opera* (1728) transforms the high Court into the low world of common criminals, both motivated by the desire for gold. The Beggar playwright observes: "Through the whole piece you may observe such a similitude of manners in high and low life, that it is difficult to determine whether ... the fine gentlemen imitate the gentlemen of the road, or the gentlemen of the road the fine gentlemen" (III.xvi.236). In this "Newgate Pastoral," Walpole appears in many guises: the womanizing highwayman, Captain Macheath; Peachum, who buys and sells the lives of his gang-members according to their level of productive corruption; and a gang-member referred to by Walpole's nicknames, "Robin of Bagshot, alias Gorgon, alias Bluff Bob, alias Carbuncle, alias Bob Booty" (I.iii.185).

Gay's opera also included a song which touched on how careful a satirist had to be when criticizing the government:

> When you censure the age,
> Be cautious and sage,

Lest the courtiers offended should be:
If you mention vice or bribe,
'Tis so pat to all the tribe;
Each cries – "That was levell'd at me."
(II.x.Air XXX.211)

The song "was so clearly a reference to the government's sensitivity to criticism that the audience supposedly stared and laughed at Walpole in his box when it was sung" (Goldgar 69). The following year, the Lord Chamberlain, who approved new plays for the stage, banned Gay's sequel, *Polly*. It was suspected that Walpole himself was responsible for its suppression.

Pope's *Dunciad* (1728) was not an obvious political satire, concerned as it was with the artistic and intellectual decay of Britain; however, most of the duncers named in it were ministerial hacks, writing for Walpole. Pope blamed the degeneration of the age on its rulers, stating that "Dunce the second reigns like Dunce the first" (I.6), an oblique reference to the two king Georges. The descent into Dullness, finally realized in the *New Dunciad* (1742) with Book Four's "Universal Darkness" which "buries All" (line 656), envisions Britain swallowed up in anarchy, corruption, and stupidity, a direct consequence of the Court administration and stifling of artistic merit.

Anti-Walpole fictions continued to pour out of the presses throughout the 1730s and into the 1740s; Jerry Beasley counts "almost three dozen different works of prose fiction" over twenty-two years featuring the minister as their focal point ("Portraits" 407).[2] Some of the less well known writings contemporary with Haywood's *Eovaai* are the anonymous *Secret History of Mama Oello* (1733), an amatory novel with Walpole as a conniving Peruvian head of state who thwarts true love in order to enforce a politically advantageous arranged marriage (see Appendix D); George Lyttelton's *Letters from a Persian in England to his Friend at Ispahan* (1735), an epistolary novel satirizing

---

2   Beasley mentions by name twenty-one such prose fictions in his article "Portraits of a Monster." Though many of the titles are obscure and anonymous, Garland's Foundations of the Novel series has reprinted facsimile editions of several, such as: *A Voyage to Cacklogallinia* (1727), *A Trip to the Moon* (1728), *Memoirs Concerning the Life and Manners of Captain Mackheath* (1728), *The Secret History of Mama Oello* (1733), *A Court Intrigue* (1741), and, of course, *Adventures of Eovaai* (1736).

many of Walpole's economic policies (see Appendix E); and *A Court Intrigue: Or, The Statesman Detected* (1741) (narrated by the "Oraculous Ship") in which Walpole, as the tyrannical first mate, endangers his ship's (the state's) welfare.

In 1742, as Walpole retired from the political scene, Henry Fielding published *The Life of Mr. Jonathan Wild the Great*, a sustained ironic piece in which Wild is praised for his Greatness which allows for no taint of Goodness. Once more, Walpole is identified as a legendary criminal, but where Gay's Beggar rescued Macheath from the gallows to appease the ladies and satisfy the rules of opera, Fielding hangs Wild who picks the hangman's pocket of a corkscrew even as he dies.

As Wild/Walpole exalts in his unadulterated evil, Fielding implies that virtue, goodness and "Christian heroism" ("Portraits" 430) must prevail. Eliza Haywood, in her anonymous *Adventures of Eovaai*, similarly suggests that Walpole's political corruption must be overcome by the very virtue it oppresses.

Life and Related Works

Almost two decades before she published *Adventures of Eovaai*, Eliza Haywood had blazed into literary prominence as the author of the amatory novel, *Love in Excess* (1719). Immensely popular, Haywood's first novel was as successful as *Gulliver's Travels* and *Robinson Crusoe* (McBurney 250). Over her thirty-seven year career, the "Great Arbitress of Passion" as she was dubbed in an early dedication, authored many amatory novels, several plays, periodicals, pamphlets, translations, domestic novels, and political satires. She was also at various times a wife, mother, actress, and lover. But only the sparsest details of her life have come down to us.

David Erskine Baker, Haywood's first biographer (in *Biographia Dramatica*, 1764) stated that Haywood did not want the facts of her life recorded for posterity: "from a supposition of some improper liberties being taken with her character after death, by the intermixture of truth and falsehood with her history, she laid a solemn injunction on a person who was well acquainted with all the particulars of it, not to communicate to any one the least circumstance relating to her" (cited in Blouch 545).

Past biographers of Haywood, like George Whicher, have tended to blur the writings with the woman, so that even Whicher's title – *The Life and Romances of Mrs. Eliza Haywood* – suggests a relation between the amatory works and the lifestyle of the author. Alexander Pope performed the same kind of ellision in his *Dunciad*, referring to Haywood's two scandal novels – *The Memoirs of a Certain Island adjacent to the Kingdom of Utopia* (1725) and *The Secret History of the Present Intrigues of the Court of Caramania* (1727) – as her "two babes of love," an ambiguous phrase which implied that she had two bastard children. Pope, as Scriblerus, labelled Haywood the most prominent "of those shameless scriblers (...of That sex, which ought least to be capable of such malice or impudence)" (II.119, note 149), capable of producing only illegitimate, second-rate works. Personally incensed that Haywood had portrayed two of his friends in her scandal chronicles, Pope made her first prize in the *Dunciad*'s pissing contest, comparing her to a chamber pot whose function as an empty vessel was to be filled up by men. Pope's anxiety over hack-writers in general, and his cruel, personal satire of women writers in particular, manifest an almost territorial concern with the arts.

While many critics have speculated that Pope's scathing portrayal of Haywood as a "Juno of majestic size,/With cow-like udders, and with ox-like eyes" (II.165-6) forced her into silence in the 1730s, Haywood simply returned to her first love of acting and stage-writing. And in 1736, she anonymously authored her satire of Sir Robert Walpole, the *Adventures of Eovaai*.

As Pope's footnotes to the Haywood portrait in the *Dunciad* attest, Haywood's two early scandal novels serve up sexual gossip about slightly fictionalized figures while purportedly exposing the profligacy of the Court. Martha Blount appears in Volume One of *The Memoirs of a Certain Island* as Lady Marthalia (I.12-13), while Lady Henrietta Howard figures prominently in *The Secret History of Caramania* as Ismonda, mistress of Prince Theodore, a thinly disguised George II. Despite Pope's reaction, these two scandal novels were not as politically incendiary as Delarivier Manley's *New Atalantis* (1709) had been earlier in the century. That novel had resulted in Manley's arrest by the Whig government for libel.

Rather than attacking specific Whigs as Manley had done, Haywood contrasted Court culture with Country innocence, using the paradigm of virtue seduced and betrayed by powerful vice. As Rosalind Ballaster points out, through this binary opposition of city and country, Haywood keeps the "over-arching structure of a Tory ideology ... in place" (156); however, she also avoids any real political targets. "[T]he seduction/betrayal motif was now exploited for the purposes of a more general moralism and Haywood betrays no interest in direct political intervention or allegiance to other opposition figures or forces" (Ballaster 156).

In *The Memoirs*, Haywood relates tales of undone women and husbands devoted to lascivious wives, including many examples of incest, suicide, and wife-pandering. She dishes out the familiar story of her friend Richard Savage's unnatural mother, Anne Mason, Lady Macclesfield (I.151-183), and ugly gossip about his mistress, Martha Fowke (I.43-49;183-187), to which Savage retaliated in his *Author to be Lett* (1729). The two volumes do not take aim at prominent political figures but at acquaintances and court personalities. The result is an entertaining, though repetitive barrage of illicit sexual liaisons, rapes, and revenges, loosely held together by the narration of Cupid who complains of how the island has been corrupted by lust, self-interest, and the dreams of wealth as the inhabitants worship at the Enchanted Well (the South Sea Company). At the conclusion of Volume One, Astrea and the genius of the place return to the island to expose and destroy the Well, but Volume Two continues with more salacious stories as Cupid tells his traveller companion,

Of mortal Race thou art alone found worthy to partake Celestial Privileges, and inspect Secrets conceal'd far, far beyond the ken of weak Humanity – the most hidden Frailties, –Vices with utmost skill disguis'd, the finest Web of fraudful Artifice and deep Deceit, 'tis given to thee to fathom and unravel! – Before thy Eyes the gaudy Hypocrite shall stand expos'd, the Mask of Virtue shall be worn in vain – and each offending Fellow-Creature appear, not as he *seems*, but as he truly *is* (*Memoirs* II.2).

Haywood's first scandal novel, then, functions not as political satire but as exemplary literature, revealing the maliciousness of human nature and the victimization of the weak and the loving.

Stylistically, *The Court of Caramania* is a much more integrated work, manifesting more narrative cohesion than the episodic *Memoirs* as it centres around the many sexual escapades of Prince Theodore and his continual returns to his patient mistress. Though Haywood again concentrates on Court life, this time portraying the love lives of Theodore (George II), Ismonda (Henrietta Howard), and Marmillio (Earl of Scarborough) among others, *The Court of Caramania* is still an investigation of male-female relationships rather than an exposé of political figures or philosophies.

While Josephine Grieder has pointed out that some of the various female characters in Caramania correspond to real life mistresses of George II, it is actually Haywood's own moral advice that is the focus of the scandals. Queen Hyanthe (Queen Caroline), Ismonda, and Barsina (the Duchess of Argyle) each experience the unfaithfulness of a husband or lover, and each must decide on the proper conduct to maintain the respect of her beloved. Hyanthe is the most sympathetic of the three. She did not entertain any

> thoughts of revenging it in the manner some Wives would do, nor vented her Discontent in Revilings, and Exclamations, as it is ordinary for Women to do on those occasions. ... She consider'd, that to fly into Passion, would but render her Condition worse, by exposing to the World her Husband's Weakness, and her want of that Power she ought to have over him ...; and that to accuse the Prince with any terms of Wrath, would but provoke him to avow his Crime to her face, and by that means lay her under the necessity either of coming to an open Rupture with him, or, by brooking such a Contempt tamely, testify a meanness of Spirit, which was not in her nature. She chose therefore not to seem to know what, acknowledging to know, she must resent, but had not the power of redressing (*Caramania* 303-4).

The Queen proves admirable in her loving stoicism; however, Haywood makes it clear that a woman has little other choice. "Few Men, if ever were, are twice enamour'd of the same Object; their whole Life indeed is one continued Series of Change, but then it is still to new Desires" (277).

Although Haywood explores the politics of sexual relationships in her two court-oriented scandal novels, she does not explicitly advocate changing them. Neither does she seem interested in creating an analogy between the government of the state and the government of the passions as Manley had done in *The New Atalantis*. In her 1729 tragedy, *Frederick, Duke of Brunswick-Lunenburgh*, Haywood does become more politically conscious as she demonstrates that the alternately callous and cowardly way in which the Prince treats his former mistress, Adelaid, is indicative of the poor rule he will exercise in the state. Adelaid complains, "Hear him, just Heav'n! with Patience, if you can!/ This Prince, for Virtue so rever'd and fam'd,/ Thinks Perj'ry and Ingratitude no Crimes!" (Act 2, 16).

Haywood was disappointed that the royal family did not attend her play; however, her portrayal of their ancestor was equivocal to say the least and unlikely to win her royal patronage. Her Dedication to Frederick Lewis, Prince of Wales, reminds him of his duties to the people, while the closing speeches of Act 5 advise the protagonist's descendants (George, Caroline and the Prince) "That to be truly Great they must be good"; and that they must be taught "to merit, not desire Dominion" (see Appendix B.iii and iv). Interspersed with politically didactic messages and advice, *Frederick, Duke of Brunswick-Lunenburgh* illustrates that Haywood was moving toward merging politics and amatory themes.

By 1736, a decade after the appearance of her scandal novels, Haywood's style, message, and artistic merit had matured considerably. Haywood had learned from her critics, her predecessors, associates, and experience.

Critical Background of *Adventures of Eovaai*

While Eliza Haywood's works are currently enjoying great popularity since being rediscovered by scholars, *Eovaai* has not yet garnered much critical attention. The attention that it has attracted is certainly mixed: its hybrid form, amatory conventions, anti-ministerial politics, and feminism have been attacked and lauded. Over the years, *Eovaai*'s oriental fantasy form has been dismissed and derided as: "a moral allegory, [that] soon lapses into mere extravagant adventure" making "immoderate use of magic elements" (Whicher 99); no more "than a pastiche of romance and magic" with "nonsensical magical trappings" (Grieder 5-6). As uncomfortable as its oriental form made some early critics, its underlying political message has always been regarded as an important one.

As the prolific Haywood did not publish any novels for six years after *Eovaai*, George Whicher felt that Haywood's satire of Walpole must have been so stinging to the minister that she was either bought off by the government or exiled herself from England to avoid prosecution (104). Whicher overlooks the fact that Haywood turned to writing for the stage and to acting during those years. Still, though not a real threat to Walpole's government in 1736, *Eovaai* did function as a challenge to its readers and critics.

In her introduction to the Garland facsimile edition of *Eovaai* in 1972, Josephine Grieder appreciated the novel's "sustained and mature consideration of politics and political philosophy" (5). Jerry Beasley identified it as a savage attack on "Robert Walpole as a private man and public figure" ("Politics and Moral Idealism" 225) and as "one of the more complicated of the anti-Walpole narratives, at least in its plotting" ("Portraits" 422). Mary Anne Schofield saw *Eovaai*'s political nature in a more feminist light as belonging to a group of Haywood's early works "examining the female tensions between submission and aggression" and "the question of womanhood as a moral and social issue" (*Quiet Rebellion* 42, 45).

Schofield's desire to read Haywood as an angry feminist tended to over-simplify Haywood's works and characterized her depiction of the sexes as observing a strict and distinct polarity: good women and the bad men who take advantage of them. Read in this way, *Adventures of Eovaai*

> becomes Haywood's strongest criticism of the position of women in society. By displaying the total licentiousness to which women can descend if they are continually bound, Haywood reveals the harm that is being done to them. Since this is surely one of the most rage-filled of Haywood's novels, it is well that it is disguised in a fairy-tale aura, for what it reveals about the female condition is truly shocking (*Eliza Haywood* 80).

While it is true that Haywood has a strong feminist message to impart in all of her novels including *Eovaai*, it is wrong to overlook her other social and political concerns. It becomes obvious that *Eovaai* is many things, but to delimit its concerns as exclusively sexual or political is to restrict Haywood's discourse.

In *Seductive Forms* (1992), Rosalind Ballaster offered a solution for the critics, a theory that would accommodate political *and* feminist interests. Ballaster suggested that eighteenth-century women's amatory plots

> attempt to articulate sexual and party political interest simultaneously, with reference both to the struggle for a specifically female authority in sexual and party political representation and to the more general struggle to resolve ethical and epistemological crises in the social order through narrative form (16).

Ballaster points out that "the readers of women's amatory fiction are required to read by a process of constant movement between sexual and party political meaning, rather than strip off the cloak of party political satire to reveal the 'true' narrative of sexual opposition" (19). *Eovaai*, as the disparate critical readings indicate, does just this: it displaces contemporary politics onto a grid of sexual conflicts, and illustrates through its narratological constructs — romance, oriental fantasy, erotica — that life, like literature, is subject to authorial control.

The text of *Eovaai* consists of seven parts and almost as many genres: the Dedication and Preface; the political satire of Walpole in the History of Ochihatou, the evil magician; the political-amatory plot of Queen Yximilla's forced marriage; the philosophical Harangue of the Patriot Alhahuza; the Republican's monologue of political utopia; the oriental tale of the Atamadoul monkey; and the fairy-tale life of Prince Adelhu. Enveloping all of these are the adventures of Eovaai as she fends off the sexual advances of Ochihatou who aims to possess both her body and her kingdom. The structure of the novel, with its intertwining political and amatory story lines, balances the narrative and makes political and sexual conflict analogous. *Eovaai* sexualizes politics and politicizes sexuality; but its hybrid nature due to its use of so many literary genres also stresses the dispersion of governing energies and draws attention to the politics of representation. One of the most effective devices for conveying this theme is Haywood's textual apparatus.

The title page and Preface of *Eovaai* perform the usual distancing of the work from real-life contemporary events while making a claim to historical fact. The topos of the discovered ancient manuscript was employed by many anti-government authors to avoid prosecution for libel (Gallagher 505-510); however, by the 1730s it was a transparent device. *Eovaai*, we are told, is a "Pre-Adamitical History" (that is, pre-dating the creation of Adam by God), originally written in the "Language of Nature" before being translated into Chinese which was believed by some to be "the original 'Adamitic' language ... [as] Noah settled in China" after the flood (Gibson 54). Already the reader is attuned to the pretence of historicity and realizes that the text is a satire on her contemporary society even as it protests it is not. The text begins then with a lie that the author and the reader both wink at.

The son of a Mandarin who has purportedly translated the work into English lives in London. He does not participate in Eovaai's adventures; he merely renders them into English and offers commentary, but through his notes he also makes occasional observations on English society. In this way, he is the ideal spectator – aloof, nonjudgmental, unbiassed, and separate from the action. In fact, the Translator is a feminized figure, observing but not truly participating in the events which draw his attention. He has much in common with an eighteenth-century woman: as she is a liminal figure in society and politics, the Translator is similarly marginalized – to the bottom of the page in the book. In addition to this, the reader, who already does not believe that the novel is really a translation, is drawn further into the text by the perception of a disguised author – that is, one who cannot speak in her own voice. An ambience of intrigue which makes the reader suspicious of the Authorities with which she is presented, is part of Haywood's point that we must learn to read through political and social representations of Truth.

As the voices in the footnotes multiply to include the original Author, the Commentator Cafferero, the Historian Hahehihotu, the Cabal of philosophers who translated the history into Chinese, among others, the notes become argumentative, contradictory, and lacking in authority. The reader will most often concur with the son of the Mandarin Translator's interpretation, but, at times, even his reading of events is questionable. Two examples will serve here: one on women, one on politics.

The Commentator, who is usually misogynistic in his observations, states that in Atamadoul, an older, vain woman still driven by sexual desires, "her whole Sex is decypher'd." The Author also remarks "that a Woman is the *first* in believing herself *handsome*, and the *last* in finding she *grows old.*" Our Translator then offers that "as we see no antiquated Coquets in our Days, we must suppose these Reflections are only just on the Ladies of former Ages" (125). The Translator is judged by the reader as being coyly ironic, smoothly flattering, or simply wrong.

Earlier, in the section following the Harangue of Alhahuza, the Commentator, whom the Translator suspects "to have been a Republican in his Principles," condemns the monarchy as "no more than Pageantry, a kind of gaudy Shew, to attract and amuse the Vulgar." The Translator admits that he might agree. He has seen "Mock-Monarchs on the Stage" that so clearly resemble some real-life Kings that had the Commentator seen them, he would have asked "Where is the essential Difference?" But the Translator quickly retracts this assertive observation and points out "this is only my own Imagination; it's possible the Courts of *Europe* might have reformed his Sentiments, and render'd him as very a Worshipper of Royalty as a *Frenchman*" (110). Without any final authority figure to interpret the events and editorial comments for her, the reader is left to form her own opinions rather than accept the representations offered by these men, authors, and politicians.

Haywood's point that representations bear the impressions of those relating them and should, therefore, be subject to careful interpretation and scrutiny, is further enhanced through the interspersed, "curious and entertaining novels" (as they were called in the 1741 edition) about Yximilla and Atamadoul. The reader is presented with these histories and the many commentators' remarks on them but is ultimately responsible for examining the facts as far as she can discern them and interpreting their significance for herself. Yximilla and Atamadoul function to offer behaviours different from the ones Eovaai exhibits:

in this way, Yximilla works as a moral rebuke to Eovaai's desire to succumb to Ochihatou's seduction, while Atamadoul shows to what depths passion can sink a woman. But these histories simultaneously convey a political theme: they reflect the vulnerability of women and nations to the powerlust of their governors.

The enforced marriage or brutal treatment of a woman by a man was a familiar literary topos in the eighteenth century, investigating the power imbalance between rulers and their subjects and demonstrating that a corrupt governor can control a nation as a man controls his lover. Once Ochihatou, in Whig-like fashion, has regaled Eovaai with the sensual and luxurious pleasures of music, dance, food, and material comforts, he takes her to his garden to complete the seduction, but their consummation is interrupted by the controlling narrator who states "we must quit her and *Hypotofa* for a while, and see what Mischiefs were occasioned in Countries far distant from it, by the Wickedness of ambitious and unsatiable Man" (79). We are then introduced to Yximilla, who, unlike Eovaai, resists the advances of Broscomin and who even goes to war to protect her country and her right to choose her own husband. Yximilla's forces are too weak to combat the combined armies of Broscomin and his allies, and she becomes his "ravished Bride" (88).

Haywood's use of the textual apparatus is especially effective in this episode as it mirrors Yximilla's disempowerment: even her story is taken from her and controlled by the self-serving commentators in the footnotes who literally undercut her. The notes are concerned with banal points unrelated to the Queen's tragic situation, such as "there is nothing more common than for People to ascribe the Success of their Purposes, of whatever kind, to the Favour of the Gods; tho', perhaps, permitted them for very different Ends than what they imagine themselves, or would have others" (83); or with petty points of translation such as the disagreement between the Cabal and our Translator who quibble about the phrase "that Thirst of Power" which could be "the Plague of Sovereignty" or "*Itch* [which] comes nearer the Original; but the Word was rejected, on account of its being too gross" (90). Yximilla, subjected to this thirst, plague, or itch of the tyrants around her, is forgotten in the debate over semantics. Just as Broscomin wages international war to achieve the personal satisfaction of gaining Yximilla's kingdom, so do the textual commentators make self-interested emendations without considering the value of the original history. The reader must remember and hold on to the suffering of Yximilla who has become an elaborate footnote in the history of Ochihatou. The reader realizes that the retelling of the Queen's story does nothing to help Yximilla, but that it is retold only for the benefit of the storyteller. By extension, Haywood points to the importance of controlling one's own history, relating one's own story because events, actions, and words can be artfully, willfully constructed for, and represented to, an audience and a nation.

Atamadoul, whom Eovaai meets after she has been recaptured by Ochihatou, does relate her own history. In comparison with Yximilla's history, Atamadoul's story is relatively unhampered by textual commentary; however, the reader still finds discrepancies. In fact, the reader comes to doubt Atamadoul's own narration and must examine carefully her language to decipher her character. The older Atamadoul describes her younger self as a vain and cool woman who enjoyed seeing the pain she gave her would-be lovers. When finally afflicted herself with a "burning Passion" for Ochihatou who was courting her mistress, Atamadoul substituted herself in the young lady's place to enjoy the minister's embraces. Once discovered, Atamadoul was transformed by the outraged magician into a monkey to "deter all woman-kind from aiming at Delights they are past the power of giving" (131). But his curse goes even farther. As a monkey chained in the corner of a room, Atamadoul must watch as Ochihatou makes love to other women. He also subjects the Atamadoul monkey to the attentions of "a very ugly and over-grown Baboon" which "is sometimes very near taking an entire Possession" of her (132). Much to the amazement of Eovaai and the reader, Atamadoul's love for Ochihatou does not cease, and she is tortured by her inability to consummate her passion.

Again, Haywood exploits the analogy between sexual and political relationships as she plays with the idea of power lust through images of physical lust: both deny reason and extol appetite for personal satiety. Atamadoul offers to save Eovaai from the threatened rape by Ochihatou by substituting herself in the princess's place in the darkness. While Atamadoul and Ochihatou fornicate surrounded by spectres who "with obscene and antick Postures animated their polluted Joys," Eovaai watches through her magic telescope (135). The employment of the pornograhic genre underscores the power motif while it also demonstrates the degeneration of morality under Walpole's government.

Haywood's portrayal of Atamadoul illustrates that in order for Ochihatou to dominate, he must have victims who are willing to be subservient. The sexual relationship reflects on the contemporary political situation in which, in Haywood's view, Walpole is empowered by a nation willing to be tyrannized. Alhahuza, in his Republican harangue, makes the same point:

> "'Oh *Hypotofans*! ... which of you has not, for a shew of private Advantage, consented to give up Publick-Good? – Which of you has not been a Factor for his own Slavery, and that of his Posterity? – Which of you has not, at some time or other, been corrupted by the Gold of *Ochihatou*? – '" (104).

Unlike Eovaai, Yximilla, and the Republicans in Oozoff, Atamadoul makes no resistance against evil and passion; she is concerned only with personal vengeance and satisfaction through power. However, the brief glimpse that the curious Eovaai takes of the copulating pair (for which she is chastized by the Commentator) suggests that she, too, is not entirely exempt from the primal urge for power. Having sex in the dark, Ochihatou believes he exerts control over Eovaai, while Atamadoul exercises her power over him. Only Eovaai has ultimate power by watching both in their undisguised forms. She drops the magic telescope, sickened by the animal lust she has witnessed and escaped. But it is the reader, the final voyeur, who possesses the real power, being in the position to view and judge all of the action. Haywood, who allows her readers this superior perspective, continues to employ her wild blend of genres and the sub-textual notes to challenge her readers into making up their own minds on literature and life, politics and sexual power-plays.

Eovaai's fall into anarchy and civil war after the ideal government of her father, the hedonism of Ochihatou's tyrannical state, and her enlightenment about Republicanism each reflects simultaneous sexual and political awakenings in the princess. The evil magician "brought her to believe, that every thing was Virtue in the Great, and Vice confined to those in low Life. ... *Eovaai*, in an Instant, became so wholly abandon'd to this pernicious Doctrine, that she thought all the Time lost, which she had spent in endeavouring to subdue her Passions" (77). Her rejection of her father's teachings and "the natural Modesty of her Sex" leads Eovaai to the brink of being debauched. Eovaai is representative here not only of Court libertinism and Authority, but also of what Nancy Armstrong identifies as "the aristocratic woman [who] represented surface instead of depth, ... material instead of moral value, and [who] displayed idle sensuality instead of constant vigilance and tireless concern for the well-being of others. Such a woman was not truly female" (20). Not doing her duty to her people, not behaving femininely, Eovaai runs the risk of becoming not another Ochihatou, but another Atamadoul monkey.

The ancient Republican tells her that "'Humane Nature is not to be trusted with itself: all Men have in them the Seeds of Tyranny'" (112) and therefore a King is bound to become a despot. Eovaai attempts to refute his arguments and defend the monarchy by stating that a balanced government would protect the people from a tyrannical ruler. She claims that a King is "'the Head of a large Family; for whose Happiness he is perpetually contriving, who *watches* for *their Repose*, *labours* for *their Ease*, *exposes himself* for *their Safety*, and has no other Recompence for all his Cares than that Homage, that Grandeur, which he ought not to be envied'" (114-115). Her words are applicable to the perfect monarch and the ideal husband. Even the reader is aware that such perfection is rarely encountered in real life. The ancient man smiles at Eovaai's naivete before he embarks on an intelligent rebuttal to which she cannot reply. "[S]he found so much Justice in the latter Part of his Discourse, that, she was at a loss in what manner she shou'd do so" (118).

The commentators in the footnotes condemn Eovaai's fickleness in being swayed first by Ochihatou and then by the Republican. But the reader finds this judgment harsh and misogynistic. Eovaai seems to find the middle way through these philosophies as she hopes to implement the ideals of a limited monarchy in her own government. Haywood, through her text and sub-text, has been equally critical of all political views.

The historians, Rabbins, Cabal members, and Author each intrude upon the Republican's monologue to add their views and opinions. Because the notes lack any single, final authoritative voice, they mimic a Republican government which lacks a single, authoritative monarch (for which Eovaai yearns). Although Haywood does not explicitly condemn Republicanism as she does Walpole's ministry, she uses her textual apparatus effectively to demonstrate that simply replacing one form of government with another is fraught with still other problems. In real life, political and sexual differences are not easily resolved. In the *Adventures of Eovaai*, they are, and the blatant artificiality of the novel's conclusion again attunes the reader to the differences between reality and representation.

Eovaai and Adelhu marry, unite their kingdoms, and live happily ever after, unlike Yximilla and Atamadoul whose histories lack such happy closure. To emphasize the fictionality of her tale, Haywood's final footnote draws attention to the artificiality of her text. As Eovaai relates her adventures to Adelhu, the commentators argue whether she told him of her garden dalliance with Ochihatou. If she did not (as one cannot imagine a woman divulging such sexual indiscretions), then how did the Author come to know about the event? The Translator surmises that someone in the magician's garden could have overheard them, or Ochihatou himself could have bragged about it. Thus, the *Adventures of Eovaai* concludes by reminding the reader that it has been yet another representation of Truth, conveyed by an Authority figure who is just as capable of manipulating perceptions as any politician. The reader, woman, citizen must learn not to accept passively everything that is presented for her consumption, but to question, challenge, and interpret those representations which may be artfully constructed illusions.

Eliza Haywood: A Brief Chronology

[There is no complete biography available on Haywood, though George Frisbie Whicher and, more recently, Christine Blouch have pieced together many significant and personal details about her life. See the Selected Secondary Sources section.]

?1693   Born Eliza Fowler in London to a merchant family; an undated letter suggests that she was "nearly related" to Sir Richard Fowler of the Grange near Shropshire.

1715   Appeared on stage in Smock Alley, Dublin, as Chloe in Thomas Shadwell's adaptation of Shakespeare's *Timon of Athens*. EH may have married in Ireland, though her husband is unknown.

1719   No longer living with her husband. *Love in Excess* Parts 1 and 2 (Part 3, 1720). *The Life of Duncan Campbell*, one of a series of pamphlets on the deaf-mute prophet.

1720   *Letter from a Lady of Quality to a Chevalier*, translated from the French.

1721   Undated, unaddressed letter signed "Eliza Haywood," seeking patronage for the publication of a "Tragedy" (probably *The Fair Captive*), states that an "unfortunate marriage" had reduced her to the "melancholly necessity" of writing to support herself and two children under seven years of age. *The Fair Captive* (tragedy) acted.

1722   *The British Recluse. The Injured Husband.*

1723   *Idalia. A Wife to be Lett* (comedy) acted; performed the role of Susanna Graspall to less than rave reviews. Became acquainted with Richard Savage. *Lasselia. The Rash Resolve. The Works of Mrs. Eliza Haywood, consisting of Novels, Letters, Poems, and Plays.* 3 vols.

1724   *Poems on Several Occasions* (vol. 4 of *Works*). *A Spy upon the Conjurer. The Masqueraders* (Part 2, 1725). *The Fatal Secret. The Surprise. The Arragonian Queen. La Belle Assemblée*; translated from the French (vol. 2, 1726). *Memoirs of a Certain Island adjacent to the Kingdom of Utopia* (vol. 2, 1725), a scandal romance in the tradition of Delarivier Manley's *New Atalantis*. Its depiction of Richard Savage's mistress led to a quarrel with him and Haywood was satirized in his poem "The Authors of the Town." *Bath-Intrigues. Fantomina. The Force of Nature. Memoirs of the Baron de Brosse. Secret Histories, Novels and Poems* (4 vols.).

1725　*The Dumb Projector. The Lady Philosopher's Stone*; translated from the French. *The Unequal Conflict. The Tea Table* (Part 2, 1726). *The Fatal Fondness. Mary Stuart, Queen of Scots.*

1726　*The Distress'd Orphan. The Mercenary Lover. Reflections on the Various Effects of Love, According to the Contrary Dispositions of the Persons on whom it Operates. The City Jilt. The Double Marriage. The Secret History of the Present Intrigues of the Court of Caramania* (her second scandal novel). *Letters from the Palace of Fame. Cleomelia.*

1727　*The Fruitless Enquiry. The Life of Madam de Villesache. Love in its Variety*; translated from the Spanish. *Philidore and Placentia. The Perplex'd Dutchess.*

1728　*The Agreeable Caledonian* (Part 2, 1729; reissued as *Clementina* in 1768). *Irish Artifice. Persecuted Virtue. Some Memoirs of the Amours and Intrigues of a Certain Irish Dean. The Disguised Prince*; translated from the French (Part 2, 1729). Satirized in Book II of Alexander Pope's *The Dunciad.*

1729　*The Fair Hebrew. Frederick, Duke of Brunswick-Lunenburgh* (tragedy) acted; "an indifferent success." Satirized in Savage's *An Author to be Lett.* He suggested that "*too homely for a Strolling Actress, why might not the Lady, (tho' once a Theatrical Queen) have subsisted by turning Washer-woman? ... the sullied Linnen ... an Emblem of her Soul, were it well scoured by Repentance for the Sins of her Youth.*"

1730　*Love-Letters on all Occasions Lately Passed Between Persons of Distinction.* Satirized as Mrs. Novel in Henry Fielding's comedy, *The Author's Farce and The Pleasures of the Town.* Performed the role of Achilles' ex-mistress, Briseis, in her lover William Hatchett's *The Rival Fathers.* Performed the role of Mrs. Arden in *Arden of Feversham*, which she may have adapted.

1733   *The Opera of Operas* (collaboration with Hatchett), a musical adaptation of Fielding's *Tragedy of Tragedies* (1731), with music by John Frederick Lampe, performed; ran for eleven nights and then published.

1734   *L'Entretien des Beaux Esprits, Being the Sequel to La Belle Assemblée*; translated from the French.

1735   *The Dramatick Historiographer; or, The British Theatre Delineated* (7 editions by 1756).

1736   *Adventures of Eovaai*, a political satire of Sir Robert Walpole (reissued in 1741 as *The Unfortunate Princess*).

1737   Joined Henry Fielding's Great Mogul's Company of actors (Little Theatre Haymarket); appeared as Mrs. Screen in Fielding's *Historical Register for the Year 1736*; appeared as the Muse in Fielding's *Eurydice Hiss'd*; benefit for Haywood on 23 May 1737, the night before Walpole brought the Licensing Act before the Commons.

1741   Established at the Sign of Fame in Covent Garden as a publisher; published and probably wrote *Anti-Pamela; or, Feign'd Innocence Detected*. *The Busy Body*; translated from the French and published.

1742   *The Virtuous Villager*; translated from the French.

1743   *A Present for a Servant Maid*, the first of her overtly didactic, moral works.

1744   *The Fortunate Foundlings*. *The Female Spectator* (monthly periodical published from April 1744 to May 1746).

1746   *The Parrot*, by the Authors of *The Female Spectator* (weekly periodical, 2 August to 4 October).

1747   *Memoirs of a Man of Honour*; translated from the French.

1748   *Life's Progress through the Passions*. *Epistles for the Ladies* (monthly periodical published from Nov. 1748 to May 1749; vol. 2, 1750).

1749   *Dalinda: or, The Double Marriage.*

1750   *A Letter from H—— G———g, Esq*. Because of the political, Jacobite theme of this pamphlet, EH was arrested by the government and held in custody for several weeks.

1751   *The History of Miss Betsy Thoughtless* (4 vols.).

1753   *The History of Jemmy and Jenny Jessamy* (3 vols.). *Modern Characters*.

1754   *The Invisible Spy*, by Exploribus (4 vols.).

1755   *The Wife*, by Mira, one of the Authors of *The Female Spectator*, and *Epistles for Ladies*.

1756   *The Husband. The Young Lady*, by Euphrosine. (Weekly periodical lasting 7 weeks.) In a postscript appended to the last number of *The Young Lady*, EH mentions that she was taken ill when she commenced the periodical and that the illness had "increased so much as to incapacitate her for going on with it." Died 25 February; buried at St. Margaret's Church, Westminster.

1772   *A New Present for a Servant Maid.*

1778   *The History of Leonora Meadowson*, by the Author of *Betsy Thoughtless*.

A Note on the Text

The *Adventures of Eovaai, Princess of Ijaveo* was published in 1736 in London by S. Baker. A "Second Edition" appeared in 1741, printed for T. Wright, bearing the title *The Unfortunate Princess, or, The Ambitious Statesman* and showed Eliza Haywood's name on the title page. The second edition is, in fact, a reissue of the 1736 edition and does not contain any corrections or additions to the first edition.

The present text is based on the University of Western Ontario's D.B. Weldon Library's first edition (1736) of *Eovaai* which I have checked against the 1972 Garland facsimile edition of the Bodleian Library's first edition (shelf mark 250 q 232) and the 1741 "second edition" (retitled *The Unfortunate Princess*) in the Mills Memorial Library of McMaster University, Hamilton, Canada.

For this Broadview Literary Texts edition I have eliminated the long "s" throughout and replaced it with the modern "s." This leads me to defend my employment of "Hypotofa" in my text rather than the "Hypotosa" which earlier scholars (Grieder, Beasley, Ballaster, Gibson) have used but which I believe is based on the perpetuation of an erroneous reading. My readings of the 1736 copy and 1741 reissue lead me to conclude that the letter is an "f" rather than an "s." George Whicher, in his 1915 biography of Haywood, also uses "Hypotofa."

I have omitted the full capitalization of the first word of each paragraph observed by Haywood's printers. The printer's typographical errors have been silently corrected but grammatical idiosyncrasies and unusual apostrophes (her's, your's, Icinda's), as well as variations in spelling (Ijaveans/Ijaveons, antient/ancient, supream/supreme, Humane/Human), are unaltered. I have also retained the original punctuation and spelling, neither of which I feel proves difficult for the modern reader. Haywood's style does not include quotation marks to distinguish one speech from another; however, she readily identifies which character is speaking. The style is imitative of dialogue, rushing in upon the words of the previous speaker as it mimics the rush of interactive conversation with all of its accompanying emotions. In only two places have I made any changes to Haywood's original text in order to facilitate understanding. In the "Translator's" footnote on page (143) I have made my alterations in square brackets and have included the original phrasing in my notes; and on page (150) I have added the word "do" in square brackets to make the sentence easier to read.

Eliza Haywood's footnotes to *Eovaai*, purportedly by the Translator and including many fictional commentators on the text, are identified by me as [E.H.] after each of her notes. I have left the superscripted numbers in the text in exactly the same place Haywood had her symbols – often preceeding the words or phrases she glossed. When it has been necessary to explain a point within Haywood's footnote, I have identified my own remarks with [Ed. note:].

My own notes to the text are designed to help the modern reader with unfamiliar vocabulary, eighteenth-century politics and personages, and social practices.

ADVENTURES

OF

EOVAAI,

PRINCESS of *Ijaveo.*

A

Pre-Adamitical HISTORY.

Interfperfed with a great Number of remarkable OCCURRENCES, which happened, and may again happen, to feveral EMPIRES, KINGDOMS, REPUB-LICKS, and particular GREAT MEN.

With fome Account of the RELIGION, LAWS, CUSTOMS, and POLECIES of thofe Times.

Written originally in the Language of Nature,
  (of later Years but little underftood.)

Firft tranflated into *Chinefe*, at the command of the EMPEROR, by a Cabal of SEVENTY PHILOSO-PHERS; and now retranflated into *Englifh*, by the Son of a MANDARIN, refiding in *London.*

LONDON:

Printed for S. BAKER, at the *Angel* and *Crown* in *Ruffel-Street, Covent-Garden.* M.DCC.XXXVI.

Title page to 1736 edition

J. Mynde Sculp.

Frontispiece to the 1741 edition of *The Unfortunate Princess, Or, The Ambitious Statesman.*

THE
UNFORTUNATE PRINCESS,
OR, THE
Ambitious Statefman.
CONTAINING
The LIFE and furprizing ADVENTURES
OF THE
Princefs of *Ijaveo*.

Interfpers'd with feveral curious and entertaining NOVELS.

By Mrs. ELIZA HAYWOOD.

Minds that will mount into fuperior State,
Climb Mifchiefs Ladder, virtuous Actions hate.

The SECOND EDITION.

L O N D O N:
Printed for T. WRIGHT, at the *Bible*, in *Exeter*
Exchange, in the *Strand*. 1741.

Title page to the 1741 edition of *The Unfortunate Princess, Or, The*
Ambitious Statesman.

To Her GRACE,
The DUTCHESS Dowager of
MARLBOROUGH.[1]

MADAM,

I presume to present Your GRACE with a small Sketch of the World
before *Adam*; and indeed, to whom could I so properly inscribe such
a History, since how Romantick soever any Adventures of those Days
may appear to the present Age, they cannot be more incredible than
some Transactions of our own Times will seem to Posterity: Our Eyes
have seen a MARLBOROUGH![2] – We feel the Benefits of his Valour and
his Counsels; but hereafter, when, perhaps, some ambitious, or avaritious Favourite, void of Abilities as of Morals, shall have spread a general Corruption thro' the Land, and destroy'd all the Blessings that
Godlike Man bestow'd; when the Love of Liberty, Glory, Virtue, shall
no more be the distinguish'd Passion of the *British* Genius; how
difficult will it be for that degenerate Race, to believe what they find
themselves so little able to imitate. *Then* will the Records of *Blenheim,
Ramillies*,[3] &c. be read but as those of the *Trojan* Wars[4] are *now*; and
your GRACE's shining Character, even by your own Sex, whose Honour is so deeply interested in supporting the Reality, be look'd upon
as that of an *imaginary* Heroine. This, I confess, must be said in their
Vindication, that it requires something more than bare Tradition, to
convince them there cou'd be so much Perfection on this side the
Grave.

---

1 DUTCHESS Dowager of *MARLBOROUGH*: Sarah Churchill (1660-1744). Haywood had satirized the Duchess as Marama in her 1726 scandal novel, *Memoirs of a
   Certain Island* (II.249); however, by 1736 Haywood admired Sarah as a virulent
   opponent of Walpole.
2 MARLBOROUGH: John Churchill, first Duke of Marlborough (1650-1722), husband of Sarah.
3 *Blenheim, Ramillies*: Two great victories for the English under Marlborough in the
   War of the Spanish Succession (1702-14). In the Battle of Blenheim (1704), the
   Anglo-Austrian army under Marlborough defeated the French and Bavarian
   armies; the Battle of Ramillies (1706) was a victory for Marlborough commanding
   the allied British, Dutch and Danish armies.
4 *Trojan* Wars: The subject of Homer's epic poem, *The Iliad*. The abduction of Helen
   of Troy, wife to Menelaus, provoked the ten-year siege of Troy by the Greeks.

O Highly-favour'd! O most Illustrious Wife, and Parent of the Greatest, Best and Loveliest! it was not sufficient for you to adorn *Prosperity* with the Amiableness of every Virtue; the Divine Wisdom thought fit to shew, he had also form'd you able to undergo, with the same Sweetness, the *severest* Trials: – Trials! to which no other Woman was ever liable, because no other Woman ever *possess'd*, and *lost* such Treasures. – Those who know there was a MARLBOROUGH! – TWO BLANDFORDS![1] a SUNDERLAND![2] a BEDFORD![3] know too with what Patience, what Fortitude you stood, calm and resign'd, amidst a weeping, an almost distracted World, and beheld Heaven resume what it had given; but who, unseeing, can conceive the Greatness of that Courage and Magnanimity which cou'd sustain so many and such dreadful Separations?

But this is a Theme I should not dare to touch upon, had not the Almighty left you still some Branches,[4] truly worthy of the glorious Stock from whence they sprung; and from whom, 'tis to be hoped, new Generations of Heroes and Heroines will arise, to propagate the Name and Virtues of their great Progenitors, till Time shall be no more.

That your GRACE may live to see, like *Job*,[5] all you have been depriv'd of doubly restored to you, is the sincere Wish of every honest Heart; and, in particular, of one, who, tho entirely unknown to your GRACE, has the Honour to be, with the most profound Duty and Submission,

---

1   TWO BLANDFORDS: The Duchess's son, Jack, Marquis of Blandford, died in 1702 of smallpox; her grandson (by her daughter Henrietta), William "Willigo" Godolphin, died in 1731 after overeating.

2   a SUNDERLAND: The Duchess's daughter, Anne, Countess of Sunderland, died in 1716 of tuberculosis.

3   a BEDFORD: The Duchess's favourite grandchild (by her daughter Anne), Diana Spencer, Duchess of Bedford, died in 1735 of consumption. Sarah had planned to wed Diana to Frederick, Prince of Wales, with a dowry of £100,000 after his differences with George II became public in 1727; however, Walpole put a stop to this scheme. Diana married Lord John Russell in 1731.

4   some Branches: The Duchess's grandsons, Johnny and Charles Spencer (who became the third Duke of Marlborough), and five granddaughters were still alive in 1736.

5   *Job*: In the Old Testament, Job was a good man, blessed with great prosperity, who lost everything and was struck with a terrible disease. The *Book of Job* tries to reconcile the sufferings of the innocent with the wisdom and justice of God.

May it please your GRACE,
Your GRACE 's
Most Humble, most Obedient,
and most zealously
Devoted Servant,
The TRANSLATOR.

PREFACE, BY THE TRANSLATOR.

Tho, since my Residence in England, *I have made it my Observation, that Addresses of this nature are generally look'd upon as design'd only to encrease the Bulk of the Work; yet, when any thing out of the common road is exhibited, I cannot help thinking it necessary to stop the mouth of Censure, by answering before-hand, all the Cavils*[1] *that, with any shew of Reason, can be made against it.*

I know the Chinese *Account, concerning the Æra of this Earth's Formation, is so much exploded all over* Europe, *that any Relation of Facts, before the Reign of* Adam, *will appear fabulous; the* Reader *therefore, who wou'd be either instructed or diverted by this Book, must divest himself of the Prejudice of Education, and consider it as no Impossibility, that our Calculation should be more just than that he has been instructed in; or, if he cannot persuade himself to this, (as nothing is more difficult) to take at least a Trip to* Nanquin, where *in the famous* Library *of* Lamazahuma, *he will find such authentic Testimonials, as cannot fail of convincing him, if he understands the Characters, that the* World *bears date higher, by many thousand Years, than the narrow Chronology of other Nations extends. We do not say it was in the same Model as when governed by* Adam; *the Maps and Geographical Tables of it in the first Ages, compared with those of his, plainly demonstrate the contrary: But as all the Learned allow, that afterward, in the Time of* Noah,[2] *it underwent a prodigious Alteration, by being overwhelmed by* Water, *and will, hereafter, go through a much greater one, by* Fire; *why may we not as well suppose, it formerly experienced some such Revolution by* Air, *an Element of no less force than either of the other? Might not that powerful Body diffuse it self, by imperceptible degrees, into the Bowels of the Earth, where gathering greater Strength, by being confined, and receiving* Permission *from the* Author of Nature, *it at last burst open its Prison-Doors, and, by a general Earthquake, overturned all that opposed its Passage? − Or, might not some neighbouring Planet, for example, the* Moon, *as being nearest to us, by a Motion* seemingly *irregular, but directed by the* Supreme Hand, *press so*

---

1   *Cavils*: Frivolous objections (*OED*).
2   Noah: In *Genesis* 8, God sent a rain of forty days and nights to drown the world. Noah and his family, and two of every creature, were saved from the deluge when God directed Noah to build an ark.

hard upon our *Atmosphere, that the condens'd Vapours, struggling for room, might crush the Globe, and destroy, by Suffocation, every thing that had life? Then, retreating all at once, and the pure Æther*[1] *succeeding, occasion that sweet Serenity which rendred it* Paradisiacal, *and a fit Reception for that Favourite of Heaven, who, by being the first who enjoyed it, is stiled,* The Father of Mankind. *But as these things are only conjectural, and not intended for the Foundation of any new Hypothesis, I shall leave every one to judge of them as he thinks fit. Not so little tenacious am I in maintaining, that the* Antiquity *of the History I have taken upon me to put into* English, *ought to be no Objection to the Veracity of it; because there are Records yet extant, in the above-mentioned Library, which prove the World existed upwards of 5000 Years before the Birth of* Eovaai; *and, what is infinitely more strange, that, in the Infancy of Time, all the Parts of this great Universe had a free Intercourse with each other, and the different Inhabitants past from World to World, with the same Facility we now do from Kingdom to Kingdom. We have, in the Possession of the Holy* Chiaca, *a Crystal Tablet, containing a Letter from a great Lady to her Husband, then gone on some Business into that Planet, which, in later Ages, is distinguish'd by the Name of* Mercury; *but at that time was call'd* Oye, *as appears by the Direction. In what manner indeed those surprizing Voyages were made, is not transmitted to Posterity; I suppose, because the Discovery would be wholly useless to us in our present Situation: we must, alas! content ourselves with such things as are permitted us in this narrow Boundary between Sky and Sky, and wait till Death shall set open the Adamantine Gates, and give the enfranchis'd Soul her Liberty to range on more glorious Disquisitions,*[2] *in the Bosom of Infinity. In the mean time, some Reflections on the extensive Faculties of the former Possessors of this Earth, methinks, wou'd not be amiss, to humble the Pride of our modern Travellers, who look down, with a kind of scorn, on their less curious, or less happy Fellow-Creatures; and think themselves vastly accomplish'd, if, after a great Expence of Time and Money, they attain to the Knowledge of four or five Languages, and have visited as many Courts: but as this might seem too presuming, among a People who, if I judge rightly, are not fond of Remonstrances; and besides, is not at all material to testify the Truth of the succeeding Narrative, where no Description is attempted of any other World than the*

---

1   *Æther:* Clear sky (*OED*).
2   *Disquisitions:* Diligent, intellectual investigations (*OED*).

sublunary one; I shall only desire, that as I shall relate many things out of what is called the ordinary Course of Nature, every Reader will so far mortify his own Vanity, as to believe them not less real, because he is unable to comprehend them.

But as the Language spoken in those remote Ages, is now quite out of use, a second Objection, of equal weight with the former, may arise, concerning the true reading of the above-mentioned Records; and consequently, the Truth of all extracted from them, be liable to Suspicion; I think myself obliged to give an exact Account of the Means by which we arriv'd at the understanding those valuable Remains.

In the Year 13799, from the Creation of the World, according to our Chronology, and 4237, by that of the European, we had an Emperor in whom every Virtue worthy of a Throne was center'd; this illustrious Monarch, instead of attempting to enlarge his Prerogative, or fill his Coffers[1] by unnecessary or unjust Taxes, as too many of his Successors have since done, placed his whole Pride and Pleasure in the Opulence and Welfare of his Subjects: His Glory was to be at the head of a brave, a wise, and a free People; and was far from envying those of his Contemporaries, however large their Dominions, who, with a Rod of Iron, ruled over a servile and enervate Race: He chose rather to be loved for the Benefits he dispensed, than feared for the Punishments it was in his power to inflict; and that he might have as little occasion as possible of exercising the latter, he endeavoured, by Example and Precept, to encourage Virtue, and a Desire of Knowledge: His Court seemed a School of Science; and the only way to be admitted to any extraordinary Favour, was to be eminent both for Learning and Purity of Manners.

The Language of Nature being, even in his days, grown obsolete, those Annals of the first Ages, which (to the Glory of the Chinese) had been carefully preserved, were, by length of time, and the Remissness of former Emperors, rendred unintelligible. This excellent Prince, therefore, proposed great Rewards to any who should be able to draw them out of that Obscurity in which they had too long remained: His Liberality and Justice were so well known, that, in a short time, Pekin was crouded with the most Eminent Philosophers of all Nations; 70 of whom were selected for this Work, and the others sent back, but in such a manner as left them no room to regret the Preference given to their Companions.

---

1   Coffers: Treasure-chests (OED).

Full Ninety and seven Moons did the Cabal[1] *(for so was this learned Body entitled) employ themselves in the orduous Task; but the good Emperor then dying, and his Successor taking little pleasure in Discoveries of this nature, their Labours ceased, and they dispersed themselves each to his Native Country; having, in all that time, been able to translate no more than three, out of twenty one Histories committed to their Inspection.*

As I brought with me a very correct Copy of that which is esteem'd the best, I thought I cou'd do no less, in gratitude for the many Favours I have received from the English, *since my sojourning among them, than to give them, in their own Language, so curious a Piece of Antiquity. If this Acknowledgment is taken as it is meant, I shall think my Time well laid out; and perhaps, hereafter, make them another Present equally worthy their Attention.*

---

1   Cabal: A small body of persons engaged in secret or private schemes or intrigues (*OED*).

ADVENTURES OF EOVAAI,

PRINCESS OF *IJAVEO*.

THE Kingdom of [1]*Ijaveo* was once among the Number of the most rich and powerful of any that compose the sublunary Globe; almost impregnable by its Situation, and more so by the Bravery and Industry of the People. The Earth produced all kinds of Fruits and Flowers: the Rivers abounded with the most delicious Fish: the Air afforded a vast Variety of the feather'd Race, no less beautiful to the Eye, than exquisite to the Taste; and to crown all, the Climate was so perfectly wholesome, that the Inhabitants lived to an extreme old Age, without being afflicted with any Pain or Disease.

This happy Spot of Earth was govern'd by a King call'd [2]*Eojaeu*, in whose Family the Scepter had remain'd for upwards of 1500 Years, in all which Time no Wars with foreign Foes, nor home-bred Factions had disturb'd the Land. So long a Series of Tranquillity produced Blessings too valuable for a good Prince not to wish earnestly for the Continuance of them; and it was with an infinite Concern, the illustrious *Eojaeu* knew, by a [3]Science in which he was a Perfect Master, that with his Life would end the Felicity of his Subjects, or at least suffer a long and terrible Interruption. As he had no Son, and was to be succeeded by an only Daughter, he took care to educate her in such a manner as he thought might most contribute to alleviate the Calamities, which he foresaw the Fates had decreed for her, and the

---

1   This Kingdom, according to a Map annexed to the History, was situated near the South Pole: if so, it must be, within a few Degrees, the *Antipodes* to *England*, and Part of that huge Continent, now call'd *Terra Australis*, or the unknown Land. The Cabal were of Opinion, that by the Name of *Ijaveo* is meant, Opulent and Magnanimous.[E.H.]

2   Father of the People.[E.H.]

3   Magick, of which the learned Commentator on the *Chinese* Translation observes, there were two kinds practised by the People of those Days; the one had for its Patrons the *Genii*, or Good Powers; the other was Diabolical. The Conduct of *Eojaeu* proves the first of these to have been his Study. [E.H.]

Nation she was born to rule. He employed no Masters expert in the Arts of Singing, Dancing, Playing on the Musick, or any other the like Modes of accomplishing young Ladies; nor, indeed, was there the least Necessity for it, even had the Business of her Life been no more than to please; for she had a Mistress capable of instructing, or rather of inspiring every thing becoming of her Sex and Rank: *Nature* had given so graceful, so enchanting an Air to all her Motions, and taught her Voice to issue in such harmonious and persuasive Accents, that any *studied Forms* must have diminished instead of adding to her Perfections; but there was nothing of which he so much endeavour'd to keep her in Ignorance as her own Charms. To this end, he suffer'd her to converse but little with her *own Sex*, and strictly forbad those of the *other*, to mention Beauty, or any Endowment of the *Body*, as things deserving Praise; the Virtues of the *Mind* were what he labour'd to inculcate, and therefore took all possible care to render amiable to her. *Pride* and *Avarice* he taught her to detest from her most early Years, as Vices the most shameful in a crown'd Head; and as her Understanding ripened, laid down to her those Precepts of Government, which no Prince, who does not punctually observe, can make his Subjects happy, or be long safe himself, from their just Resentment. He represented to her, that the [1]greatest Glory of a Monarch was the Liberty of the People, his most valuable Treasures in *their* crowded Coffers, and his securest Guard in their *sincere Affection*. Take care, therefore, said he, that you never suffer yourself to be ensnared by the false Lustre of *Arbitrary Power*, which, like those wandering Fires, which mislead benighted Travellers to their Perdition, will, before you are aware, hurry you to Acts unworthy of your Place, and ruinous to yourself. – Remember, you are no less bound by *Laws*, than the meanest of your Subjects; and that even *they* have a *Right* to call you to account for any Violation of them: – You must not imagine, that it is meerly for your *own Ease* you are seated on a Throne; no, it is for the *Good* of the Multitudes beneath you; and when you cease to study *that*, you cease to have any *Claim* to their *Obedience*.[2] – Let

---

1   This implies, that the *Ijaveans* were a free People, tho' under Monarchical Government. [E.H.]

2   greatest Glory of a Monarch...their Obedience: Eojeau's philosophy echoes John Locke's *Second Treatise on Civil Government* (1689) which explains that government

then your *Ear* be ever *open to Complaints*; your *Mind* inquisitive into the Ground of them and your *Eye* swift in seeing their *Redress*. But this will be impossible, if you suffer yourself to be engrossed by any *one Man*, or *Set of Men*; above all things, therefore, beware of *Favourites*, for Favour naturally implies *Partiality*, and *Partiality* is but another Name for *Injustice*. All Passions deceive us, but none more than the Goodwill we bear to such whose Sentiments seem to fall in with our own: we know not our selves the wrong we do to others, by loving these too well, nor can ever be sufficiently assured, they really merit to be thus particularized. – 'Tis a Fault to rely wholly on the most virtuous and approv'd Minister, because the best may err; but that Prince is unpardonable, who suffers himself to be guided in Matters of Government by one who has incurr'd the *general* Hatred. – The common and universal Voice of the People is seldom mistaken, and in all Affairs relating to the *Publick*, the publick *Opinion* ought to have some Weight. He illustrated this Truth by many Arguments, as well as by a great Number of Examples from the History of *past* Times, and his own Observation of the *present*; and that what he said to her might be the more deeply imprinted on her Mind, he obliged her every day to repeat to him the Subject of their Conversation the preceding one, with what Remarks she had been able to make upon it.

This excellent Father having thus done every thing in his power to form her Mind for governing in such a manner as shou'd render her Reign *glorious* for *herself*, and *fortunate* for her *Subjects*, his next Care was to instruct her in the Mysteries of *Religion* and *Philosophy*, that, whatever should befall, she might have so just an Indifference for all terrestrial Things, and so entire a Dependance on her future Inheritance in that World above the Stars,[1] as neither to be too much elevated or dejected at any Accident below.

---

is a free contract between governors and people, that the governors hold their power in trust, and that if that trust is abused or broken, the people have the right to revolt against that tyranny. See Chapter 8, "Of the Beginning of Political Societies," section 111, on the golden age; Chapter 11, "Of the Extent of the Legislative Power," section 137, on the purpose of laws; and Chapter 18, "Of Tyranny," section 200, King James's addresses to Parliament in 1603 and 1609.

1 This denotes the *Ijaveans* to have a Notion of Futurity, not much differing from what most Nations now agree in. [E.H.]

Eovaai[1] (for so was this young Princess named) profited so well by these Lessons, that, in a short time, she was look'd upon as a Prodigy of Wit and Learning; and her Beauty, tho' far superior to that of any Woman of her Time, was scarce ever mention'd, so greatly was the World taken up with admiring the more truly valuable Accomplishments of her Mind. But alas! the Precepts she received were yet green, there wanted Age to confirm and spread their Roots, so as to enable her to bring forth the Fruit expected from her; she was but in her fifteenth Year, when *Eojaeu* found himself summon'd, by a Power whose Calls no Mortal can resist, and the only Excuse can be made for her Conduct after his Decease, is, that she became Mistress of herself too soon.

When this truly good and great King perceived his last Moment was approaching, he commanded her to kneel by him; and, having tenderly embraced her, I need not tell you, said he, how dear you are to me; my Behaviour to you, and the Care I have taken to instruct you in such Things as alone can make you happy, by enabling you to discharge the Duties of your Place with Dignity and Honour, has abundantly convinced you of my Paternal Affection: but, because no human Guards are sufficient to ward against the Blows of Fate, receive from me a Jewel of more Worth than ten thousand Empires. – A Jewel made by the Hands of the divine [2]*Aiou*, the Patron of our Family, and most powerful and beneficent of all the *Genii*. This, if you preserve entire, and in its present Purity and Brightness, will avert the most malevolent Aspect of the [3]Stars, and even the inveterate and incessant Attempts of the fiery *Ypres*[4] themselves; and defend you, and the Nations under you, in all the Dangers with which you are threatned. In speaking these Words, he took off a Carcanet,[5] which he had constantly worn upon his Breast, and put it upon her's.

---

1   By interpretation, *The Delight of Eyes*. [E.H.]

2   The Cabal differ'd very much concerning the Signification of this Name, and at length left the Matter undetermined. [E.H.]

3   By this Passage it is evident, the *Ijaveans* had Skill in Astronomy, and depended on future Events from the Influence of the Stars; but the System by which they studied is now utterly lost. [E.H.]

4   By what is said of them here, as well as in many other Places of this History, the Ypres are no other than infernal Spirits, who are sometimes permitted to torment the People of the Earth, and are always at enmity with them. [E.H.]

5   Carcanet: An ornamental necklace (*OED*).

Let neither Force nor Fraud,[1] resumed he, deprive you of this sacred Treasure: Remember that what ought to be infinitely dearer to you than your Life, your eternal Fame, and the Happiness of all the Millions you are born to rule, depend on the Conservation of it. He cou'd no more; and perceiving his last Breath issuing from his Lips, he laid his Hands upon her Head, by way of enforcing the Command he had just given her, and graciously bowing his Body to the Nobility, who were weeping round his Couch, expired without any of those Agonies which make Death terrible.

Eovaai now assumed the Throne of her Ancestors, amidst the Acclamations of a shouting and almost adoring People: Novelty has in itself so many Charms for the Populace, that nothing is more common than to see all the Benefits of a deceased Prince, buried in the Hopes of greater from his Successor; and the unequalled Beauty, and rare Qualifications of this young Queen, prepossessing even the most wise and penetrating in her favour, it's not to be wonder'd at, that *Eojaeu* was soon forgot. It was, however, by regulating her Conduct after the Model of that illustrious Instructor, that she a while so fully answer'd all the great Expectations conceiv'd of her, that the *Ijaveons* had reason to think no Addition cou'd be made to their Felicity, except that of seeing their excellent Sovereign married to a Prince worthy of her, and by whom she might have Children to inherit her Dignity and Virtues.

This was a Happiness to which several potent Princes, and other great Men aspired; but whether it were, that she found no Inclinations in herself to Marriage, or that she thought none of the Alliances yet offer'd were for the Interest of her Kingdom, she gave no ear to any Proposal of that kind: And so great was the Reverence paid her, that not even those of her own Sex, who most shared her Confidence, nor those of the other, whose Birth and Employments placed them nearest to the Throne, durst presume to urge what they so earnestly desired.

Thus loved, thus obeyed, did she live and reign, till the Satellite of Earth had seven times lost and renewed its silver Crescent; so truly

---

1   Force nor Fraud: Haywood suggests a sexual subtext for the jewel by employing this phrase which is often used to describe the means by which men take advantage of a woman's virtue – rape or seduction. In Pope's *The Rape of the Lock*, the Baron "meditates the way,/By force to ravish, or by fraud betray;/For when success a lover's toil attends,/Few ask if fraud or force attained his ends" (I.31-34).

happy in herself, so good to all beneath her, that to wish beyond what they enjoy'd, was a thing unknown either to Queen or People. O, to what a Height of Glory might such a Kingdom have arrived! What Examples to Posterity might the Annals of that Reign have afforded, if, by a fatal Inadvertency, every *present Enjoyment*, and *future Hope*, had not been subverted, and all Degrees of People, from the Cottage to the Throne, involved in one common Calamity?

As she was one day sitting alone in her Garden, ruminating on the last Words of her Father, and the strict Injunction laid on her concerning the Carcanet, Emotions, to which hitherto she had been a Stranger, began to diffuse themselves throughout her Mind; she took it from her Breast; she examin'd it over and over, and the more she did so, the more her Curiosity encreased: She saw the Stone contain'd in it was of an uncommon Lustre, but cou'd not conceive how it shou'd be of so much consequence to her Happiness as she had been told; and perceiving some mystic Characters engraven on the Inside, which yet were seen through the Clearness of the Stone, she resolv'd to consult all the learned Men of her Kingdom, for the Interpretation. So presuming is human Nature, that we cannot thankfully and contentedly enjoy the Good allotted us, without prying into the Causes by which it comes about: The *wherefore*, and the *why*, employ the Speculations of us all; and Life glides *unenjoyed* away in fruitless Inquisitions.

She continu'd still pondring on the mysterious Words,[1] flatter'd perhaps with the Imagination, that her own Ingenuity would enable her to unfold the Meaning, when, to her inexpressible Amazement, the Jewel drop'd from the cemented Gold, and only the exterior Ornament, which had encompass'd it, remain'd between her Fingers: She stoop'd hastily to take it up, hoping to replace it; but, in that instant, a little Bird that, unregarded by her, had been all this while

---

[1] The Commentator will needs have it, that these Words imply a Vanity, or kind of Self-sufficiency in *Eovaai*; and infers from thence, that it's an Error to trust Women with too much Learning; as the Brain in that Sex being of a very delicate Texture, renders them, for the most part, incapable of making solid Reflections, or comparing the little they can possibly arrive at the knowledge of, with the Infinity of what is beyond their reach. But as old a Man, and as rigid a Philosopher as he was, I am apt to think, he wou'd have spared this Part of his Animadversions [Ed. note: hostile criticisms – OED], had he been honour'd with the Acquaintance of some *European* Ladies. [E.H.]

hopping about her Feet, snatch'd it in his Beak, and taking wing, immediately bore out of sight the sacred Prize. In vain her Eyes pursued the Track in Air, as far as she was able! in vain her Tongue, in screaming Accents, invoked the Powers that ruled her Birth. All seem'd deaf to her Entreaties, and her Misfortune certain and irremedible. Horror and wild Astonishment now seiz'd every Faculty; she stood motionless, and even bereft of Thought for some Moments; but cruel Recollection soon bringing to her mind the Value of what she had been deprived of, the Manner of her Loss, and the Mischiefs which were to ensue, an adequate Despair succeeded: Philosophy was incapable of affording her any Relief, and all her Reason served only to paint the Unhappiness of her Condition in the stronger Colours. With her Lamentations she could not restrain herself from mingling Repinings: Since so much depended on the keeping that fatal Jewel, said she, why was it intrusted to one of my weak Sex?[1] Why was it not rather enclos'd in a brazen Tower, guarded by fiery Dragons, and inaccessible to all the Efforts of Man, or Beast, or Fiend? – Why did not the divine *Aiou* protect his Workmanship? – Why suffer so [2]silly, so inconsiderable an Animal, to prophane the hallowed Relique? – Or why, continued she, in the bitterest Anguish of Soul, did he at all make what he foresaw the Fates were resolute to destroy? – And why, O why, was it ordain'd, that the Blessings of fifteen hundred Years must end in me? – Why am I alone, of my whole Race, born to feel and give Calamity, who am the least able to sustain it in my self, or afford Relief to others?[3]

As the Extremity of her Grief forced from her these and the like Exclamations, the Firmament grew dark, and was at length quite

---

1   my weak Sex: The analogy between Eovaai's jewel and her chastity continues here. In both cases, the woman's loss leads to some social chaos. Eovaai's lamentations over the loss of the jewel echo eighteenth-century conduct books such as Halifax's *Advice to a Daughter* (1688; but reprinted at least 14 times in the eighteenth century) which advised that, as the weaker vessel, woman needed the moral guidance and protection of parents and husband. Eovaai's "Extremity of ... Grief," her histrionics in this speech, illustrate Haywood's point that women are taught to behave in this self-deprecating manner. Eovaai's "Calamity" leads to her ultimate social, sexual, and political awakening through experience of the world outside her father's dominion.

2   This shews, that the greatest Mischiefs frequently owe their birth to what seems to us the most minute Causes. [E.H.]

3   These Expostulations, says a learned and religious Author, perhaps added to the Miseries destin'd for her. [E.H.]

covered with a thick and sulphurous Cloud. So strange a Phænomenon, in a Country where the Sun was used to shine with uninterrupted Splendor, struck Terror to her Soul; but, how greatly was that Terror encreas'd, when, from the dreadful Gloom, she beheld unnumber'd Fires burst forth in forked Darts, crossing each other with such Rapidity, and accompanied with so horrible a Noise, as tho' the whole Frame of Nature were unhing'd, and every Crack snap'd in sunder the Axis of the World: [1]She thought no less than that the *Ypres* had got the better of the *Genii* of Mankind, that the eternal Barriers between them were thrown down, and each contending Element was broken loose, and had free Liberty, by turns, to o'erwhelm each other, for a final Dissolution of all things. – Nay, her Imagination carried her so far, as to make her think, that she verily heard Rocks banging against Rocks, and saw them whirling about in wild Confusion through the Air.

As Solitude naturally enhances every Danger, the Horrors of this Tempest had double Force on poor *Eovaai*, by having none near to comfort her, or bear a part in this Affright: She call'd to her Attendants, who were in another Alley in the Garden; but they, no less terrified than herself, either not heard or not regarded her Voice and she was expos'd alone, and without any other Defence than the Boughs of a spreading Oak, to Shocks she had never felt, nor cou'd have any Notion of before this Hour.

At length the Elements, as having spent their Fury, sunk into a Calm; the Vapours dispers'd; the blue Screen again appear'd; and the bright Planet of the Universe returned to gild the Hills: Nature seem'd now recover'd, and smil'd in all her Works. All but the Princess, who being still disconsolate for the loss of her precious Stone, hasted to the Palace; and having summon'd a Council of all the great Men of her Kingdom, acquainted them, with Tears, of the Accident had befallen her; and entreated their Advice how to behave, that the Woes denounced against her by the last Words of *Eojaeu*, might be averted.

But how great a Change did the Recital of this Adventure occa-

---

1   This was the first Thunder and Lightning that had ever been known in *Ijaveo*, or perhaps in the World; for all the Pre-Adamitical Writers agree, that, in the first Ages, none of the Elements transgressed the Bounds set to them at the Creation. [E.H.]

sion in them? She immediately perceived the Influence she had been made to fear, already had begun to operate; and found her first of Sorrows in the loss of that Respect had hitherto been paid her: Instead of humble Attentiveness, a confused Murmur ran thro' the whole Assembly, all the time she was speaking; and as soon as she had given over, every one rose sullenly from his Seat, and left the Chamber without making any Answer to what she had said.

The Event being made known, the Body of the People were not less dissatisfied; a general Discontent diffused itself throughout the Country, the City, and the Palace; all the Love and Reverence with which she had been treated, was now no more; and wheresoever she turn'd her Eyes, she met with nothing but upbraiding Looks, or cold and inforced Civilities. The Consequence of this sad Alternative were secret Plots, or open Rebellions against her Government: *Ijaveo* became the Scene of Civil War, Father against Son, and Brother against Brother, now hurl'd the fatal Dart; the crystal Rivers received another Colour tinctur'd with human Gore: The Streets were so encumber'd with the Dead, the Living had no room to pass, but over the Bodies of their slaughter'd Friends; and even the Temples of the Gods had no longer Power to protect the Wretches who flew to them for Refuge.

Amidst this general Uproar, *Eovaai* was safe only from the Contention between the Heads of her rebellious Subjects, who, each ambitious of the sovereign Sway, prolong'd her Life but to intimidate his Competitor; she being held in the most strict Captivity, with no other Variation in her Fortune, than that she was sometimes in the power of one Faction, and sometimes of another, all equally her Foes.

In such a Circumstance, what had Life of value? A thousand times she wish'd to throw the Burthen off, and had doubtless eased herself of it, by means no way agreeable to the divine Will, if the natural Timidity of her Sex had not restrain'd her; but her Melancholy, by degrees, grew into a Despair, which wou'd have been no less effectual for that purpose, had not a sudden Change happen'd in her Affairs, which gave her another, and very different Turn of Mind.

Among all the Princes who had sollicited her Affection, while in her prosperous State, not one had offer'd his Assistance in her Misfortunes; and she imagin'd her self entirely forgotten by them: But, in this, her Conjectures deceiv'd her. One there was, over whose Heart her Beauty still retain'd its Empire; he was call'd *Ochihatou*, and had, for many Years, ruled every thing in [1]*Hypotofa*, tho' *Oeros*, the King thereof, was living; but, as he had so great a Share in the Adventures of *Eovaai*, it's proper to give a more particular Account of him.

---

1 According to antient Geography, upwards of an hundred Leagues southward of *Ijaveo*. [E.H.]

The History of OCHIHATOU,
Prime Minister of Hypotofa.[1]

THIS great Man was born of a mean Extraction, and so deformed in his own Person, that not even his own Parents cou'd look on him with Satisfaction: To attone, however, as much as was in their power for the Imperfections of his Body, they endeavoured to cultivate his Mind with all possible Improvements. And, to that end, put him under the Tuition of a virtuous and learned Master; but he proved of too arrogant and impatient a Spirit to endure Controul, or go through the tedious and gradual Forms by which Youth ordinarily arrive at Knowledge: He therefore set himself to the Study of the worst Sort of Magic, renounced the Powers of Goodness, and devoted all his Faculties to the service of the *Ypres*; by whose assistance, he became, in a short time, so expert in the pernicious Science, that he was capable of putting in practice the most difficult Enchantments. As he was extremely amorous, and had so little in him to inspire the tender Passion, the first Proof he gave of his Art, was to transform himself into the reverse of what he was: Not that he had Power to change the Work of Nature, or make any real Alteration in his Face or Shape, but to cast such a Delusion before the Eyes of all who saw him, that he appeared to them such as he wished to be, a most comely and graceful Man.[2]

With this Advantage, join'd to the most soothing and insinuating Behaviour, he came to Court, and, by his Artifices, so wound himself into the Favour of some great Officers, that he was not long without being put into a considerable Post. This he discharged so well, that he was soon promoted to a better, and at length to those of the highest Trust and Honour in the Kingdom. But that which was most remarkable in him, and very much contributed to endear him to all Sorts of People, was that his Elevation did not seem to have made the least

---

1   Ochihatou, *Prime Minister* of Hypotofa: This "great Man" is a satire of Sir Robert Walpole.
2   comely and graceful Man: In 1736 Walpole was 60 years old. Not physically deformed as described here, he was short, coarse featured, and weighed almost 300 pounds.

Change in his Sentiments. His natural Pride, his Lust, his exorbitant Ambition were disguised under the Appearance of Sweetness of Disposition, Chastity, and even more Condescension, than was consistent with the Rank he then possest. By this Behaviour, he render'd himself so far from exciting Envy, that those, by whose Recommendation he had obtained what he enjoy'd, and with some of whom he was now on more than an Equality, wish'd rather to see an Augmentation, than Diminution of a Power he so well knew to use; and so successful was his Hypocrisy, that the most Discerning saw not into his Designs, till he found means to accomplish them, to the almost total Ruin of both King and People.

The Places he held, giving him frequent Access to the King,[1] it was easy for a Penetration, such as his, to discover what Failings had harbour in the Royal Breast; and finding a little Vanity in Dress was most predominant, was continually inventing new Fashions, and communicating them to him for his Approbation. Among other gay Ornaments, *Oeros* was particularly fond of Feathers; several of which he always wore either on his Breast, or Shoulders, or about the Hilt of his Dagger; nay, he would sometimes have them fastned to his Scepter. *Ochihatou* seeing this, by his [2]*Æriel* Agents, procured one pluck'd from the Phœnix Wing, and having dipt it in a pernicious Liquor, which his execrable Art had taught him to compose, presented it to the King, who, charmed with the Rarity and Beauty of it, immediately stuck it in his Crown, while the cursed Magician uttered some mystick Words to himself, and so firmly bound the Charm, that *Oeros* had no sooner put the infected Wreath of Royalty on his Head, than a sudden Infatuation seized his sacred Mind: all his nobler Faculties were perverted, his Reason was lull'd into a Lethargy; nor had he Eyes or Ears for any thing that was not presented to him by the Enchanter; so that he became, in effect, no more than the Executioner of his Will.

---

1   the King: Oeros is representative of King George II. The feminized portrait of him here, his vanity and his obsession with fashion, suggest that Oeros is a composite of George and Caroline, especially as it was Queen Caroline who was so close to Walpole.

2   Spirits, under his Subjection, of much the same Nature with the Ypres, and frequently employed for the same Purposes. [E.H.]

Having thus attain'd an absolute Power of disposing every thing in *Hypotofa*, he oblig'd *Adelhu*, the only Son of *Oeros*, a young Prince of great Expectations,[1] and who already began to testify his Dislike of his Proceedings, to remove from Court, and afterward sent him, under the pretence of improving him in his Exercises, into the Kingdom of [2]*Huaca*, under the Care of a Person in whom he could confide, and who had Orders to make him privately away, as soon as the Murder could be perpetrated without Suspicion. Every thing seem'd to agree in flattering the Wishes of this artful Minister: He received News that his Commands were obeyed in a much shorter time than he could have imagined, and he now experienced in the fullest manner the Force of his Spell; for the King instead of making any Enquiry concerning the untimely Fate of an only and most deserving Son, appeared wholly unconcerned when it was related to him.

Ochihatou being now freed of this Impediment to his ambitious Views, got himself created a Prince, and, by a publick Edict, Vicegerent of the Kingdom.[3] After which, all who were eminent for their Birth, Virtues, or Abilities, were turn'd out of their Employments, whether Civil or Military, discharged from their Attendance at Court, and their Places filled up with Wretches, whom natural Baseness, or occasional Indigence, had rendered subservient to his Interest. He next proceeded to seize the publick Treasure into his own Hands, which he converted not to Works of Justice or Charity, or any Uses for the Honour of the Kingdom,[4] but in building stately Palaces for

---

1 Young Prince ... Expectations: Frederick, Prince of Wales (1707-51), whose enmity for his father, George II, became a public scandal in 1727, was courted by government Whigs and the opposition. The Prince, influenced by Bolingbroke's patriot philosophy, allied himself with William Pulteney and the opposition in 1737. Rosalind Ballaster suggests that the Prince is the Pretender, James Edward Stuart, who has been deprived of his birthright (157); however, in view of the novel's ending, I think her reading is too overtly Jacobite for Haywood.

2 The Land of Regret. [E.H.]

3 Prince, ... and Vicegerent: In 1720 Walpole became the First Lord of the Treasury and Chancellor of the Exchequer; he received a Knighthood of the Bath in 1725; and in 1726 George I conferred on him the Garter. Vicegerent: A person appointed by a king to act in his place or perform some of his administrative functions (*OED*).

4 The judicious *Hahehihotu*, in Volume the first, pag. 32d of his Remarks on this History, takes notice that our Author might have saved himself the Trouble of particularizing in what manner *Ochihatou* apply'd the Nation's Money; since he had said enough in saying, he was a *Prime Minister*, to make the Reader acquainted with his Conduct in that Point. [E.H.]

himself, his Wives, and Concubines, and enriching his mean Family,[1] and others who adhered to him, and assisted in his Enterprizes. All, however, being too little for his exorbitant Expences, he laid most grievous Imposts on the People, who taxed beyond their Ability, at length began to murmur loudly against the Government; but he had the Address, by a Shew of Pity for their Calamities, and shrugging up his Shoulders, as tho' he wish'd, but had not the Power to ease them, to throw the Odium[2] of all on the [3]Royal Authority; and pretending he was no more than an unwilling Instrument of the King's Pleasure, preserv'd the good Will of some, even among those whom most he had impoverished and abused.

Thus was the sacred Name of Majesty prostituted to screen the most enormous Crimes; and a Prince whose Heart abounded with Justice, Clemency, Magnanimity, and every Kingly Virtue, made to appear with all the Vices of a Tyrant and most cruel Oppressor. The poor *Hypotofans*, tho' naturally the most loyal and obedient People in the World, had at length their Patience quite exhausted: they grew ripe for Rebellion, and wish'd a Change of Affairs on any Terms, since no Slavery could be worse than what they now endured. *Oeros* had certainly been deposed, if *Ochihatou*, who knew his own Safety depended on that Prince's Reign, had not found out the only Expedient which could have prevented it amidst that general Disaffection. He kept in continual Pay a great Number of [4]armed Men, some Foreigners, some Natives, but all under the Command of Chiefs, who were entirely his Creatures, and were dispersed through every part of

---

1   Stately Palaces...mean Family: The stately Chelsea Hospital and the ten-acre garden of Orford House was Walpole's London residence. Houghton, his Norfolk residence, was pulled down and elaborately re-done in the Palladian style. The renovations included rasing his boyhood village and rebuilding it a mile away. Walpole's first wife (married in 1700) was Catherine who died in 1737. He housed his mistress, Maria Skerrett, and his illegitimate daughter in a government residence in Richmond Park in 1725. He elevated his son, Robert, to a barony in 1723 and made him Ranger of Richmond Park. In 1730, Walpole's brother, Horatio, was brought home from his diplomatic position in Paris to receive a post at court as well as a privy councillorship.
2   Odium: Hatred; aversion (*OED*).
3   This indeed seems to be an Artifice of a more modern Date, and therefore might well be looked upon as somewhat wonderful in those early Times. [E.H.]
4   This shews that a Standing Army was the Refuge of evil Ministers some thousands of Years before *Adam*. [E.H.]

the Kingdom, in order to awe the People into Submission.[1] Besides these, he had a kind of Civil Army, composed of the lowest and most profligate of Mankind; they were call'd[*2] and employ'd in gathering a certain Tax,[3] which gave them a full Power to enter the House of any Citizen, inspect into the Secrets of his Trade, and know to a [4]single Todo how much he was worth; so were in the Quality of Spies on every Family, as well as Soldiers in case any Insurrection should require them to join the military Forces, to whom they were little inferiour in Number. But this execrable Statesman, thinking himself not sufficiently secured by impoverishing and enslaving a People, who, till this dreadful Æra, had boasted of more Wealth and Liberty than any Nation in the World, took Measures also to corrupt their Morals, and to render all kinds of Vice so universal, that his own might pass unremark'd. To this end, he chose the *Hiahs*, or Chief Priests, out of different Sectaries, of which at that time there were many in *Hypotofa*. These held publick Disputations concerning some nice Points in Divinity; and each exclaiming virulently against the Tenets of the other, so puzzled the Understanding of the weaker sort, that many of them began to think, there was no Necessity of observing any Rules of Devotion, and that all Religion was an Artifice, invented only by a Set of Men, to hold an Authority over the Soul. This brought every thing sacred into Contempt; Men openly despis'd the Gods, laugh'd at the Influence of the Genii, and no longer invok'd the Protection of the Celestial World. *Ochihatou* found his Designs perfectly compleated by this Stratagem; for the great Barrier against

---

1 armed Men ... Submission: In 1730, Walpole's ministry proposed to keep a standing army of 12,000 Hessian troops on the British payroll in case of war with France over the Pretender. In 1735, the ministry called for an increase of 10,000 seamen and a land force of 25,000.

2 Many things in the Original being express'd by Character, the *Chinese* Language could not always afford Words to translate them; and this, among others, was so abstruse, that the Cabal thought proper not to attempt an Explanation; which after all their Care, they might possibly have been deceived in. [E.H.]

3 a certain Tax: Reference to the unpopular Excise Bill of 1734 which proposed the taxing of tobacco and wine. The "kind of Civil Army" refers to the opposition's belief that the general excise would create more excise officers who would be granted the power to search all businesses and even private houses for contraband goods.

4 A Coin worth about the 10th Part of an *English* Farthing. [E.H.]

human Propensity to do Evil being removed, the *Hypotofans* were easily led to the Commission of any Crimes, which gratify'd their Passions, so became fit Instruments of so wicked a Minister, and worthy of the Miseries inflicted on them.

Things were in this Position, when the Fame of *Eovaai*'s Beauty and Accomplishments fired *Ochihatou* with a Desire of enjoying a Princess of such uncommon Perfections; and former Successes encouraging him to look on every thing he wished as easy to be accomplished, he committed the Care of the Kingdom to *Zunzo*,[1] a Wretch, whose Nearness of Blood and Conformity of Principles made entirely his own, and took a Journey to *Ijaveo*, where he immediately listed himself among the Adorers of the Princess; but that Kingdom being then under the Protection of the divine *Aiou*, all his Enchantments were of no Efficacy, to delude the Eyes, or ensnare the Reason of any there. So that appearing in his real Deformity of Body, his Talents of Wit and Eloquence did him no further Service, than just to preserve him from Contempt; and he returned to *Hypotofa*, cursing Nature, himself, and his Masters the *Ypres*, for this Disappointment. But his Rage was converted into Rapture, when he was informed by his Art, that *Eovaai* had lost that Jewel, by the sovereign Virtue of which she had hitherto been protected from all the attempts of Men, or *Ypres*. He now resolved, nor Heaven nor Earth should bar her from his Embraces; and having devoted [2]seven times seven Hours, seven Minutes, and as many Seconds, to the Mysteries of Darkness, he at length obtained a Spirit, who brought her to *Hypotofa* in the following manner:

Amidst the Calamities, in which we left the Princess of *Ijaveo* involved, it had often been Matter of very melancholy Reflection to her, that, since the Death of *Eojaeu*, she had never been blest with the sight of his illustrious Shade,[3] either in Dream or Vision, and she now languished under the Apprehensions of being eternally abandon'd by

---

1   *Zunzo*: Horatio Walpole, Sir Robert's brother.

2   This Division of Time was not therefore an Art invented by the modern World, but only revived after it had seem'd lost for some thousand Years. [E.H.]

3   The *Ijaveons* looked on the Spirits of their deceased Friends as a kind of Guardian Angels to them; and therefore thought, when they did not appear, no good Fortune was to be expected. [E.H.]

him; when, one Night, contrary to her Hopes, he appeared to her, with a Visage wholly free from Severity, and looking stedfastly on her, spoke these Words: *Eovaai*, be patient – be watchful – be resolute – be constant – doubt of all you see – hope in what you see not – you must be more unhappy to be happy. He said no more, but at that Instant vanished in a Stream of Light. She quitted her Bed immediately, and having returned Thanks to *Aiou*, by whose [1]Intercession this Favour was permitted her, sat down to contemplate on what he had uttered. She knew very well she had sufficient Occasion to practise the Lessons he had given her, while he remained on Earth, and which his immortal Part had now reminded her of; but could not conceive, that there was a Possibility of being more unhappy than she already was. Deposed, a Prisoner, subjected to the Will of those she was born to rule, not only herself, but her whole Kingdom, plunged in present Confusion and lasting Infamy, meerly by her own Fault: What Woes, cry'd she, yet ever equal'd mine? What more can the utmost Rigour of the Fates inflict? *If to be happy, I must be more unhappy*, never, never must I hope Relief! 'Tis not in Heaven, or Earth, to add to what I suffer; and 'tis but to make my present Miseries seem lighter, that my Father would have me think there can be greater. She was thus going on to set Bounds to Infinity, and measuring the Power of the immortal Beings, by her own shallow Comprehension of them, 'till Day appeared, when casting her Eyes on the unclouded Sky, she beheld at a great distance a small black Spot, which coming nearer by degrees, and extending itself as it approached, at length took the Form of a Body, part Fowl, part Fish. From the enormous Sides were stretched out Wings of a prodigious Size, underneath which, instead of Feet, grew Fins, reaching to a Tail, in Shape and Breadth like that of the Leviathan.[2] Head it had none, at least that was discernable; for just above the Neck was placed a Globe of bluish Fire, which, to the astonish'd *Eovaai*, seem'd one huge tremendous Eye. But small was the

---

1   It was Part of their Religion to believe the Supream Powers conferred no Favours on Mortals, but by the Intercession of Beings, of a middle State, whom they called *Genii*; and to whom they supposed the Government of the Stars was committed. [E.H.]

2   Leviathan: A whale, but also, biblically, Satan (Isaiah 27:1). The name was used by the opposition to signify Walpole.

Time allowed her for Examination, had the Terror she was in permitted her to make any: The dreadful Apparition came just over her, and she could only know thus much, that she perceived a thick Vapour enter the Room, which immediately inveloping her, she felt herself taken from the Place, and presently after heard the Wings of her ærial Carriage sing with the Rapidity of its Flight; then the Fins and Tail lash among Waves, as forcing a Passage through mighty Waters; but the swift Transition gave her no room for Thought, till on a sudden every thing was hush, she found her Feet on Earth, and her Eyes had liberty to look abroad. She turned herself about in search of the Machine, in which she had been conveyed; but the hideous Phantom vanished in the Instant she was set down, nor could she perceive the least Traces of her Journey, any more than form any Conjecture into what Part of the World she had been thus miraculously transported.

She looks round, and finds every thing delightful as the Dwellings of the Blessed, when, after a Life of Care, they receive their Virtue's Recompence in the World of *Eos*[1]: The Verdure of the Plains, enamell'd with the most beautiful Flowers, charm her on the one side, and magnificent Buildings on the other: As she advances toward the latter, she is more and more struck with the Grandeur and Elegance of every thing she sees, and is so taken up with Admiration, that she forgets she is a Stranger, destitute of Servants, Friends, or even the Means of supporting herself. Nor had the Thoughts, in what manner she shou'd live, once enter'd her Head, when she beheld, at a distance, a Chariot coming towards her, richly adorned, and drawn by twelve Antelopes, white and shining as the Morning-Dew, and attended by a great Number of Lacqueys, in very splendid Liveries.[2] The Equipage stop'd within three or four Yards of the Place in which she stood, and a Person, whose Aspect inspired an equal Share of Respect and Reverence, alighted from the Chariot, and falling on his Knees before her, accosted her in these Terms: Permit me, *Divinest Princess*, said he, to be the first to welcome you to a Land, which cannot but be bless'd while

---

1   Or *Jupiter*, in which Planet, they supposed, were those pleasant Fields, by modern Poets, call'd *Elysium*. [E.H.]

2   Lacqueys ... Liveries: Servants dressed in clothes bestowed by their master so that they could be recognized as his; lacqueys were servants who ran before their master's carriage and waited on him at table (*OED*).

you continue on it, and to conduct you to a Palace less unworthy of you than that you lately left.

Not all the Changes *Eovaai* had experienced since the Death of *Eojaeu*, had fill'd her with greater Consternation than she now felt, at hearing the Voice of him that spoke: She knew the Accents to be the same she had often heard from the Mouth of *Ochihatou*, when he had sollicited her for Marriage in *Ijaveo*, and who, at that time, had so disagreeable a Form, as to render all the fine things he said to her scarce to be endured. She now beheld the most mishapen of Mankind, converted into one of the most lovely; and the Uncertainty, whether she shou'd give credit to her Eyes, against the Testimony of her Ears, rendered her unable to make any Answer to the obliging Salutation he had given her. But he, who was no Stranger to her Suspense, nor wanted Artifice to solve any Difficulty, endeavoured to ease her of it in this manner: *Charming Princess*, resumed he, I perceive, that different Sentiments make a kind of Conflict in your Bosom; that a thorough Contempt for a Person can hardly be worn off, and that the Remembrance of what I once appeared, occasions in you a Regret to do Justice to what I really am: It might therefore be my Interest to deny I am the Man, who had the Boldness to address you under that forbidding Form; nor cou'd you disprove such an Assertion, since there is nothing impossible in two People's having the Organs of Speech formed so exactly alike, as to make not the least Difference between their Voices; but I will not go about to deceive you in any thing: I am *Ochihatou*, and no less your Adorer, now restored to the Shape that Nature gave me, than when a cruel Enchantment made me seem an Object more proper to excite your Loathing than your Love. How fortunate shou'd I be, (continued this Deceiver, looking on her with Eyes all languishing) if this Change in my Person cou'd make any Alteration in your Sentiments!

Here he left off speaking; and *Eovaai* blushing, between Modesty and Pleasure, replied in Words to this effect: So many and such surprising Accidents have of late befallen me, said she, that it is not to be wondered at, that I want Words to express myself as I ought. All I can do, is to assure you, I rejoice in any thing that may contribute to the Happiness of a Prince whom I always esteemed for his good Qualities, and was never unjust enough to hate, for what was not in his power to avoid.

Ochihatou, charmed with an Answer that seemed so favourable to his Wishes, took the liberty of kissing that Hand she had stretched out to raise him; and then, I flatter myself, most lovely *Eovaai*, resumed he, that the Proofs I shall hereafter give you of a Passion without Bounds, will, in due time, convince you, I merit somewhat more than you vouchsafed to grant at our last Meeting. In the mean time, refuse me not the Blessing of attending you to that Repose your late Fatigues require. With these Words he made a Motion to lead her to the Chariot, which she not opposing, he seated himself by her; and having commanded the Servants to proceed in their Journey, renewed the Conversation, by telling her, that knowing, by his Skill in Magic, that she was threatned with greater Woes than any she had yet endured, if she remained in *Ijaveo*, he had compelled a Spirit of the Air to remove her from so ungrateful a Country; and concluded with a thousand Protestations of his eternal Services. He then pointed out to her several stately Edifices, as they pass'd along to the Palace; but when they arrived at that Rival of the celestial Orbs, all he had remarked to her on the Road, or all she had seen in *Ijaveo*, seemed Cottages. The lofty Battlements, the gilded Spires, the Alabaster Columns supporting the capacious Structure, filled her at once with Wonder and Delight. Soon as they approach'd, the brazen Gate open'd with an hundred Folds, to give them entrance; as many Slaves, habited in flowing Robes of Green and Gold, strewed various Perfumes beneath their Feet; while, ushering them into a magnificent Gallery, at the End of which was an Apartment ornamented with all the Rarities of Art and Nature: Whatever either in Air, or Sea, or Earth, is to be found of rich and curious, might here be seen; and the unsated Eye for ever gaze, yet still be ignorant of half the gorgeous Magazine.[1] *Eovaai* wou'd fain have past some time in examining what she beheld; but *Ochihatou* thinking Rest would be more proper, would not permit her: And calling for Women-Attendants, forced her, in an obliging and most tender manner, to suffer them to conduct her to an inner Chamber, where they put her into Bed.

All the time she was undressing, these Creatures entertain'd her with the Merits of *Ochihatou*; one extoll'd his Wit, another his Generosity, a third his Gallantry and agreeable Person, and a fourth, more

---

1 Magazine: A storehouse or repository for goods or merchandise (*OED*).

bold than her Companions, after having equall'd him almost to the celestial Beings, cried out in a sort of Rapture, Happy, beyond Expression, will be that Lady who has the Secret to gain and keep his Heart! Bless'd will be her Days, and doubly bless'd her Nights. – Such a Transcendency of Good-Fortune can neither be merited nor possess'd by any but so charming a Princess as *Eovaai*. The fair Stranger was a little surpriz'd to find her Name and Rank already so well known; but she soon perceived, that every Circumstance of her Life had been the common Topick of Discourse in *Hypotofa*, long before her Arrival; and that these Women had been instructed to receive and obey her as their Mistress. From the Praises of *Ochihatou*, they proceeded to the most gross Flattery of her Beauty; and laying her on the Bed, the Canopy of which was lined with Looking-Glass: [1]Cast up your Eyes, most lovely Princess, said one of them, and behold a Sight more worthy the Admiration, even of yourself, than any thing this sumptuous Palace, or the whole World can shew. – Your own heavenly Person. – Ah, what a ravishing Proportion! – What fine-turned Limbs! – How formed for Love is every Part! – What Legs! – What Arms! – What Breasts! – What – She was going on, as one may imagine, to particularize every Charm, but *Eovaai*, whose Modesty would not allow her to seem pleased with Discourses of this nature, desir'd to be covered, and left to her Repose. Her Commands were immediately obey'd, and the moment the Women were withdrawn, a Concert of the softest Musick she had ever heard, struck up in an adjacent Room; and while it charm'd her Senses, lull'd them into that Supineness[2] she before but counterfeited.

On her awaking, she found the same Women obsequiously waiting to clothe her in Apparel, to which that she wore on the Solemnity of her Coronation, or any she had ever beheld in *Ijaveo*, was mean and contemptible. She now, for the first time, considered the Perfections of her Person: She viewed herself with pleasure: She no longer doubted if the repeated Panegyricks[3] of her insinuating Attendants were

---

1   We find by this, that Court-Bauds [Ed. Note: those employed in pandering to sexual debauchery; women who keep a place of prostitution – *OED*] were the same before the Days of *Adam* as since. [E.H.]

2   Supineness: Negligence; inattention; carelessness (*OED*).

3   Panegyricks: Elaborate praise.

just;[1] and, from this moment, assumed an innate Vanity, and outward Haughtiness, to which hitherto she had been a perfect Stranger.

Dazling as those superior Beings which rule the Stars, and tread the lofty Mansions of the Skies, did *Ochihatou* find her at his Morning's Visit; and his Passion growing more furious, by this Addition to her Charms, he omitted nothing that might serve to convince her of the Greatness of it; and having said and protested all that the extremest Love, and most persuasive Wit could dictate, took the boldness at length to press an immediate Gratification of his Desires. But that Pride,[2] which the sudden Consciousness of her own Beauty had inspired, was now, perhaps, of more service to her than all the grave Lessons of Virtue and Philosophy she had been so long instructed in; she was pleased with the Person and Address of her Lover; her Heart confessed the Impression he had made on it; the tender Impulse thrill'd in every Part; she languish'd; she almost died away between his Arms: Nature and Inclination pleaded strongly in his behalf; yet, when she remembred what she had been told she was, the most lovely and accomplish'd Woman upon Earth, the Boast of the Creation, and formed to be adored by the whole World, she thought the Man who should be happy enough to possess her, ought to purchase the Blessing by a long Series of Hopes, Fears, Perplexities, and, at last, Despair. This Consideration made her vigorously repel his Efforts, and tell him, in a majestic Tone of Voice, that she too well knew the Value of the Favour he required, to grant it on such easy Terms; that the Service of a thousand Years, if the Fates allow'd so long a Term of Life, wou'd, in the Scale of Justice, be found too light in Merit; and that it was sufficient that she listned to his Suit.

Ochihatou soon perceived his Error, in having done any thing to excite in her this high Idea of herself; but as he was well acquainted with all the Passions, he soon bethought him how to retrieve it, and

---

1   This Passage gives the Commentator an Opportunity of exerting his usual Severity: He makes a long Dissertation, to prove Vanity is so much a Part of Woman, that tho' Precepts of Education may prevent its Appearance for a time, it will sooner or later burst into a Blaze; and often, on the most trifling Encouragement. [E.H.]

2   This Supposition so much justifies the foregoing Reflection on the Fair Sex, that I wou'd fain have omitted it, cou'd I have done so without incurring the Censure of an unfair Translator. [E.H.]

render even his present Hindrance the Means of his future obtaining. But not to appear too precipitate, he feign'd a Repentance of his late Presumption; and having, with some affected Difficulty on her side, received his Pardon, led her to the Royal Apartments, entertaining her as they pass'd along the Court, only with such Discourses as gratify'd her new Passions of Pride and Vanity.

It being then the Hour, when those who were permitted to do so by *Ochihatou*, came to pay their Compliments to the King, or rather to himself; for the other was merely for the sake of Form: she found the Antichambers crouded with a gay Multitude, attired in various-fashion'd Habits, but all so rich in Gold and Jewels, that she took each of them for no less than a sovereign Prince, till the Homage they paid to *Ochihatou*, convinced her of the Error she had been in; and, at the same time, involved her in a good deal of Surprize, which desirous to be eased of, she asked him, of what Rank and Country those Persons were? He told her with a smile, that they were all *Hypotofans*, and Creatures entirely devoted to his Will: Some, said he, are of the Nature of Dogs, and when I cry, *Halloo*, will fly at any thing; nay, tear one another in pieces: Others are a kind of two-legg'd Asses, and, for a golden Trapping, yield to any burden I think fit to lay upon them. *Eovaai* could not help laughing at these Words, and looked on the Wretches with the Contempt they merited; but still testifying some Suspense concerning the Difference of their Habits, We have here, said he, no established Fashion in Garb or in Religion: Every body wears what he thinks will best become him, and professes that Worship which is either most agreeable to his own Opinion, or most consistent with his Interest: All that is required from the People, is to be satisfied with whatever is done by the Government, to pay an implicite Obedience to all Edicts from the Throne, and never to enquire into the Actions of the Ministers: In all things else, the *Hypotofans* enjoy a profound Liberty.

That *Ypre*, which inspires the Lust of arbitrary Sway,[1] now twisted its envenom'd Tail round the Heart of *Eovaai*; and, in an instant, erased all the Maxims the wise *Eojaeu* had endeavoured to establish there: so

---

1 Lust of arbitrary Sway: In Pope's "Epistle to a Lady" the two ruling passions in women are described as "The Love of Pleasure, and the Love of Sway" or power (line 210). Here, Eovaai suffers the two passions in tempting combination.

easy is it for the best Natures to be perverted, when Example rouses up the Sparks of some darling Inclination. She despised the Lessons of her Youth; looked on it as a Meanness of Spirit, to study for the Good of Inferiors; and considering Subjects as Slaves, thought it the just Prerogative of the Monarch, to dispose at pleasure all their Lives and Properties. As she was in this little Resvery, the Doors flew open, and the King appeared, seated on a Throne, blazing with Jewels brought from all Parts of the habitable Earth; the servile Throng immediately fell prostrate, crying with one Voice, Long live *Oeros*, and his great Minister *Ochihatou*. This Salutation his Majesty returned with a little declining of his Head, in token of Approbation; for since his receiving the enchanted Feather from *Ochihatou*, he had not opened his Lips to any Subject but himself. Then the Courtiers retired, and the Lover of *Eovaai* presented her to the King in a manner, which secured her a Reception every way flattering to her now high-rais'd Ambition.

A magnificent Collation[1] was served in by Waiters, habited like Children of the Sun; and *Eovaai* being placed on the right hand of the Throne, and *Ochihatou* on the left, they fell into those entertaining Conversations, which revive decaying Appetite, and give Luxury a second Course, after the Calls of Nature have been satiated with the first. *Ochihatou* told so many pleasant Stories, that the King laugh'd excessively, and the fair Guest was transported with the Wit and Humour of her Lover.

The Repast over, all the great Courtiers of both Sexes were admitted, and having placed themselves, according to their Ranks, on Seats erected on each side the Room; the middle was immediately filled up with a great number of Men, Women, and Children, who, some by singing, some by dancing, and others by a Variety of humourous Postures and lascivious Jests, which they before had studied, but seemed to speak *Extempore*, gave great Diversion to this illustrious Company. This Entertainment ended, and the Performers withdrawn, the Noblemen, who had all this time been toying with the Ladies, rose up, and every one singling out his favourite Fair, formed a kind of antick Dance.[2] *Ochihatou* taking *Eovaai* by the Hand, would needs have her mingle with them: She at first excused herself as being no

---

1 Collation: A light meal or repast (*OED*).
2 antick: Grotesque, bizarre (*OED*).

Proficient in the Art; but he would not be denied: and as she could do nothing which had not in it a peculiar Grace, the Sweetness of her Motions, join'd to the Liberties the Example of others seem'd to authorize him to take with her, added new Fires to his already too much enflam'd Bosom. Over these Revels the *Ypre* of loose Desires presided: All Sense of Shame, all Modesty was banished thence; not a Man but discovered himself ready to ravish what his kind Partner shewed an equal Propensity to grant; they ran, they flew into each other's Arms, and exchanged such Kisses, as the chaste Reader can have no Idea of. And the Princess of *Ijaveo* having now lost all that could be a Curb to Nature, scrupled not to do as she beheld others of her Sex; and great Part of the Assembly going out in Pairs, suffered herself to be drawn by the impatient *Ochihatou* into a Garden behind the Palace; where, as they walked, he entertained her with the most passionate Discourses, interspersed with others, which served as Baits for her Ambition. *Oeros*, said he, is old; he is without Children, or any immediate Successor. Whenever he dies, the Measures I have taken, will infallibly make the Crown devolve on me; it will then be in my power to reduce your rebellious Subjects, and *Hypotofa* and *Ijaveo* united, will form one of the greatest Empires in the World. What Wives I have, though the Custom of this Country allows as many as we please, I will be divorced from, and the Divine *Eovaai* shall reign sole and absolute Queen of my Soul, and all its Faculties, as well as of the adoring Nations. The former Part of these Insinuations seemed so probable to the deluded Princess, and her Vanity so ensnared her into a Belief of the latter, that she listned to all he said with a kind of Rapture; and so much had his Artifices debilitated her Reason, and lull'd asleep all Principles of Virtue in her Mind, that she neither felt, nor affected any Reluctance to be led by him into a Place, the Gloom and Privacy of which might have been sufficient to let her know for what Ends it was designed.

It was a thick Grove, where all the different Fragrancies of Nature seemed assembled: The Trees which composed it being Cinnamon, intermixed with Roses, Honey-suckles, Oranges, and the finest Limes in the World. Camomile, Balm, and Tansy, spread themselves beneath their Feet, becoming still more sweet by pressing. A Bank covered with Violets, Pinks, Daisies, and every Flower which crowns the

Spring, assisted the Invitation *Ochihatou* made the Princess to recline herself a while on this delectable Seat. 'Tis in Shades like these, said he, that true Felicity is only to be found. The Pomp of Grandeur, when seated on a glittering Car, the Rival of the Sun in Brightness, and at once the Envy and Adoration of the inferior World, tho' it exalts the Mind, and makes us think ourselves of a different Species from the gazing Crowd, is far from affording those sweet Transports which Love and soft Recess bestow. An elevated Station is therefore chiefly to be desired, as it is a Sanction to all our Actions, indulges the Gratification of each luxurious Wish, and gives a Privilege, not only of doing, but also of glorying in those things which are criminal and shameful in the Vulgar: – Bound by no Laws, subjected by no Fears, we give a Loose to all the gay Delights of Sense; and, if like the wandering Stars, our Motions seem a little irregular to those beneath, the Wonder we occasion but serves to add to our Contentment.

With such-like Discourses, he brought her to believe, that everything was Virtue in the Great, and Vice confined to those in low Life. As there is no Sentiment more flattering to human Nature, than that of being above Controul; there requires but few Arguments to convince us of what we wish. *Eovaai*, in an Instant, became so wholly abandon'd to this pernicious Doctrine, that she thought all the Time lost, which she had spent in endeavouring to subdue her Passions, and the Pains she had been at for that purpose, an Injustice to herself. – Not all the Principles of Religion and Morality, given her by *Eojaeu*, not a long Habitude of Virtue, nor the natural Modesty of her Sex, had power to stem the Torrent of Libertinism,[1] that now o'erwhelm'd her Soul. To live without Restraint, is to live indeed, cry'd she, and I no longer wonder, that the free Mind finds it so difficult to yield to those Fetters, Priests and Philosophers would bind it in, and which were never forged by, nor are consistent with Reason. – Reason bids us aim at Happiness, and can it be Happiness to waste our Days in denying ourselves the Blessings we were formed to enjoy, to support a continual Conflict in our Bosoms, between our Desires of Pleasure and the Mortification of them. No, from henceforth I

---

1 Libertinism: Disregard of moral restraint, especially between the sexes (*OED*).

renounce all Rules but those prescribed by my own Will – all Law, but Inclination.

There needed no more to make *Ochihatou* assure himself of obtaining, one day, all he could desire; but the Policy of his Love,[1] as well as the Impatience, forbid him to let slip a Moment so favourable as the present: Time and Consideration might possibly return her to her first Principles; nothing was to be risqu'd in such a Circumstance; and a Lover, infinitely less violent, wou'd scarce have refrained the Gratification of his Passion, even tho' she had put on a more resisting Air than she was now capable of. His Vanity, however, suggesting to him the Hopes of a full Consent, he repeated those Efforts on her Chastity, which, in the morning, she had, with such seeming Severity, reprimanded; but the Case was now entirely altered: Nor will it be thought strange it shou'd be so, by any who gives himself the trouble of reflecting on the Situation of this unhappy and perverted Princess.[2]

She was young, and full of all those tender Languishments, which, to keep within due Bounds, stand in need of the utmost Exertion of those Principles she had now thrown off: To heighten this Propensity of Nature every thing had conspired: Rich Viands,[3] delicious Wines, Musick, Dancing, Dalliance,[4] and, above all, the ardent Pressures of a Man, whom if she cou'd not be said to *love*, she infinitely liked. After such Excitements, the Sweetness and Privacy of the Recess they were in, could not fail of inspiring her with that dissolving Softness which *Ochihatou* wished to find in her; he saw the melting Passion display itself a thousand different ways; her shining Eyes swam in a Sea of Languor: her rosy Cheeks received a livelier and more fresh Vermillion: Dimples before unseen, wantoned about her Lips: her Bosom heav'd more quick: a sweet Confusion reigned in every Part: the transported Lover snatch'd her to his Breast, printed unnumbered Kisses on her Lips, then held her off to feast his Eyes upon her yielding Charms: Beauties which till then he knew but in Idea, her treach-

---

1 Policy of his Love: Implying that Ochihatou's courtship is a strategically and cunningly planned procedure rather than an honest passion. The word "policy" hearkens back to Machiavelli's use of it for the Prince's statecraft.

2 perverted Princess: Not used here in our modern sense to imply sexual perversion, but meaning that Eovaai has been turned away from the truth to wicked error.

3 Rich Viands: Foods, victuals (*OED*).

4 Dalliance: Amorous caressing and petting; wanton flirting (*OED*).

erous Robes too loosly girt revealed: his eager Hands were Seconds to his Sight, and travell'd over all; while she, in gentle Sighs and faultering Accents, confessed she received a Pleasure not inferior to that she gave. There wanted so little of her Ruin, that one can only say, it was not quite compleated; but the Prevention of it being brought about by other Events, no less worthy of Remark, we must quit her and *Hypotofa* for a while, and see what Mischiefs were occasioned in Countries far distant from it, by the Wickedness of ambitious and unsatiable Man.

The History of YXIMILLA; and the Motives which drew on the long War in Ginksy, that by degrees spread it self over great Part of the World.[1]

YXIMILLA ascended the Throne of *Ginksy*, after the Death of her Father *Protoobi*: She was a Lady of uncommon Perfections, and from her Youth had loved and been beloved by *Yamatalallabec*, a Native of that Country, and a Prince whom all the manly Graces seem'd to vye with each other, in rendring the most accomplish'd of his Time. The Conformity of their Tempers first created a mutual Respect, which, by swift degrees, increas'd, till it grew into a more tender Passion; but the Laws of *Ginksy* not permitting the Heir of the Crown, much less the Person in actual Possession of it, to marry without the Consent of the People, cast an Impediment in their way to Happiness, which not all the Valour of the one, nor the Constancy of the other, was able to surmount.

Not that the *Ginksyans* had any Reasons to alledge against the Choice their Queen openly made of him: On the contrary, his Virtues had rendered him no less reverenced by the whole Nation, than endear'd to her: He was perhaps the only Person in the World, of whom no body spoke ill; and even those who were prevailed upon by Avarice and Ambition, to oppose his Interest, cou'd not in their hearts approve of what they did; and afterwards had, without all question, come over to his side, if other Difficulties, then unforeseen, had not arose, to render a Declaration in his favour destructive to themselves, and not in the least serviceable to him.

Broscomin, the Sovereign of a petty Principality, had long aimed at being the Husband of *Yximilla*, or rather the King of *Ginksy*; for his whole Conduct testified it was not the Woman, but the Crown she wore, with which he was enamoured: To back his Pretensions, he had the Interest of *Oudescar*, King of *Habul*, whose Tributary and Creature

---

1   *History of* YXIMILLA I have been unable to identify who the main characters in this love story – Yximilla and Yamatalallabec of Ginksy, Broscomin, and Tygrinonniple – might represent. I suspect that they do not have real-life counterparts, but are "entertaining" fictions as the 1741 edition refers to this, and the Atamadoul episode, as "curious and entertaining novels."

he was: This powerful Monarch it was, who partly by Promises, partly by Threats, had influenced some few of the *Ginksyan* Lords to protest against the Marriage of *Yamatalallabec* with *Yximilla*, in order to impede the Completion of it, and give him time to raise an Army, which shou'd enforce that Princess to receive *Broscomin*. In this unjust Enterprize joined *Tygrinonniple*, Queen of the *Icinda*'s, a Woman every way qualified to govern a great People, and might have made as amiable as conspicuous a Figure in History, had she been less implacable in her Hate, or fierce in her Resentments. In a word, had she been more, or less a Woman; but she had all the Malice of her Sex, without any of the Softness: Compassion was a Stranger to her Nature, unless instigated by Favour; no Misfortunes, no Calamities of a Foe cou'd excite it in her: She took the same Pleasure in revenging the slightest Injuries, as in retaliating the greatest Benefits; both equally gratified her darling Passion of making known her Power. – But her Behaviour in relation to the Affairs of *Ginksy*, will better delineate her Character, than any Description can be given of it.

An old Spleen she had a long time bore to *Yamatalallabec*, on account of his Friendship with a Person at enmity with her, tho' he had never assisted him in any Designs against her, made her gladly enter into the Measures *Oudescar* had taken for the Establishment of his Favourite; and before *Yximilla* had any warning of her Danger, the Forces of these two potent Princes poured down upon her Kingdom. *Yamatalallabec* was not idle in the defence of his Country and his own Pretensions; he gathered together, he disciplined, he harangued the *Ginksyan* Troops, and knowing how vastly unequal they were to the Enemy in Number, implored the Assistance of *Osiphronoropho* King of *Fayoul*, with whom he had long lived in the strictest Amity, and who at that time was one of the most powerful Princes in the World.

This Monarch, who took more pride in succouring the Distress'd, than in the vast Extent of his Dominions, cou'd not refuse what was desired of him, on such reasonable Motives as that of relieving a Kingdom from its most cruel Foes, and giving to a Woman and a Queen that Liberty of chusing a Husband for herself, which the meanest of her Subjects enjoyed. He enter'd with vigour into the War, and caused also several other Princes his Allies to do the same; but *Ginksy* being at too great a distance to send the whole Body of the

Army thither, they marched into *Habul*, part of which lay not many Leagues from *Fayoul*, in order to oblige *Oudescar* to recall his Forces for the defence of his own Territories. This Design had the wish'd Effect; but brought not the least Advantage to the People for whose sake it had been form'd; the dreadful Banners of *Tygrinonniple* being still displayed upon their Borders, and her Army reinforced by Numbers not at all inferior to those that were withdrawn.

These were the Methods taken by *Broscomin*, for the Attainment of his Ends; and as they were so contrary to those of the Passion he profess'd must naturally turn the Dislike *Yximilla* before had for him, into the most fixed Aversion, and excite an Abhorrence in all those Princes who were not moved by Principles of Self-Interest, or partial Favour, to espouse his Cause. Those of the *Ginksyan* Lords, who by his Artifices, and the Promises of *Oudescar*, had been wrought upon to oppose *Yamatalallabec*, now saw their Error, but too late repented of it; and finding no Means of Safety even for themselves and Families, but by publickly joining with those whose Designs they before had secretly carried on, went over to the strongest Party: The same Timidity made others less criminal follow their Example; and *Yximilla*, being deserted by some even of those whom she most confided in, beheld her fruitful Plains laid waste by their own Lords, her Cities depopulated, her Fortresses, her Palaces, her stately Temples levell'd with the Earth, by those whose Hands had help'd to rear them. Yet did not all this Misery, this direful Scene of Ruin, once shake her Resolution: She remain'd constant to her first Vows, and was determined to perish with her Kingdom, rather than yield herself to the injurious *Broscomin*.

Seven hundred and seventy seven times had the great Eye of the Universe waked and reposed on the Slaughter of the loyal *Ginksyans*, before the sad Decision was made in favour of Cruelty and Ambition; but at last the Lot was cast, the Arms of *Tygrinonniple* gain'd an entire Victory, *Yximilla* was taken Prisoner, and the brave unfortunate *Yamatalallabec*, oppress'd by Numbers, was compell'd to fly, for the Preservation of a Life, which was no longer dear to him, but in the hope it might one day, in spite of the present Misfortunes, be of service to his infinitely dearer Queen and Country.

To attempt any Description of the Sorrows of *Yximilla* in this dreadful Situation, wou'd be too tedious; and besides, all that cou'd be said wou'd be little expressive of what she felt: It must therefore be left to the Reader's Imagination, when he shall be made acquainted with the Manner in which she was treated in her Captivity.

When first she was presented to *Tygrinonniple*, Well *Yximilla*, said that imperious Princess, I hope you now repent of your late Errors, and are ready to submit to what those, who know your real Interest much better than yourself, have decreed for you? If I have been guilty of any Errors, reply'd the *Ginksyan* Queen with a becoming Majesty, 'tis to the World above alone, I ought to be accountable; and while I remember what I am, shall never regulate my Conduct by the Will of any Power on Earth. You speak as you were still upon a Throne, rejoin'd the other scornfully: Enjoy while you may this imaginary Dignity of Mind; Time and constrain'd Obedience will abate this Pride. *Yximilla* was about to make some Answer to this Insult, but was prevented by *Broscomin*, who came that Instant into the Room, and with an affected Humility accosted her in these Terms: Madam, said he, since the immortal ¹Gods have declared, by the Success they have given my Arms, that it is their Pleasure I should enjoy the Sovereignty of *Ginksy*, and a much greater Happiness in the lovely *Yximilla*, I cannot doubt your Readiness to comply, and shall therefore order the necessary Preparations for our Marriage and Coronation. – He would perhaps have added something farther, having assumed an Air of Tenderness for that purpose, if *Yximilla*, who was deprived of all her Stock of Patience, at the sight of him, had not interrupted his Proceeding. If any thing, cry'd she, with an Air of Indignation, could heighten that Aversion your odious Pretensions, and the Measures by which you have pursued them, has kindled in my Soul, this present Impiety would do it. – How dar'st thou, continued she, raising her Voice beyond its accustom'd Pitch, impute the Destruction thou hast brought on an unhappy and defenceless Nation, to any Merit in thyself or Favour of the Gods? No, 'tis the Transgressions of the People have incurr'd their Vengeance, and thou art the Scourge appointed to inflict it. – But as for me, believe not I will be ever wrought upon to countenance thy Tyranny. – Triumph,

---

1 The Commentator observes that there is nothing more common than for People to ascribe the Success of their Purposes, of whatever kind, to the Favour of the Gods; tho', perhaps, permitted them for very different Ends than what they imagine themselves, or would have others. [E.H.]

while 'tis permitted thee, over ruin'd *Ginksy* – Reign King of Misery and Wretchedness – Yet know the divine [1]*Kinwallah*, from her celestial Dwelling, sees, and, in due time, will quell thy Arrogance and Cruelty; till then, be assured, that *Yximilla* regards thee with a Contempt, which nothing but her Hate can equal.

Here she concluded, and turned from him with a Look which shewed she meant much more than she was able to express. *Broscomin* stood motionless, and had his Eyes fixed on Earth all the time she was speaking, the Force of her just Reproaches had struck him to the Soul: 'tis possible, that in this moment he felt something like Remorse, but wanting Virtue to repent, was soon emboldned by the Fierceness of *Tygrinonniple*. You use with too much Gentleness, said she, the Wretch by Heaven and Earth given to you for a Slave; but I have that will bend her stubborn Heart. In speaking these last Words, she made a Sign to the Guards, who, having received Orders before in what manner they should behave, immediately seized on the unhappy Princess, and carried her to a Dungeon, which had no other Light than just enough to shew the Horror of it. There was she stript of all her Regal Ornaments, and in their stead her delicate Limbs loaded with massy and corrosive Fetters. What Sustenance she received was Scraps from the Table of her cruel Persecutors, brought to her by the Hands of Men, whose very Aspect was sufficient to strike Terror in any Heart less resolute than her's; but she appeared so far from being daunted, that even in this deplorable Situation the Majesty of her Deportment inspired those, who had the Care of her, with a Reverence, which rendered them scarce capable of executing the Commands of their unrelenting Mistress. The truth is, *Yamatalallabec* so took up all her Thoughts, that she had no leisure to reflect on any Calamities which related immediately to herself: for him alone she trembled; for him alone she offer'd up her Vows; and the Dangers to which she knew he must necessarily be exposed, were all the Ideas of

---

1   Supposed to be that Power in later Times call'd *Astrea* [E.H.] [Ed. note: In Delarivier Manley's scandal novel *The New Atalantis* (1709), Astrea, the self-exiled goddess of Justice comes back to Earth to review its moral condition. Haywood also employs the figure in her 1724 *Memoirs of a Certain Island adjacent to the Kingdom of Utopia* in which Astrea, Reason, and the Genius of the Isle expose the fraud of the Enchanted Well (the South Sea Bubble).]

her waking or her sleeping Hours. It is a Tradition credited by many, that the Constancy and Patience with which she supported this miserable Bondage, gave more pain to *Tygrinonniple* and *Broscomin*, than their most studied Malice could inflict on her. However that be, perceiving all their Severities were unavailing, they had recourse to other Means. They removed her from that loathsome Prison to a handsome Apartment in the Palace, they placed Women about her for Attendants; the Guards waited at an humble Distance, nothing but Liberty was denied her. *Tygrinonniple* sent Compliments to her befitting one Princess to another; and *Broscomin* visited her with all the Obsequiousness of the most respectful Lover. But her Soul, which had so magnanimously stood the Shocks of Cruelty, was also too well guarded against the Insinuations of Flattery, for this sudden Change in their Behaviour, to work any Alteration in her Sentiments. She looked on their Insults and Civilities with a like Indifference, and scorning to imitate them in Dissimulation, declared by all her Words and Actions, that she was still the same, and ever would be so.

The natural Haughtiness of *Tygrinonniple*, and the Impatience of *Broscomin*, to see himself confirmed on the Throne of *Ginksy*, would suffer neither of them to remain long in this Uncertainty; and the Messages of the one, nor the personal Addresses of the other, having been able to draw no Answer from the Mouth of *Yximilla* suitable to their purpose, they resolved to put an end to the Affair by other means.

They gave Orders that the chief Temple should be illuminated, the sacred ¹Bough brought forth, the Sacrifice prepared, and the Priests ready at the Altar; then went together to the Apartment of *Yximilla*, who having no Warning of their Approach, was a little surprized at sight of them; but suspecting, that there was some fatal Meaning in this joint Visit, summoned all her Courage for the Event. Princess, said *Tygrinonniple*, the little Gratitude you have shewn for the Lenity with which you have been lately treated, makes us know, you have a

---

1   The Branch of a certain Tree, feigned to be the first Thing created, and was always held over the Kings of *Ginksy* during the Ceremony of their Marriage. Some believe it to have been Myrtle; others Palm, as the one is the Emblem of Love, the other of Peace; but *Hahehihotu* imagines it rather a Plant, unknown in the present State of Nature. [E.H.]

Soul as incapable of Tenderness, as it is of Discernment; but you have been strangely deceived in your Conjectures, if you imagine our Determinations are to be altered or prevented by so perverse and senseless an Obstinacy. – No, we are weary of entreating, where we may command, and come now not to *ask* but to *compel*. – You must this Instant give yourself to the King. No Words can give any just Idea of that Scorn with which *Yximilla* turned her Eyes on *Broscomin* at these Words; and then, He may indeed, reply'd she, assume the Pageantry of that Title, but never can possess the real Dignity, since that must be conferred by me alone: which when I do, may Heaven, and all good Things, forsake me, and I have as little hope in the eternal *Eos*, as the Injustice of Mankind has left me here on Earth. Words are but vain, rejoin'd *Tygrinonniple*, and made a Signal to her Guards to seize on her; but *Broscomin* somewhat more mild, or affecting to be so, interposed, and taking her gently in his Arms, Madam, said he, you ought not to condemn what is the Effects of the most ardent Passion. – Too well I love to support a longer Delay; therefore, I beseech you, to resign willingly that Hand you see I have the power to force. Nor Force, nor Fraud, cry'd *Yximilla*, struggling, has power to move a Mind disdainful of your pretended Passion, as of your experienc'd Barbarity. Then, Madam, reply'd *Broscomin*, sullenly, I shall waste no farther Time in attacking so impregnable a Fortress: this unconquerable Mind shall be left to its own liberty; and I must content myself with the means which more indulgent Heaven has given me of becoming Master of your more defenceless Part. He said no more, but permitting the Guards to lay hold on her, she was forcibly carried to a Chariot, in which being placed between *Tygrinonniple* and *Broscomin*, and surrounded by a great number of armed Men, and preceded by loud Musick of various kinds, neither her Shrieks, nor any other Token of the Distraction she was in, was regarded as they passed along.

Being arrived at the Temple of the [1]Seven Great Gods, she was

---

1 All those Books which contained the Articles of the *Ginksyan* Faith being lost in the Conversion of Earth into Paradise, for the Reception of *Adam*, the Cabal found themselves unable to determine what Gods they worship'd; but look'd on this Misfortune as a Proof of the Fallacy of their Religion, since had they entertained any Notions of a true Divinity, some of those Volumes by one Miracle or other had doubtless been preserved. [E.H.]

rather dragg'd than led up to the Altar, where stood the Chief Priest ready to receive her at the Head of his venerable Band. At sight of him a Dawn of Hope began to beam once more upon her: That holy Man had been Witness of her Contract with *Yamatalallabec*,[1] had always encouraged her to keep it unviolated, and had testified himself a thousand ways one of the greatest Admirers of that Prince's Virtues. As she had a long Experience of his Principles, and knew he had an entire Command over the Inferior Officiates at the Altar, she imagined he neither would perform the dreadful Ceremony of giving her to *Broscomin*, himself, nor suffer them to do it; and as soon as she came near enough to be heard by him; Father, said she, you behold here your wretched Queen, dragg'd by inhumane Violence to be dispos'd of, contrary to her Inclinations, and to the Vows you have heard her make. Espouse her Cause, I conjure you, by your sacred Order, by all those Gods whose Representative on Earth you are, and by that *Genius* under whose Protection this Kingdom heretofore has flourish'd. – Confirm not the Title of Tyranny and Usurpation, nor pour the hallowed Unction on the Head of the Oppressor, the Undoer of your Country; but rather denounce the Woes his wild Ambition merits, and make him tremble at ensuing Fate.

Thus with streaming Eyes, and Accents which might have melted the most inexorable Heart, did this unhappy Princess enforce a Suit, she thought there was but little cause to urge, to one so much resolved as he had ever seemed: But alas! she too soon found what wicked Power can do, and saw in him a great and sad Example of human Frailty. This saint-like Man, this Herald of the Gods, this Dictator to the Souls of a whole People, worn out by a severe Captivity, and terrified with the Prospect of a still worse Treatment, had assured *Tygrinonniple* and *Broscomin* of his Readiness to perform whatever they enjoin'd; and as he expected no less from the Courage and Constancy of *Yximilla*, than what she now expressed, was prepared with Arguments for his Excuse: He told her, that he had received a Mandate from above; – That it was the Will of the Celestial World, *Broscomin* should be King, and by no other Method of proceeding

---

1   Contract with *Yamatalallabec*: In eighteenth-century church law, a formal agreement to marry, expressed in the present tense in front of witnesses was tantamount to a legal marriage and therefore indissoluble.

Ginksy could be restored to Peace. He added, no Man had a more true Regard for the Person and good Qualities of *Yamatalallabec* than himself, but must submit to the supreme Beings, who had revealed to him in Visions their Decrees in favour of the other; and therefore he desired she would conform her Sentiments accordingly, and not attempt any Disturbance of the Sacred Rites. He might have spared this last Remonstrance; for *Yximilla* perceived herself so cruelly deceived in the only Refuge she had flatter'd herself with, was immediately deprived of all her Spirits, and fell motionless, and in a Swoon, at the Foot of the Altar.

Broscomin raised her, and supported her between his Arms, while the High Priest, taking this Opportunity of the Absence of her Senses, pronounc'd the mystic Words which indissolubly united her to the Man she most abhor'd. Their Heads were shadowed with the sacred Bough; the [1]consecrated Balsam rubbed upon their Hands, and all the Solemnities of Marriage nigh perform'd before this unhappy Queen return'd to a Condition of knowing what had happened; and when she did, in vain were all Protests, her Cries, or Imprecations. She was born back to the Palace in the same manner she had been brought thence, and put into Bed; where, in spite of all her Opposition, she became the ravished Bride of the triumphant *Broscomin*.

The Hardships all this while endured by the virtuous and most accomplish'd *Yamatalallabec*, were little inferior to those of his dear Mistress, and such as to support with Patience and Fortitude proved him more the Hero than all the Battles he had fought. To escape the close Pursuit made after him in his Flight, he was constrain'd to experience Variety of Climates and of Dangers. Sometimes, thro' trackless Desarts, he made his painful Marches; sometimes, in strange Disguises, thro' the Camps of his most inveterate Enemies; now climbing Hills of Ice, then panting, and almost breathless, on Sands; scorched with eternal Heat; one while conceal'd in Fens,[2] another plung'd in mighty [3]Waters, whence his own nervous

---

1 Supposed to be the Gum of the Tree before-mentioned, and used in Marriages as a Type of that close Union, which ought to be between the Hearts of the Persons, by this Cement of their Hands. [E.H.]

2 Fens: Marshes.

3 This wou'd entirely overthrow all that some late Writers have endeavoured to prove, that there was no Sea before the Flood which happened in the Days of *Noah*, if the Cabal, in their Annotations, had not made it appear, that the Earth

Arms[1] alone bore him to a less inhospitable Shore; did Heaven, long unrelenting, behold this great, this excellent Prince; till, having made sufficient Trial of his Courage and Resignation, it at length directed him to take shelter in *Bazzuli*. The King thereof was brave, warlike, generous and just; and tho' (as Monarchs are not always permitted to act according to their Inclinations) the Interest of his People had obliged him to remain neuter in this War, he truly lamented the Miseries of *Ginksy*, detested the Injustice of *Tygrinonniple*, and the Ambition of *Broscomin*, and had the highest Esteem for *Yamatalallabec*; which growing still greater by the Knowledge of his Misfortunes, and the Manner he had supported himself under them, he received him as a Brother and a King, established a Court for him, and omitted nothing which he thought might be any kind of Consolation.

There was he, from day to day, informed by Couriers dispatched for that purpose, of all the Particulars of *Yximilla's* Captivity, and at length her forced Marriage: All which he bore with the Anguish of a Lover, but with the Resignation also of a Philosopher, and a Man wholly devoted to the Will of the Gods. But it was remarkable, that what not all the Woes of his Queen and Country had been able to draw from him, the [2]Infidelity of the High Priest extorted. O ye immortal Beings! cried he with a deep Sigh, and smiting his Breast when the Tidings were reported to him, who shall believe your Truth, when the great Oracle of your Dispensations makes it a Merit in us to be false!

While these illustrious Lovers, in Climates far remote, were thus regretting, more than their own, the Misfortunes of each other, *Oudescar* was not without his share of the ill Consequences of a War he had so unjustly commenced, the Arms of *Osiphronoropho* pierced even to the Heart of *Habul*. Several fine Provinces were taken, and divided among those Powers who had assisted the *Fayoulian* Monarch in his Conquests; his antient Allies made Excuses for refusing him the Succours he desired of them; and some, even of his own Tributaries,

---

received as great a Change before *Adam*, as it can have done since; but of that I have sufficiently made mention, in the Introduction to this Book. [E.H.]

1   nervous: Muscular.

2   The Priesthood of those Days so well maintain'd the Dignity of their Character, by a Sanctity of Manners, and Contempt of all temporary Things, that it was looked upon as a Prodigy, when any of them had been prevail'd upon, either by Promises or Threats, to act against the Dictates of his Conscience. [E.H.]

such as the Princes of *Laglah*, *Mizha*, and *Zalma*, but trifled with his Distress. *Tygrinonniple*, extending her Hate to all who took the part of *Yamatalallabec*, indeed remain'd firm to the Engagements she had made with him; but as her Dominions were at a great distance, the Forces she sent arrived not till too late, to prevent his being well-nigh over-run by the numerous and impetuous Foe.

In such a Situation, who can believe he wou'd not readily have listned to Proposals of Peace, and chose rather to have seen *Yamatalallabec* possess'd of *Yximilla*, and the *Ginksyan* Crown, than himself deprived of that of *Habul*, had any Motion to that purpose been made? but *Osiphronoropho* and his Allies, flush'd with repeated Victories, seem'd now to have forgot the first Occasion of the War, or the Motives which induced them to take Arms. Ambition, and that Thirst of Power which is the [1]Plague of Sovereignty, turn'd all their Thoughts on enlarging their own Territories; nor cou'd the Tears of *Yximilla*, or the pressing Instances of *Yamatalallabec*, obtain more than a verbal Assurance, that when *Habul* was entirely reduced, their Wishes should be accomplish'd.

Nothing could be more plain, than that *Osiphronoropho*, and [2]*Fanharridin* King of *Narzada*, had laid a Scheme for engrossing universal Monarchy between them;[3] and this made the Politick of all Nations begin to look about them, and think it was time to put a stop to the Progress of Arms, which one day might be turned against themselves.

None had greater reason for Apprehensions of this kind than the *Hypotofans*; those two powerful Princes having each of them, in their turns, given frequent Proofs, that they wanted but an Opportunity of invading that Kingdom: But *Ochihatou*, knowing the universal Hatred his Measures had incurred, wou'd not suffer the Army he so long had kept in Pay to depart; and thought it a less Evil to expose his King

---

1 *Itch* comes nearer to the Original; but the Word was rejected, on account of its being too gross. [E.H.]
2 The most powerful of all the Princes in league with *Osiphronoropho*. [E.H.]
3 universal Monarchy between them: This suggests the Family Compact between the Bourbon dynasties of France (Fanharridin of Narzada) and Spain (Osiphronoropho of Fayoul) in November 1733. The agreement was that Spain would help France against Britain while France would help Spain regain its territories in Italy. From 1733 to 1735 France was assisted by Spain in the War of the Polish Succession against Austria (Habul).

and Country to the Violence of a rapacious Conqueror and antient Enemy, than himself to the just Resentment of a People he had injured. However, to prevent *Oudescar*[1] from resenting this Treatment, he pretended, that the Succours he required shou'd be sent; but desired leave first to try, if there was a Possibility of adjusting the present Differences in an amicable Manner; and to that end, tho' he very well knew nothing cou'd be more impracticable, enter'd into various Negotiations with the contending Powers: His Creatures were continually posting from Court to Court, as if some great Affair were carrying on; and one was no sooner discovered to be fruitless, than he had another ready on the Carpet.

This Stratagem, for a while served to amuse the King of *Habul*, but cou'd not be of any long continuance; and finding himself in the extremest Necessity both of Men and Money, and the Rapidity with which his Foes pursued their Conquests, not in the least abated by all that had been done; he sent Orders to his Residentiary at the Court of *Hypotofa*, to demand the Assistance they had made him hope,[2] in Terms which shou'd oblige *Ochihatou* to give a direct Answer: but that Minister was too artful for the *Habulian*, and still found Evasions to put him off, till *Oudescar*, thinking himself trifled with, remanded him home in a manner as wou'd admit of no delay. This Order, and his Preparations for quitting *Hypotofa*, happened in that very Point of time when *Ochihatou* had just brought the Princess of *Ijaveo* to grant all that luxuriant Love could ask: *Zunzo* knew where and to what end he had retired with her; but his Unwillingness to disturb him in his Pleasures, was obliged to give place to the Necessity which required it: He foresaw the Departure of the Ambassador must unavoidably occasion a Breach between the Kings of *Habul* and *Hypotofa*, and con-sequently, draw the Resentment of both Nations on *Ochihatou*; he therefore hasted to the Grot,[3] and found the Lovers in such a Posture,

---

1   *Oudescar.* Emperor Charles VI of Austria.
2   Assistance they had made him hope: The 1731 Treaty of Vienna stipulated that Britain would support Austria with troops against France and Spain; however, Wal-pole wanted to keep Britain out of a war until after the general election of 1734, and therefore found ways of evading its obligation to Austria.
3   Grot: Or grotto. A picturesque structure made to imitate a rocky cave, often adorned with shell-work, and serving as a cool retreat (*OED*). Alexander Pope's grotto at Twickenham is among the most famous.

as assured him nothing cou'd be more unwelcome than this Intrusion. *Ochihatou* was at first all Fury; but the other no sooner made him acquainted with the Cause, than his Reproaches were turn'd into Praises; he immediately quitted *Eovaai*, who chose to remain in that agreeable Solitude, rather than be conducted to the Palace, and flew to the *Habullian* Statesman, in order to put a stop, if possible, to his going.

The Princess of *Ijaveo*, now at liberty to give scope to Meditation, all the Particulars of her strange Adventure were again acted over in Imagination; but when the Words spoke to her by the Spirit of *Eojaeu*, just before her being brought to *Hypotofa*, came into her mind: To what purpose, cried she, did the Vision enjoin Patience, Watchfulness, Resolution? I see no occasion for the Exercise of those Virtues. Why was that Menace of ensuing Woes? What *Unhappiness* have I endured in attaining the highest *Happiness* a Mortal can possess? – Am I not in *Hypotofa*, the Seat of Bliss! – Is not *Ochihatou* all that can be wish'd in Man! and is he not mine, for ever mine! and gives he not with himself all other Pleasures that can charm the Sense, Power uncontroul'd, Wealth, Homage, Adoration. – O, if I stand in need of any of those Lessons taught me in *Ijaveo*, it's Temperance to bear so vast a Surcharge of Delight, without such Extasies as might distract my Reason, and render me incapable of enjoying the glorious State allotted me by the Stars.

A Thousand rapturous Ideas did her perverted Fancy, and the imaginary Felicity of her present Condition, excite in her; and 'tis uncertain to what extravagancies they might not have transported her, had she been permitted much longer to indulge them: but short are the Joys which have not Virtue for their Guide, and lasting the Anxieties, when we too late are sensible of our Misconduct. Those warm Inclinations which the Behaviour of *Ochihatou* had raised, demanded Gratification; she languished for his return, and was beginning to feel [1]such Emotions, as might very well deserve the Name of

---

1   The Cabal were at a loss for the Author's Meaning in this Expression; and having consulted the Ladies about it, were assured by them that the Sex is wholly free from any Inquietudes of that nature. As it would be unmannerly to doubt their Veracity in this Point, we must either believe it Malice in the Historian, or that the Women of those times were of Constitutions very different from the present. [E.H.]

painful, when a sudden Gloom obscur'd those Beams of the Sun, which before were here and there suffer'd to peep thro' the Trees, and illuminate the Grot; and with this Darkness came a hollow rustling Wind, spreading a solemn Horror over all the Place. *Eovaai* was seized with an unusual Chillness; she trembled, tho' ignorant why she did so: but the Darkness lasting but a few Moments, a Stream of Light succeeded, not less glorious, but more moderate than the great Orb of Day, and presented to her amazed Eyes, a Form altogether new, yet such as excited more of Admiration than Affright. It seemed a Woman, but of a Stature far exceeding every thing in human Nature: She was neither so naked as to offend Decency, nor so habited as to conceal the fine Proportion of her Legs, her Arms, or Breast; a flowing Robe, which seemed borrowed from the Firmament, when no ascending Vapours sully the azure Tincture, being all that mantled any Part: Hair, more shining than the purest Gold, fell in careless Ringlets o'er her Brow, and gave a necessary Shade to Eyes whose Lustre wou'd else have been too divinely bright for *Eovaai* to have safely seen. Millions of glittering Atoms, such as appear, when the in vain excluded Sun, thro' some round Crevice, darts his Radiance, form'd a kind of Wreath, on which the heavenly Vision seemed to stand, about some five Foot elevated from Earth. The astonished Princess fell upon her Knees, but had not power to speak, nor lift her Eyes, till a Voice, infinitely more harmonious than the softest Musick, somewhat re-assured her in these Words:

Rise, *Eovaai*, unhappy happy Maid! said the celestial Being, whom in spite of thy Inadvertency, and late Neglect of every sacred Principle instilled into thy Youth, art yet too dear to the supream Powers, to be permitted to fall into that Destruction thou hast seemed to covet. – Know, I am the Genii [1]*Halafamai*, Sister of *Aiou*, the Protector of your Race, and sent by him to save you from yourself, and those detestable *Ypres* who have ensnared your Virtue. Therefore ascend with me, continued she, stooping to take her in her Arms, and see to whom, and what you were going to be abandon'd. While she spoke, a Chariot drawn by Doves appeared above their Heads, into which the Genii

---

[1] By this Name is signified *Truth*, according to the Cabal; but both the Commentator, and *Hahehihotu* are of opinion, that *Mercy* is more agreeable to the Original. [E.H.]

lightly springing with *Eovaai*, they shot quick as Thought over a Summer-House, where *Ochihatou* was in conference with the Ambassador of *Oudescar*. There hanging suspended between Æther and the grosser Air, Take this, said *Halafamai*, presenting a small Perspective[1] to the Princess, and behold your Lover as he really is: all Delusions of the *Ypres* vanish before this sacred Telescope, nor can even they themselves, invisible as they are to human Sight, escape detection by the Eye that looks through this: Nay, it has moreover this wondrous and peculiar Property, that, tho' envelop'd with the Shades of Night, the visual Ray becomes so strengthned by it, that you see all as clearly as at Noon-day. *Eovaai*, who had not yet assum'd Courage enough to open her Lips, obeyed in silence; but that reverential Awe, which had hitherto obstructed the Passage of her Words, now subsided at the more poignant and instantaneous Emotions of Horror and Surprize. She not only saw *Ochihatou* as she had seen him in *Ijaveo*, crooked, deformed, distorted in every Limb and Feature, but also encompassed with a thousand hideous Forms, which sat upon his Shoulders, clung round his Hands, his Legs, and seem'd to dictate all his Words and Gestures. Oh, all ye Rulers of Earth, Sea, and Air, cried she, what dreadful Vision is this? 'Tis not a Vision, answer'd *Halafamai*, but the real Person of *Ochihatou*, and those the *Ypres* to whom he is devoted, and at whose Instigation Rapes, Murders, Massacres, Treasons, all Acts which tend to universal Ruin, are committed by him. Can it be possible! resumed the Princess, turning her Eyes from so offensive an Object, and at the same time gave a great Sigh, either to ease her Heart from the Pain it received from her late Fright, or that the Pleasure she had experienced in loving, and being beloved by this seemingly agreeable *Ochihatou*, made her endure this forced Conviction of her Error with Reluctance. She wou'd have return'd the Glass, but the Genii bid her keep it. Things in this World are so little what they appear, said she, that you will have sufficient Occasion to make use of it, with People of all Professions and Degrees: By this alone you can be able to distinguish the Hypocrite from the Saint, the Betrayer of his Country from the Patriot, the Fool from the Politician, the

---

1   Perspective: Identified in the next phrase as a "Telescope," it also refers to the smaller spy-glass.

Libertine from the Priest, the Coward from the Brave, or the Foe from the pretended Friend: By this alone you can be preserv'd from falling the Victim of Deceit, which waits in every Shape, and every State, to lure the Unwary to Perdition. But it's time, continued she, we leave this Place, lest the Magician should practice Arts for the detaining you, too strong for all the friendly Genii to oppose. She had no sooner spoke these Words, than the wing'd Charioteers took their flight; and immediately brought them to a huge uncultivated Plain, where neither Tree nor Shrub was to be seen: No Cattle browz'd, nor cheerful Bird sought Food on the inhospitable Wild; but, far as the Eye cou'd reach, rough craggy Stones, and parch'd up Sands, confess'd a barren Soil, and an inclement Clime. Alas! cried *Eovaai*, what dismal Country are we now upon? That which you lately term'd the Seat of Bliss, replied *Halafamai*, you still are in *Hypotofa*; nor ought you to think it strange, that the private Luxury you have been witness of, shou'd occasion publick Misery. These now unfruitful Lands, not many ages since, produced every Necessary for the support of Man; but Pride and Idleness having spread a general Corruption thro' the Owners Hearts, each grew above his honest Labour, forsook his home, to wait at the ¹Levees of the Great,² and preferr'd Slavery, accompanied with Splendor, to the plain and simple Freedom of his Ancestor. Thus was all Husbandry, all Trade, all honest Occupations lost, and, in their room, a shining Beggary, a painted Wretchedness established. – Wou'd the Fates permit, I wou'd entirely remove you from so ruinous a Place; but here my Commission ends. – Here must I leave you to yourself. – Nor can my Power do more than warn you of the Dangers are to come, by the remembrance of what are past. As she left off speaking, *Eovaai* felt herself, by an invisible hand, set down on the Earth, and in that moment both Chariot and Genii vanish'd from her sight.

What more dreadful than this Solitude can Imagination figure out! No Mark of any Footstep, no Path to direct the forlorn Princess in

---

1 This was certainly a Term unknown to the Antients; but, at present, there is no Word which so well expresses a Place of Attendance and Dependance. [E.H.]

2 Levees of the Great: A morning or early afternoon assembly held by a prince or person of distinction (*OED*). Halafamai refers to this practice disdainfully as it usually involves unprincipled toadying to the socially or politically "great."

her uncertain Pilgrimage, no grassy Bank on which she might repose, nor Tree to shelter her from the rude Winds, or more injurious Sun, but all around a Scene of Desolation. She expected no less than to perish, nor indeed was there the least Appearance she should do otherwise; yet did she wander on for several Hours, tho' altogether unsustain'd by Hope; sometimes falling thro' Faintness, and at every Step her tender and delicate Feet smearing with Blood the sharp and flinty Way. At last overcome by Hunger, and Thirst, Pain, and Weariness, Nature could no more; and the Soul of this fair and bewildered Traveller was just about to yield up all its Faculties, when casting her almost dying Eyes a little towards the Right, she imagined somewhat like a Building presented itself to view, but at so great a distance, that she could not be assured it was so. The bare Possibility however so much renewed her Strength, that she was enabled to advance that Way; and soon found by the Aid of the valuable Present made her by *Halafamai*, that she had not been flatter'd with a vain Conjecture. She saw a spacious Castle, ancient, but not ruinated, built all of Stone, and seemed no less durable than the Rock on which it was situated. No Painting, Gilding, or carv'd Work, adorn'd this Structure, erected for Use not Ostentation; yet had in this plain Magnificence something which shamed the pompous Geugaws[1] invented by Luxury and Pride. *Eovaai* found so much difficulty in climbing the steep Ascent, that she began to fear she should be obliged to pass the Night, which now drew on, only with the Consolation of knowing herself near to a Place of Rest, without being able to partake any of the Benefits of it. But Time and Patience assisting her Endeavours, at length she gain'd the Summit, from whose commanding Height, she had a full Prospect of the direful Vale beneath; and having in a short Ejaculation acknowledg'd her Deliverance from all the Dangers of it, turned her Sight on a more pleasing View. On a huge Oak,[2] which grew just before the Castle Gate, she saw a Silver Trumpet hang, and beneath it a Tablet of the same Metal, on which was engraved in large Capitals these Words:

---

1   Geugaws: Or gewgaws. Gaudy trifles; knick-knacks (*OED*).
2   Oak: Oak boughs were "tory emblems to recall their part in the Restoration [of Charles II who, as a prince escaping to France, had hidden in an oak tree to avoid the Cavaliers after the execution of Charles I] to offset the whig glorification of the Revolution" (Plumb, 1960, 322, note 1).

Here the Remembrance of those abominable Principles she had so
readily imbibed from the Mouth of *Ochihatou*, and from the Practice
of which, she had rather been terrified than persuaded, drew Tears
from her Eyes. She thought the Task imposed on Human Kind, by the
Supreme Powers, was too severe: O why, cry'd she, can nothing but
our Torments be acceptable to Heaven? Why must our Pains alone be
Virtue, and all our Pleasures Vice? But these prophane Expostulations
lasted not long; they were but the Dictates of perverted Nature, and
Reason assisting the Lessons of her Youth, enabled her to look up to
Joys more noble and refined, than can be found in the utmost Gratification of the Senses. Being now resolved to fly Corruption, and have
an Abhorrence for Vice, she took Courage to sound the Trumpet; on
which the Gate was immediately opened, and she received into a
spacious Hall, adorn'd with Statues and Busto's[1] of those illustrious
Persons, who, in Times of Tyranny and Oppression, had happily been
the Deliverers of their Country, or bravely perished in the great
Attempt, immortal Men, true Sons of Fame, and worthy of the Name
of Heroes! Each aweful Head was graced with a Wreath of Laurel, but
none encircled with a Diadem; on which *Eovaai* testifying some
Surprize, a Servant who had been explaining to her the different
Hieroglyphicks engraven on the Pedestals, told her with a Smile, that
it was the Business of *True Patriots* to *humble* the Pride of *Crowns*, not
wear them. These Words to one who was a Queen herself, were not
altogether so grateful as the Person who spoke them intended, and
with a grave Air, I always thought, said she, that a *good* Prince was the
first of *Patriots*; the Happiness of the People over whom he had
Dominion, being of infinitely more Consequence to *him*, than it can
be to any *Subject* how great soever. Nothing can be more true than
what you say, reply'd he; and when a Monarch thinks as you do, he
merits living, not only more Adoration than he is willing to receive,
but also when he dies, to have his Image placed in [2]the Theatre of the

---

1   Busto's: Busts; sculptures representing the head, shoulders and chest of people (*OED*).
2   A Temple dedicated to the whole Hierarchy of Celestial Beings, and never entered
but on solemn Days, or to give thanks for some National Blessing. [E.H.]

Gods. With some such we have been blest; nor is the Owner of this Castle unjust to their Memory, as you shall be convinced. In speaking this he threw open an Ivory Door, and conducted her into a Room, or rather Chapel, which seemed cut out of one entire Marble, with such admirable Skill were the Quarries joined, the extraordinary Neatness of the Workmanship had doubtless engag'd her Attention, if something more interesting had not immediately drawn it off.

Two majestick Figures representing a King and Queen, filled an Arch just opposite to the Entrance; beneath the Feet of each a Monarch lay in Chains, yet seemed not to regret his Captivity, while his generous Conqueror, with stretch'd out hands, restored that Crown he had lost. The Gratitude, the Reverence, which appeared in the Faces of the Suppliants, and the blended Dignity and Sweetness in those of the Bestowers, demonstrated the great Skill of the Sculptor. *Eovaai* was charmed with the Beauty of the Piece; but much more so, when she was acquainted with the History of it. *Glaza* and *Ibla*,[1] said her obliging Informer, whose statues you see there enthroned, were King and Queen of *Hypotofa*, when it was invaded on the North and South sides, at the same time, by the Kings of *Tolzag* and *Bitza*. The dreadful News no sooner arrived, than *Glaza*, without losing time in consulting Ways and Means to raise Money from his Subjects, made use of his own Revenue for the enlisting a great Number of Men, with part of whom he marched against those of *Tolzag*; while *Ibla*, throwing off all the Delicacies of her Sex and Rank, went at the head of the other, to encounter the *Bitzians*. The Courage of this Royal Pair was rewarded with the Success it merited: *Glaza* not only rid his Dominions of so formidable an Enemy, but carried the War into *Tolzag*, subdued many fine Provinces, and took the King Prisoner. *Ibla* gained an entire Victory over the *Bitzians*, and brought also that Monarch in triumph to *Hypotofa*. The Royal Captives, sensible of the Injustice of their Cause, expected no less than the most severe Treatment; but our generous Princes made them see, that Hospitality, and a Readiness in forgiving Offences, were Virtues in which, as well as Bravery, the *Hypotofans* excell'd all other Nations in the World;

---

1   *Glaza* and *Ibla*: These may be King William III (who ruled jointly with Mary, 1688-1702) and Queen Anne (1702-14), respectively. William was at war with France ("Tolzag") for most of his reign (1689-97), while Britain under Anne fought the War of the Spanish Succession with France and Spain ("Bitza") from 1702-13.

exacting no other Ransom for their Liberty and forfeited Crowns, than an Assurance, from the one, never more to disturb the Peace of this Kingdom; and, from the other, a formal Resignation of some of those Cities taken in the War, which were of service to our Commerce.[1] Thus were all the Acquisitions of these Conquests turned to the advantage of the Subjects, while our glorious Sovereigns contented themselves only with that Love and Reverence, which the Power and Will of doing good can never fail to excite.

The Character given to the Princess of *Ijaveo*, of this excellent King and Queen, was so conformable to what *Eojaeu* had always told her a Monarch ought to be, that it drew Tears from her Eyes; but the Gentleman repelled those regretful Meditations she was about to fall into, by obliging her to turn her eyes on another scepter'd Hero, not far distant from the former. He seem'd in that Bloom of Life, which, one may say, is but just arrived at Maturity; yet, with the Fire of Youth, was mingled all the Wisdom of Old-Age; fierce, but yet sweet: So admirably were the commanding and beseeching Air united in every graceful Feature, as render'd him awefully lovely, and delightfully austere. As scorning Ease he stood, not sat upon a Throne: In one extended Hand he held a Sword of more than common Size; in the other, a Scepter ornamented with Doves, the Emblems of soft Peace. On either side was erected an Adamantine Pillar reaching to the Ceiling, on which were engraven the History of his Battles, and his Sieges, the many Dangers he had escaped, and the Victories he had gained. But because it wou'd have taken up too much time for *Eovaai*, to have examined every Particular of these curious Hieroglyphicks, the Gentleman continued to satisfy her Curiosity in as brief a manner as he could. This, said he, is *Amezulto*, a Monarch who excelled not only all the Princes of his own time, but also all that had gone before him, in every Virtue both of War and Peace, and left a Pattern for Posterity, more easily admired than imitated.[2] The whole Business of his

---

1   Assurance ... Commerce: The Treaty of Utrecht (1713) stated that King Louis XIV of France must renounce the Pretender to the British crown, James Edward Stuart; it also demanded that Spain hand over Gibraltar and Minorca to England and grant the *asiento* (the slave trade to South America) to Great Britain for 30 years.

2   *Amezulto*: The Catholic Stuart King, James II (ruled from 1685-88, or approximately "50 moons" – four years). Haywood's portrait of James suggests Jacobite sympathies (which surfaced again in her 1750 pamphlet *A Letter from H— G—g, Esq.*). However, it is more likely that she is simply romanticizing the figure in a nostalgic way to contrast with the political corruption of her day.

glorious but short Life, was to render his People happy at home, and reverenced abroad: With a Handful of Men, in comparison of the Number of his Enemies, he over-run one of the most potent Empires of the Earth, annex'd the Crown thereof to that of *Hypotofa*; and, in the space of 50 Moons, perform'd the Work of as many Ages. Oh! how transporting an Idea do you give me of this young Conqueror, cried *Eovaai*; but how came you to lose the Advantages procured by his Valour? How comes it that your Kings, in later days, enjoy only the Shadow of that Grandeur he acquired, and left to his Posterity? The Gold and Luxury of the conquer'd Nation, answer'd he, with a Sigh, undid their Conqueror, corrupted the lower Class of People, and Envy and Ambition divided the Great: A different Branch of the Royal Family pretended a Right to the Crown;[1] the reigning Prince was weak, wholly ruled by his Queen and Minister, who regarded more their private Interest than the Publick-Good, and were suspected to live in a more than becoming Intimacy: By this means the royal Authority fell into contempt; the Noblemen set themselves up for Heads of different Factions, the Populace lifted under their several Banners; and, while domestick Jarrs took up the Minds of all, foreign Acquisitions were no longer supported, and consequently reverted to their former Owners.

Eovaai was about to testify her Surprize at so fatal a Negligence in a whole People, but was prevented from it, as well as from examining some other Images of Monarchs who had reigned in *Hypotofa*, before and after *Glaza* and *Amezulto*. Word was brought, that the Lord of the Castle attended, to give welcome to his fair Guest; on which she immediately presented her Hand, in order to be conducted where he was.

[2]*Alhahuza*,[3] for that was the Name of this truly great Man, accosted

---

1   different Branch ... Right to the Crown: After James II fled England, Parliament invited William and Mary to take the throne. After Queen Anne's death, the crown went to King George I, from the House of Hanover, Austria. The "reigning Prince" is George II, ruled by his Queen, Caroline, and Minister, Walpole. Caroline and Walpole were suspected of having a love affair, but this was an unsavoury rumour meant to stir up more hatred for the Minister.

2   A Complication of all Virtues, and particularly of Patriotism. [E.H.]

3   Alhahuza: Probably Henry St. John, Viscount Bolingbroke (1678-1751) who, in 1725, organized with William Pulteney and Sir William Wyndham opposition to Walpole's government.

her with Civilities which had nothing in them of Reserve or Affectation; and, after she had imparted to him the whole History of her Misfortunes, from her being brought to *Ijaveo* till that moment; It wou'd be my Happiness, as well as Glory, Madam, said he, cou'd I assure you of an Asylum here; but alas! so great is the Power of *Ochihatou*, throughout all *Hypotofa*, that I dare not flatter myself even this Castle can sufficiently secure you. He then proceeded to inform her of all the Particulars of that Traitor's Life, and by what execrable Arts he had rais'd himself to a Condition not only to give Laws to the whole Kingdom, but also to the King himself. The Princess listned to his Discourse with the utmost Attention; and perceiving by it, that he had constantly opposed all the Measures of that perfidious Statesman, cou'd not conceive how he had been able to preserve himself from the Malice of so artful and so powerful an Enemy. And having given some Hints of her Sentiments on this head; It would have been impossible for me, replied he, by any human Wisdom, to have escaped the many Snares laid for my Life and Reputation, by that wicked Politician; but, from my youth, I have bent my whole Application to the Study of that kind of Magick which is [1]acceptable to the celestial Beings: My early Proficiency in that Science, made me see the black Designs of *Ochihatou*, long before he had an opportunity of putting them in execution; and tho' I could not prevent what the Fates, for the punishment of a wicked and corrupt Generation, had resolved to permit, I procured for myself and a few Friends, who, to avoid the Vices and Follies of the Times, have accompanied me in this Retirement, some Sprigs of a certain Herb that grows in the Gardens of the Genii [2]*Hemha*, of sovereign Virtue against all Efforts of the *Ypres*, or those devoted to them. I wish, continued he, seeing a kind of Entreaty in her Looks, the sacred Plant cou'd be of the same defence if worn by you; but that is impossible, you have renounced the Protection of a far greater Power, the ever-blessed [3]*Aiou*, by suffering that Jewel, which

---

1   This proves what the Commentator asserts concerning two very different kinds of Magick. [E.H.]

2   Some interpret this *Prudence*, others *Veracity*: *Hahehihotu* thinks the latter, as does also a more modern Author. [E.H.]

3   The Commentator imagines they looked on *Aiou* as the Prince or General of the whole Species of Genii; and that he was Ruler of that Galaxy of Stars, now call'd *Ariadne's Crown* [E.H.] [Ed. note: According to Greek myth, when the god Bacchus fell in love with Ariadne, daughter of King Minos, he tossed his golden crown into the

was the Pledge of Safety to your Race, to depart from your Breast; and till it be restored, no inferior Being, however benevolent by Nature, dares interpose in your behalf. The beautiful Eyes of *Eovaai* were overwhelm'd in Tears at these Words; and, after a short Pause, she burst into this Exclamation: Then am I doom'd to everlasting Misery, cried she, for never, never must I hope to see again the hallow'd Gift! Be not too rash in pronouncing Judgment on yourself, replied *Alhahuza*, it is not given us Mortals to fathom the deep Mysteries of Futurity, or scan the Fates immeasurable Decrees: By means entirely unforeseen, and least expected, the greatest Events are usually brought about; and what seems most remote, is frequently the nearest to us. Your wonderful Deliverance from *Ochihatou*, convinces me, that you are not wholly abandon'd by the great Patron of *Ijaveo*; nor ought you to offend, by despair, a Power whose Goodness you have so lately experienc'd.

To these he added many other consolatory Expressions; and a handsome Repast being served in, entertain'd her all the time with such Discourses as entirely brought her back to those Principles from which the Delusions of *Ochihatou* had made her swerve; and, at the same time, establish'd so perfect a Harmony in her mind, that she scarce felt any Remains of the Fatigues she had undergone. So great is the Power of Wisdom over a Soul capable of tasting its Joys, that while she heard him speak, she forgot all Causes of Inquietude, and cou'd have listned to him, with an Infinity of Pleasure, a much longer time, if he had not reminded her, that it was proper for her to allow Nature some Repose.

She was then attended by Women to an Apartment, neat, but not curious, and there left to herself, to ruminate on the Wonders of the Day.

The Adventures which had befallen her, and the Uncertainty of her present State, gave her sufficient Matter for Reflection; yet did not all the Misfortunes she had sustain'd, nor those she had reason to apprehend, give her half that Anxiety, as the Shame of having abandon'd her self, tho' but for a few moments, to Pleasures so contrary to the Modesty of her Sex, and so much beneath the Dignity both of

---

heavens to remind mankind of Ariadne's beauty. The star Gemma, which Haywood may be associating with Eovaai's lost jewel, sparkles at the front of the tiara. When Ariadne married Bacchus, she became immortal and lived on Olympus. The crown, designed by Venus, the goddess of Love, and created by Pluto, the god of the underworld, is the constellation Corona Borealis, or the Northern Crown (Staal 210-211)].

her Birth and Understanding: but as she cou'd not think how near she was to being lost, without remembring she was not wholly so, the Disquiets occasion'd by the one, were easily dispersed by the sweet Contentment which the other afforded; and she sunk, by degrees, into that calm Repose, which a Mind, devoted to the pursuit of guilty Joys, strives but in vain to find.

Soon as the Goddess of the Morn displayed her blushing Cheeks, *Eovaai* rose, no less refresh'd and cheerful than herself; and finding the same Women who had waited on her the Night before, were now ready to receive her Commands, by their assistance, was more than half-dress'd, when a confus'd Noise, and the murmuring of many Voices, made her almost relapse into her former Terrors: but one of the Women perceiving an Alteration in her Countenance, put an immediate stop to the progress of her Apprehensions by these Words: I hope, Madam, said she, respectfully, you will never have more real Cause for fear than at this moment; be assured, your Pity is all can be interested in this Affair. The Sounds you hear, proceed from the distress'd and discontented Citizens of *Hypotofa*, who, on some appointed Days, come in Crowds to this Castle, expecting, from the Wisdom and Virtue of *Alhahuza*, a Mitigation of their Woes. They are now in the [1]Hall of Patriots, where he will presently descend, and make an Harangue to them. On this, *Eovaai* resumed her Serenity of Mind and Air; and being desirous of hearing what *Alhahuza* should deliver, made the utmost expedition in getting herself ready. Soon as she was so, and her Request made known to him, he gave orders she should be seated in a Gallery which overlooked the Place, and from which she could easily see and hear all that pass'd. The Cries of these poor People, and the Hardships they complain'd of, drew bitter Sighs from the Heart of the Princess of *Ijaveo*; she griev'd for them, but much more for what she imagin'd might be the Sufferings of her own Subjects, whom she had left in the most distracted and divided State; and had perhaps fallen into a Melancholy, from which it wou'd have been difficult to rouze her, had not the Contemplations that occasion'd it been timely interrupted by the Presence of *Alhahuza*, who that instant appear'd, and having taken his place on an Eminence, in the middle of the Hall, for the Convenience of being heard by all, began to speak to them in this manner:

---

1   The same in which *Eovaai* was first received. [E.H.]

The Harangue of ALHAZUZA
to the Populace of Hypotofa.

Friends and Countrymen,

I grieve to see so many of you repair daily to me for Advice in the present Calamities, yet so few among you arm'd with that Resolution, and true Spirit of Patriotism, which alone can redress the Grievances you complain of. – Examine yourselves. – Look back on your past Conduct, and attone for it by the future. – Your Oppressors laugh at your Misery, and when you ask redress, are not ashamed to tell you, that [1]*if you are undone, it is by your own Act and Deed*; they tell ye Truth, Oh *Hypotofans!* for which of you has not, for a shew of private Advantage, consented to give up Publick-Good? – Which of you has not been a Factor for his own Slavery, and that of his Posterity? – Which of you has not, at some time or other, been corrupted by the Gold of *Ochihatou?* – The Gold of *Ochihatou*, did I say? No, 'twas your own Gold, the Remains of what your careful Ancestry had left you, drawn from you under various Pretences, and then returned in shameful Bribes, to make you accessory to your own Perdition. What Taxes has he not invented out of that detestable Maxim, That the way to keep you obedient is to make you poor?[2] – All the Necessities of Nature, all the Indulgencies of Luxury, are but so many Hands to feed his Avarice or Ambition. – Can you eat or drink, or sleep, or work, or play, in safety, beneath those Roofs rear'd with the Sweat of your industrious Predecessors, unlicens'd by this sole Director of all things. – Does not the very [3]Air you breathe, encrease his Treasures? – Are you not

---

1   The Commentator observes from this, that the *Hypotofans* must have naturally a mean-spirited People, to brook so bare-faced and impudent an Insult, as this mention'd by the Patriot. [E.H.]

2   keep you obedient ... to make you poor: In 1730 the House of Commons wanted the Salt Tax repealed to help the poor and merchant classes. Walpole favoured reducing the Land Tax to benefit the upper classes. He wanted the poor, the manufacturing, and merchant classes taxed and their wages kept low so that they would be compelled to work.

3   Of what nature this Tax was, is hard to guess; nor have we the least Light to guide us: but *Aristotle*, a *Greek* Philosopher, in his *Politics*, tells us, that one *Cypselus*, a Governor of *Corinth*, invented an Impost to be laid upon the People, which, in less than ten Years, brought all the Money of that State into his Coffers; and mentions the

excluded from the Light of the Sun, without paying Tribute to his Coffers? – What all the brute Creation freely enjoy and batten in,[1] O miserable Citizens, is denied to you! These are the Means by which those Sums were raised, which, parcell'd since among some leading Men, have prevailed on you to resign your dearest Privileges, and become Slaves by Law.

But you will answer, That you were unwarily drawn in, to do you knew not what. – Most certainly very many of you were so, I hope the greater Number; but now your Eyes are open'd by the dreadful Consequences, how poor is the Excuse you make, for not being as vigorous in your Endeavours to remove the Burthen, as you were tame in suffering it to be laid? – What if some few of the [2]mercenary Great-ones purchase a share in the Plunder of the Nation, with the dear Price of their own Honour, and subvert, by their Vices, that Liberty their glorious Progenitors reared and settled by their Virtues; are you to see the Morsel taken from your Childrens Mouths, because those *Tools of Power*, prophanely blending the Cause of sacred Majesty, with that of him who usurps the Authority of it, tell you it's Treason to oppose? Are any of you so unletter'd in the Laws, as to believe it criminal to defend your natural Property from the hands of Robbers? Or, can you think these Men less Robbers, because dignified with certain Characters? – They shew you indeed a Schedule signed with the Royal Signet: But who is the Keeper of that Signet? Is it not *Ochihatou*? – *Oeros* is generous, benevolent, compassionate, and full of all those Virtues that render Kings a kind of Gods on Earth: His Royal

---

Tameness of those Citizens with admiration. That *Ochihatou* then cou'd contrive so many, and of so severe a kind as the History implies, with impunity, will scarce gain credit in these times of *Liberty*. [E.H.] [Ed. note: Although Cypselus is mentioned in Aristotle's *Politics*, Book V, chapter x, there is no mention of his use of taxes. Aristotle includes him in his discussion of tyranny and the downfall of monarchy (monarchy meaning "the rule of one") which does have much in common with Walpole's government. "A tyrant...does not look to the public interest at all, unless it happens to contribute to his personal benefit. The tyrant's aim is pleasure: the king aims at what is good.... [T]he tyrant grasps at money, the king at honour. A king's bodyguard is made up of citizens, a tyrant's of foreigners" (V.x.335-336). Walpole's Excise scheme and his use of standing armies could easily be substituted.]

1   batten in: To thrive, grow fat, prosper (*OED*).
2   The Cabal were of opinion, these were of the Nobility of *Hypotofa*; but *Hahehihotu* thinks otherwise, because they are immediately after stiled, *Tools of Power*. [E.H.]

Heart wou'd weep Tears of Blood, to know one half of your Suffer-ings; but, alas! he is entirely ignorant of what is acted in his Name. You are represented to him as a People factious, and repining without a Cause, depreciating his Authority, and forming Plots against his Government; and tho' he decrees not the Punishments inflicted on you, believes you justly merit them. – Who then but *Ochihatou* is the Source of all your Evils! – By whom but *Ochihatou* are you impoverish'd, beggar'd and abus'd! By whom but *Ochihatou* are you deluded to relinquish the Rights to which you were born! by whom but *Ochihatou* are you banish'd the Royal Ear and Favour! Whom but *Ochihatou* is at once your Undoer, your Betrayer, and your Scourge! and on whom but *Ochihatou* ought you to seek Revenge? Rouze then, for shame, encounter the Oppressor, while there is yet any thing to save! Remove the Enchanter from before the Throne, – drive him from those Pleasure-Houses, those Palaces, erected on [1]the Ruin of your Fellow-Citizens, those Gardens [2]water'd with the Widow and the Orphans Tears, and, with his Blood, wash away the Barriers which divide you from your King! Think not, by Prayers or lazy Wishes, to retrieve what you have lost, or avert the Mischiefs yet impending. – You still have Hands; and, O *Hypotofans*, you once had Hearts to undertake the most daring Enterprizes. What is become of all that Spirit, that noble Thirst of Fame, which rendered your Forefathers so glorious? – Did you inherit nothing from them but those Lands, which you have either meanly yielded to the great Devourer, or riotously wasted in the Luxury he has introduced among you? – What will Posterity say, when they read over the Annals of these Times? Will they not blush to compare the soft and silken Days of their immediate Predecessors, with the brave Roughness of more dis-tant Ages? Will they not tear out the shameful Page, erase from their

---

1 A Manuscript almost as antient as the History itself, and which serves as an Expla-nation of it in many places, acquaints us, that *Ochihatou* compell'd the People to sell their Lands to him at very low Rates, and built several magnificent Palaces on them. [E.H.]

2 There is also an Account, that the Money appropriated by the Publick, to pay such Arrears as should be owing to Persons that died in the service of their Country, to their Widows and Orphans, was seized by *Ochihatou*, and laid out on Ornaments for his Gardens. [E.H.]

Escutcheons[1] all the Blazonry derived from you, and leave a Gap in History?

It therefore lies upon you, if you have yet remaining any Sense of the Honour of your Country, your Religion, your Laws, your Liberties, your own Welfare, and of those to whom you have, or shall hereafter give Being, to throw off the Yoke, which wants but a very little of being fastned beyond all possibility of removing; – to exert your selves once more; – to be unanimous in your Resolves, and vigorous in the execution. – Remember, it is the Cause of Heaven, of Loyalty, of Glory, and of Freedom, which urges you to Arms, and will be rewarded with their united Blessings: But if you continue much longer in this Inactivity, this Coward Passiveness, Chains, Slavery and Wretchedness will be entail'd upon you from Generation to Generation: Woes, of which yet no Description can be given, will be your Portion while alive, and everlasting Infamy attend your Names when dead.[2]

Here *Alhahuza* ended, and the Applauses given to what he said, were such as might have made any one believe, his Advice was about being put into immediate execution. When the Crowd was dispersed, *Eovaai* came down, and congratulated him on the Success of his Declamation. Ah! Princess, answered he, with a Sigh, you judge too favourably of this degenerate Race; their very Souls are debilitated with their Bodies; all Ardor for Glory, all generous Emulation, all Love of Liberty, every noble Passion is extinguish'd with their Industry. They imitate the Lion in his Roar, are Heroes in *Words*, but when call'd forth to *Deeds*, start like the timorous Hare, sculk into Corners, hide themselves in Caverns, and have nor Hands nor Hearts to combat with Oppression; so fatal a Damp has Luxury, and its Attendant *Sloth*, cast on their wonted Fire, that, without the Interposition of some supernatural Power, *Hypotofa* must fall, to rise no more.

He then led her into another Room, where having taken part of a

---

1   Escutcheons: Shields on which a coat of arms is depicted (*OED*).
2   Alhahuza's speech echoes many of Bolingbroke's opposition writings urging patriotism, mixed government and the upholding of the constitution. See his *Dissertation upon Parties* (1733) and "A Letter on the Spirit of Patriotism" (1736).

small Collation, he informed her, that having consulted the [1]celestial Science on her account, he found that *Ochihatou*, enrag'd beyond measure at her departure, was exerting the whole Force of his Art to bring her back; and consequently, there cou'd be no Safety for her in the Confines of *Hypotofa*. I wou'd, therefore, advise you, continued he, to take sanctuary in [2]*Oozoff*; that Republick[3] is under the Protection of a Genius, at whose powerful Name the *Ypres* and their Adherents tremble. No wicked Magick was ever of any force against it; and I flatter my self, you may remain there in an undisturbed Security, till Heaven relenting, shall vouchsafe to restore you to *Ijaveo*. The Terrors which the Beginning of this Discourse had excited in *Eovaai*, being dispersed by the latter Part, she readily prepared for her departure, without any other Anxiety than what was occasioned, by finding herself oblig'd to quit the Conversation of so wise and good a Man.

The Castle of *Alhahuza* being on the very Borders of *Hypotofa*, and separated, on the western Side from *Oozoff* but by a small River, he caused a Bridge, he had made in case of any Extremity, to be let down; over which the Princess easily passed; and, in a few minutes, reach'd a Place, in all things so vastly different from that she had lately left, that it seem'd to her almost another World; and indeed nothing cou'd be more amazing, than that People, such near Neighbours, born under almost the same Climate, professing the same Religion, and living together in the strictest Amity, shou'd be the direct Opposites to each other in their Manners. In *Hypotofa*, nothing was to be seen but excessive Grandeur or extreme Wretchedness; for a fruitless Attempt to arrive at the one, naturally produced the other: In *Oozoff*, a happy Sufficiency appear'd throughout, and Luxury and Poverty were things equally unknown. All Pride, all Vanity, all Ostentation, were banish'd hence: 'Tis true, the Desire of Riches seem'd the ruling and universal Passion among them; but then, they sought not the Gratification by mean Arts, or Projects destructive to their Fellow-Citizens, or shame-

---

1   It is supposed by several, and with good reason, that Astronomy was a Branch of this Science. [E.H.]

2   The Interpretation of this Name engag'd the Cabal in a Dispute, which took up five Moons. Some wou'd have it *Wisdom*, but the Majority were of opinion, that *Impartiality* came nearer the Meaning. [E.H.]

3   Republick: A commonwealth; the supreme power resting in the people rather than in a king.

ful to their Country, but by honest Care, and painful Labour; by adhering strictly to their Promises; by being just in all their Dealings abroad, and frugal at home; by never delaying till to-morrow, what was in their power to accomplish to-day; and by suffering no Drones to eat up what the others laboured for. Thus every Individual, like the industrious Bee,[1] while he acted for his own Interest, acted also for that of the Publick; and all no less unanimous than vigorous in the common Cause, they so well knew how to profit by the Sloth or Timidity of other Nations, that they became almost the sole trading People, extended their Commerce even to the farthest Parts of the habitable Globe; and, from a small beginning, arrived to such a height, as, at the time of *Eovaai's* sojourning among them, to be look'd upon as one of the most formidable Commonwealths beneath the Influence of [2]*Akibar.* Nor indeed is it at all to be wonder'd at, that they were so; they had always maintain'd an inviolable Freedom, whenever any Man, how much endeared soever to them, by his Name or Services, discover'd an Inclination to deprive them of that sacred Right, all he was, and all he had done, were no more remem-bred, and he was certain to meet that Fate his unjust Encroachment merited; and I think it may be established as a certain Maxim, that the Love of Glory is more or less prevalent, according to the Liberty of the People; for true Bravery can never be the Companion of Servi-tude. But to return:

As *Eovaai* found herself treated with an extreme Civility, without the least Appearance of any Inquisitiveness into her Affairs, she for-bore discovering either her Name or Rank. The many Advantages, however, she possest, above all those Persons who had ever taken shel-ter in that Republick, entitled her to the highest Respect among a People who regarded only Merit, and contemned those pompous Titles which are falsly call'd *Honourable,* when worn by Persons of

---

1 industrious Bee: An allusion to Bernard Mandeville's *The Fable of the Bees: or, Private Vices, Publick Benefits* (1714). Mandeville, who criticized the opposition's humanist and nostalgic values, asserted in his poem and the "Remarks" appended to it in 1723 and 1724, that "Fools only strive/To make a Great an honest Hive./.../ Fraud, Luxury, and Pride must live/Whilst we the Benefits receive" ("The Moral").

2 By the Cabal supposed the Sun; but *Hahehihotu* and several other Authors believe it has a further Meaning. Perhaps *Liberty,* all Republicks enjoying that Blessing in its full Extent; but as I am a Stranger, and in a Place where Monarchical Government is established, I shall forbear inserting what they have said on this head. [E.H.]

mean and corrupt Principles. She received frequent Visits from the Heads of the Common-wealth, and found them Men of such profound Wisdom, Virtue and Probity, as made it not seem strange to her, that the State under their Direction shou'd acquire so high a Reputation; but in spite of the great Qualities she observed in those who had the care of publick Business, the prodigious Respect paid to them by the Ambassadors of the greatest Kings, the Weight their Voices had in foreign Councils, and the Advantages they made from every little Incident that happened in the World, for the aggrandizing their own Country, the Prejudice of Education which most People imbibe for that kind of Government under which they are born, made her think there wanted something to compleat the Grandeur of this Nation, and that it was pity some one of those noble Personages, so august in every Action, shou'd not be dignified with the Name of [1]King.

As she made no scruple of declaring her Sentiments on this head, an antient Man, but infinitely less venerable for his length of Days, than Extent of Knowledge, took upon him to rectify the mistaken Ideas she seem'd to him to have conceived concerning Government.

I know not, said he, but some Nations, and on some particular Occasions, may have found their advantage in a Monarchical Government; but am very certain, that few Instances can be produced of Kings who have really acted according to the Ends for which they were originally made so. Yet there are People so bigotted to the

---

1 The Commentator, who I shrewdly suspect to have been a Republican in his Principles, lays hold on this Passage, to lash, with a good deal of Severity, that Veneration which weak Minds, as he calls them, pay to Kings merely as Kings. The Crown, the Sceptre, the Robes, and other Formalities of Regal State being, he says, no more than Pageantry, a kind of gaudy Shew, to attract and amuse the Vulgar; and the Person thus dress'd up no more, perhaps *less*, brave and honest than the meanest Gazer. I must confess, since my abode in *England*, I have seen some Mock-Monarchs on the Stage, so much resembling those who wear that Title to their Life's End, that I am apt to think, had the Commentator been present, he wou'd have look'd on both alike with his Philosophical Spectacles; and cried out, Where is the essential Difference? Both are Men, made of the same Clay, incident to the same Passions, same Diseases, same Infirmities of Mind and Body: Both equally make it their chief Business to get Money: Both enjoy their Dignity but for a time; and if the one continues longer than the other, yet both alike will have an end, and, after Death, be converted into the same undistinguishable Dust. But this is only my own Imagination; it's possible the Courts of *Europe* might have reformed his Sentiments, and render'd him as very a Worshipper of Royalty as a *Frenchman*. [E.H.]

Name, that they imagine, whoever is invested with the Robes of Majesty, becomes immediately divine in his own Person, and has also the Power of conveying the sacred Influence to his Posterity from Generation to Generation, how unworthy soever to succeed him: Hence follow those wild Notions of hereditary, indefeasible and unalienable Right, which for many Ages have set the World in Confusion. – But to trace this Matter to its Source. –

When the Almighty Powers peopled this terrestrial Globe, to *Man* they gave the Sovereignty over all other living Creatures; and to that end, endued him with a superior *Reason*, and Dignity of Soul worthy to command, and proper to enforce Obedience: but have we from History or Tradition any Proof, or even Hint, that they said to [1]one particular Man, *Be thou above the rest*: – *The whole Species shall adore* thy *Smiles, and tremble at* thy *Frowns*: – *From* thee *all Honours, all Promotions, all Happiness shall flow as from their Source*: – *In* thee *shall center all Rewards and Punishments, and* thou *shalt be a* God *on Earth*? – No, on the contrary, they reserved this State of Dependance, as a proper Token of Subordination to themselves alone; and Mankind confess'd himself sufficiently favoured in the Rule assign'd him over inferior Beings, without once thinking of exalting himself above those of his own kind. Whatever is against *Nature*, is against *Reason*; and that this is so, I think is obvious to the meanest Capacity, however prejudiced by Education, or more powerful Interest. – But I will not go about to impose my own Opinion, but endeavour to convince your's. In the Infancy of Creation, as I have already said, and consequently the time of the most perfect Innocence and Integrity, there was no Precedency, no Subordination; but when the *Ypres* broke loose, and got the better of the *Genii* appointed for the Guardians of the World, Self-love, Discord, Avarice, the Lust of Power, and every kind of Vice, corrupted the native Simplicity of our Manners: We no longer regarded the Welfare of our Neighbours: We quarell'd on the most trifling Occasions: We coveted what we wanted not; grew arrogant and assuming, and at length rapacious; seizing by *force* what *Fraud* cou'd not obtain. Then, dividing ourselves into Parties, Wars ensued; various

---

1 This is an Argument that they believed, as we in *China* do to this day, that a great Number of Men were created at the same time; and I have had the pleasure to find several learned *Europeans* of the same opinion. [E.H.]

Instruments were every day invented, to destroy the Workmanship of Heaven; and Death triumph'd in those Plains where Love, and Peace, and sweet Society before had reign'd. In these Skirmishes, he who had shewed himself the boldest, or most cunning in the fatal Science, was look'd upon with the greatest Respect: Here began *Distinction*; and such a Man, in a future Engagement, was put at the head of the others, by their joint Assent, and, as they then believ'd, for their *Common-Good*: This Chief, this Captain, this General, or by what Name soever you call him, happens to be successful, and having tasted the Sweets of Command, is loth to relinquish it. By Bribes, and Promises of sharing with him in his Power, he secures a Majority to his Interest; the Continuance of his Authority is decreed, which he afterwards maintains by the same Artifices; the People thus unwarily brought under Subjection, make a Virtue of Necessity, and seem pleas'd with what they cannot remedy; they extol their new Mode of Living; the neighbouring Nations, deceived by appearances, follow their Example; choose a Chief to whose Authority they vow Obedience; and thus came *Kingship* into fashion: thus was *Usurpation* converted into *Law*, and thus was *Slavery* establish'd, and the Body of Mankind render'd a Prey to the insatiable Pride and Avarice of a few. A dreadful Æra, and which shou'd, methinks, inspire us with Horror, rather than Veneration.

Yet, cried *Eovaai*, interrupting him with some warmth, as you confess the supreme Authority was at first lodg'd in one Person, for the *Good* of the Community over whom he was placed; and that many Benefits accrued from such a Delegation: I cannot but think it highly unjust, that Authority shou'd afterward be depreciated, because some Kings may not have discharg'd the Duties of their Place, so well as might be expected.

Madam, replied he, I have not admitted that the Superiority of any one Man above the rest could be of general Service but on extraordinary Exigencies; and never can admit that it ought to be continued, when those Exigencies are past. Humane Nature is not to be trusted with itself: all Men have in them the Seeds of Tyranny, which want but the warm Sun of Power to be enabled to shoot forth in proud and undisguis'd Oppression. It is therefore the Business of a wise People to endeavour, as much as possible, to keep every one on the same Level with each other, in which they were born; and on which, 'tis evident, Heaven, by setting no Mark of Distinction between them, intended they should remain. – Nor do I give it as a Reason, that because ¹many Kings have been bad, the Regal Authority ought to be abolish'd; but because such an Authority seems to me to be established on Principles both absurd and prophane: Contrary to Nature, Common Sense, Religion and Universal Liberty. – Can any thing be more ridiculous, than to see Millions of free-born Souls prostrating themselves beneath the Feet, and submitting their Lives and Fortunes to the ²arbitrary Will of one of their own Species, and whose Intellects are perchance weaker than any of the servile Throng? – Or can any thing be more injurious to the immortal Gods, than to give to a created Being those Marks of Adoration, which are due only to themselves? who, if they pleased, could strike dead in a moment this Ape of their Divinity, or render him a more piteous, and at the same time a ³more dreadful Example of the Folly of Human Grandeur: Nor does it at all answer the Objections made against monarchical Government, that there have been ⁴many very excellent Princes, true Fathers of their People, and strict Observers of the Laws; our Quarrel is not to the *Person*,⁵ *but the Function* of a King: for suppose we could

---

1   *Hahehihotu* says, the Cabal have grosly misinterpreted this Passage, which he brings a great Number of Arguments to prove is, *all Kings*, instead of *many Kings*. [E.H.]

2   As the Cabal undertook the Translation of this History at the Request of our Emperor, and expected from him alone the Reward due to the Pains and Time bestowed on it; 'tis thought, by the last mentioned Author, the Commentator, and several others, that the Words *Arbitrary Will* were added to the Original in Compliment to our Form of Government, which at that time was far from being despotick, and our Emperors however pompous in their Titles, enjoyed little more real Power than the most petty Magistrates now assume. [E.H.]

3   Later Times have presented us with an Instance of this kind in *Nebuchadnezar* King of *Assyria*, who, for his Arrogance, was converted into an Ox. 'Tis probable, some such Transformation had happened before, that gave rise to this Expression; which, in my mind, seems to imply something of a Remembrance of what *had been*, as well as a Conjecture of what *might be*.[E.H.] [Ed. note: In the Old Testament, God punishes the proud King Nebuchadnezar by driving him from his kingdom, and making him "eat grass as oxen...till his hairs were grown like eagles' *feathers*, and his nails like birds' *claws*" (*Daniel* 4:33). After this, the king "blessed the most High, and...praised and honoured him that liveth for ever, whose dominion *is* an everlasting dominion, and his kingdom *is* from generation to generation" (*Daniel* 4:34).]

4   This I think destroys the Assertion of *Hahehihotu* concerning the false Interpretation of *many Kings* for *all Kings*, unless you will understand by this Passage (which I must confess is a little Equivocal) that *excellent Princes* make *bad Kings*. [E.H.]

5   *Quinpodol*, an eminent Writer of our Nation, and Cotemporary with *Japhet*, the Son of *Noah*, from whom, after his settling in *Cilicia*, he received a great Insight into the original Language transmitted carefully by *Adam* to his Posterity, has left behind

find a Hero, in whom all the Virtues met, and little inferior to the Celestial *Genii*, he certainly would both merit and possess a Throne in every honest Heart: He would be loved and respected; which is as much as any *Man* can deserve, or ought to desire from his Fellow-Creature; but we should be well satisfied he was something *more* than *Man*, before we paid him *divine* Honours, made him a Sacrifice of those dear Rights given us by Heaven and Nature, and levied Contributions from the Bowels of our Posterity, to dress him up a gaudy Shew, and maintain a vast number of People in Idleness, who might, by their Industry, be useful to their Country, meerly to fill the pageant Pomp of Royalty. His Courage, his Prudence, his every good Quality would be at least of the same Service without all this Expence; and, as I before observ'd, there are too many Temptations in the *Power* of doing whatever we *will*, for the best to confine himself always to the doing what he *ought*.

Where Kings are invested with so absolute and uncontroulable a Sway as to have the Power of acting in all things according as Ambition prompts, said *Eovaai*, I wonder not the Nations under them have good Reason to regret the cruel Necessity of submitting to it. But in those Monarchies, where *Power* is limited by *Laws*, where the *Tenure*, by which the *Prince* holds his Crown, is the *Observance* of those Laws, where he can raise no Armies without the Consent of his People, enter into no Leagues, transact no Treaties, either of War or Peace, without laying the Motives of his having done so before them, where he is obliged to give an Account of the publick Treasure to them, and where even his private Expences are bounded by their Regulations; such a King surely cannot be said to act by the Instigations of his *own Will* (unless he happens to have no Will, but for the Service and the Interest of those beneath him.) He is indeed the Head of a large Family; for whose Happiness he is perpetually contriving, who *watches* for *their Repose, labours* for their Ease, exposes himself for *their Safety*,

---

him a large Treatise of the Policy and Customs of *Oozoff*; in which he tells us, it had at first been subject to the Kings of *Narzada*; but being used by them in a most cruel and tyrannick manner, had at length thrown off the Yoke, and converted itself into a Common-wealth. If so, as there is no Reason to doubt the Sincerity of this Author, we cannot wonder at the Bitterness with which the old Republican inveighs against Kingly Government. [E.H.]

and has no other Recompence for all his Cares than that Homage, that Grandeur, which he ought not to be envied; and, which in my Opinion, is of no less Benefit to the State in general, than to himself, by adding Weight to its Counsels abroad, and supporting that Order at home, which is the Beauty of Government.

Hold, Madam, cry'd the Republican, with a Half-Smile, you are advancing Positions which, I am very certain, to maintain, will put all the fine Wit you are Mistress of to a Task too difficult. As to the first it is meerly visionary; for tho' I grant there are many Kingdoms, where the People boast of perfect Liberty, where the Power of the Prince is said to be bounded with certain Conditions, which if he attempts to violate, he is no more a King, and all Obedience is void by Law; yet I deny there is any such thing in *Fact*, or that the People there in reality enjoy a jot more Liberty, than those in Monarchies, which are term'd Absolute. The Name, indeed, the Shadow of it they possess; but are as very Slaves, as those they affect to pity. What if their Kings do not directly say *I will, because I will*, and think their Pleasure a sufficient Sanction for the most unjust Decrees; Is their Power of acting in every thing according to their Will less great, for their not openly avowing it? No, I can easily prove the contrary. Is not the Power of conferring all Titles, Honours, and Badges of Distinction, entirely lodged in every one of these limited Monarchs, as you call them? And are there not always to be found Men of corrupt and mercenary Principles, who will consent for a present Advantage to themselves to any Scheme, tho' never so detrimental to their Country? Are not all Employments of any Note, whether civil or military, in the Disposal of this bounded Prince, and cannot he, when he finds Persons[1] refractory to his Designs, discharge them, and fill up the vacant Offices with others more conformable? – What avails it, that he is tied by Oath to do nothing against the Consent of the People, when those who represent the People are his own Creatures, and entirely devoted

---

1 *Cafferero* laments the ill Consequence of this Power in the Prince; it seems it had been fatal to Liberty, even in his Time, which is no more than seventeen Centuries ago. These are his Words: What dreadful things may we not expect, when we see the Favour of the Prince the only Standard of Merit; when all things are governed by Caprice, and Flattery is the chief Plea for Promotion! when the brave and experienced Officer remains without any Mark of Honour, but the Wounds he has

to his Interest, or perhaps, that of a first Minister, which is still worse; for I verily believe, that Ambition of Princes was never so fatal to Liberty, as the Avarice of Ministers: But that is another Argument, tho' none of the weakest, might be alledg'd against monarchical Government; because where there is not a King, there cannot be a Minister; at least one vested with an Authority capable of being prejudicial to the Publick.

But supposing any Instance cou'd be brought of a Kingdom, where Integrity and Love of Country was so universal, that [1]no Man in it cou'd be found so much infatuated with the Charms of Grandeur, as to serve the unlawful Interests of either King or Minister, such a People wou'd certainly be very jealous of their Liberties: This wou'd occasion perpetual Struggles between them and the Prince: The Balance of Power cou'd never be so equally pois'd, but that one Side or other wou'd have some little reason for Complaint; and the strict Guard both ought to keep against Encroachments, wou'd unavoidably make them frequently too quick-sighted, and cry out on Insults which had no existence but in their own Apprehensions: Misinterpretations wou'd be put on every thing: Heart-burnings wou'd rise to Animosities, and these break forth at length into open Ruptures, which might probably know no end, but with the Ruin of one of the contending Parties; and which-ever got the

---

received in fighting for his Country; while the beardless Boy, who never drew his Sabre, but to smell of the Perfume, is advanced to the highest Dignities in the Army; when Buffoons are made Counsellors, and wise Men are oblig'd to keep Silence? [E.H.] [Ed. note: It was a common complaint that nepotism and bribery gained inexperienced, unqualified "boys" high-ranking positions in the military in the eighteenth century. Haywood may have in mind the particular example of the advancement in 1711 of Abigail Masham's ineffectual brother, Jack Hill (died 1735), to brigadier-general over the Duke of Marlborough, which enraged Sarah, Duchess of Marlborough (to whom *Eovaai* is dedicated).]

1 As ideal as this Supposition seems, *Tatragraoutho* the Rabbin, in his History of Revolutions, gives us an Account of a certain Country, but in what Part of the World situate I remember not, where the Prince aiming at despotick Power, was continually changing all his great Officers, in the hope of getting a Set subservient to his purpose; but all alike maintaining their Probity, and communicating to the People the Temptations had been laid in their way: The King was dethroned, Monarchy abolish'd, and the Nation from that time, governed by a Council of 50, who were annually nominated by the Publick. [E.H.]

better, the Commonwealth must be a Loser. So that, put a Monarchical Government on the best foot you can, the Dangers attending it will be still demonstrable.

Then, as to the other Part of your Assertion, concerning the Name of King, adding weight to the Councils of a Nation abroad, or supporting Order at home; you need but look round the World, to be convinced of that Mistake. Do we not see some Kings sending Ambassadors, whose Behaviour in foreign Parts, has made the Manners of their own the common Topick of Ridicule? Have they not been publickly, to their very Faces, laugh'd at, nay hiss'd? Have not their Credentials been contemn'd, spurn'd at? Whereas those of several Republicks are received with the greatest Veneration; and, tho' dignified with no vain-sounding Titles, the Pageantry of Words, been consulted in the Cabinet, while those glaring Nothings were left to toy with the Women, or play with the Pages in the Antichamber. And as to Order at home, I hope the Place you now are in, discovers no want of any Regulation, which should render a first Magistrate necessary to our Peace. What Disorders, what Indecencies have you observed among us? Have we not Laws sufficient for preserving a due Decorum? And are not those Laws strictly observ'd? Or, when violated, the Offender, without Partiality, made to suffer the Punishment of his Crime? Do our Magistrates, who are truly and indeed appointed by the People, meet with less Respect from the Commonalty, because, like them, they live in a plain simple manner, and are void of all Ostentation? Does any one here endeavour to encroach on the Rights, or any way exalt himself above his Fellow-Citizen, and not meet with the Humiliation he justly deserves? Not but we have Honours here paid to particular Persons; but then they are such who have either very remarkably distinguish'd themselves in the Service of the Republick, by their Wisdom or Bravery; or who, having enrich'd themselves by an honest and indefatigable Industry, make a proper Use of the Treasures they have acquired. In fine, those who know how to command their Passions, who make the Happiness of Mankind their Care, who labour without ceasing for the Common-Good, are with us the *Great Men:* On them we confer all the Badges of Honour in our power to give, without injustice to others of equal

Merit; but then this Distinction[1] descends not to their Posterity, unless they tread in the same Steps: 'Tis not enough to have been begot by such a Man, or born of such a Woman, without following their Example. Nay, we expect more from a Person of an eminently virtuous Extraction, he must improve on the illustrious Model, or we look on him as a kind of bastard Offspring, and unworthy of his Parent's Name or Respect.

A long Pause here gave *Eovaai* an opportunity of replying; but she found [2]so much Justice in the latter Part of his Discourse, that she was at a loss in what manner she shou'd do so; and was almost ready to give up the Dispute: Which the other perceiving, wou'd not pursue the Argument, thinking he had done enough in convincing her Mind, without obliging her to confess she had been in the wrong; and contented himself with concluding in these Terms:

Much more, Madam, continued he, might be added, to prove that a Republick has in it all the Advantages of a Monarchy, without any of the Inconveniencies; but as Observation and Experience are the best Instructors, I dare believe, that on comparing the one Form of Government with the other, nothing will be wanting to make you judge as I do.

After this, the Conversation turned on different Subjects; and the Princess of *Ijaveo*, from this time forward, forbore to say any thing which might give rise to Arguments she found herself so little able to confute. The truth is, that if she were not a Convert to all the Republican Principles, she at least thought some of them so highly reasonable, that she resolved, if she was ever happy enough to regain her Crown, she wou'd make them Part of the Constitution; and to live in such a manner herself, as should render the Expences or Regal State no way oppressive to the People.[3] How fluctuating is Human Nature!

---

1   The Commentator, *Hahehihotu*, and almost every Author who takes any notice of this History, of whom there are a great Number, launch into vast Encomiums on the Justice of this Law. *Quinpindol*, in whose time it began to be exploded, earnestly wishes the revival of it, as the most effectual Method to encourage Virtue, and put Vice to shame, that can possibly be taken. [E.H.]

2   By this we may imagine, that the Historian himself was a Favourer of the Republican System of Government; and from thence infer, that in those times it seem'd best calculated for the Happiness of Mankind. [E.H.]

3   Regal State ... People: While Eovaai has not been convinced by the Republican to abandon the monarchy, she is willing to adopt some of Bolingbroke's tenets out-

how variable in its Inclinations! How little able to withstand the Force of Persuasion and Example! She who, by the Insinuations of *Ochihatou*, had imagin'd Princes might exalt themselves to Gods, and had a right to tread on the Necks of Millions, ruin'd to support that Arrogance; was now, by this Republican, brought into as great an Extreme of Humiliation, and ready to resign even that decent Homage and respectful Awe which were the Requisites of her Place. But as it is impossible for the most discreet and scrutinous Examiner into himself, when *out of Power*, to know what he will do when *in*, the present Notions of *Eovaai* cou'd have given but slender Assurances to her Subjects of her future Conduct; and had she been immediately restor'd, wanting that [1]sacred Director of her Will, and of that of all her Family, the Gift of the divine *Aiou*, it is probable her Head, grown [2]giddy with the Elevation, might have lost all Memory of what she had determined in her low Estate. But not to anticipate the Reader's Curiosity:

While she was thus forming Projects for the Happiness of a People, over whom, tho' by means she cou'd not foresee, she hoped once more to be established, Designs were laid to render her entirely and eternally incapable of any thing but the lowest, most abject, and withal, the most unpitied Wretchedness. *Ochihatou* was not of a Disposition to give up any Point he had once fix'd his Heart upon, and that of enjoying *Eovaai*, was of so much Consequence to his Peace, that he cou'd not abandon it, without trying all the Stratagems that his own fertile Invention, or wicked Art, could suggest. He had, by his usual

---

lined in his *Dissertation upon Parties* (1733), namely, to cut some of the crown's costs to the people, primarily the civil list. "Our kings, since the establishment of the civil list, have not only a private and separate estate, but receive a kind of rent-charge out of the public estate, to maintain their honor and dignity, nothing else" (*Works*, II, 157-58).

1 The Jewel left her by *Eojaeu*; and, by what has been said before concerning the Virtues of it, and now enforced by this Passage, it certainly must have contain'd some Mysteries which we, in these latter Ages of the World, how wise soever we think ourselves, can have no Idea of. [E.H.]

2 Methinks, this Supposition is a little unjust to one who was born to a Throne, and had really been in possession of it; since it is the sudden and unexpected Transition from Meanness to Grandeur, which, according to the received Opinion, intoxicates the Brain, and renders the Person so raised insolent, cruel, avaritious, and full of all Dispositions of a Tyrant. [E.H.]

Artifices, prevail'd on the Ambassador of *Habul*, to retard his intended Departure for a few days, within which time he doubted not but to find some [1]Expedient to set all right again with that Monarch. And having thus got off, at least postpon'd an Affair which threatned him with so much Mischief, returned hastily to the Grove where he had left the Princess: His Rage, at finding she had quitted not only that Place, but the whole Kingdom of *Hypotofa*, cou'd be exceeded by nothing but that which seized him, when, on consulting the *Ypres* concerning her retreat, he was informed she was in *Oozoff*, a Country which, as *Alhahuza* had truly told her, was wholly out of the reach of wicked Magick. Neither aerial, terrestrial, nor infernal Spirits, cou'd, in this juncture, be of service to him: He rav'd, he curs'd the Insufficiency of his Science; and, for some Moments, behaved little like that artful Politician, whose Subtilty had enslaved the bravest Nation in the World, and seduced the wisest. But this Gust of stormy Passion blowing over, he endeavoured to banish all Thoughts on what was impossible to be done, to make way for those on what was not so; and after comparing, examining, and condemning an infinite Number of Projects, which, by turns, presented themselves for Approbation, he at length made choice of the following one.

He caused twenty of his Dependants, [2]Wretches capable of under-taking any thing for Hire, to attire themselves in mean Habits, and repair to *Oozoff*, pretending they took shelter in that Republick from the Calamities brought on *Hypotofa*, by the Avarice and Cruelty of himself; which he knew would readily enough gain Credit with a People, who, tho' they carried fair to him, as indeed they did with all the World for their own Interest, he was sensible, knew very well the little Trust was to be reposed in him either at home or abroad. These Men he ordered to take up some Occupation, as Persons that intend-ed to settle there, and had no means of living but an honest Labour; and to take up their abode as near as possible to the Residence of *Eovaai*, to the end they might observe all her Motions, and be ready to bear her off when they saw a fit Opportunity: the means by which

---

1   The before-mentioned Manuscript informs us, that this Minister was excellent at temporary Expedients. [E.H.]

2   He who has the Treasures of a plundered Nation in his hands, can never be without such Instruments; whom our Author very justly terms Wretches. [E.H.]

they should do so, he left to them as most proper Judges, being on the Spot, of what was likely to succeed, and what was not.

As he was equally liberal, even to Profuseness, to the Agents of his Will, and implacably and cruelly revengeful to those who failed in the Execution of it; it is not to be doubted, but that the Persons employed in this Enterprize, were indefatigable in every thing that seemed to promise the Accomplishment of it. They were incessant Spies on all the Actions of this unfortunate Princess, and having discovered that, imagining herself in a Place of perfect Security, she frequently walked alone, indulging Meditation in an adjacent Wood, they thought a more fair Occasion could not present itself for the Execution of their Design; and therefore resolved not to let it slip. They provided a ¹Scahi, and seven or eight of them concealing it with themselves behind the Trees till her Approach, rush'd forth at once, seized and bound her upon it with Cords, stop'd the Cries she was about to make, with an Instrument they thrust into her Mouth, and covered her over with Moss and Branches of Yew and Willow; then carried her forth, uttering the most bitter Lamentations all the way, as if for the Loss of one of their Countrymen, who they said was dead, and they were going to interr without the City-Walls. This Pretence had the wish'd Effect; none had the least Suspicion of the Deceit, and they passed the Gates without Molestation or any further Enquiry. Being arrived into an open Plain beyond the Jurisdiction of the Republick of *Oozoff*, they were met by their Companions, according to Appointment, with a Chariot, into which having relieved her of her Bonds, and given her Tongue that Liberty, which they now no longer feared, they compelled her to enter, and in that manner equally regardless of her Supplications or Exclaimings, brought her to the Palace of *Ochihatou*.

'Twould be more the Business of a Paraphrase than a History, to go about to relate the various Emotions which rose in the Mind of *Eovaai* at this sudden Turn of Fate; nor is it at all necessary for the better understanding her Adventures, since any one who remembers she was now happily restored to Virtue, will naturally infer, they must

---

1   A sort of Carriage on which dead Persons were ordinarily laid; but whether any thing like those now in use, it is impossible to be ascertain'd. [E.H.]

be all made up of Shame, Fear, Detestation, and the most shocking Apprehensions. She was conducted into an Apartment, where she past the little time of her being left alone in imploring the Protection of the Celestial *Genii*, and in particular that of *Aiou* and *Halafamai*. On the first Appearance of *Ochihatou*, she found indeed that she had suffi- cient Occasion for so doing. His very Looks at his Entrance made her tremble for the Actions she expected would ensue. You see, my fair Fugitive, said he, with a Countenance in which triumphant Villany was painted to the Life, with how much Ease I surmount whatever Difficulties are thrown in the way of my Desires. – Your pretended Tenderness, 'tis true, deceived me for a time, and I was willing to owe my Happiness rather to your Inclination than my own Power; but since you have forfeited all Claim to my Complaisance, by an ill- judg'd Flight from *Hypotofa*, you must now resolve to aid my Pleasures in the way others have done before you. – I shall no more entreat where I have so full a Command; and if you hope to regain any part of that Respect I before treated you with, you must employ the Hour I give you in contriving some new Method of heighthing the Rap- tures of Enjoyment, out-do all I have ever found in the warmest and most artful of your Sex, be more than ever Woman was, and force me in unexperienced Extacies to pardon what is past, and own you merit future Favour. He waited not her Reply, but with these Words, accompanied with an insolent Toss of his Head, flung out of the Room, leaving the Princess in a Condition which it would be impos- sible to express. The shameful Remembrance of those indecent and vicious Liberties she had indulged him in, becoming more poignant at his Presence; the Horror of those she now was threatened with, and the little possibility there seemed of avoiding being subjected to his Will, almost stupified her Spirits, and by despairing of Relief, she became incapable of imploring it.

As she was in this sad Situation, a Monkey which was fastned by a Chain to one Corner of the Room, and was before unnoticed by her, leap'd suddenly against the Wall, and having pulled down a [1]Tablet,

---

1   The Manuscript giving an Account of the various Enchantments practised by *Ochi-hatou*, tells us the Spells given him for that purpose by the *Ypres*, or infernal Spirits, were engraved on Tablets of the Boles of Yew [Ed. note: trunks of a type of large evergreen tree – OED], and petrified into Stone, by lying a certain Time in a par- ticular River, dedicated to the Powers of Darkness. [E.H.]

came and presented it to her between its Paws. The Oddness of this Action made her a little recover the Power of Reflection, and perceiving the Creature pointed to some Words engraven on it, and at the same time put itself into a Posture more expressively beseeching, than could be accounted for, in an Animal void of Reason; she could not help believing there was some extraordinary Mystery couch'd under this seeming Accident; and examining the Characters, and endeavouring, if possible, to comprehend their Meaning, she repeated them three times over; which she had no sooner done, than, to her inexpressible Amazement, she saw before her, instead of the Monkey, a Woman, of a very graceful Appearance, tho' pretty far advanced in Years. This sudden and strange Transformation deprived her for a Moment of the use of more than half her Faculties; she was all Eyes, and those were fixed rather in a stupid than enquiring State; which the other perceiving, Let not your Surprize, said she, render you incapable of the only means the Immortal Gods allow for your defence against the Power of *Ochihatou.* – If you are indeed desirous of avoiding his Embraces, rouze from this Lethargy of Mind, and prepare yourself to do as I shall direct. What are you? cry'd the Princess, not yet recovered. A Woman, as you are, reply'd the late-seeming Monkey, a Virgin too; but by the Cruelty and Revenge of the implacable *Ochihatou,* compell'd to languish out my Days under that ridiculous and detested Form you just now saw me in; and to which I must again return. It is however in my power, and in mine alone, to preserve you from the Effects of that wild Passion your Beauty has inspired him with. – Listen therefore, with Patience and Attention, to my Story; and whatever may be your Opinion of my Conduct, forbear to blame those Errors which are fatal only to myself, and extremely fortunate for you.

Eovaai having testify'd her Readiness to comply with all her Injunctions, the other resumed her Discourse in these Terms.

The History of ATAMADOUL, *Maid of Honour, and afterwards first Woman of the Bedchamber to* SYLLALIPPE, *Princess of* Assadid.

MY Name, said she, is *Atamadoul:* I am descended by my Father's Side from a Family almost as ancient as the World itself, and by my Mother's, from a Branch of the Blood Royal of *Assadid.* It was in that Court where I first saw Light, where I was bred in all the gay Delights of Life; and where I might still have dwelt in Pomp and Honour, had I either sooner, or not at all, experienced a Passion, which has no Medium in its Consequences, and never fails to render the Person possest of it extremely happy or extremely miserable. As I never could boast an extraordinary Beauty, so I wanted not enough of the Agreeable to make me very much admired. My Youth, besides that Chearfulness which is almost inseparable from it, was accompanied with a certain Air; which I have been told, even by those least concern'd to please me, had something in it more attractive than the most dazling Whiteness of Skin, or Regularity of Features. However it was, no Lady about Court was treated with more Respect and Obsequiousness by her Lovers, or had a more numerous Train of them. Had they been fewer, and their Devoirs[1] less flattering, perhaps I had not been the Wretch I am, but my Vanity was swell'd till it overwhelm'd my Reason: I began to fancy myself born only to be adored, and that I merited more than all Mankind could pay. I could not think of parting with my Power over so many Slaves for any Consideration; wholly untouch'd by any soft Emotion, in the pain I gave them consisted my chief Pleasure; and never reflecting that every Day stole from me something of my Charms, that a terrible Decay would soon ensue, and all my Triumphs wither with my Bloom; I looked on all the Overtures of Marriage made me by my Friends, as so many Indignities to my Beauty's Prerogative; and declared myself so great an Enemy to that State, that in time they forbore pressing me. I was two and twenty when I entered myself among the Number of those Virgins who attended the Princess *Syllalippe*, then an Infant of five Years

---

1   Devoirs: Dutiful respects, courteous attentions.

old; and tho' I had frequent Hints from my Companions of the Disparity of my Age with theirs, none of them exceeding sixteen or seventeen, I [1]took all they said as the Effects of Envy for my superior Perfections; and tho' I hated them for it, was far from being mortified myself. Thus did I suffer Years after Years to roll away without one serious Thought, nor would be prevailed upon to quit my Post of Maid of Honour, till by remaining in it I became the Derision of the whole Court; and the Queen herself, in pity of my Weakness, obliged me to exchange it for first Woman of the Bedchamber, the Princess being now arrived at an Age to have her Houshold settled, in a manner befitting the Heiress of Empire, she being the only Child; and indeed it was done with a Splendour not at all inferiour to that of her Royal Parents. To express the Charms of that young Beauty would be impossible; so I shall only say, none but those you are Mistress of could come in any Competition with them; nor were those of her Mind less to be admired. She had all the Softness of our Sex, without any of the Affectation; Wit, unaccompanied by Vanity; and Virtue, without Pride. She beheld half the Princes of the Earth dying at her Feet, with a Pity excited by the Generosity of her Nature, but entirely free from that Sensibility of their Passion, which each endeavour'd to inspire. As she had no Aversion to Marriage, so she yet discovered not the least Inclination to it; and the King and Queen, who loved her with the Tenderness so many amiable Qualities merited from them, would not urge her overmuch upon a Theme they found not pleasing to her. But at length the fatal Moment arrived, which was to convince both her and the unfortunate *Atamadoul*, that Love, by being long repulsed, triumphs but the more. *Ochihatou* came to *Assadid*, and had the Boldness to declare his Pretentions to my Princess: the Gracefulness of his Person, the engaging Manner of his Address, his Wit, his Gallantry, and perhaps his Science, had so powerful an Effect, that he no sooner came, than conquer'd; her Heart that had withstood the Assaults of so many Sovereign Princes, yielded to

---

1   The Commentator will have it, that in the Character of *Atamadoul*, that of her whole Sex is decypher'd. The Author of the Remarks also adds, that a Woman is the *first* in believing herself *handsome*, and the *last* in finding she *grows old*. But as we see no antiquated Coquets in our Days, we must suppose these Reflections are only just on the Ladies of former Ages. [E.H.]

the first Summons of a Man no way her equal; and as she was of a Humour averse to all kinds of Deceit, she endeavoured not to disguise the Tenderness he had inspired her with, but gave him all the Proofs of it that Modesty would permit. Their Majesties, however, were so highly offended at his Presumption, that they forbad him the Court and Kingdom, and strictly enjoin'd the Princess to hold no farther Communication with him, either by Letters or Messages. She was too dutiful a Daughter to do any thing contrary to their Will, and resolved a perfect Obedience to this Command, tho' much the severest she had ever received. The Agonies she endured in the Conflict, between Virtue and Inclination, were so violent, that to behold them, would have drawn Tears from any Eyes, but those of a Rival; but I must confess my Cruelty in this Point, I loved *Ochihatou*, had envied her the Conquest of his Heart, and felt the extremest Satisfaction in finding there was a Bar, which I knew would be indissoluble, put between the Completion of their mutual Desires. As the Gratification this gave my Malice was all I could hope; so, for some moments, 'twas all I wish'd: But alas! the burning Passion, for I can call it no other, with which I was inflamed, soon reminded me, that Revenge afforded but an imperfect Bliss. I found, I could not live without the Sight of *Ochihatou*, and as he was obliged to quit *Assadid* for ever, the Pain my beautiful Rival sustained, wou'd but serve to shew my own Misery in the stronger Colours, who languished in the same Calamity, without the Consolation of being pitied, or even thought on by the dear Author of our common Woes. Reflections, such as these, put me on racking my Invention how to make the Disappointment of their Loves subservient to my own Aim; and *Syllalippe*, honouring me with a perfect Confidence, I persuaded her, that neither Duty nor Reason demanded she shou'd be so far ungrateful to the Passion of *Ochihatou*, as to suffer him to depart, without letting him know at least, that she bore an equal Share in his Misfortune. Overcome by the Arguments industrious Love inspired me with, she at length consented I shou'd go to him in her Name, and say every thing I thought proper for his Consolation. I cannot say, that I flatter'd my self with any thing further in this Visit, than the Pleasure of seeing him again, and talking to him; my Vanity had received so many Mortifications of later Years, that I cou'd not hope he wou'd turn his Addresses to me, since disappointed in them to my Princess: yet did I spare nothing that day, which I thought might contribute to the rendring me agreeable; but alas! his Behaviour to me soon convinced me, the Errand on which I came, was all that recommended me to his Civilities. He expressed so much Despair, at the Thoughts of never seeing *Syllalippe* more, that I was ready to burst with spite; and the violent Emotions of my Heart making a visible Alteration in my Countenance, he, little suspicious of the real Motive, imagined it proceeded only from my Compassion. Kind *Atamadoul!* said he, how obliging is the Concern you testify for my Sufferings; and how infinitely bound shou'd I be for ever to your Goodness, if you wou'd exert that Influence I know you have over your adorable Mistress, to prevail with her to recede yet a little more from that severe Duty, which wou'd tear her from me. These Words were accompanied with so tender a Pressure of my Hand, that my very Heart thrilled, every Pulse was in confusion; and, without considering what I spoke, Wou'd to Heaven, cried I, it were in my power to give your Sorrows ease. Endeavour it then, resumed he impatiently, if *Syllalippe* loves as she a thousand times has made me hope, she will rather chuse to abandon *Assadid* for ever, than resolve to see me fall the Victim of Despair: Nor need she fear a Diminution of her State; she shall live adored, and be more than Queen in *Hypotofa*, cou'd my fond Passion but persuade her to fly with me to a Place where I, in effect, rule all, and all shou'd be at her Devotion. I wish, answered I, there were a Probability of her complying; but I have been told, you are a Master of a Science, which enables you to become, in all things, the Master of your Aim, without the slow Result of any Choice but your own: If so, methinks, it's easy for you to bear the Princess hence, yet save her the Guilt of yielding.

You will doubtless be surprized, continued *Atamadoul*, to be told, I gave advice so contrary, in appearance, to the Interest of my Passion; but the Sequel of my unhappy Story will convince you, I acted, in this point, a Part, as I imagined, extremely artful: I knew it was in my power, by betraying all to the King, to disappoint whatever Measures shou'd be taken for the accomplishment of their Loves, provided I was apprised of them; which I cou'd no way be, but by winding myself into his Confidence. I had also a half-formed Idea of a farther Design, which alas! I afterward had an opportunity of compleating, to my own everlasting Shame and Ruin. But I will hasten to a Catastrophe, which I see you are impatient for, and which is indeed too shocking to me to suffer me to dwell long upon.

My Behaviour working the intended Effect, of making him believe, I wish'd nothing more than to see him possest of the Princess; he open'd his whole Heart to me without reserve. He told me, he was indeed so great a Proficient in Magick, that there were but few things he cou'd not obtain by it; but that having consulted his Agents in that Art, he found two things; first, that *Syllalippe* was under the Guardian-ship of a *Genius*, from whose Protection she was not to be wrested without her own Consent; and secondly, that shou'd she yield to make an escape with him, and the Design, by any Accident, be frus-trated, all Attempts afterward wou'd be in vain: I therefore, added he, must obtain her by her own free Will, and at once, or never hope to do it. He then proceeded to entreat me to urge her on this Theme, which I as readily promised, nay, swore to do; and took my leave, as going on the Performance: But, in truth, to put the finishing Stroke to that Plot, which I told you on the beginning of my Conversation with him, had started into my head, and was of no less consequence than putting myself in the Princess's place, and being conveyed away by him in her stead.

'Twou'd be unnecessary to detain you with Particulars; so I shall only say, my Stratagem was but too successful: After having left him only so long a time, as he might imagine it might take me to prepare *Syllalippe*, I returned to him, told him my Intercession, join'd with her extreme Tenderness, had got the better of her Duty and Allegiance; that she consented to leave *Assadid*, and wou'd come into the Palace Garden when it grew dark; where, if he cou'd provide any means for her escape, she wou'd put her self under his direction, for her whole future Life. The Joy with which he received these Tidings is not to be express'd; he called me the Preserver of his Life, the sole Bestower of all the Happiness he wish'd on Earth, and tho' he never wants Words to declare his Meaning in the most efficacious Terms, never did I hear his Tongue flow with such harmonious Eloquence as on this occa-sion. As a Testimony of his Gratitude, he put a Ring upon my Finger, of sovereign Virtue to preserve an eternal Gaiety of Desire and amorous Warmth; This, said he, whenever you think fit to make a Man happy in your Embraces, will bind him to you in the most last-ing Chains; she who wears this, will never know a Decay of Inclina-tion; and, by being capable of *receiving*, will also *give* the highest

Raptures Nature can support, or Love afford. Small was the need I had of such a Present; I gladly accepted it however; and the time for his meeting *Syllalippe* being fixed for thirteen Seconds and a half after the Noon of Night, I flew as to acquaint her with it; but, in reality, to get every thing ready for my own departure.

The wish'd-for Moment being arrived, I went into the Garden, wrapp'd up in a Veil he had often seen the Princess wear, and had taken notice of for the Curiousness of the Work, it being the finest blue Net in the World, embroider'd all over with silver Stars. There was so little difference between us in Shape and Stature, that a Person, less prepossess'd that it cou'd be none but herself who came to meet him, might have been easily deceived: He enter'd at the same time I did; and perceiving me at a distance, ran to me, catch'd me in his Arms, press'd me to his Bosom with an Ardor which shew'd the Vehemence of his Passion; I trembling, between the Extasy his Caresses gave me, and the Fears of being discover'd, had now little the Power of making use of any Artifice; yet the Confusion I was in, appeared so like what might be expected from the Modesty of *Syllalippe*, that perhaps it was of greater service in carrying on the Deception. This, however, not being a Place for Congratulations, he utter'd some mystick Words, on which a Chariot, which seem'd made of one entire Emrald, and drawn by six wing'd Horses, immediately presented it self before us: We went into it, and were no sooner seated, than our aerial Steeds bore us far above the Tops of the most lofty Turrets. Not Thought it self was quicker than our Flight; my Head was giddy with the Rapidity; but he, more accustomed to such Ætherial Voyages, shewed not the least Alteration, but continued kissing and embracing me, with Transports such as leaves me no room to doubt, he wou'd have proceeded, even in that hurrying moment of our Passage, to the last Gratification of his furious Desires, had he not been deterr'd by the knowledge that the Vehicle which contain'd us, unable to sustain the Rapture, wou'd have [1]burst in pieces, and thrown us headlong down.

Tho' *Assadid* is some thousands of Leagues distant from *Hypotofa*, we were here in less than seven Minutes: I need not tell you in what

---

1   This seems to prove what several Naturalists of later Ages have endeavour'd to maintain, that the Emrald is a Stone of such Purity, as to endure no unchaste Endearments. [E.H.]

manner I was received, since it was just the same in which you your self was usher'd in. He led me immediately into this Chamber; and having made a sign to his Attendants to retire, Now, my dearest *Syllalippe*, I may call you mine! said he; now do I triumph over the *Genius* that would have withheld you from me! now is it not in the Power of Heaven, or even [1]*Fate* itself, to hinder me from being the happiest of Mankind! He had scarce made an end of pronouncing these Words, when seizing me with an Extasy which no Language can describe, he threw off my Veil! – But, Oh Gods! how is it possible for me to represent, in what manner he looked, when, instead of the young blooming *Syllalippe*, he found the decayed, the wither'd *Atamadoul*. – He let me fall from his Arms; – he stood speechless, motionless; wild Horror wandered over every Feature, a Paleness, like that of Death, o'erspread his Lips and Cheeks, and his Eyes seem'd to start with Fierceness inconceivable. Tho' I had expected little less from the Shock I believed must attend the first Discovery of this Disappointment, yet was I frighted beyond all measure at it; but still flattering my self, that when he shou'd consider there was no remedy, he would forgive and pity a Fault, occasioned only by my too violent Love; I fell upon my knees, I kiss'd his Feet, I set forth the Influence his Perfections had made in my Heart, in the most tender and most passionate Terms, and begged he would rather *kill* than *hate* me for what I had done. The Extremity of his Rage not permitting him to speak, I had full Opportunity to say every thing that I thought might move him to Compassion; and sure, my Love inspired me, at that time, with the softest and most endearing Expressions that Tongue e'er utter'd. At last, his Mouth open'd, and the struggling Passion, which I believe wou'd else have choak'd him, vented it self in the most unheard of Curses, Imprecations, and Revilings: Thou Toad, cried he, thou Serpent, or, if there be any thing more loathsome, *that* shall be thy Name – how darest thou add to the Mischief thou hast done me, the Persecution of thy nauseous Love? – the very Word is odious, coming from Lips like thine. – Coud'st thou imagine thy stale, thy fulsome Embraces, cou'd compensate for the Joys thou has deprived me of

---

1   *Hahehihotu* infers from this, that the *Hypotofans* believed the Gods themselves were in subjection to a superior Power, which they call'd *Fate*. [E.H.]

with the incomparable *Syllalippe*? Or, that I should ever be prevail'd upon to take a thing like thee into my Arms? No, all the Pleasure thou art capable of affording me, is the Gratification of my Revenge, which I will exercise in such a manner, as shall deter all Woman-kind from aiming at Delights they are past the power of giving. With these Words he spurn'd me from him, and turned away. I followed him still on my knees, hung upon his Robe, and answered these cruel Reproaches but with Tears, and Beseechings; but I soon found, that if these Humiliations had any effect at all on his Heart, it was but to render it more remorseless; and, after a long Pause, Thou shalt not die, said he, but live a lasting Monument of thy own Shame. Be, continued he, in shape of *Body*, what thou long hast been in *Mind*: Then spit upon me, and spoke some [1]Words, the Meaning of which I was utterly unacquainted with; but they were no sooner out of his Mouth, than I found my Tongue deprived of all articular Sounds, my Skin was covered with Hair, my Limbs contracted, and, in fine, my whole Person transformed into a Monkey. Now, resumed he, for thy greater Curse, be still possest of those Desires thou ne'er canst gratify. – Love me with greater Violence than ever; and, in this Chamber, be witness of the Extasies I shall indulge with others. After this, he call'd a Servant, who chained me in the manner you saw, and in which I have ever since remained.

You will suppose nothing cou'd have been added to so cruel a Punishment; but the Magician has Arts of Torture beyond all Comprehension but of those they are practised on. 'Twas not enough to turn me into so obscene[2] a Form; – 'Twas not enough to compel me to hear the Vows he gives to others in this fatal Chamber, and the Raptures he shares with them, when every Kiss, when every Sigh Excess of Pleasure causes in them, pierces to my Soul! when wild Desires, Despair, and unavailing Rage, racks every Fibre in this wretched Frame, and makes me all o'er Agony! Yet this, all this, he

---

1   The Cabal were very careful to suppress these Words; fearing that, by design or accident, they might be repeated, and cause other Transformations of this kind; but we fear their Caution has been in vain, and the Secret is by some means or other discovered for, tho' we have no Magicians in our days, we see a great many *Atamadoul* Monkeys. [E.H.]

2   obscene: Offensive to the senses or to taste or refinement; disgusting, repulsive.

looks on as insufficient for his Vengeance; and taking no less a Delight in the gratification of his Malice, than any other Lust, diverts himself with my Misery, in a manner impossible to be guess'd at. He causes a very ugly and over-grown Baboon to be brought into the Room to me, which taking me for one of his own Species, leaps upon me, caresses me after the way of those Animals, till my Strength is wearied out with struggling; and, in spite of my Horror at suffering so detestable an Action, the Brute is sometimes very near taking an entire Possession of me. The cruel *Ochihatou* is all this while laughing, and deriding me with the most opprobrious Reflections; nor consents to relieve, but in order to renew my Affliction. Day after Day is the same shocking Scene repeated; and, as his Hatred to me seems rather to augment than abate, I shudder with the Apprehension, lest it should at length carry him so far as to permit the odious Animal to gain an entire Victory over me.

To compleat my Misery, resumed she, I still languish in the most consuming Fires for my inhumane Persecutor; and it is this Propensity in me, which must preserve you from becoming an immediate Victim to his Passion: Counterfeit therefore a yielding to his Will; if you are not sufficiently practised in the Arts of Dissimulation, to act the part of one who is really in love with him, pretend at least that your Virtue recedes to Necessity, and that you think it better to submit patiently to what you find is unavoidable, than, by fruitless Resistance, incense a Person in whose power you are; only make it your Request, that, for Modesty's sake, he will suffer the Lights to be extinguished, the first time at least that you receive him to your Embraces. This obtain'd, the wretched *Atamadoul* will take your place. The Ring which keeps alive in me those vehement Desires, will also render me capable of gratifying, in the most extatick manner, those in him; and, in spite of his Disdain, I shall be once happy.

Eovaai now perceiving she had done, and expected, with some Impatience her Reply; I want Words, said she, to express the Astonishment your Story has given me; nor will I waste the time, so precious now, for both our Purposes, in any Testimonies either of my Disapprobation of your Behaviour, or Compassion for your present State: I shall only say, I am ready to come into any Measure that shall preserve my Virtue, and make you Mistress of your Wishes.

In brief then, said *Atamadoul*, shewing her the Tablet a second time, behold these Characters engraven by the Fingers of the most subtil *Ypre* all [1]*Caihou* affords: These on the Top are to *Transform*, those at the Bottom to *Reform*; there is a necessity I must return to that Shape his Cruelty has fixed upon me, that when he enters the Room he may see me as I was, and suspect nothing of what has past between us; you must therefore utter these Words, (in speaking this, she pointed to her the Lesson) and I shall be in that instant a *Monkey*; – and afterwards, when to avoid his Love you wou'd have me a *Woman*, pronounce distinctly, but so as not to be overheard by him, these Words which you have already repeated, and the Effect of which you have experienced.

Eovaai examined carefully the Characters, but to be more perfect in her Instructions, repeated them various times, and as often as she did so, converted the *Woman* into a *Monkey*, and the *Monkey* into a *Woman*. Having made sufficient Tryal of the force of these Words, *Atamadoul* resumed her Corner, and fell to gnawing her Chain, as she was wont; and the Princess of *Ijaveo* set down to consider in what terms she should deceive *Ochihatou* into an Opinion, that she had quitted all Thoughts of opposing his Desires.

She assum'd, at his Entrance, an Air, neither gay nor sad, but perfectly composed; and when he demanded if she had resolved on Compliance, where the means of resisting are denied, said she, The Question might be spared. I see the *Genii* themselves yield to your superiour Arts: Virtue is found too weak to protect her Votary;[2] and all I trusted in for my defence has left me. – But if you really think my Embraces can afford you any Pleasures capable of compensating for the pains you have been at, abuse not, I conjure you, the Power you have over me by any Act of Force; but suffer me, by those Degrees becoming of my Sex and Birth, to resign to you a *Soul* as well as *Body*; the one without the other would be unworthy of you, and bestow no more than an imperfect Bliss and fleeting Rapture.

Princess! answered he, looking on her with Eyes that seemed to penetrate her inmost Thoughts, I am not to be twice deceived by the

---

1   The Cabal had a long Dispute on the Meaning of this Word; some would have it *Hell*; others, *the Bowels of the Earth*: nor did they at last agree. [E.H.]

2   Votary: A devotee.

same Person. – Who would have imagined, after what past between us in the Garden, I should not have found you at my Return disposed to grant the only remaining Joy Love had in store. – Yet did you leave me, fly from me with the most cruel Enemy of my Happiness, and betrayed by the Insinuations of *Halafamai*, resolve to see me no more. – How then is it possible I should now give Credit to your Words? – My past Behaviour may have sufficiently convinced you how loth I was to use Compulsion, and that my Ambition was to become Master of your Heart; but if by pretending to yield to me by *Degrees*, you mean only to gain Time, expecting perhaps a second Deliverance, you flatter yourself with a vain Hope; for by the Powers that rule the Realms of Darkness, I swear I will this moment enjoy your *Person*, dispose your *Heart* by what *Degrees* you please.

From the very Beginning of this Discourse *Eovaai* had reason to fear she should not be able to put her intended Stratagem in execution; and wholly dispair'd of it, when at the Close of it, he took hold of both her Hands, and endeavour'd to force her to a Couch, which was placed at the farther End of the Room. Her Confusion permitted her to utter only half form'd Words, nor indeed was this a time, had she been possest of Power, to urge her Request; but the Lady *Monkey* having greater Presence of Mind, and perceiving all was now at stake, leap'd to the String, on which hung a great Lamp enlightning all the Chamber, and making use of her utmost Strength, threw it out of the Pully; whereby falling to the Ground, the Flame went out, and left them all in Darkness. *Eovaai*, in spite of her Disorder, comprehended the Meaning of this Action; and while *Ochihatou* ran to the Door to call Servants, that this Accident might be remedied, and the Light renew'd, she hastily pronounc'd the Words *Atamadoul* had taught her, then followed him, and catching hold of one his Arms; Since Chance, said she, with a Voice which had nothing of Severity in it, has thus far favour'd my Modesty, all I beg is, that you will suffer us to remain in the Obscurity we now are, nor see my Shame till I have enough overcome it to endure the Light.

'Tis not to be suppos'd, that the *Ypres* acquainted *Ochihatou* with every Transaction that happened, nor that he gave himself the Trouble of consulting them on all occasions; especially on this, where there seem'd so little need of supernatural Assistance to render him Master of his Wishes. Far, therefore, from imagining *Eovaai* had any other Design in this Petition than what she appear'd to have, he made no Scruple of granting it; and as he turned to take her again into his Arms, *Atamadoul*, who having now regain'd her own Shape, stood close to *Eovaai*, had the Dexterity to put herself between them, and was carried instead of the other to the Couch. The Impatience of *Ochihatou* to reap the Joys he had so languish'd for, and the Fury of his Extacy in the supposed Attainment of them allowing him no Breath for Words, as well as the Disorder of the Lady, render'd the profound Silence she observed, not in the least suspected by him, and either by virtue of the Ring he had given her, or that she had in herself sufficient to gratify the most riotous Luxury of Love, he found her all that his warmest Imagination had suggested to him of the Princess of *Ijaveo*.

That Princess had all this time a strange Flutter about her Heart, occasion'd by vastly different Emotions: Those of her late Fright; those of her Joy, for having escaped so imminent a Danger, were neither of them yet quieted; but she had others also more difficult to repel. – The tumultuous Pleasures she found the amorous Pair were involved in, the Fierceness of their Bliss alarmed Nature (for Nature will be Nature still) and shot unusual Thrillings thro' every Vein. Happy was it for her, that she bethought herself of the Perspective given her by *Halafamai*, tho' perhaps [1]Curiosity had the greatest share in her making use of it at this Juncture. She no sooner look'd through it, than instead of the smiling Loves she expected to have seen, she beheld two frightful and mishapen Spectres, hovering over the Heads of *Ochihatou* and *Atamadoul*, and pouring upon them Phials of sulphurous Fire; while a thousand other no less dreadful to sight, stood round the Couch, and with obscene and antick Postures animated their polluted Joys. Sick to the Soul, and quite confounded with the horrid Prospect, she put her Glass again into her Pocket, and bless'd the Darkness which defended her from so shocking a Scene. She was beginning to make some Reflections on the Meanness of suffering Passions of any kind to get the Mastery of Reason, when a

---

[1] The Commentator employs no less than three whole Pages in the most bitter Invectives on this Propensity, which, he will have it, is only natural to Woman-kind. [E.H.]

sudden and tumultuous Noise rouzed her from this Resvery, and the Lovers from the Slumber they were just fallen into. *Ochihatou* started from the Couch to enquire into the Cause of this Disturbance, and that Instant seven or eight Servants came running hastily into the Room, crying, Where is my Lord? and as soon as they saw him, added, Fly, fly, my Lord, and escape the Mischief that is intended you. – The City is in Arms – the Soldiery have join'd them – *Alhahuza* your mortal Enemy, with a chosen Band surrounds your Palace, and has already forced the outer Gates. While these were speaking, others followed, confirming the same thing, and all had Terror and Confusion in their Faces. 'Tis difficult to say, whether *Ochihatou* was more alarm'd at the News they brought, or amazed to find by the Lights they had in their Hands, that it was *Atamadoul* had fill'd his Arms; for, in this hurry, *Eovaai* had forgot to pronounce the mystic Words, which should have reduced that Lady to a Monkey. Never was any Rage equal to what he felt, and had not the Consideration of his Safety interveen'd, even the Princess of *Ijaveo* herself might possibly have experienced the Effects of it, for having join'd in the Deception put upon him. Go, said he, to his Attendants, – 'tis in vain to make head against them – the inner Door will presently be burst – my Life, I know, is what they aim at – therefore let some of you delude their Search – direct them to find me in a different Apartment, while I bestow the Moment is allowed me in thinking what to do. The Servants went out of the Room, having received these Orders; and *Atamadoul* perceiving by the Countenance of *Ochihatou* great part of what pass'd in his Mind, threw herself trembling and all in Tears at his Feet, conjuring him, by all the Pleasures of their late Endearments, to pardon the Fault of her unbounded Love. *Eovaai* also interceeded; but he refused to listen either to the one or the other, and casting the most furious Looks at both, It would require more time, said he, than I have now to waste, to inflict the Punishment your Crimes deserve, and which neither of you ought to hope to escape. But as for thee, continued he, turning to *Atamadoul*, thou most detested Thing! be henceforward in the sight of all Eyes the most hateful of all domestick Vermin. With these Words, he took a little Wand out of his Pocket, with which having struck her on the Head, she immediately became a huge grey Rat; and as if fearful of something yet worse than this

Transformation, ran and hid herself behind the Tapistry. *Eovaai* was ready to die at this sight; and without being able to speak, fell upon her Knees, endeavouring, by that submissive Posture, to avert any Design he might have of exercising his magick Power over her in the same manner; when *Ochihatou*, putting up his Wand a little, reassured her, in these Words, No, said he, ungrateful as you are, I shall for some time at least suspend my Resentment against you. Then turning from her, he muttered some Words in a very low Voice, tho' had he spoke much higher, they would have been wholly unintelligible to the Princess; which ended, he took her in his Arms, and bore her down a Pair of Stairs which led into the Garden. A large Machine, in form like a Lanthorn, and seemed made of Crystal, stood at the Entrance of one of the Walks, into which having thrown her, with the Air rather of a Tyrant than a Lover, he went in himself, and the same Instant an invisible Hand lifted them up in Air, and they went with the Rapidity of Lightning many thousand Leagues above all the Globes visible to mortal Sight. *Eovaai* had been so terrified with what she had seen happen to the unfortunate *Atamadoul*, that she had suffered herself to be put into this enchanted Lanthorn, without making the least Resistance, and was but now beginning to reflect on the Miseries that threatned her, thus entirely subjected to the Will of the Enchanter, when all at once they descended, and the Vehicle which had conveyed them in a moment vanish'd. *Ochihatou* all the time of their Passage had not once opened his Mouth, nor even cast his Eyes on the Princess of *Ijaveo*, but seem'd involv'd in some deep and important Thought. The horrid Gloom, which still sat on his Brow, encreased the Apprehension of his fair Companion; and tho' at first she was glad to find herself once more on Earth, yet when she look'd round and saw no Prospect of Relief from the Force he was at liberty to use her with, she fell into a kind of inward Agony, which no Words are able to describe. His Meditations at present were however employed on very different Subjects from that her Fears suggested: his amorous Inclinations receded to those of his Ambition and Revenge. – The Recovery of his lost State, and turning the Mischief intended against him on the Heads of his Enemies, were the Designs he was now forming; and when he had brought them, as he imagined, to some Maturity, Princess, said he, I will not go about to recapitulate the many

Indignities with which you have treated my Passion, and hope you will equally forget those Transgressions, which the too great Violence of it has made me guilty of to you. – Be assured, I will henceforward endeavour to gain your Affections only by such means as may become the most submissive Lover. – All I desire of you, is to mention nothing of what is past, nor contradict what you shall hear me say at the Court where we shall immediately arrive, and where I do not doubt, but you will be received in a fashion worthy your Birth and Virtues. Whether *Eovaai* really gave any Credit or not to the Promise he made her of regulating his Conduct, it certainly behoved her, in the present Situation, to seem as if she did; and rejoiced to find that there was a Necessity at least for his dissembling any ill Designs he might have on her, answered him in terms which gave him no reason to apprehend either his past, or future Projects, would be betray'd by her. After some little Discourse, which served to assure both the one and the other of their mutual Dependance, he told her the Place they now were in, was the Kingdom of *Huzbib*; that *Haminha* the Sovereign thereof, had long maintained the strictest Amity with *Oeros*; and that he doubted not, but thro' his Interest, to recover his former Greatness, to the Confusion of those who had attempted to overthrow it.

With this Discourse they arrived at the Gates of a magnificent Palace, where *Ochihatou* making himself known to the Officers of the Houshold, the King was immediately informed, and they were conducted to his Presence. He received them very graciously, but testified some Surprize to behold so great a Man as *Ochihatou*, and a Lady such as *Eovaai* appear'd to be, Visitors at his Court, without Attendants, Equipages[1] or any other Mark of Distinction; but the Statesman soon put an end to it by these Words:

It may justly be a Matter of Astonishment to your Majesty, said he, that a Man who so lately ruled, under *Oeros*, one of the most potent Kingdoms in the World, should be at once divested of Power, Friends, and reduced to take shelter in a foreign Court. – Yet so it is, – A Set of ambitious Men, who distinguishing themselves by the Name of *Patriots*, (tho' they are the rankest Traitors in their Hearts) by private

---

1   Equipages: Carriages, horses, servants of an upperclass person.

Cabals and Insinuations, have so poison'd the Minds of the *Hypoto-fans*, that even the most beneficent Actions of the Administration, seem to these deluded People as so many Oppressions; and, enflamed by their designing Leaders, they are become weary of [1]kingly Government, – they envy their Neighbours the *Oozoffians*, – cry out for Liberty, and resolve to throw off the Yoke of Sovereignty. – My firm Attachment to the Crown was too well known, to give any room for hope, I cou'd ever be drawn into such detestable Projects, the Ruin of my sacred Master was to begin with mine. Accordingly, in the dead of Night, when I was sleeping in my Bed, *Alhahuza*, the Head of the Rebel Faction, with a tumultuous Mob, surrounded my Palace, broke down the Gates, and had certainly made me the first Martyr to that Loyalty they had so shamefully thrown off, if my Skill in a Science, too abstruse for any of my Opposers to be Masters of, had not furnished me with the Means of escaping their wild Fury. Amidst the dreadful Disorder of that Hour, continued he, presenting *Eovaai*, I met this Princess, whose Virtues shou'd I attempt to describe, must greatly suffer; so I shall only say, to engage a Welcome from the gracious *Haminha*, that being born Queen of *Ijaveo*, and driven thence by her rebellious Subjects, she took refuge in the Court of *Hypotofa*, and alarmed at the Confusion so like to that she before had been Witness of at home, entreated I wou'd make her the Companion of my Flight from that destructive Scene. I fearing, that neither her Rank nor Virtue might be a sufficient Defence against those Desires her Beauty might inspire, consented to her Request, and doubted not but she wou'd find a certain Asylum in the Goodness of your Majesty. All I entreat for myself is Protection here; but for the Royal *Oeros*, my much wronged Sovereign, I have much more to urge; I who was his chief Bulwark against the Assaults of Faction, being beaten down, he is now defenceless from the Storm; and if not timely assisted by your Majesty, his most faithful Friend and Ally, must be depos'd, become a Slave to Slaves, and perhaps murder'd, for the better Security of those Traitors, who, having proceeded thus far, will be intimidated from nothing. O Royal *Oeros!* most dear Master! sacred Sovereign! added

---

1 The common Artifice of wicked Ministers in all Ages, to render any Opposition to themselves an Attempt against the Monarchy. [E.H.]

he, bursting into well-dissembled Tears, what Shocks, what Insults may'st thou not, even while I am speaking, undergo! How may the Majesty of Kings be trampled on, if Rebels, such as these, are permitted to enjoy the Benefit of their Crimes!

Here he ceased, and had the pleasure to find this artful Tale had all the effect he cou'd desire; *Haminha* express'd the utmost Abhorrence at the Proceedings of *Alhahuza* and his Adherents; and having given Orders that *Eovaai* and *Ochihatou* shou'd be conducted to Apartments, and waited on according to their Dignities, dispatch'd an Ambassador to *Hypotofa*, with a Commission to denounce War against that Nation, if they did not immediately return to their Allegiance.

Eovaai was now entirely freed from the Persecutions of *Ochihatou*; he saw her not but in publick; and when, at any time, he visited her, it was accompanied by some Lord or other of the Court; and if, by accident, either walking in the Gardens, in the Temple, or in any other Place, he happened to have an opportunity of speaking to her, unheard by any but herself, his Discourses were such as tended only to convince her, that he was ashamed of his past Conduct, and had now for her an Affection worthy of her Virtue. He acted his part with so admirable a Dexterity, that the Princess of *Ijaveo*, tho' Mistress of a greater Share of Penetration than was usually found in a Person of her Sex and Age, had doubtless been deceived into a belief of his Conversion, had not the Perspective of *Halafamai* informed her of the contrary. Indeed, never had he practis'd a greater Self denial, than in the Restraint he put on his Desires for the Enjoyment of this Princess; but she was now continually surrounded with the Ladies of the Court, who were charm'd with her Society, and in their absence had Attendants which served as a kind of Guards to her; besides, he had experienced the little Cause he had to hope she wou'd consent to gratify his Passion, and to attempt Force, wou'd have rendered him odious to *Haminha*, and been the total Ruin of his Designs: he therefore resolved to confine himself within the Bounds of Decency, till he had her once more in a Place where nobody shou'd have the power to call him to account for any thing he did. This he was far from despairing to obtain; for he doubted not but *Oeros* wou'd give such an Answer to the Ambassador of *Haminha*, as should engage that Monarch to send a sufficient number of Forces into *Hypotofa*, to expel, or put to the Sword *Alhahuza*, and all his Party, and he should then return in Triumph.

But things had taken a Turn in that Kingdom the Reverse of what he expected; and even much worse for him than, in his most timid moments, his Imagination had ever suggested to him.

When *Alhahuza*, and the Patriot Band had every where searched in vain for *Ochihatou*, they flew transported with an honest Zeal to the Houses of all those who had assisted his wicked Schemes, and rioted in the Spoils of a plunder'd and almost ruin'd Nation. None of the Associates of that pernicious Statesman was more trusted by him than *Zinky*;[1] he therefore was designed as the first Sacrifice: but this Wretch, who exceeded *Ochihatou* himself in Acts of Cruelty, Rapine, and Oppression, who knew neither Love nor Pity, and was so swell'd with Pride, while Villany was successful, that he disdained to hold Converse even with his Fellow-Monsters, if less opulent than himself, now all at once [2]became the most abject Creature breathing, he prostrated himself beneath the Feet of *Alhahuza*, confess'd his Crimes, and begg'd his Life with such Submissions, as were below the Dignity of Man. But not all the Contempt, which such a Behaviour must naturally excite, could make the virtuous Patriot think him beneath the Punishment his enormous Crimes had merited; he therefore ordered he should be hang'd in Chains, till he died, from one of the highest Windows in his own House. The enrag'd Populace immediately seized on him, and were hurrying him away to Execution; when he cried out, with a loud Voice, Hear me, hear me, I have that to discover will well deserve the Life I beg. – *Ochihatou*, in me alone, has reposed the Secret of the Enchantment, which has so long deprived you of your King. – In me it lies to restore him to you such as he was before the Ambition of the Minister poison'd his Faculties, and threw Reason into a Lethargy. – Let me but live, and I will tell you all. – *Alhahuza* was too loyal, and too truly attach'd to the Interest of the King, to suffer any Considerations to outweigh those of serving him:

---

1   *Zinky*: I have been unable to identify Zinky, if, in fact, he represents a real life figure.

2   The learned and judicious *Usquimlac* set it down as an infallable Maxim, that a *Mean-bearing in Adversity*, is the infallible Consequence of *Insolence in Prosperity*; and indeed, I never found any one Example, which contradicted the Truth of it. [E.H.]

He commanded the Traitor to be brought back, and having assured him of a Pardon, at least so far as concern'd Life, if he could make good what he had promised, *Zinky* related the whole Story of the Magic Feather; and concluded with saying, that whoever should have Courage to pluck it from the Crown, and throw it into the Fire, would immediately see *Oeros* such they wished him to be. This Task *Alhahuza* took upon himself, and having committed *Zinky* to the Care of some he could confide in, till he should experience the Truth of his Information, went directly to the King's Palace, accompanied with the Chief of his Forces. The Guards had Orders to oppose their Entrance; but as they obeyed without Inclination, their Resistance was too feeble for the others Courage and Resolution, and the Patriots penetrated even into the King's private Cabinet. – At first he branded them with the Name of Rebels, audacious Traitors, and swore he would chastise their Insolence; but *Alhahuza* wasted not the Time in Arguments, which he too well knew would be in vain, while the Enchantment remain'd in force; and stepping boldly up to him, took the Crown from off his Head, and drew out that pernicious Feather, which having burnt, as *Zinky* had directed, returned the Diadem, and falling on his Knees, Resume, O sacred Sir, said he, this Wreath of Royalty now worthy of your Head, since freed from that which robb'd you of yourself and all your faithful Subjects Hearts.

Oeros during this Transaction had appeared in the utmost Consternation; and when it was concluded, and the Crown again set upon his Head, started and look'd wildly round him, like one just waking from some frightful Dream. Tis probable, he either not heard, or at least in his present Confusion, not understood the Words of *Alhahuza*, for nothing could be got from him for some time, but *What is all this? – Wherefore do I see you here? – Where is* Ochihatou! Reason however at last resumed her full Dominion. – The execrable Spell was now totally dissolved, and the recovered Monarch listned attentively to what *Alhahuza* and the rest said to him concerning the Arts had been practiced on him, and the dreadful Effects they had produced over an almost ruin'd Nation. The sad Relation drew from him Tears of mingled Rage and Grief; nor was it easy even for himself to determine, whether Indignation for the Abuse he had sustain'd, or Sorrow for the Calamity of his People, was the most predominant. He resolved to do Justice to both these Passions, which if he had not felt, would have rendered him as undeserving the Regal Dignity, as he was really the contrary. He put all the Friends and Creatures of *Ochihatou* to death, *Zinky* excepted; who was suffer'd to live, because of *Alhahuza's* Promise, but was kept a close Prisoner the whole Remainder of his Days, and his amassed Treasures, with those of his Confederates, divided amongst those Families who had been most oppressed. This done, a Proclamation was issued out, requiring all who had any Grievances, to repair to the Palace; the Gates of which were ordered to be kept open for the meanest Suppliants to have Access, and none returned without full Satisfaction. All heavy Taxes were taken off; the Army raised by *Ochihatou* was disbanded, tho' not without Reward for turning against that perfidious Minister, when convinced he aim'd at subverting the Liberty of his Country. In fine, all who had the least Claim to favour, either by their Services or Distresses, were certain of obtaining it.

Never was Joy so universal as that, which now diffused itself through all *Hypotofa*. The Name of *Oeros*, attended with millions of Blessings,[1] echoed from every Mouth. The ancient Nobility, who had long shut themselves up in their Castles, to avoid, as much as possible, seeing the Vices and Follies of the Times, now returned to Court, with Hearts full of loyal Transport. The Artificers,[2] and those employ'd in cultivating the Earth, went chearfully to work, secure of enjoying the Labours of their Hands. Encouragement of Arts and Sciences, Hospitality, Benevolence, and Charity, Virtues for which the *Hypotofans* had been famous, but had lain dormant during the Tyranny of *Ochihatou*, seem'd now to [3]revive with their Liberty; and tho' all People could not be rich, yet none feared Poverty, secured in any Exigence of Supply from those enabled to afford it.

---

1   This is indeed the *true Grandeur* of a King, and ought to afford him more Satisfaction than the vain Pomp of exterior Homage; [which is given] when [the public is] conscious [that] his Actions [do not] deserve...[that]...[their blessings] should proceed from the Heart. [Ed. note: Original reads: "This is indeed the *true Grandeur* of a King, and ought to afford him more Satisfaction than the vain Pomp of exterior Homage; when conscious his Actions deserve not it should proceed from the Heart."] [E.H.]
2   Artificers: Artisans, craftsmen, mechanics.
3   The Commentator observes, that there cannot be a more distinguishing Mark of a Free Government than Liberality and Charity; because, where the People are under one or more Tyrants, they know not how far the Demands of absolute Power may extend; and fear to part even with a little, lest they should be reduced to the want of it themselves. [E.H.]

As *Alhahuza* had been the chief Instrument in bringing this happy Change to pass, he was no less careful to make it perfect,[1] he prevailed on the King, who call'd him his Deliverer, and could deny him nothing, to repeal whatever Laws could possibly be made use of by any succeeding Prince, to the Detriment of the Subject, and got new ones in their room; restraining the Regal Authority to such Bounds, as had never before been set, yet left sufficient to content a virtuous Prince: and, in every thing he did, so exactly preserved the Dignity of the Crown, and the Freedom of the Subject, that both had reason to be highly satisfied.

Things were in this position in *Hypotofa*, when the Ambassador of *Haminha* arrived. *Oeros* was exceedingly rejoiced to find that Monarch still retain'd his former Friendship; but much more so, when he heard that *Ochihatou* had taken shelter in his Court; because he doubted not, but he would readily deliver him up to those Punishments his Guilt deserved. He made a brief Recital of all had past; and the *Huzbibian* was amazed beyond measure, at the Timerity of that Statesman, who, knowing what he had done, durst expect his injured Sovereign should continue of his Party; but the Consternation he was in ceased, when he was reminded, that he knew not the Enchantment was broke: which had it continued, said the King of *Hypotofa*, with a Sigh, I must most certainly have answered your Embassy in Terms wholly in his favour. But as I am restored to myself, pursued he, Thanks to the Immortal Powers, I have nothing now to wish, but that my Royal Brother of *Huzbib* will give me this Testimony of his Friendship, to send that Traitor to me, in such a manner, as shall render it impossible for him to escape the just Revenge of a People, whom his wild Ambition and insatiable Avarice had well nigh reduced to the last Extremity of Wretchedness.

The Ambassador assured his Majesty of his Master's Readiness to oblige him; and a Courier was that Instant dispatched with a Catalogue of all the Crimes of *Ochihatou*.

---

1 Some Fragments of the Life of *Alhahuza* inform us, that this great Patriot never ask'd any thing for himself; and was so strictly just to his Country, that he gave up his own Brother, finding he had been corrupted by *Ochihatou*.[E.H.] [Ed. note:The "own Brother" is not identified, if indeed, it refers to a specific man. In 1735, Bolingbroke left for France because the opposition was so fragmented in its fight against Walpole.]

In the mean time, that Minister, tho' he little suspected the Cowardice of *Zinky*, had Curiosity enough to know how Matters went in *Hypotofa*; and one Night when all the Court were drowned in sleep, he stole out of the Palace, and repair'd to a wild barren Heath, at a small distance from the City. There,[1] having utter'd horrid Incantations, and performed all the Rites necessary to raise the subterranean Powers, and enforce them to obey his Will, he was by them informed of all had passed between *Oeros* and the Ambassador of *Haminha*. He found he was undone, and all his high-rais'd Hopes of returning to *Hypotofa*, and the Confidence of his abused Master, were but delusive Shadows. He raved, cursed Heaven, Fate, and the better Genius of Mankind, for putting a stop to his destructive Aims, added fresh Invocations to the *Ypres* to assist him with means to pluck the Sun forth from its fiery Orb, and set the World in flames,[2] to dash in pieces the Crystal Globes which beautify the Sky, to compel the Ocean to break down all Fences set by Nature, to anticipate Destruction, and either drown or burn the whole Creation; but the dreadful Groans, and Yellings, he received in answer to this wild Petition, soon convinced him, that great as was their Power, there was [3]a Being of yet infinitely greater, and who had prescrib'd Bounds, which it was impossible for them to pass.

The Magician having vented some part of his Rage in Exclamations, began to consider how he should avert the Evil which seem'd just ready to burst upon him; he found the Courier of *Oeros* would arrive at the Court of *Huzbib*, within eight and forty Hours, and that on the delivery of the Message he brought, he should be immediately secured and sent to *Hypotofa*. Some Asylum must therefore be thought upon, and what Place promised so secure a one, as the Kingdom of *Ijaveo?* He knew by his Art, that the People had sadly experienced the Effects of Rebellion and Anarchy, and wished earnestly for the Return of their lost Princess, whom, since her strange Departure

---

1   It is observable, that the Ministers of Darkness bring no Intelligence to their Votaries, without being demanded in a peculiar manner. [E.H.]

2   This Passage seems to be a Proof, that even in those early Times, they had a Notion that the World should in succeeding Ages go thro' the Revolutions both of Water and Fire. [E.H.]

3   The Words *a Being* implies they believed in one great Supreme Being, who commanded the *Genii*, and kept the *Ypres* in awe; but by what Name they distinguish'd him, or what kind of Worship was paid to him, is no where specified. [E.H.]

from among them, had never been heard of. Could *Eovaai* be prevailed on to marry him, he saw no Difficulty of living and reigning there; so he set himself to put on all that might conduce to bring her to this Point; to which indeed the Modesty of his late Deportment seem'd not a little to contribute.

Early the next Morning, he sent a Messenger to entreat a private Audience in her Apartment. As he had not since their coming to *Huzbib* made the like Request, this a little alarmed her; but as she had always Attendants within Call, she yielded to it with the less Scruple, and he approach'd her with an Air so perfectly submissive, as entirely banish'd all unquiet Apprehensions from her Bosom. Madam, said this Master of Dissimulation, I come now to give you an uncontestable Proof of the Purity of my Intentions toward you. – The *Ijaveans* repent their ill Treatment of so excellent a Queen. – Loyalty is rekindled in their Hearts. – A vacant Throne attends your Presence, and I should add to my past Offences a much greater yet, could I be capable of detaining you one moment from your impatient People. No, Madam, pursued he, I swear to you by the immortal Gods, I will defer my Longings to return to *Hypotofa*, and the Revenge due to my Persecutors, till I have seen you re-established in all those Dignities you were born to wear. – Be pleased then to permit me to exert that Science, which I shall esteem more than ever, if serviceable to you, for your Conveyance hence; and before the Sun has passed half his Diurnal Progress,[1] you shall behold yourself in the Confines of *Ijaveo*.

It was with an inexpressible Confusion of Ideas, that *Eovaai* heard this Discourse: Wonder and Joy, and Hope and Fear, joined with a certain Suspence proceeding from them all, left her not the Power of making any immediate Answer. *Ochihatou* gave her some time to recover herself; and when he perceived she grew more composed, I doubted not, Madam, resumed he, if the Tidings I brought would fill you with the extremest Surprize; but then I expected it would be a Surprize wholly made up of Transport, nor can see any reason why you should hesitate, even for a moment, to accept the Offer I make of restoring you to your Kingdom, and by that means attoning for some part of my past Conduct.

---

1   Diurnal Progress: Daily; in the course of a day.

Before these last Words, the Princess of *Ijaveo* had brought herself to resolve in what manner she should behave: She knew nothing of what had happened in *Hypotofa* since their Departure from that Court, and could not but look on his Desires of setting her on her Throne, before his own Re-establishment, as the highest Testimony of an unfeign'd Affection and Respect. She imagined indeed, that he was not without some interested Designs, both on her Person and Kingdom; but then she thought she should be much more secure from any thing he should attempt amongst her own People than she could possibly be in the Court of *Oeros*, where every thing had been so entirely at his Command, and she expected would be so again at his Return to it. She thought it therefore much better to agree to his Proposal, by which she seem'd to hazard but little, in comparison with what she might be exposed to, if carried back to *Hypotofa*; and perceiving he had done speaking, and seem'd impatient for her Reply; To be told, said she, that the unfortunate *Ijaveans* are at length sensible of their Faults, and willing to repair the Injuries done to me, their lawful Queen, is a Blessing I so little expected, or even hoped, that it might well put all my Faculties to a stand: But since you have assured me of the Truth, I should be ungrateful to the relenting Gods, to neglect any possible means of laying hold on the Bounty they, thro' you, present. If I have therefore hesitated, it is only occasioned by an Unwillingness to abuse your Generosity, in suffering you to bestow any of those Labours for my Establishment, at a time when your own requires them all.

Ochihatou reply'd to this little Compliment, in Terms full of Respect; and when he found she was no less impatient for this Journey than himself, Madam, said he, as you have potent Enemies among the Stars, who are continually at war with those who would pour down auspicious Influences on your Head, it is not at all Times, nor by all Methods, you can possibly attain any good. – This present Hour is governed by the most benignant[1] of all the shining Train that fill the great Expanse above us. – Let us not lose it. – The next perhaps may render all Endeavours fruitless. – We must depart this moment; and to do it with safety, we must both of us exchange the Forms given us by

---

1 benignant: Benign, benevolent; exhibiting kindly feeling towards inferiors or dependants (*OED*).

Nature, for those of a less noble Part of the Creation. – Excuse me therefore, continued he, with a well-affected Modesty, and yield to the Necessity of plucking off your Habit. – We must be free, entirely divested of all that Pride, or Luxury, or Convenience invented for us, before we can assume the Shape of those less guilty Animals, who content themselves with appearing such as they were born.

Here followed a long Debate: *Eovaai* could not think of being naked, without a Confusion, which made her look on all the Benefits she might receive as too little a Recompence for the Shame she must undergo; but *Ochihatou* having utter'd unnumber'd Imprecations, that while she was undressing, he would not so much as turn his Eyes that way, she was at last prevailed on, and screening herself behind a Curtain, slowly pull'd one thing off, and then another; *Ochihatou* urging her all the time to be more speedy, by crying out, Dear Princess, the happy Moment is almost elaps'd. At last, she was wholly stript of every thing but the Shell, which had contain'd the mystic Jewel given her by *Eojaeu*, and the Perspective of *Halafamai*; the last of which she carefully conceal'd in the Palm of her Hand, and the former being tied about her Neck, had never quitted her Breast; and tho' she thought it of no Value, the Stone being lost, was now happily forgotten by her.

Having thus done what was required from her, she told him, with a faint Voice, that she was ready. His Clothes were immediately torn off; and when they were, he threw back the Curtain where *Eovaai* stood cowring down half dead with Shame: but he forbore to add to it, and without seeming to be at all affected with her naked Charms, spoke some Words altogether unintelligible to her, and at the same time struck her on the Forehead with his magic Wand; on which, she immediately became the most beautiful white Pigeon that ever was seen: That done, he gave a Blow to himself, and clapping the Wand between his Teeth, was turned into a huge Vulture; then seizing the Princess between his Talons, yet, in such a manner, as not to hurt her tender Body, took his Flight with her out of the Window, which he before had opened for that purpose.

Full many a League thro' Air the Vulture, with unwearied Pinions, bore his lovely Prize, nor perch'd for Rest on any Pinnacle, or Cloud-topt Rock, till he had reached *Ijaveo*; the sight of whose well-remember'd Towers, gave a strange Flutter to the Heart of *Eovaai*.

It was in a lone and unfrequented Forest *Ochihatou* chose to alight, and as soon as he had eased himself of his fair Burthen, took between his Talons the Wand, which he had all this while held carefully in his Beak, and having smote himself with it, instantly recovered his former Shape; then doing the same to *Eovaai*, she also saw herself as she was before: but tho' she was glad to have resumed Humanity, yet when she considered she was naked and in the presence of a Man, who was so too, she was ready to sink into the Earth. She ran behind a Tree to avoid looking on *Ochihatou*, or being looked upon by him, and cried out, Oh, my Lord! what shall we do for Habits? – Why did you not rather conduct me, modestly array'd in Feathers, to some Place where Conveniences might have been provided for us, the moment we returned to ourselves, and so have spared this most indecent Act? Call it not so, my Dear *Eovaai*, reply'd he, laughing, as I flatter myself you intended, when you accepted my Service, to reward it with no less than your Person, I see no Crime in anticipating my Happiness. Oh, all ye Stars! exclaimed the Princess, trembling, What is it you mean, my Lord? I mean, said he, to make myself Master of a Blessing, I have but too long waited for. With these Words he catch'd her in his Arms; but perceiving that unable to sustain the Shock of Shame and Fear, she was just fainting, he endeavour'd to extinguish those Passions, so much Enemies to the Desires he aimed to inspire, and far from proceeding to any greater Liberties than a Kiss, Be not alarm'd, my dear Princess, said he, I have brought you to *Ijaveo*, your native Climate, brought you to live and reign over a People, who long for nothing more than to testify their Submission to you; but I will now avow the Truth: I did you not this Service, without hope of a Recompence; and what other Recompence would be worthy of me, but to share your Crown and Bed? – Yes, Madam, continued he, you must make me King of *Ijaveo*, and your Husband. Stay then till I am Queen, answer'd she, a little more assured, does this wild Forest afford us Regal Ornaments? Where is my Throne, the State I should be treated with? Soon shall you find it all, resumed he; but tho' this Place has none of the Glare of Greatness, it may however produce a more delightful Bridal Bed. – What can be sweeter or more soft than this enamell'd Verdure beneath our Feet? What Canopy so magnificent as the high Arch of Heaven, where the gorgeous Sun embroiders with his Rays the pure Serene? What Musick more enchanting than the Birds, which, from the neighbouring Thickets, attend to chant our Nuptials in a thousand different Notes. Yield then, my Love, added he, (now growing more vehement) be mine – all Nature joins with my fierce Desires to tempt you to be happy, and you must. – Here grasping her more closely to his Bosom, he was about to render all Denials fruitless; but *Eovaai* summoning all her Strength, both of Resolution and Limbs, broke from his Arms, and with a Tone of Voice, which had more in it of the commanding than beseeching, Hold, I conjure you, cry'd she; if, as you would have me think, your Desires are legal, lose not the Merit of them by violating that Virtue it should be your Interest to preserve. – Let me be carried to my Palace, cloathed according to the Modesty of my Sex, and then when Marriage-Rites shall have made us one – No, Princess, interrupted *Ochihatou*, I have already too much experienced the little Consideration you have for me, to flatter myself with any Gratification, which must depend upon your Choice; and therefore resolved to make sure of my Reward before my Service is compleated. Hear me then, continued he, with a stern and determined Air; if you [do] not resign yourself willingly to my Embraces, I shall forgo all the Respect my foolish Passion has hitherto made me observe, and seize my Joy; which done, I shall despise and hate – give all my Soul up to revenge. – Yield then, and be a Queen, or by refusing, cease to be a Woman. – This Wand, whose Power you know, shall strait transform you to a Weazel's loathsome Form;[1] under which you shall pass the whole Remainder of your wretched Days.

This Menace entirely destroyed all the Courage poor *Eovaai* had assum'd, but not her Virtue, which never was more powerful in her than at this dreadful Moment – tho' nothing could be more terrible to her than the Thoughts of such a Transformation; tho' she doubted not but he would really inflict it on her, yet she resolved to hazard

---

1 Weazel's ... Form: Remarkable for its slender body, ferocity and bloodthirstiness; also, according to Ovid's *Metamorphoses* Book 9 (The Story of Hercules' Birth) the servant girl, Galanthis, who tricked the goddess Juno, was transformed into a weasel which was able to reproduce through its mouth. This transformation reflects the misogynistic attitudes of Ochihatou who reduces women to creatures defined by biological function or, as in the case of the Atamadoul monkey, as merely mimicking the behaviour of superior beings.

every thing, endure every thing, rather than consent to sacrifice her Chastity to the Enchanter's Will. The Distraction of her Thoughts keeping her from making any Answer to his last Words, he inferr'd from her Silence, that tho' she could not bring herself to tell him she would be devoted to him, she had at least given over all Resistance; and abating somewhat of his late Austerity, he again approach'd her, and taking her tenderly in his Arms, endeavour'd to dissipate her Tremblings with repeated Vows of making her Queen of *Ijaveo*, as soon as, by having possest her, he could assure himself she would suffer him to reign with her. But she, who abhorr'd a Throne with such a Partner, continued firm in her Resolution, and as he was about[1] to perpetrate the Ruin he intended, O divine *Aiou*, cry'd she, this once afford me Relief! – Let not the Remains of thy Favourite *Eojaeu* become the Prey of Lust, nor the Princess of *Ijaveo* be polluted in that Land which gave her[2] Birth! In speaking these Words, she seemed inspir'd by the Power to whom they were address'd, she sprung a second time from the Arms of *Ochihatou*, in spite of his superior Strength; and seeing the dreadful Wand, the Instrument of his Mischiefs, lying on the Grass, she ran to it, snatch'd it up, and broke it in sunder before his Face. The Suddenness with which she did this Action, left *Ochihatou* not the Power of preventing it; and he saw himself undone, before he had the least Thought of being so.

The Moment *Eovaai* had broke the inchanted Wand, a dark'ning Mist fell from the Regions of the Air, and huge Claps of Thunder rattled over their Heads, a thousand frightful *Ypres* kept in subjection by *Ochihatou's* Power, now freed, express'd their Joy in antick Skippings round him, then vanish'd; while he, loud as the Storm, blasphemed the Gods, and uttered such Impieties, as would be horrible repeated after him. What otherwise indeed could be expected from him? He had renounced Heaven and all the Powers of Goodness: his Crimes had render'd him detestable to Earth; and the *Ypres*, who for his Ruin had become his Servants, now deserted him; the magick

---

1   The Commentator observes, that either *Ijaveo* must be a very warm Climate, or *Ochihatou* of an uncommon Constitution, to retain the Fury of his amorous Desires, considering the Position he was in. [E.H.]

2   The same great Author also takes notice that since the Loss of her Jewel, this was the first time *Eovaai* had ever assumed Courage to offer up any Prayer to *Aiou*.[E.H.]

Wand broken, his Spells no longer were of use; and all his Skill in Necromancy[1] but made him know how much accursed he was. He who so lately could command the Elements, convert the Moon to Blood, and even annoy the Celestial *Genii* in their starry Palaces, had now no means of procuring for himself or Lodging, Food, or Rayment,[2] much less of executing that Revenge his Soul was big with. *Eovaai*, of all created Beings, seemed only in his power, and on her he resolved to inflict all the Torments he was able. That poor Princess had hoped to conceal herself from his Fury in a little Thicket; but he presently discover'd, and dragg'd her forth, then tied her up by her delicate Hair on one of the Boughs of a spreading Tree, where, as she was hanging, he got Bundles of stinging Nettles, and sharp-pointed Thorns, with which he intended to scourge and tear her tender Flesh, till Death should ease her Anguish: but even of this Mischief, of which he thought himself so sure, was he disappointed. Just as his Arm was stretch'd for beginning the Execution of his barbarous Purpose, a young Man, richly habited, and of a most majestic Form, rush'd forth from the inner Part of the Forest, and seizing him by the Shoulders, Inhuman Monster! said he, what more than savage Fury has possest thee, thus to abuse the fairest and most perfect Part of the Creation? *Ochihatou* was surprized at the nervous Gripe[3] but much more so at the Sight of the Person from whom he received it; he hung down his Head, and now for the first time shewed some Marks of Shame. Can it be possible! cry'd he, have I been then betrayed, has *Hoban* too deceived me! Oh Heaven! said the other at the same time, is it then the Villain *Ochihatou*, whom indulgent Fate has put into my power! – O for ever blessed be the Influence that directed my Steps this Way, and made me the happy Avenger of my own and Country's Wrongs. As he spoke this, he hastily plucked off a Gold and Crimson Belt, with which he was girded, and bound the vainly struggling Wretch fast to the Body of a huge Oak, near to that on which the Princess was still hanging. – There, most accursed of all that ever bore the Shape of Man, resumed the brave Stranger,

---

1 Necromancy: Magic, enchantment, conjuring (*OED*).
2 Rayment: Clothing.
3 Nervous Gripe: Muscular, strong hold or grasp (*OED*).

recollect the horrid Catalogue of thy enormous Crimes, and think what Tortures Justice requires should be inflicted on thee. Then turning to *Eovaai*, Pardon, divinest Creature, continued he, that I deferr'd releasing you from a Condition so unworthy of your Sex and Beauty; till I had secured that Traitor to all Goodness; for should he have escaped, nor Heaven, nor Earth, nor you, ought to have forgiven my Remissness. While he was speaking, he gently untwisted her Hair from the Bough, and taking from his Shoulders an azure-colour'd Robe embroider'd with Silver Stars, in part cover'd the blushing Charmer. The first Use she made of Liberty, was to cast herself at the Feet of her Deliverer; but he obliging her to rise, received such Testimonies of her Gratitude, as made him see it was a Person of no mean Condition, whom he had the good Fortune to preserve.

Many Compliments had not pass'd between them, before they were surrounded with a numerous Band of the *Ijaveon* Nobility, who express'd the extremest Joy at seeing the gallant Stranger safe, having been separated from him in the late Storm and Darkness. They accosted him with such a Respect, as well as Love, that *Eovaai*, who very well knew them, and their Quality, was at a loss to guess of what Rank he must be, to whom they paid such Homage. Being unwilling to reveal herself till more ascertained how Affairs went in *Ijaveo*, she drew part of the Robe over her Face, while her Protector was informing the Company in what manner he found her. The Relation of this Adventure made every one turn with Eyes of Horror on *Ochihatou*, whose Character in the World yet they knew not, nor did the Deliverer of *Eovaai* acquaint them; contenting himself with saying, he would hereafter divulge a Secret concerning himself, as well as that Captive Villain, which would amaze them all. He then gave Orders, that he should be tied with Cords to a Horse's Tail, and in that manner dragg'd to Prison, till he had consider'd of his Execution.

But the unavailing Rage of *Ochihatou* being now converted into the most horrible Despair, he no sooner found himself loosed from the Tree, than before the *Ijaveons* could fasten the Cords about him, in order to carry him, as they were commanded, he broke from the Hands which held him, and running furiously against a knotted Oak, dash'd out his Brains, and by that means shun'd the publick Shame design'd for him.

Thus ended the Life of this pernicious Man, to the great Satisfaction of *Eovaai*, who could not think herself safe while he was yet in Being; but her Defender could not forbear testifying some little Uneasiness, that he had thus escaped the Punishment of his Crimes, for the least of which he thought Death by far unequal. He seemed however entirely submitted to the Will of Heaven, and having commanded that the Chariots, which attended them, should be drawn as near as possible to the Edge of the Forest, in consideration of *Eovaai*, he put the Princess into that which belonged to himself, and being seated in it by her, Madam, said he, I look on it as an inexpressible Favour of the Gods, that they have ordain'd me the happy Instrument of delivering you from that dead Wretch's Cruelty; and the more so, that the Accident happen'd in a Place where, having the sole Command, 'tis in my power to accommodate you in such a fashion, as your Perfections seem to merit.

This Discourse, meant for a Comfort, was the severest Corrosive to the Heart of *Eovaai*; it seem'd to confirm what she before believed, that he was King of *Ijaveo*; but she made no shew of Discontent, and when they arrived at her own Palace, where he bid her welcome with the utmost Gallantry and Politeness, scarce could she refrain from bursting into Tears; and finding herself unable to return his Civilities in the manner she fancied he would expect, pretended a sudden Illness came over her Spirits, and entreated she might be put to bed.

The late Fatigue and Terror he was Witness she had endured, made this Request not seem strange to him. Women-Attendants were therefore immediately called, and she was by them ushered into a very rich Apartment, where she had enough to exercise her utmost Wit to keep herself from their Knowledge. She was obliged to feign a Weakness in her Eyes, which would not bear the Light, to make them darken the Rooms so far as not to render her Features discoverable; and as they all of them had waited on her when Queen, and might easily remember her Voice, she spoke no more than she was compell'd to do, and that in such disguised Accents, that they had not the least Notion they now served a former Mistress.

Being left to her Repose, a thousand sad Ideas ran through her troubled Mind, which at length burst out in these Complainings: Are these, said she, my promised Joys at my Return to *Ijaveo*, to find my

Throne in the Possession of another? – And, wou'd cruel Heaven allow me no means of Preservation, but from the Usurper of my Dominions?

To render, as she thought, her Misfortunes compleat, and capable of no Addition, the Charms of her Deliverer, when in that dreadful Moment he rush'd between her and impending Fate, had taken such fast hold of her Heart, that she now in vain struggled to get free; and indeed never were there such seeming Causes for Love and Hate blended in one Object. She could not harbour a revengeful Thought against the Invader of her Right, without being guilty of Ingratitude to the Preserver of her Life. Reason, had she been more the Mistress of it, than she was at present, had not the power of extricating her from this Labyrinth of Perplexity. – She knew not what she ought to do; but found too well for her Peace of Mind what she must do: – She felt she loved, and loved to that degree, that to live without him would be a Misery greater than in all her Sufferings she had ever before had any notion of. The first moment she beheld him, she wished he might be of a Rank that might not disgrace her Choice in making him King of *Ijaveo*; but as she now believed him already so, the Pride of Blood and conscious Title made her disdain the Thought of reigning with him, if even, to sanctify his Claim, he should make her that Offer, when who she was should be discovered.

The various Agitations of her Thoughts were such, as would permit no Sleep: she long'd for Morning; but when Morning came, was as dissatisfied, as disturbed as ever. The Women brought her Habits, not inferior in Magnificence to such as would have been presented had they known her for *Eovaai*; but she continuing resolute to conceal herself for a while, refused to rise, and desired they would leave the Chamber. When they were withdrawn, she quitted her Bed, drest herself, and watch'd at the Window, in hope of seeing a Lady, call'd *Emoe*, who had been formerly of her Bedchamber, and who, of all her Women, she loved best, and could repose most Confidence in; to her alone she was willing to make herself known; and as she knew her Lodgings faced those she was in, was not without hope of an Opportunity of speaking to her. In this, her Conjectures deceived her not; *Emoe* at length appear'd, and she calling her by her Name, and shewing her Face to her, the other, full of Amazement, rather flew than ran

cross the Court, and was in a moment at her Feet, crying, Royal
Eovaai, my dearest Queen, do I then live to see you! *Eovaai* interrupted her Acclamations, by saying, Ah *Emoe!* who is King? – King!
reply'd that Lady, what means your Majesty by such an Interrogation?
Heaven forbid the *Ijaveons* should have a King ungiven by you. – We
indeed have a Protector, one who is truly worthy of that Name. – The
Nobility, the Populace strove to outvye each other in laying waste this
unhappy Land – all things were in Confusion, and to make perfect
our Undoing, the offended Gods sent among us a dreadful Monster,
who in a short space of time devour'd thousands of your wretched
Subjects. – No mortal Courage or Strength, was thought capable of
subduing him, and setting free the Country; but when our Hopes
were at the lowest Ebb, and Despair began to invade every Heart, a
gallant Stranger arrived, and with his single Arm laid dead this Terror
of the Earth, as did his Wisdom afterward reconcile the jarring Factions, and what before was Discord converted into Harmony. Such
Services well merited the Distinction paid him: he was unanimously
chose Guardian of the Kingdom, in which high Station he has
behaved with so much Justice, Prudence, and Humility, as has
endeared him to all Degrees of People in such a manner, as, I am certain, they would exchange him only for yourself.

Thus ended *Emoe* her little Narrative, and returned to her former
Demonstrations of Joy, for the sight of her Royal Mistress; but how
impossible is it to describe the Transport with which her Words had
fill'd the Soul of *Eovaai*: to find, in the Preserver of her Life, the Preserver of her whole People also, to have such infinite reason to love
the Man, whom she cou'd not have avoided loving, had it been otherwise, was such a Surcharge of Felicity, as Sense cou'd hardly bear.
While she was in this Flow of Spirits, a Page enter'd the Chamber, to
let her know the Prince Protector desired leave to wait upon her: A
more welcome Message cou'd not have been brought. Impatient now
to see him, she immediately dispatched an Answer of Consent; and his
Entrance on it was so sudden, that she had only time to command
Emoe, as she withdrew out of respect, to keep the News of her Arrival
entirely secret till farther Orders.

The Meeting of this illustrious Pair had something in it very peculiar: They stood for some moments gazing at each other at a distance;

then bow'd and approach'd, but without speaking; the extraordinary Emotions which hurried thro' their Souls, (as they afterwards confess'd) kept both in a profound Silence. At length the Hero recover'd himself; and, with an Air full of Respect, address'd her in these terms: Madam, said he, the Service I had the Honour to render to you yesterday, would be uncompleat, without taking care to have you conducted to some Place where you may promise your self a safe Retreat: Therefore, as I shall quit this Kingdom in a few hours, and cannot answer for any thing after my departure, entreat you will accept of a Guard before I go, to wait you to whatever Residence you intend to bless.

How, my Lord! cried *Eovaai*, shock'd beyond measure, are then the *Ijaveons* so ungrateful for the Happiness you have procured them, as to have been guilty of any thing might justly occasion them so great a loss? The *Ijaveons*, Madam, answered he, have too much acknowledged the little I have done for them, not to make me regret leaving so deserving a People; nor cou'd I be drawn hence, if summon'd by any Calls less powerful than those by which I am. A Wife, perhaps, or Mistress, said the Princess, trembling for the Reply he might make to this Interrogatory? No, Madam, rejoined he with a Sigh, were it permitted me to follow my Inclinations, all that I know of Love for your Sex wou'd rather prevent than hasten my Journey. – But – As he was proceeding, an Attendant came to inform him, that the Lords of the Council being met according to his Orders, waited his Approach. On which, I go, said he, to fix the Government of this Kingdom, if possible, in such a manner, as shall prevent it from falling again into the Confusions I relieved it from; that done, will renew my Visit to receive your last Commands. He went out of the Room with these Words, leaving *Eovaai* in such a Perplexity of Mind, as may more easily be conceived than represented; it seem'd extremely strange to her, that he should abandon a People by whom he was so much esteem'd, and who had given into his hands the sole Reins of Power; especially when she remembred, that the Day before he seemed to be far from having any such Design; this sudden Resolution she therefore thought must proceed from as sudden an Excitement; – she found he was not married, and the Eyes with which he had regarded her both at the time of his delivering her from the Rage of *Ochihatou*, and in this Morning's Visit, made her think it not impossible he might have found something in her worthy of the most violent Passion; and that imagining she was not of a Birth which might justify his Choice, he had no other way of expelling her Idea, but by Absence. She was the more confirm'd in this Opinion, when *Emoe*, who returned as soon as he was gone, told her he had never been observed to treat any Lady of the Court with a particular Distinction, tho' he behaved with an Infinity of Respect to all. She ask'd this Confidante a thousand Questions, to all which she gave such Answers, as served to heighten the Affection she had for him, and far from discouraged the Hope of an adequate Return, when he shou'd come to know who she was. She was however less delicate in the Point of Rank, than she supposed him to be; for tho' *Emoe* informed her that he kept every body in ignorance of his Descent, and let them know no more, than that he was of noble Blood, and called *Ihoya*; yet she determined to offer him her Crown and Person, *as she said*, to recompense him for what he had done for herself and People, but *in reality* to gratify[1] the Passion she was enflamed with for him; and as it never enter'd her Head that she shou'd be refused by him, or that all the Motives for his departure wou'd not recede to being King of *Ijaveo*, and her Husband, she had now no other Disquiet than what arose from her Modesty in making this Proposal.

Never was Impatience greater than that she felt for his Return from Council; at last he came. Well, my Lord, said she, have you brought the *Ijaveons* to consent to your departure? We all must yield to Fate, Madam, answered he: But tho' I am certain, they suffer much less than I do by it, yet has the Concern they testify been such, as greatly adds to mine. They, nor yourself, resumed she smiling, can search into the Seeds of dark Futurity, and see the Events of Time. – Who knows but some strange Revolution may happen in a Moment to fix you ever here? Come, my Lord, pursued she, perceiving he

---

1 The Historian, methinks, might have spared giving his Opinion in this Matter; but, if it were as he suggests, that Passion cou'd not be blameable in *Eovaai*, which had Gratitude for its Source, and was encouraged by an appearance of the greatest Virtue and Bravery in the Object.[E.H.] [Ed. note: According to contemporary conduct books which advised on the correct behaviour for women, gratitude and esteem, not sexual attraction, were the proper reasons for a woman's admiration for a man.]

look'd surprized, be seated, and add to the Obligations you have conferred upon me one more; it is that of relating to me by what Adventure you first came into this Kingdom, and on what Motives you now so rashly quit it. – Be assured it is not womanish Curiosity, but the strongest Reasons that prompt me to desire this Narrative; and that it shall be recompensed with another from me, no less deserving your Attention. These Words were delivered with such an Emphasis, and accompanied with so extraordinary a Look, that the noble Stranger had not the power of resisting them. Madam, answered he, tho' I cannot conceive how any thing relating to a Person utterly unknown to you, and who till this hour has been so to all the World, can be of any service to you; yet I think it sufficient to be commanded by you, and shall content my self with an implicite Obedience. Prepare then, Madam, to hear a Story so full of Wonder, as may justly make you more than once call my Veracity in question; I shall however utter nothing but what I can, without Impiety, call the immortal Gods, and those [1]second celestial Beings, to whom I owe my Preservation, to attest the Truth of. He then placed himself on the Couch, opposite to the Chair the Princess was sitting on, and began to satisfy the Demand she had made, in these or the like Words:

---

1   The *Genii*, or guardian Angels, are supposed to be meant here.[E.H.]

The History of ADELHU, *only Son of* OEROS, *and Heir apparent to the Crown of* Hypotofa.

I WAS born a Prince, said he, and only Son of *Oeros*, King of *Hypotofa*: In my younger Years, I looked on myself as happier in a Father's Love, than in the hopes of one day enjoying his vast Dominions; but when I arrived at the age of nineteen, the most artful of all that ever was brought up in the School of Villany, got possession of the Royal Ear; but I need not waste time in giving you his Character, since it was no other than that Wretch, who I found using you with a Brutality, which nothing but himself could have been guilty of: This *Ochihatou*, by misrepresenting all my Actions, robb'd me of Paternal Affection;[1] – and when I refused to come into some Projects proposed to me by the Creatures of that wicked Statesman, which I knew were detrimental to Liberty, and the Good of the People; I was sent by his Artifices from Court, and, in a short time, out of the Kingdom, under the Care of a pretended Tutor, but who was indeed design'd for my Murderer: *Huaco* was the Place in which the Scene of my Death was to be acted, and I had not been there many Days, before *Hoban*, for so he was called, came into my Chamber, with a Countenance which informed me his Mind laboured under some great Disturbance; and, after some previous Discourse, acquainted me with the whole black Design in which he had been engaged; but which Remorse wou'd not suffer him to perpetrate: He told me also, that *Ochihatou* had endeavoured, by his horrid Art, to transform me into some Part of the inferior Creation; but that being, from my Birth, committed to the Care of [2]*Uieah,* the *Ypres* were too weak to combat with that powerful *Genius*, and Magick cou'd have no effect on me; and concluded with assuring me, that there was no Hope of Safety for me, but in my supposed Death. It was therefore agreed between us, that I should depart privately, and he shou'd deceive that accursed Politician, with a

---

1 Paternal Affection: King George II and Caroline never seemed to have loved their eldest son, Frederick, Prince of Wales, and were often involved in farcical quarrels with him. Walpole, as first minister, took the side of the King in these differences, while the opposition courted Frederick.

2 Fortitude, or true Greatness of Mind. [E.H.]

feign'd Tale of having executed his Commands. Late at night, I quitted *Huaco* in disguise, and changing my Name, which is really *Adelhu*, into that of *Ihoya*, by long and painful Journeys I at last arrived in the Kingdom of *Narzada*, just at the time when *Hyalard* was about to set out on an Expedition against the Provinces of *Tacty* and *Benla*. The natural Propensity I ever had to martial Exploits, induced me to lift my self under the Banners of this young Prince: Our Arms obtain'd a Conquest, indeed, but too easily; for most of the Cities and great Towns, having, as they imagin'd, been severely dealt with by their former Sovereigns, surrendered themselves gladly to one who promised them many Liberties and Immunities they before had been debarred from: but they soon found, that where a People consents to a Change of Government, for the sake of Freedom, the Person to whom they submit takes but the more care to rivet their Chains the faster. *Hyalard* had been educated in the Principles of arbitrary Sway, and no sooner was made King, than he began to exercise his Authority in the same manner his Father did in *Narzada*. Nothing now was to be seen but Pride, Luxury and Oppression among the Great, and Remorse, Beggary, and Wretchedness, among the Populace. This made me grow weary of that Court. – I took my leave of the new King, and travelled into *Habull*, where I was yet more mortified; *Oudescar*, the King thereof, had been compelled to make Peace with the *Fayolians*,[1] very much to his Prejudice, merely on the account that *Hypotofa*, his ancient Ally, had seen his Provinces laid waste, his Armies routed, and himself distress'd beyond measure; yet, sent no Forces to his Aid, nor seem'd any otherwise concern'd, than to offer a fruitless Mediation.[2] I very day heard my Royal Father spoken of, in Terms which stabb'd me to the Heart. – They said he was in his Dotage, a second time a Child, and under the Tutorage of one of the meanest Wretches in the Kingdom, meaning *Ochihatou*; that there was neither Honour, Wisdom, Faith nor Courage, left in *Hypotofa*, and seemed to hint, that, at a proper time, the Affront offered to *Habull* should be returned

---

1   *Habull, ... Fayolians*: In October 1735, Austria (Habull) had to surrender Naples and Sicily to Spain (Fayoul) when peace was made in the War of the Polish Succession.
2   fruitless Mediation: In 1733, Britain offered itself, with Holland, as a mediator in the War of the Polish Succession rather than coming to Austria's aid with troops as the Treaty of Vienna stipulated.

with Interest. Unable to support this Insolence, and far from a Condition to resent it as I ought, I went to *Fayoul*; not doubting but I should *there* hear only Praises of the Moderation observed by *Oeros* in this nice Conjuncture: but, on the contrary, they only laugh'd at his Supineness; and what yet more alarm'd me, were entering into Leagues with his most cruel Enemies to invade *Hypotofa*, which by the Degeneracy of its Morals was now looked on as an easy Conquest. I wrote several Letters, as from a Person unknown, of all I had discovered, to some whom I knew were still sollicitous for their Country's Welfare, but fear they were intercepted by the Vigilance of *Ochihatou*, who was more careful of nothing than to keep the true Knowledge of Affairs from the People.

From *Fayoul* I travell'd into *Ezba*, where the generous *Yamatalallabec* perceiving himself deserted by *Osiphronoropho*, *Fanharridin*, and all those Princes, he had depended on, and that the Efforts he could make of himself, for recovering his betroth'd Mistress *Yximilla*, would only serve to render her yet more unhappy, wrote her a Letter, in the most moving Terms I ever read, to persuade her to that due Resignation the Gods require from all their Creatures. He made her see that it was in vain to struggle with superior Powers, and that the Aid to be expected from Man was altogether uncertain, and promised but with a View of Self-Interest; which once ceasing, those, who pretended the most Zeal to serve, were often the first that joined in the Destruction of the Hopes they had raised. Since, therefore, the Hand of Fate had torn them from each other, he advised her to endeavour to love his happy Rival, and to an entire Forgetfulness of himself, and all the flattering Expectations her Affection had inspired him with.

The Condition of this Prince, abandon'd by even those who had the most binding Obligations to him, served to shew me the Faith not only of Princes, but of Mankind in general; and I could not forbear making Reflections on it, which may hereafter contribute much to my Security.

After I had quitted *Ezba*, I intended to pursue my Journey to *Pentnah*, and take a View of the many Curiosities, with which that famous City is said to abound; but being attended only with one Servant, who happened to know less of the Road than he pretended, we lost our Way in the vast Desart of *Bamre*. We wandered long till faint with Hunger; and Darkness coming on, we at length lay down to take such

Repose as that wild and naked place would permit. Here I had an Opportunity of observing how little the Toils of the Body are to be held in competition with those of the Mind: The poor Fellow having nothing to disturb his Thinking Faculties, immediately fell into a profound Sleep; while I, tho' much more fatigued, as I had been less accustom'd to such tiresome Journeys, could not indulge one Moment's Slumber; the Unkindness of a Father, the exiled and distrest State to which I was reduced by the Villany of *Ochihatou*, the Miseries of a Country I was born to rule, and the little Probability there seemed of any Turn of Fortune in our favour, ran too strongly in my Head to suffer me to close my Eyes. But intent and fixed as I was on this melancholly Entertainment, I was rouzed from it by an Apparition too tremendous to be remember'd, without a Horror scarce to be conceived. Huge whirling Clouds, black as the direful Shades[1], where Tyrants and Oppressors mourn their past Crimes in everlasting Anguish, covered the whole Hemisphere, and blotted out the Stars: then bursting suddenly, high in the Air, two Forms of more than Giant-size by their own Lightnings showed themselves plain to my wond'ring Eyes. – Enraged, and fierce, they seemed in Combat: – the Weapons with which they fought, were Thunders and Elemental Fires: – A while the Victory was doubtful. – Earth shook, as fearful of the Event. – Noises, of which no Description can be given, eccho'd from the Arch of Heaven, and I expected no less than that the End of all things was approaching; when, from the Firmament, a mighty Comet darted from a superior, but unseen, Hand, fell upon one of the Contending Powers, and with its Excess of Blaze, struck me for a moment blind. My Sight restored, I cast my Eyes up again, and saw all was serene, and but one of the majestic Figures remained. – I fell upon my Knees, and would have implored the Protection of the Celestial Conqueror; but Amazement had locked up Utterance, and internal Devotions were all I was able to offer. Rise, Prince, said a Voice, which had in it somewhat that inspired Rapture, and take up what you see before you. – Preserve it with more Care than you would do your Life, till you find a Virgin who has the Case, which once contained it. – It is a Jewel of more Value than all the Empires in

---

1   It was an established Article of Faith in those Days, that all who made use of the Power they had to oppress their Fellow-Creatures, were condemned after Death to eternal Darkness. [E.H.]

the World can purchase. – But beware how you cast your Eyes on Beauty, till your propitious Stars shall bring to you the Owner of that Gem. – 'Tis she alone is destin'd to make your Happiness, and that of Thousands yet unborn. – Fame, Honour, Glory, Peace, and Everlasting Bliss, will be the Consequences of your Union; but if you seek to anticipate your Lot, and give your Heart to any other, Shame, Disgrace, Discord, and Contempt, must be your Portion here, and keen Remorse dwell with you to Eternity.

The Vision ceased to speak or to be seen, and all was as before: I stoop'd and found this Stone, which glitter'd like a Star beneath my Feet, and I have ever since kept it as my Defence from Ill. With these Words the Prince took a small Purse out of his Pocket, from which he drew the precious Relique, and shewed it to *Eovaai*; who no sooner cast her Eyes upon it, than she was assured of what she before had pleased herself with the Hopes of, that it was the very Jewel given her by *Eojaeu*, and which she had so strangely lost. Scarce could she refrain bursting into the Transports her Soul was full of; but a sudden Jealousy that moment taking possession of her Thoughts, And have you, cry'd she, (interrupting the Prince hastily) have you indeed obey'd the Dictates of the heavenly Being? Have you not suffered your Heart to be usurp'd by the Charms of some Beauty? – Is it yet entire and pure from any Impression?

Adelhu seemed a little surpriz'd at these Interrogatories, and, with some Confusion, Madam, answered he, till yesterday I might have boasted an entire Obedience to the Divine Will; and if I since have swerved from it, I hope to be forgiven, since no Eyes less powerful than yours could have made me guilty; and as I am resolved, in spite of the Pleasure I take in gazing on them, to condemn myself to an eternal Absence, and to do every thing in my power to obliterate all Ideas from my Heart, that may render it an unworthy Offering to the Owner of this Jewel.

Eovaai having this Confirmation of what she wish'd, no longer cou'd restrain herself: Behold her then before you, cried she, I am the true Owner of that Jewel; and, as a Part of the Happiness you were promis'd with me, take the Kingdom of *Ijaveo*, of which none will dispute with me the Title. Excess of Joy wou'd suffer her to utter no more; and the Prince, quite lost in wonder, was as little able to reply: but what she cou'd not do in Words, she supplied with Action; she untied the Ribband from her Neck, and putting the Stone into the Socket from whence it had drop'd, he saw they not only were exactly fitted to each other, but also that moment they were join'd, the Cement closed upon the Jewel, as it never had been loosened. What Words, what Ideas can be equal to the mutual Transports of this happy Pair! *Eovaai!* – *Adelhu!* – Queen of *Ijaveo!* – Prince of *Hypotofa!* – Divinest Woman! – Charming Hero! were all was to be heard between them for some time; but as *Adelhu* imagined his dear Princess cou'd not be without a good deal of Curiosity, to know by what means they met together in *Ijaveo*, and he was not free from some Impatience himself, he gave a Truce to Extasy, in order to satisfy her's, by resuming the History of his Adventures in this manner:

After the Prophecy, already in part so happily fulfill'd, said he, I waked my Servant, who had all this time been in a death-like Sleep, and obliged him to prosecute our Journey, tho' I knew not which way; for as I had no material Business any where, all Places were alike to me, and I resolved to give my self entirely to the Conduct of Fortune. – We travell'd all the remainder of the Night, and early in the morning found ourselves on the Borders of a fine Country, which I was presently informed was called *Ijaveo*. I heard likewise, at the same time, of a Monster which did much mischief to the Inhabitants. Charm'd with an Opportunity of testifying at once both my Courage and Compassion, I undertook to rid the Land of such a Grievance, and happily effected what I promised. I know you did, cried *Eovaai*, and thank the divine Beings, who inspired my People with the Gratitude your Services merited from them. She then told him, she had heard from *Emoe*, every thing that had pass'd since his coming into that Kingdom; and, on his desire, proceeded to inform him[1] of every

---

1   As People (tho' bound by Honour to tell nothing but the Truth) seldom think themselves obliged to tell all the Truth, when it wou'd be a disadvantage to their Interest or Reputation, the Commentator imagines *Eovaai* concealed that Part of her Behaviour with *Ochihatou* in the Gardens of *Hypotofa*. This he is blamed for by *Hahehihotu*; because, says this Philosopher, had she kept it a Secret, how shou'd the Historian come to the Knowledge of it? But I must here be of the Commentator's side; there might possibly, in that amorous Season, be others on the same Errand, in some adjacent Grove or Arbour, who might overhear what passed between them; or *Ochihatou* himself, being naturally vain, might more likely divulge to some of his Friends, the Condescensions she made him, than she repeat them to any one; much less to a Person whose Esteem she was so desirous of preserving. [E.H.]

thing had happened to herself, since the Death of *Eojaeu* till that moment. After which, the Nobility of both Sexes were called into the Room, who, with Tears of Joy, congratulated the Return of *Eovaai*, and the Choice she had made of a Prince so justly dear to them. They were married the next Day, with a Magnificence worthy of their Virtues and their Births; and all things being in a profound Tranquillity, the wedded Pair took a Journey to *Hypotofa*, the pious *Adelhu* being in the utmost Impatience to see his Royal Father. To describe the Satisfaction of *Oeros*, in embracing a Son, whom he had so long thought dead, or that of the People, in seeing their Prince with his beautiful Consort, would fill a Volume; so it shall suffice to say, that never was greater or more universal Transport.

Soon after their Return, the good *Oeros* died, as full of Comforts as of Years; and the Scepters of *Hypotofa* and *Ijaveo* being united in the Persons of *Adelhu* and *Eovaai*, compos'd the most powerful, most opulent, and most happy Monarchies in the World.

FINIS

Appendix A:
Selected Literary Portraits by Eliza Haywood.

i. From *Memoirs of a Certain Island Adjacent to the Kingdom of Utopia.* **Vol. II (London, 1726): 249-250.**

[A description of "Marama," a satirical portrait of Sarah, the Duchess of Marlborough, to whom Haywood dedicated the *Adventures of Eovaai* in 1736.]

Mark (*continued the Deity*) with what sullen Pride the Duke Severus[1] walks, disdainful of his Fellow-Peers: He is indeed of a Family the most antient among the Nobility, and has not, by any known or remarkable Vices, disgrac'd the Honour of his truly noble Ancestors. Add to this, that he has many Perfections both of Mind and Body, but a too great Haughtiness of Temper eclipse their Lustre, and render terrible what else would be engaging to the World. – There are two things which at present sit heavy on his Soul; the one is, that he sees the Man whom most he hates, prime Minister,[2] and is by that means entirely depriv'd of any part of the management of publick Affairs. – The other, that he is disappointed of his Aim in marrying *Marama*,[3] who tho' no more than a titular Princess, has a Revenue which might entitle her to a Match with the first Monarch in the Universe. Tho' in possession of a vast Estate, and a large Tract of Land which calls him Lord, his greedy Eyes are eager after more; and to have gratified the Lust of his Ambition, gladly would have wedded where not one

---

1   Duke *Severus*: Charles Seymour, 6th Duke of Somerset (1662-1748). He became known as "the proud duke." He fined his daughter, Charlotte, "20,000l. of her inheritance for having sat down in his presence. ... His domestics obeyed him by signs, and, when he travelled, the country roads were scoured by outriders, whose duty it was to protect him from the gaze of the vulgar" (Secombe, *DNB* 17:1235-37).

2   prime Minister: Sir Robert Walpole.

3   *Marama*: Sarah, Duchess of Marlborough. She was left immensely wealthy upon the death of her husband, John, Duke of Marlborough, in 1722.

Charm but Wealth could tempt Desire. *Marama* has been for many Years a Grandmother;[1] but Age is the smallest of her Imperfections: – She is of a Disposition so perverse and peevish, so designing, mercenary, proud, cruel, and revengeful, that it has been matter of debate, if she were really Woman, or if some Fiend had not assumed that Shape on purpose to affront the Sex, and fright Mankind from Marriage. Such as she is however, she has in her possession Charms which to him exceed the loveliest Eyes, or softest Nature;[2] and never Man sollicited with greater Ardency, the brightest and most blooming Beauty, than did he this wrinkled Hag. – The Affair went on so far between them, that she made him a Promise to be his Wife, but on some secret Disgust,[3] she revoked it, and forbad his visiting her any more. So unexpected a Repulse has made him, who was before the worst-natur'd Man breathing, arrive at such a height of Discontent, and Sourness of Behaviour, that he is unfit for Conversation, and shuns, and equally is shunn'd by all Society.

ii. From *The Secret History of the Present Intrigues of the Court of Caramania* (London, 1727): 337-345.

[Marmillio,[4] Prince Theodore's[5] trusted advisor and arranger of his extra-marital affairs, has been asked by the monarch to persuade the virtuous Violetta[6] to sleep with him. Marmillio, having tried in con-

---

1   a Grandmother: The Duchess was sixty-three years old in 1723 when the Duke of Somerset proposed marriage to her.

2   Charms ... exceed ... Eyes, or ... Nature: Haywood satirically refers to the Duke's falling in love with the Duchess's estate and money; however, the Duke of Somerset admits in his correspondence with Sarah his desire for her "most charming Person." "All contemporary records agree that Sarah maintained beauty and grace to an advanced age" (Butler, 304). Haywood, though, is intent on exposing the Duke of Somerset as a fortune-hunting hypocrite and Sarah as an aged monster.

3   some secret Disgust: The Duchess of Marlborough may have refused Somerset because of his involvement in 1711, as one of the independent Whig Dukes who joined Harley to destroy Marlborough. She referred to Somerset in her memoirs as "a man of very mean qualities, but of an inflexible pride and resentment never to be conquered" (Butler, 306).

4   Marmillio: Theodore's friend since childhood; a satire of the Earl of Scarborough.

5   Prince Theodore: King George II.

6   Violetta: The name suggests shyness and delicacy. If Violetta is based on a real-life mistress of the King, she is not identifiable; however, her rape, which is the last

versation the virtue of the young woman, realizes that persuasion and seduction are out of the question.]

To save his Credit therefore with the Prince, he had recourse to the most cruel Stratagem that ever enter'd the Heart of Man. Despairing to corrupt her Principles, or inspire her with any Tenderness for a Man, of whose Heart she could not hope to possess above a third share;[1] after having told THEODORE that all the Arguments he could use had been of no effect, he persuaded him to force the Joy, which he found it was impossible for him to obtain by any other means.

Rash, amorous, and ungovernable as this Prince was in all his Passions, such a Proposition extremely shock'd him: he had an inimitable share of Good-nature, and as much Honour as was consistent with the Inconstancy of his Temper; and told MARMILLIO, that he could not consent to such an Action, though the perpetrating it was all for which he wish'd to live, and charg'd him to renew his Endeavours to make her his by other means than those. The other promis'd him to obey, not daring to let him know the reason why he believed they would be eternally in vain.

In fine, without uttering one syllable of the Prince's Passion to her, he continued every day to assure him, that he found her Heart impregnable as a Rock, that he had try'd her every way, and that there was now no remaining hope, but in the course he had before advis'd. What will not the subtile Insinuations of the Person one loves,[2] when concurring with one's own Inclination, in time prevail on one to be guilty of!

The Prince, impatient to possess, and made to believe that nothing but Force could afford the long'd-for Bliss, at last half yielded to the Persuasions of his Favourite; who, to remove the only now remaining Scruple, that of the thing being known, contriv'd this Stratagem, that

---

episode in the novel, suggests the King's increasing lust and drive for power. That the rape is not his idea but the suggestion of another shelters Haywood from the libel laws, but it is clear that she feels that the King is misusing his power and authority, while his subjects, represented by the overpowered and over-awed Violetta, are abused by him.

1 third share: Theodore is married to Queen Hyanthe and is the long-time lover of Ismonda.

2 the Person one loves: Marmillio. Theodore loves him as a trusted friend.

he should not appear in his own shape, and the destin'd Victim of his wild Desires be ignorant to whom she ow'd her Ruin. Honour now lull'd to sleep, and all the nobler Faculties drown'd in the Excess of an o'erflowing and tumultuous Passion, he consented with pleasure to the Proposal, and left the management of it to him, who promised to accomplish it in a very short time.

Nothing could be more easy, than for him, who was so intimate with her, to betray her in this manner: And the Method he took to do it was this; he caused an *Egyptian* Habit[1] to be made for the Prince, and a tawny Mask, so artifically contriv'd, that whoever had it on, would appear to have no other Face, than that which Nature had bestow'd: And intreating the Prince to come into his Apartment, You must condescend, my Lord, *said he*, like JUPITER,[2] to assume a Shame unworthy of you, when you attempt an Enterprize of this kind. The things being try'd, and fitting exactly, never Man was more delighted than THEODORE; but yet could not conceive of what service this Disguise was to him, or how design'd to be made use of, till MARMILLIO pluck'd out two Letters, the one directed for himself, the other to VIOLETTA: These, *said he*, are written by a hand so exactly counterfeiting that of CARICLEA,[3] that were herself to see them, she would imagine them dictated in her Sleep. – They contain a Recommendation of an *Egyptian* Eunuch,[4] whom this careful Sister entreats the young VIOLETTA to entertain as the Guardian of her Virtue: So many Stratagems being daily contriv'd at Court to destroy the Innocence of

---

1 *Egyptian* Habit: Egyptians, at least since Biblical times, were regarded as despots. In the eighteenth century, Egyptians were also regarded as observing a special affection between the people and their pharoahs: "The virtue in the highest esteem among the Egyptians, was gratitude. ... Benefits are the band of concord, both publick and private. He who acknowledges favours, loves to do good to others; ... But no kind of gratitude gave the Egyptians a more pleasing satisfaction, than that which was paid to their kings" (Charles Rollin's *Ancient History of the Egyptians ... and Grecians* (1730-8). (Cited in Battestin, 2:668). Haywood employs irony in Theodore's disguise which is used to force Violetta to sexually satisfy her king.

2 JUPITER: The chief of the Roman gods, he was notorious for donning disguises (such as the form of a swan, a bull etc.) to make love to mortal women. One woman, Semele, demanded that he come to her in his own form; however, his godlike form proved too much for her and she was destroyed.

3 CARICLEA: Violetta's sister-in-law.

4 Eunuch: A castrated man, usually a guard of the harem as he would not have any temptation to trifle with the Sophi's wives.

a Virgin, she cannot think her safe without this watchful ARGUS,[1] who, incapable of injuring her himself, will be her Security from all others. He is therefore to lie in her Chamber, lest any Attempts should be made on her sleeping Virtue. Your Highness, *continued he*, has nothing to do to carry on this Plot, but to personate this Slave for an hour or two, for it shall be near night when I present you: and to excuse your absence, you must pretend a little Indisposition, and dismiss all but me from your Attendance. The transported THEODORE agreed it should be done that very Evening; and having appear'd in the Drawing-room long enough to give a colour to the thing, cry'd out on a sudden, that his Head ach'd, and retir'd hastily to his own Apartment; where being follow'd by all the Gentlemen of his Bed-Chamber, he order'd a profound Silence to be kept, and that none but MARMILLIO should stay in the Room.

Every body being remov'd, he began to equip himself in the *Egyptian* Habiliments, which the assiduous Favourite had before convey'd by a back way into the Chamber; by which also, as soon as dress'd, they went, and so to the Apartment, who, being not then in waiting, they found at home. MARMILLIO presented her with the Letters of the Slave; which she had no sooner read, than she blushed prodigiously, at the thoughts of permitting any thing that bore the shape of Man to lie in her Chamber; but MARMILLIO assuring her, that it was the Custom in all those Countries where the Men are jealous of the Honour of their Families, she at last consented to obey the Injunction of her Sister. But here immediately rose another Obstacle, which was, that according to the Custom of *Caramania*, she having but one Bed in her Chamber, he must lie in another till one could be put up: But this was not an Obstacle which was beyond the Wit of MARMILLIO to surmount; he presently told her, that these Slaves never lay but on Carpets, which could be spread in a moment, and as easily remov'd.

The good Opinion she had of him, the observant Care with which he had ever treated her, and her Sister's Commands, left her no room to hesitate, whether what they injoin'd was for her good, or not; and she order'd her Woman to see it perform'd. The Royal Slave,

---

[1] ARGUS: A mythological monster with one hundred eyes.

who pretended not to understand one word of the *Caramanian* Language, was entertain'd by the Servants, in as civil a manner as possible: but it was no small diversion to him, to behold the wonder with which all the Women look'd upon him, and the Mirth which his suppos'd Condition occasion'd among them, every one speaking according to the Sentiments of her Heart, without reserve before him, in confidence he knew not what they said.

But when Night came, and he saw the lovely VIOLETTA in her Bed, how difficult was it for him to restrain the Impatiencies of his burning Passion, till she was asleep, not daring to stir from his Carpets till then, lest she should alarm the Family: but a more than ordinary Drouziness, by her ill Angel cast on her Senses, made her presently fall into the Condition he wish'd; which he no sooner perceiv'd, than he quitted the uneasy Position in which he had lain, the Eagerness of Desire with which he seiz'd upon her Beauties leaving no time for the Preparatives of Kisses, and Degrees of Caresses, he in a moment became Master of too much, not to put it past her power to keep from him any part of what he wish'd. But in what words is it possible to set forth the Rage! The Horror! The Surprize with which she waked, and found this bold Intruder! She struggled, would have shriek'd for help, but Kisses stopp'd the one, and more prevailing Strength rendred the other of no effect. – In fine, she was undone, and he as happy as the full Possession of her Charms could make him; but Tears, and Vows, not to out-live the loss of Honour, allay'd the Joy, and turn'd him all into Endeavours to mitigate the Tempest of her Soul. – He spoke to her, excusing what he had done by the Violence of a Passion, which disdain'd all Bounds, and would fly to any Artifice to shun Despair.

Oh! By whom, *cry'd she*, have I been thus abus'd? – yet, if thou lovest thy Life, *continued she*, I charge thee do not tell me, for be assur'd, I will revenge this Wrong. It was not to show that he not fear'd this Threat, but believing the knowledge of his Quality would ease the present Horrors of her Soul, he discover'd to her who he was; at which indeed her Surprize increas'd, but a small Portion of her Griefs abated – the Rank of her Undoer took not away the Shame of being undone, and tho' she ceas'd to *revile*, she did not to *complain* – Oh Cruel Prince! *said she*, what could provoke you to the Ruin of a harmless Maid, who never injur'd you even in a Thought? Your Heart and Vows elsewhere devoted, how small your Satisfaction, and how immense my Woe! – Wretch that I am, *pursu'd she, after a little pause*, Death only can put a period to my irreparable Shame. In this manner did she go on, nor could less be expected from a Woman of her strict Modesty; yet had the Prince the pleasure to observe, that either the Respect she paid him as her Sovereign, or a secret Inclination to his Person, made her suffer his continued Endearments with less reluctance than before. As he was indeed one of the most lovely and accomplish'd Men on earth, it was not difficult for him to make the most favourable Impression on a Heart so entirely unprepossess'd as was her's: to add to this, he address'd her in the softest, most engaging terms that Love and Wit could dictate; and before Morning, if she was not brought to think what he had done no Crime, she was at least to wish it were not so: and though she did not in words declare so much, the tender Pressures, the Languishments, which, unawares even to herself, her Arms, and Eyes bestow'd on him, confess'd the melting God had pleaded in her Heart so powerfully in the defence of his Votary, that she now more than forgave the Effects of his embolden'd Passion. – Transported with this Discovery, he pursued his Conquest, and swore to hold her for ever Prisoner in his Arms, if she would not seal his Pardon, and consent henceforth to give a loose to Rapture. Faintly she struggled to get free from the sweet Confinement, but could not speak: A thousand, and a thousand times he repeated the same Request, before her Tongue could utter what her swimming Eyes sufficiently made known and when, to prevail on him to rise, it being now broad day, all she could bring forth was, *Yes*. Enough confirm'd that he was Master of her Soul, as well as Body, he now forsook the happy Scene of Pleasure; and having clothed himself in his Disguise, retired to his Carpets: from which, as soon as her Woman came into the Chamber, he rose, and went into another Room; whence, taking his opportunity, he pass'd to his own Apartment, where MARMILLIO waited with impatience to know the End of this Adventure.

The Prince making him a full relation of all that had pass'd, he was not a little alarm'd, when he first heard he had discover'd who he was, not knowing how far the Fury of a Woman, thus abus'd, might transport her: but when he was told how kindly she forgave the Deceit, he as much applauded himself for the Contrivance. The Prince express'd his Sense of it in terms the most obliging to him, and passionate to VIOLETTA; which let this Favourite know, that his Desires being yet unsatiated, he would still have need of his Assistance to procure their future Interviews.

iii. Dedication to *Frederick, Duke of Brunswick-Lunenburgh. A Tragedy*. (London, 1729).

To His ROYAL HIGHNESS
FREDERICK LEWIS,
Prince of Wales, *and Earl of* Chester, *Electoral Prince of* Brunswick-Lunenburgh, *Duke of* Cornwall *and* Rothsay, *Duke of* Edinburgh, *Marquis of the Isle of* Ely, *Earl of* Eltham, *Viscount of* Launceston, *Baron of* Snaudon *and of* Renfrew, *Lord of the Isles, and Steward of* Scotland, *and Knight of the most noble Order of the Garter.*
   May it Please your Royal Highness,
   Tho' your ROYAL HIGHNESS stands in Need of no Examples of Antiquity, having before your Eyes such shining Models, in your Own PARENTS,[1] of all that can illustrate ROYALTY and adorn a Throne; yet it cannot but afford an Infinity of Satisfaction, that how far soever you trace the History of former Times, you find Virtue inseparable from the House of *Brunswick*; that they seem born for the general GOOD of Mankind; and that none could be Enemies to them, without being so, to that DIVINE SOURCE of all Perfection, whose Emanations have from Age to Age so abundantly illuminated their *Truly* Princely Souls.
   To the Name of ROYALTY indeed, not only exterior Homage, but an inward Reverence is also due; but where *Power* is accompanied with *Beneficence*, it commands all the Affections of the Heart! *Inclination* outstrips *Duty*! A Kind of *Seraphick Love*[2] influences our Action! With eager *Rapture* we seek the Means of Testifying our *Obedience*, and adore *Heaven* in the Person of its *good* VICEGERENT.[3]

---

1   your Own PARENTS: George II and Caroline.
2   *Seraphick Love*: A love of the highest order of angels.
3   VICEREGENT: In this case, a person appointed by God to act in his place or exercise his functions.

How greatly would it be my Pride and Pleasure, had I the Power of Expatiating, as I ought, or according to the Dictates of my Soul, on the Obligations which the whole CHRISTIAN World lies under to the Ancestors of Your ROYAL HIGHNESS, the present peculiar Blessings these *happy Nations* enjoy under the Auspicious Reign of their most EXCELLENT MAJESTIES, and the high Ideas which all *true* Lovers of *Virtue* form of a Prince descended from such a *Lineage*, and who has given such early Proofs that he inherits, in the most full and complicated Manner, every Perfection of his illustrious Predecessors. But too much Plenty makes me poor: So vast the Theme, it only can be *felt*! Nor ought a Person of my Sex to blush in confessing herself unequal to a Task, in which the most improved Genius of the *Other* would be found defective. Every one may admire the Sun; but no Pen, or Pencil, can describe its Beauties as they are. When the Glory of Alexander[1] was at the Height, the Panegyrists[2] of those Days thought it sufficient to say, He had a PHILLIP for his Father; so I say Enough of the Blessings, which are to be expected from Your ROYAL HIGH-NESS, when I remind the World, from what a Race of Hero's you are deriv'd, and that you are the immediate Offspring of a GEORGE and CAROLINE.

But possessed, as your ROYAL HIGHNESS is, of every shining Quality, which can render the *Heir* of *Monarchy* justly dear to the People he is born to rule, I could wish, methinks, that there was added yet one more Attribute of the DEITY; that as you *Charm* all Hearts, you might at the same Time *Read* them too: Then would the mean Oblation[3] I now offer, be acceptable, as it would be found not to spring from Presumption, but the most Humble, Sincere, and *Zealous Loyalty*; and that my whole Ambition consists in attesting myself, as far as my Capacity permits, with the most profound Duty and Submission,

May it Please your ROYAL HIGHNESS,
Your ROYAL HIGHNESS'S
Most humble, most obedient,
And most faithfully
Devoted Servant,
ELIZA HAYWOOD.

---

1 *Alexander.* Alexander the Great (356-325 B.C.), son of Philip II of Macedonia.
2 *Panegyrists*: Poets who wrote eulogies of praise and commendation.
3 Oblation: An offering or sacrifice given in religious worship.

Selections from The Country Gentleman or, The Craftsman *by Caleb D'Anvers, of Gray's Inn, Esq.*

i. ["The Vision of Camilick"] *The Craftsman*. Friday, January 27, 1727. No. 16.

Having as yet given the Reader little besides grave Discourses on publick Matters, and foreseeing that, during the Session of Parliament, I shall be obliged to continue daily in the same Track, I am willing to take this one Opportunity of presenting him with something, which has no Relation at all to publick Affairs, but is of a Nature purely amusing, and entirely void of Reflection upon any Person whatsoever.

My Friend *Alvarez* (a Man not unknown to many here, by his frequent Journies to *England*) did some time since make me a Present of a *Persian* Manuscript, which he met with while he follow'd the Fortunes of *Meriweis*. An exact Translation of the first Chapter has been made, at my Request, by the learned Mr. *Solomon Negri*, and is as follows.

The First Vision of Camilick.

In the Name of God, ever merciful; and of *Haly* his Prophet. I slept in the Plains of *Bagdad*, and I dreamed a Dream. I lifted my Eyes, and I saw a vast Field, pitch'd with the Tents of the mighty, and the strong ones of the Earth in Array of Battle. I observ'd the Arms and Ensigns of either Host. In the Banners of the one were pictur'd a Crown and Sceptre; and upon the Shields of the Soldiers were engraven Scourges, Chains, Iron Maces, Axes, and all kinds of Instruments of Violence.[1] The Standards of the other bore the Crown and Sceptre also; but the Devices on the Shields were the Balance, the Olive Wreath, the Plough-Share, and other emblematical Figures of Justice,

---

1 Scourges, Chains, ...Violence: Symbols of royal prerogative and encroachments on liberty.

Peace, Law, and Liberty.[1] Between these two Armies, I saw a King come forth, and sign a large *Roll of Parchment*;[2] at which loud Shouts of Acclamation were heard from every Quarter. The *Roll* itself flew up into the Air, and appear'd over their Heads, encompassed with Rays of Glory. I observed that where ever the second Army moved, this glorious Apparition attended them; or rather the Army seemed only to move, as That guided or directed. Soon after, I saw both these Hosts engaged, and the whole Face of the Land overspread with Blood. I saw the King, who had sign'd and broken that *sacred Charter*, drink out of a golden Cup, fall into Convulsions, gasp and die.[3]

I then saw another King take his Place;[4] who, in the most solemn Manner, engaged to make the Words contain'd in the *Roll* the Guide of his Actions; but notwithstanding This, I saw both Armies again encounter. I saw the King a Prisoner.[5] I saw his Son relieve him, and I saw the Chiefs of the other Army put to Death. Yet that victorious Son himself bow'd his Head to the *Parchment*; which now appear'd with fuller Lustre than before. Several other Battles ensued, with vast Slaughter on both Sides; during which the *celestial Volume* was sometimes clouded over; but still again exerted its Rays, and after every Cloud appear'd the brighter. I observed those Heroes, who fought beneath it, tho' ever so unfortunate, not once to abate their Courage, while they had the least Glimpse of that heavenly Apparition in their

---

1   Balance, the Olive Wreath ... Liberty: symbols for the feudal barons who raised an armed rebellion against King John in 1215.

2   *Roll of Parchment*: The Magna Carta, issued by King John in 1215 after he was coerced by the feudal barons' armed rebellion to protect their liberties. The Charter became the basis for the modern English constitution.

3   broken that *sacred Charter*, ... die: Immediately after signing the charter, King John refused to acknowledge its validity. It was reissued in 1216 and 1217 by King Henry III.

4   another King take his Place: Henry III. The war that follows could be the Barons' War (1263-65) but the paragraph performs a telescoping of history, combining events and persons to show the turbulent history between the English people and their monarchs and how the balance of power achieved through the charter had been abused.

5   King a Prisoner: Charles I was beheaded by Cromwell and the Parliamentarians in 1642. His son, Charles II, was restored to the throne in 1660. The father and son pair could also represent James II (who succeeded his brother Charles in 1685) and his son the old Pretender, James Francis Edward, as there were more rebellions and battles supporting the Jacobite right to the crown.

View; and even Those, whom I saw overthrown, pierced with ghastly Wounds, and panting in Death, resign'd their Lives in Smiles, and with Eyes cast up to that glorious Object. At last the long Contention ceased. I beheld both Armies unite and move together under the same divine Influence. I saw one King twelve Times bow down before the bright Phænomenon; which from thence-forward spread a Light over the whole Land; and, descending nearer to the Earth, the Beams of it grew so warm as it approach'd, that the Hearts of the Inhabitants leap'd for Joy. The Face of War was no more. The same Fields, which had so long been the Scene of Death and Desolation, were now cover'd with golden Harvests. The Hills were cloath'd with Sheep. The Woods sung with Gladness. Plenty laugh'd in the Valleys. Industry, Commerce, and Liberty danced hand in hand thro' the Cities.

While I was delighting myself with this amiable Prospect, the Scene entirely changed. The Fields and Armies vanished; and I saw a large magnificent Hall, resembling the great *Divan* or Council of the Nation. At the upper End of it, under a Canopy, I beheld the *sacred Covenant*, shining as the Sun. The Nobles of the Land were there assembled. They prostrated themselves before it, and they sung an Hymn. *Let the Heart of the King be glad; for his People are happy! May the Light of the Covenant be a Lanthorn to the Feet of the Judges; for by This shall they separate Truth from Falshood. O Innocence rejoyce! for by this Light shalt thou walk in Safety; nor shall the Oppressor take hold on thee. O Justice be exceeding glad! for by this Light all thy Judgments shall be decreed with Wisdom; nor shall any Man say thou hast erred. Let the Hearts of all the People be glad! for This have their Grandfathers died; in This have their Fathers rejoiced; and in This may their Posterity rejoyce evermore!*

Then all the Rulers took a solemn Oath to preserve it inviolate and unchanged, and to sacrifice their Lives and their Fortunes, rather than suffer themselves or their Children to be deprived of so invaluable a Blessing.

After This, I saw another and larger Assembly come forward into the Hall, and join the first. These paid the same Adorations to the *Covenant*; took the same Oath; they sung the same Hymn; and added a solemn Form of Imprecaton to this effect. *Let the Words of the Roll be for ever in our Eyes, and graven on our Hearts; and accursed be He, who layeth Hands on the same. Accused be He, who shall remove this Writing from the People; or who shall hide the Law thereof from the King. Let that Man be cut off from the Earth. Let his Riches be scatter'd as the Dust. Let his Wife be the Wife of the People.*[1] *Let not his first-born be rank'd among the Nobles.*[2] *Let his Palaces be destroy'd. Let his Gardens be as a Desart, having no Water.*[3] *Let his Horses and his Horsemen be overthrown; and let his Dogs devour their Carcasses!* – In the midst of these Execrations enter'd a Man, dress'd in a plain Habit, with a Purse of Gold in his Hand.[4] He threw himself forward into the Room, in a bluff, ruffianly Manner. A Smile, or rather a Snear, sat on his Countenance. His Face was bronz'd over with a Glare of Confidence. An arch Malignity leer'd in his Eye. Nothing was so extraordinary as the Effect of this Person's Appearance. They no sooner saw him, but They all turn'd their Faces from the Canopy, and fell prostrate before him. He trod over their Backs, without any Ceremony, and march'd directly up to the Throne. He open'd his Purse of Gold; which he took out in Handfuls, and scattered amongst the Assembly. While the greater Part were engaged in scrambling for these Pieces, He seiz'd, to my inexpressible Surprise, without the least Fear, upon the sacred *Parchment* itself. He rumpled it rudely up, and cramm'd it into his Pocket. Some of the People began to murmur. He threw more Gold, and they were pacified. No sooner was the *Parchment* taken away, but in an Instant I saw half the august Assembly in Chains. Nothing was heard thro' the whole Divan but the Noise of Fetters, and Clank of Irons. I saw Pontiffs in their ecclesiastical Habits, and Senators, clad in Ermine, linked together like the most ignominious Slaves. Terror and Amazement were impressed on every Countenance, except on That of some few, to whom the Man continued dispersing his Gold. This He did, till his Purse became empty. Then He dropt it; but then too, in the very same Moment, He himself dropt with it to the Ground. That and the Date of his Power

---

1 *Wife of the People*: It was reputed that Walpole prostituted his wife, Catherine, for political favours. She was unfaithful to her husband, and their third son, Horace, born in 1717, was not Sir Robert's.

2 first-born ... Nobles: Walpole's eldest son, Robert, was made a baron in 1723, but he was born a commoner like his father.

3 Gardens ... as a Desart, ... no Water: Walpole's estate at Houghton.

4 Gold in his Hand: Walpole. The description that follows includes what were to become conventional symbols of Walpole's corruption.

at once expired. He sunk, and sunk for ever. The radiant *Volume* again rose; again shone out, and reassumed its Place above the Throne; the Throne, which had been darkened all this Time, was now filled with the Effulgence of the Glory, which darted from it. Every Chain dropped off in an Instant. Every Face regained its former Chearfulness. Heaven and Earth resounded with *Liberty! Liberty!*[1] and the HEART OF THE KING WAS GLAD WITHIN HIM.

ii. ["Eloquence and Rhetorick"] *The Craftsman*. Saturday, September 9, 1727. No. 62.

To Caleb D'Anvers, Esq;
SIR,
There is no Qualification which is better calculated to flatter the Vanity of Mankind, or can be a nobler Object of Ambition, than the Power of captivating the Minds of our Fellow-Creatures, and of leading them to our own Purposes by the Force of ELOQUENCE; and there being at this Time no Constitution of Government in the World which affords more frequent, more important, or more useful Occasions of exerting such a Superiority than this of *Great Britain*, I have often wondered, why so few of our *young Noblemen* and *Gentlemen* have applied themselves to, the Study of *Rhetorick*, and made so little Use of the Precepts of that Art, as laid down by the *Ancients*.

I happen'd, the other Day, to fall into Company with a young Gentleman, who, owning himself possess'd of all the other Qualities of an *Orator*, complain'd that they were render'd useless to him by the single Defect of MEMORY. I have sometimes, said he, form'd as handsome a Compliment to the *Administration*[2] as a Man could wish; but have no sooner gone thro' my Preamble, but I have utterly forgot all I had prepar'd. Upon this a Gentleman in the Company, who is really a Scholar and a Man of Wit, ask'd our young Spark if he did not

---

1   *Liberty! Liberty!*: the cry of the opposition to Walpole. The vision is a utopian one, suggesting the ultimate demise of Walpole and the resuming of order, virtue, and freedom.

2   Compliment to the *Administration*] the young Gentleman is a Walpole supporter. He is satirized for his ignorance, and his condescending attitude to learning. Like Walpole, the young man is not appreciative of the arts, nor of the ancient constitution which Cicero (Tully) represents for the opposition.

remember what *Tully*[1] writes upon ARTIFICIAL MEMORY: He answer'd, that he had not lookt into the Works of that *old Prigg*,[2] since he read them with his Tutor at the University. It might be of Service to you, replied the Scholar, to cast an Eye on his *third Book* to HEREN-NIUS; where he instructs us how to raise *Pictures* in the Mind, and, by fixing them in proper Places, to preserve the Form of a whole Speech. He gives the following Example: "A Person is accus'd of having *poison'd* a Man; he had committed this Fact for the Sake of his *Estate*; and there are *Witnesses* to prove it upon him." To remember the several Parts of this Accusation, you are to form, *says He*, this Picture in your Mind. "Place a *sick Man* in his Bed, the Person *accus'd* standing by him, and holding in his right Hand a *Cup*, in his left *Deeds* or a *Will*, and some *Lamb-stones*[3] hanging upon one of his fingers." By this *last Circumstance* you are to remember the *Witnesses*, from the Affinity of the Word in the *Latin* Tongue, *Testiculos*.[4]

Now, suppose you had a Mind to praise a *Lord Treasurer*;[5] to represent the *Plenty of Money*, occasion'd by his Administration: the *Command* he has of it; and the *good Use* he puts it to, both *at home* and *Abroad*: According to *Tully's* Method, you may paint him sitting in the *Court of Requests*, at a large Table heapt with Money, counting, and distributing from right to left, and encompass'd with *Clerks, drawing Bills of Exchange* to all parts of EUROPE. Should any one be so audacious as to insinuate, in the Debate, that some of the Members of *two great Assemblies*[6] were *brib'd* by this Minister, you resolve upon some smart Reply to that *base Aspersion*, but are afraid of forgetting a Circumstance so *groundless* and *trivial*; you have nothing to do but to add to your former Picture, *two Strings*, held in the Hand of *this Minister*, reaching into *these Assemblies*, and imagine you see a Number of *Bank*

---

1   *Tully*] Marcus Tullius Cicero (106-43 B.C.); classical author, politician, and orator. The work that the gentleman refers to here is *Rhetorica ad Herennium*.

2   *Prigg*] one who cultivates or affects a propriety of culture, learning or morals, which offends or bores others (*OED*).

3   *Lamb-stones*] testicles of a young sheep (*OED*).

4   *Testiculos*] testimonies, witnesses as in the form of papers. The visual image of lamb stones is to remind the young man of the related word for "witnesses" — testimony — who will prove the poisoning.

5   *Lord Treasurer*] Sir Robert Walpole.

6   *two great Assemblies*] the House of Lords and the House of Commons.

Bills sent along *those Strings*, as Boys send *Messengers*[1] up to their *Kites*; that Picture will be sufficient to bring into your Mind the Reflection you design to answer.

I like this very well, says the young Gentleman; but I should think it difficult, when one of the *opposite Party* says a Parcel of *scurrilous things*, to draw Pictures immediately upon the Spot, which may have such Resemblance as to bring the Matter into one's Mind. As for Example, suppose some *discontented Tory*, or *grumbling Whig*, shou'd assert that our *Trade* was in Danger of being lost; that we shou'd soon be oblig'd to give up some of the *Acquisitions* we had got by *former Treaties*,[2] and that an *indiscreet enterprizing Minister* had ventured the Dishonour of his Master, and the Ruin of the Nation; only to get – what you please, – we'll say a *Feather in his Cap*. How cou'd one form a Picture to remember such a *Heap of Absurdities?* Very well, replied the Gentleman; image to yourself that *Map of Europe*, and where the *Streights of Gibraltar* are described, place the Figure of the *Great Man* you design to vindicate, like a *Colossus*, straddling cross *those Streights*, with *Ships* sailing between his Legs, and he *p–ss—g* upon them as they pass; sinking some, and spoiling the Cargo of others; the Fortress of GIBRALTAR trampled upon the demolished under one of his Feet; add to this, his holding a *Pair of Scales*, and weighing *three Imperial*, besides *Electoral* and *Ducal Crowns*, and what else you please of that Kind, against a *Cap and Feather*. The young Gentleman was mightily pleased with this, and said he had now that Picture perfectly imprinted in his Mind, and believed he should remember it as long as he lived.

Having paused a little, he broke out, with an Oath, that he had made a *Picture* for a long Speech, in which he design'd to praise a *whole Administration*. I will celebrate, *says he, one* for his Skill in making *Treaties; another* for his *indefatigable Pains* in his Office; a *third* for his

---

1 *Messengers*] little pieces of paper sent up a kite string to become stuck on the kite.
2 *former Treaties*] After the War of the Spanish Succession, the Treaty of Utrecht (1713) acquired Gibraltar and Minorca from Spain for England. The "*discontented Tory*, or *grumbling Whig*" imagined by the young man accuses Walpole of endangering trade by intending to restore Gibraltar to Spain; by favouring the bigger trading companies over the smaller merchants; and by allowing the corrupt customs practices at Gibraltar to continue.

incessant Labours in *running about the World* to bring our Allies to Reason; and a *fourth*, for bearing the Weight of the Whole, and dexterously managing the *publick Revenue*.[1] All this I can put into one *Picture*; and I find, by *Tully's Lambstones*; that a Man is not obliged to mind by what *ridiculous Symbols* He preserves the Images. I will therefore represent to myself a *Great Man*, in the form of a *Porter*, or a *Pedlar*, carrying a *huge Pack of Treaties* on his back; in his *right Hand* I fix a bundle of *Axes* and *Halters*, to put me in mind of his Zeal for bringing *Offenders* to Justice; in his left a *Roll of Papers*, such as the Statues of the *Antient Orators* hold, that I may not forget to compliment him on his Talents in *Oratory*. Then by his side, I must hang a great *red Bag*, top full of Papers, and peeping out of it, there shall appear the Head of a *little Man*[2] who sits cram'd up to the Ears in those Papers. This will at once represent to me the close *Union* between those two *Ministers*, and also, what I am to praise each of them upon. I may fix the Image of the next upon *Pacolet's Horse*,[3] turning his Peg to fly from one part of the World to the other, dressing him up in my Mind, like a *little dirty Postilion*,[4] to represent *diligence* and *dispatch*. I place these Images on a *Globe*, not to denote the *uncertainty* of their Situation, but for the reason that follows. I will paint it the *Globe of the World*, and the other *Great Man*, I will form in my mind, carrying it like *Atlas*, with all the *former Images* upon it. I will hang him all round with *Bank Bills, Exchequer Notes, Lottery-Tickets, Tallies*, &c. and a *small Bag of Money*, to represent how, by his Skill, he can give a cirulation to a vast *Paper credit*, with a *small Proportion of Specie*. I will also paint him with his *own Pockets s[tick]ing*[5] out, that I may not forget to Compliment him upon the prudent care he has taken of *himself* and his *family*.[6] Over his *left*

---

1 *whole Administration … Revenue*: the four different ministers described here are all Walpole. He is being accused of running the whole administration single-handedly.

2 *Little Man*: Walpole's brother, Horatio, who is contrasted with the *Great Man*, Sir Robert; but it could also be Walpole's brother-in-law, Townshend. Both were involved in diplomatic, political negotiations with France and Prussia.

3 *Pacolet's Horse*: a magical horse made of wood that could transport its rider to any desired place instantly (*OED*).

4 *Postilion*: a post-boy; one who rides quickly (*OED*).

5 *s[tick]ing*: the text is illegible here, appearing as *sir tting*.

6 *himself* and his *family*: Walpole was criticized by the opposition for using his office to reward himself, his close relatives, and friends. His mistress and illegitimate daughter were housed in Richmond Park; he made his eldest son a baronet and Ranger of

Arm, I will hang a *large Roll*, on which shall be writ, OLD DEBTS TO BE DISCHARGED; and over his *right* another, intitled NEW DEBTS CONTRACTED; to shew his dexterity as well in finding out *new Funds*, as in paying off the *Old*. "But pray, interrupted the other, how is that *left Arm* to put you in mind of *Dexterity*? I hope you have not *sinister* meaning, as if *those Debts* were to be pay'd over the *left Shoulder*"?[1] Not at all, answer'd He; for that noble *Gentleman* is allowed, by all the World, to be *Ambidexter*; and it is necessary for my Picture, that I should load him on *both Arms*. "Sir, I beg your Pardon, reply'd the Scholar; indeed I think you have given him his Hands full, and have so loaded him *Head, Back, Arms, Pockets* and all, that I tremble, lest he should make a *false step*, and the whole *Machine* should be broken to pieces." Never fear that, quoth the Young Gentleman; it will hold till I have made my *Speech*, and that's all I care for.

Upon this we parted, and the *Young Gentleman*, who, through the brightness of his *Parts*, has forgot his *Latin*, is now looking out for a translation of TULLY, and is fully determined to make *a Figure*[2] in the next Session of Parliament.

iii. ["The Robinocracy"] *The Craftsman*. Saturday, October 18, 1729. No. 170.

Usbeck at —— to *Rustan* at Ispahan.

Thou knowest, *Rustan*, that in our happy Regions of the *East*, there is but one Form of Government, which is despotick and uncircumscrib'd by any Laws, except the Will of the Prince. Our mighty *Sophi's*[3] are uncontroul'd and omnipotent like the great *Alha*, whose Vicegerents they are. But in these Northern Parts of the World, where I reside, there is almost an infinite Variety of Governments. Some are

---

Richmond Park; and he gave his brother, Horatio, a post at court as well as a privy councillorship.

1 *sinister ... left Shoulder*: sinister means "on the left hand side," but also evil or corrupt; "over the left Shoulder" alludes to the superstitious practice of throwing spilled salt over the left shoulder to appease or ward off the devil.

2 *Figure*: The scholar puns on the word as it means two things: to make a distinguished appearance, to be conspicuous or notable, and also, through rhetoric, to adorn a discourse with figures of speech.

3 *Sophi's*: Mohammedan sovereigns; sultans.

called *absolute Monarchies*; but they bear no Proportion of Power to our great *oriental Empires.*[1] They have likewise what they stile *mix'd* or *limited Monarchies*, *Aristocracies*, *Oligarchies*,[2] *Democracies* and others compounded and decompounded out of two or more of These. It would be endless, *Rustan*, to enumerate; much more to describe them all. They swarm one out of another, as different Humours and Interests and Factions prevail. But there is a particular odd kind of Government, lately hatch'd amongst them, which I will describe to Thee, as well as I am able, because I know Thee to be curious in such *political Novelties*. It is called ROBINARCHY or ROBINOCRACY, from the Name of the Man, as I have been informed, who first founded it.[3] This Form of Government seems to be compounded of a *Monarchy*, an *Aristocracy* and a *Democracy*; for it consists in keeping all *Three* in a State of Dependency upon itself. The *Robinarch*, or Chief Ruler, is nominally a *Minister* only and Creature of the Prince; but in Reality a *Sovereign*; as despotick, arbitrary a Sovereign as this Part of the World affords. He does every Thing in his Prince's Name and by his Prince's Authority; except Good, which he always does in his *own Name* (whenever he happens to do any) and claims the sole Merit of it to *Himself.* His Government therefore may properly be called *ministerial Government* or *Imperium in Imperio*;[4] which hath been always treated as a Solæcism[5] in Politicks by the best Writers upon Government, even in these barbarous, *European* Nations.

These *Robinarchs, Rustan,* are commonly *new Men*, of Plebæian[6] Extraction and small Inheritance; and as their Power is a manifest Usurpation upon the Prince's Prerogative, and tends to the Oppression of the People; their Government seldom lasts long; for which Reason it is a constant Maxim amongst them to fill their Coffers as fast [as] They can. Their Measures and Methods of doing this are very

---

1   *oriental Empires*: situated in Asia, or the East.
2   *Oligarchies*: governments in which the power is in the hands of a few.
3   the Man ... who ... founded it: Sir Robert (which was often shortened to "Robin" in satirical literature) Walpole.
4   *Imperium in Imperio*: imperial rule within an empire.
5   Solæcism: an irregularity in speech; a violation of the rules of grammar or syntax (*OED*). The letter suggests that Walpole's "ministerial Government" is a paradox, a contradiction in terms.
6   Plebæian: common; not of noble rank.

extraordinary; though well enough suited to the Nature of their Government. The *Robinarch* in Possession considers very rightly that as He hath unjustly engross'd the whole Power of a Nation into his own Hands, with a View to exorbitant Gain, all the honest and sensible Part of the Nation must of Consequence be his Enemies. He therefore admits no Person to any considerable Post of Trust and Power under Him, who is not either a *Relation*, a *Creature* or a *thorough-pac'd Tool*,[1] whom He can lead at Pleasure into any dirty Work, without being able to discover his Designs or the Consequences of them. He knows that *Ignorance* is often the *Mother of Obedience as well as Devotion*. As for his Inferiour Agents and Instruments, He takes them out of the vilest of the People, whom He secures by *Corruption*. On the other Hand, He makes it his particular Business to discountenance Men of Probity, Learning and Understanding; whom He dares not trust and therefore hates. He endeavours to make *Patriotism* and *publick Spirit* ridiculous, by representing them as the Effects of *Madness* or *disappointed Ambition*. He maintains roundly that *Bribery*, when well apply'd, is an excellent, political Virtue, without which no Government can subsist; and to convince the World of his Sincerity, He makes it the sole Expedient of his own. He rules by Money, the Root of all Evils, and founds his iniquitous Dominion in the Corruption of the People.

The greatest Difficulty, which He hath to struggle with, is when He meets with a Prince of Virtue, Fortitude and Wisdom. Thou wilt wonder, *Rustan*, how the *Robinarchal Government* can subsist under such a Prince; but alas! thou knowest that even the greatest and wisest of Princes (though descended from the *Sun*, like our oriental Monarchs) are but Men; subject to the same Frailties and Imbecilities with other Men; nay their high Station is, in many Respects, a Misfortune. It puts them out of the Road of common Intelligence and Information. It lays them under a Necessity of trusting to their Servants and Favourites. They cannot see with their own Eyes; nor hear with their own Ears. On this depends the *Robinarch's* Security. He closets up his Master. He sticks close to his Ear and infuses into it whatever Notions

---

1 *thorough-pac'd Tool*: a person thoroughly trained (like a horse) to be used as an instrument for the good of someone else (*OED*).

and Prejudices He thinks fit or finds serviceable to his Interest and Ambition. He leads Him into Measures, contrary to the Interest and Inclinations of his Subjects, in Hopes of diverting the popular Odium from Himself. He represents his own personal Enemies (whom *Corruption* and *Male-Administration* have made such) as Enemies to their Kings and Country. He forges sham Plots; suborns false Evidence, and tries every Art to make the People jealous of their Prince and the Prince diffident of his People, in order to make Himself necessary to his Service.

This is not all. I told thee, *Rustan*, that none of the *Northern* Princes were properly *Monarchs* or *absolute Sovereigns*; but in those *Gothick* Countries,[1] where *Robinocracy* generally prevails, the Prince is limited and restrained by Laws, Oaths and Contracts between Him and his Subjects, who have a Share in the Legislature, and send their *Deputies* to act in Concert with Him. He can raise no Money, the great Sinew of Government, without their Approbation and Consent. They have likewise a Power to call his Ministers to Account for all their Actions, and have often obliged Him to give them up to Justice, against his own Inclinations. It is therefore necessary for a Man, who aspires to *Robinarchal Power*, to secure the *Deputies* of the People on his Side, as well as the *Prince* Himself. This, I am told, was no easy Matter in former Times, the Deputies being a numerous Body of Men, stubbornly tenacious of their Rights and Liberties; but *modern Robinarchs* have found out a Method of softening this old-fashion'd rigid Virtue to their Purposes. They do this chiefly by giving Encouragement to *Luxury* and *Extravagance*, the certain Forerunners of *Indigence, Dependance* and *Servility*. Some are ty'd down with *Honours, Titles* and *Preferments*; of which the *Robinarch* engrosses the Disposal to Himself; and others with *Bribes*, which are called *Pensions*[2] in these Countries. Some are persuaded to prostitute Themselves for the lean Reward of *Hopes* and *Promises*; and others, more senseless than all of them, have sacrific'd their Principles and Consciences to a Set of *Party-Names*, without any Meaning, or the Vanity of appearing in Favour at Court.

---

1   *Gothick* Countries: found in northern Europe; France, England, Germany.
2   *Pensions*: periodical payments as rewards, tributes, etc. for services (*OED*).

The *Robinarch*, having thus establish'd Himself in Power, begins to discover and exert his Capacities for Government. He corrupts the People with their own Money to part with their own Money; and by throwing a Spoonful or two of Water, at convenient Times, into the Well, pumps out again what Quantities He pleases. He loads them with *Taxes* to keep them from growing wanton with Wealth and plunges them into *Debt*, to secure their Affections. He negociates them into Difficulties and Distresses to make great Sums of Money necessary for what are called *secret Services*;[1] and bridles them with large, mercenary Armies to preserve them from *Tyranny, Slavery* and *Oppression*.

When He hath bled them down almost to the last Gasp, He comforts them with Assurances that They were never in so vigorous a State of Health. He desires them to judge of the Publick Prosperity by his own; and insolently endeavours to convince them that they are not miserably poor, because He is exorbitantly rich.

In the same Manner that He governs Affairs at Home, He would willingly rule them Abroad; that is, by *Money* rather than *Ability*; but in this He commonly finds Himself disappointed; They take his *Money* without doing his *Jobs*; unless when He sometimes happens to meet with *Ministers* of less Depth and penetration than Himself.

I told Thee, *Rustan*, that this new-fangled Medley of Government seldom lasts long in the Person of one Man[;] nay Thou wilt conclude, from the small Sketch which I have given Thee of it, that it cannot be of long Duration, without overthrowing the Constitution itself, and destroying the Prince, as well as the People. The *Robinarch* carries every Thing before Him, in the Zenith of his Power, which is too violent and rapid to be stemm'd; but at length the Cries of the People become loud and importunate and general as their Distresses; they reach the Prince's Ears and pierce his Heart. He makes Enquiry into their Complaints; and finding them just, rouzes Himself up to Vengeance and resolves to redress them. The *Robinarch* perceives the impending Storm. He sees it gathering over his Head and leaves no Art untry'd to break or divert it. There is something, *Rustan*, very

---

1 *secret Services*: Walpole's government spent a fortune to spy on known or suspected Jacobites and to maintain standing armies in case of war.

Tragi-comical in this Crisis of his Fate. He writhes, winces, distorts Himself and shews a manifest Disturbance in his Looks, his Words and his Actions. He sinks his proud Crest; he becomes very humble and descends to little, mean Apologies for his Conduct. He desires that he may not be answerable for *Events*, though they evidently flow from his own wild Counsels and extravagant Measures. He imputes the Calamities of his Country, which his insatiable Avarice hath occasioned, to the natural Fluctuation of human Affairs, to unavoidable Accidents, the Obstinacy of foreign Powers, or the malevolent Opposition of domestick Enemies; of those very Enemies whom, upon other Occasions, he affects to treat with Indifference and Contempt. When he is beaten out of these weak Holds, he does not scruple to lay the Blame on the *Winds*, the *Weather* and *Seasons*; and even presumes to arraign Providence as the Author of his Mismanagement. Thou can'st not be surprized, *Rustan*, to hear that such a Man will stick at nothing to secure himself in this Distress; that he is false, ungrateful and perfidious; that he cancels all Obligations, human and divine; and is willing to give up a *Friend*, a *Relation*, or even a BROTHER,[1] who hath proved faithful to Him for many Years, to the Disadvantage of his own Character, and been ready to lend his *Name* and *Authority*, upon all Occasions, to support Him in his unrighteous Power. But the People (the injur'd, enraged People) will not be satisfy'd with This. They keep their Eyes stedfastly fix'd on the *Principal* of their Misfortunes, and will not suffer them to be diverted by such a Mock Sacrifice of his *inferior Agents* and *Accomplices*. They know very well who hath been their *great Oppressor*, and expect to see Him made an Example of Justice.

The *Gothick* Governments of the North, *Rustan*, are naturally subject to these *Robinarchal* Usurpations. I have been informed that *England* itself (the best constituted of them all) hath not been intirely free from them. They tell me that even in the Time of their most Favourite Princess, Queen *Elizabeth* (who reigned about a Century

---

1 BROTHER: Walpole's brother-in-law, Charles, 2nd Viscount Townshend (1674-1738), who resigned from his office of foreign minister in 1730 after more than a decade of service to Walpole. Their fights and disagreements were satirized earlier by Gay in *The Beggar's Opera* (1728) in the scene between Peachum and Lockit, Act 2, scene x.

and an half ago) a *Robinocracy* prevail'd for some Years in the Person of the Earl of *Leicester,* her *Prime-Minister;*[1] and that several have been establish'd since that Time under some of their *best* and *wisest Princes.*

How painful a Task must it be, *Rustan,* for a brave People to submit to such a mean, Plebæian and inglorious Tyranny? Is it not much more tolerable to be Slaves, as our *Asiaticks* are, under a great, high-born Prince, whose Lineage sets Him above the Level of other Men, than to crouch and truckle[2] to a Fellow-Subject, an Upstart of Yester-day, whose only Præ eminence consists in his exalted Guilt and distin-guish'd Genius for Wickedness?

——— The 4th of the Moon
Zilcade 1726

1 *Leicester ... Prime-Minister.* Robert Dudley (c.1532-88), rumoured to be the lover of Queen Elizabeth I, and believed to have poisoned people who stood in his way either in politics or in love affairs.
2 truckle: to take a subordinate or inferior position; to be subservient (*OED*).

Appendix C:

Anonymous, The Secret History of Mama Oello, Princess Royal of Peru. A New Court Novel (London, 1733).

To the Right Honourable the Lady HUMBLE.
May it please Your Ladyship,

The Translator presents You with the *Secret History of* MAMA OELLO, Princess Royal of *Peru*; but I am afraid, deviates very much from the common Road of *Dedication*; when, instead of writing a fulsome Panegyrick[1] upon Your Ladyship, (whose superior Merits would look down with Scorn on Flattery, and whose Virtues render You sufficiently conspicuous to the World without the Assistance of an Advocate to sound them) he lays before You the Advantage You may gather from the Perusal of it.

The Design of all History in general is to improve Mankind, to stir up a laudable Emulation in us to imitate the good Actions of our Ancestors, and to detest and avoid the bad.

This, that I humbly presume to lay at Your Ladyship's Feet, is a Novel form'd from true History found some time ago by the Vice Roy,[2] amongst the Royal Commentaries of *Peru*, and wrote originally by the *Inca Garzilasco de la Vega*, Author of those Commentaries, whose Father was of a noble *Spanish* Family; and in Reality descended by his Mother's Side from the *Incas* or Kings of *Peru*. In which is contain'd Variety of pleasing Amazement. Hence Your Ladyship may learn to prize the Liberty that the *British* Ladies boast of in chusing their own Husbands, and bewail the Misfortune of the fair *Mama Oello*, with the secret Satisfaction to find Yourself free from that Compulsion.[3] The *Curaca Robilda's* Character will inform You that there

---

1   Panegyrick: Elaborate praise.
2   Vice Roy: One who acts as the governor of a country, province, etc., in the name and by the authority of the supreme ruler (*OED*).
3   Liberty ... Compulsion: An ironic statement. Although arranged marriages were less popular than they were earlier in the century, women were still not free to choose husbands for love alone.

were Evil Ministers even amongst the simple *Indians*; and the *Curacas Posinki, Sinchi* and *Cobinqui* point out the true Patriots of their Country. *Atabalipa* Prince of *Quito* will shew you that Marriage by Compulsion, or even Proxy, was altogether distasteful to the *Americans*; and the *Cacique Loque Yupanqui* will demonstrate the wonderful Effects of Love.

But I forbear mentioning any more Particulars to Your Ladyship, and only wish You may receive it with the same Intent as it was written, which was to give the World a Proof how much I am

Your Ladyship's most Devoted
And Humble Servant,
The TRANSLATOR.

The *SECRET HISTORY OF MAMA OELLO*.

In the imperial City of Cusco[1] lived the charming *Mama Oello*,[2] eldest Daughter of Inca Manco Capac,[3] by his Queen Coya Mama,[4] a young Princess of admirable Accomplishments, who possess'd a large Share of the Beauties of the Mind, as well as those of the Body, and fortunate in every but Love. How happy was the fair *Mama Oello*, till enslav'd by this inveighling Passion? How did it imbitter her Days, and make her Life become a Burden to her? Not that this lovely Princess had any Reason to complain of the Indifference of her beloved Cacique[5] (for a *Cacique* he was, and one of the noblest Extraction amongst those that adorn'd *Inca Manco Capac*'s Court, that had got the Ascendant over this Lady's Heart) he glow'd with a mutual Passion, and fell a grateful Victim to her Charms: But another Obstacle, and that unsurmountable, nipt her growing Hopes in the Bud, and made her for ever despair of enjoying her Heart's desire.

---

1   *Cusco*: London.
2   *Mama Oello*: the Princess Royal, Anne (1709-59), eldest daughter of King George II; married to William, Prince of Orange, March 14, 1734.
3   *Manco Capac*: King George II; ruled 1727 to 1760.
4   *Coya Mama*] Caroline of Brandenburg-Anspach (1683-1737), Queen Consort of King George II.
5   *Cacique*: later identified in the text as *Loque Yapanqui*. A Key to *Mamo Oello*, handwritten into the British Museum's copy, identifies Mamo Oello's lover as "Lord Carmichael, afterward E[arl] of Hyndford"; however, I have not uncovered any evidence for this.

There had been a Law enacted by the Emperor and the States of *Peru*, that no Princess, of the Blood Royal of the *Inca*'s, should be suffer'd to marry a *Peruvian* Subject, or any foreign Prince that was an Idolator,[1] but only one of the reform'd Religion, who worshipped the invisible *Pacha-Camac*, and their Father the Sun. How could the charming *Mama Oello* relish this severe Restriction, which not only hinders her from being match'd to her dearest *Cacique*, but to any one else that she might like, provided he was not of the prescrib'd Sect? She consults with herself, and contrives, but all in vain; what Method can there be left to get over such apparent Difficulties, as she is oblig'd to encounter with? Distracted with ten thousand Fears she sends for her dearest *Cacique*, to see if between them both any Expedient might be found to accomplish her Wishes, but if it is all in vain, as she has but too great Reason to suspect, yet it will be some mitigation to her Pain (and that no small one) to sooth her Cares in his engaging Company. To this Purpose she dispatches away her trusty Confidant to acquaint the *Cacique* she had something to communicate to him on which her Happiness and his did depend.

This noble Personage (who constantly attended her Royal Father's Court, as being one of his *Dica Vidida*, that is of those Nobles who belong'd to his Bed-Chamber) receiv'd the trusty Messenger, and with an ominous Concern, first kiss'd, and then unloosed the beloved Seal, which soon discover'd the Uneasiness that his dearest Princess labour'd under. He answers the Fair one's Billet[2] with all the Tenderness he was Master of, and express'd his Design of waiting on her that Evening.

Hardly was this Affair transacted, and the Confidant gone, but one of the *Inca*'s *Curacas* or Counsellors comes to the disconsolate *Cacique* with a Message from his Sovereign, which informs him, that the *Inca* had no farther Occasion for his Service and therefore dismissed him, having received private Intelligence that this *Cacique* was a greater Favourite of his eldest Daughter, the Princess *Mama Oello*, than ever he had been of his Royal Master, and thereupon forbid him the

---

1 Idolator: A worshipper of idols or images. In relation to the "reform'd Religion," it may refer to one of the Catholic faith (as opposed to the Protestant) and a Jacobite, a supporter of the House of Stuart and the Pretender, Prince James Francis Edward (1688-1766), rather than the House of Hanover.
2 Billet: Letter.

Court. The before dejected *Cacique*, now thunderstruck at these Words, stood for some time senseless and confounded, not so much on the Account of his losing his Pension (which was very considerable) but least it should debar him the Conversation of his dearest Princess; but recovering himself out of his Insensibility, return'd the *Curaca* this Answer; That it had been his highest Ambition to serve the *Inca* with the sincerest Loyalty and Affection, whilst his Majesty had been pleas'd to honour him with his Royal Favours, but since it seemed good to his Sacred Highness to withdraw them, he patiently submitted to his Sovereign's Will and Pleasure.

The *Curaca* being gone, the enamour'd *Cacique* had time to ruminate on his present Circumstances; And can there (says he) be so great a Crime in Love? If Nature has formed me of *Porcellain* Clay (as our Poets term it) of a finer Mould than the Majority of my Fellow-Creatures, how am I to blame? If Fortune has destin'd me to charm these Eyes, which charm the World besides, how is it my Fault? 'Tis decreed, 'tis decreed that I should captivate the fair *Mama Oella*, and who can resist Fate? But, alas! rigid Laws, and Reasons of State forbid the Accomplishment of our Desires, as her Letter too plainly intimates; why thought we not of this when first we embark'd in the Affair? We launch'd out in the midst of Sun-shine, on a smooth Sea, but now too late perceive the gathering Clouds portend the impending Storm, yet my dearest Princess will I hazard all to see you once more, to take a long and last Adieu, to wash thy Cheeks with Tears, to bid farewel to Pleasure, Courts and Love. Then rousing himself out of this melancholy Soliloquy, he bends his Steps towards the well-known Apartment of his dearest Princess; where gaining a ready Admittance, (for as yet the Princess had not been forbid the Sight of him) he finds his Fair one bath'd in Tears, but yet charming in Grief. Such a Sight as this soon disheartned the already dejected *Cacique* who perceived by her extraordinary Concern that something more (than she had in her Letter express'd, or he understood) distracted her Mind. Then seizing her fair Hand, and throwing himself at her Feet; Tell me my dearest Princess, says he, tell me what other killing News you have to impart worse than your Billet hinted, for I perceive by your excessive Grief, and that Deluge of Tears you pour forth, that you have conceived some extraordinary Trouble, which labours within your Breast! Arise (says the fair disconsolate *Mama Oello*) arise, my dearest *Cacique*, and I will impart to you the Torments of my Soul. When I sent (proceeds she, desiring him to sit) the trusty — [1] to you this Morning, that Letter contain'd the Sum of my Affliction; and was not that Affliction enough to think I must lose you; for ever lose you, because the Laws of *Peru* forbid? But I was in hopes that I should have greatly alleviated my Trouble by your good Company, if a fresh Cause of Grief had not demanded fresh Sorrow. O ye Gods! was it not enough for ye to debar me from the Enjoyment of my dearest *Cacique*, but must ye destine me to the Arms of one I hate: Why was I born of Royal Race? Why not rather a simple Shepherdess, then should I have been happy in the Embraces of my dearest *Cacique*. Hateful *Peru*! what are your Laws to me? Happier had I been if my Royal Father had never sway'd this Scepter, nor my illustrious Ancestors left the Province of *Hurin Capassa*,[2] their ancient Patrimony for these extensive Dominions, whereby my Sorrows are extended. Then should I have never seen my charming *Loque Yapanqui*, or not have seen him in vain. I have been rais'd higher only to be reduc'd the lower, and enjoy a miserable Greatness.

Wonder not, my dearest *Cacique* (says the charming Princess, pursuing her Discourse) at what I am going to tell you, for since I wrote to you, the *Inca*, my Father, and his chief *Curaca Robilda*[3] have paid me a Visit, to inform me, That (for what they call Reasons of State)[4] I must surrender up my Hand and Heart (which last I never can to any but you) to *Atabalipa*, Prince of *Quito*;[5] and to encourage you, says

---

1 It is not clear why the trusty servant is not named.

2 *Hurin Capassa*: Hanover.

3 *Curaca Robilda*: Sir Robert Walpole.

4 Reasons of State: The propaganda at the time was that the King was marrying Anne to the Prince of Orange to strengthen the Protestant succession to the crown and to renew a beneficial alliance with the Dutch. By uniting Holland and Britain in marriage, it was hoped that the Dutch would break their treaty of neutrality with France and join Britain as a mediator between Poland, Russia, and France and Austria over the Polish succession. The real reason for such a poor match, however, was that no other husband for the Princess Royal could be found.

5 *Atabalipa, Prince of Quito*: William Charles Friso, Prince of Orange, Stadholder of Holland (1711-51). "On the 8th May 1733 the King signified to the Parliament that the contract of marriage between the Princess Royal and the Prince of Orange was settled." [Key].

the *Inca*, my Father, chearfully to obey my Commands, I will make you a Present of Jewels of inestimable Value, which I design'd to dedicate to our Father the *Sun*: And I, says the old *Curaca Robilda*, will engage at the next Convention of the *Curacas* and *Caciques* of this glorious Empire you receive an ample Annuity out of the publick Revenues, to render you more acceptable to Prince *Atabalipa*.

Thus you see, my much beloved *Cacique*, says the Princess, giving him her Hand, I must not only be depriv'd of you, the sole Comfort I ever propos'd the Enjoyment of in this World, but be oblig'd to waste a wretched Life in a foreign Country, and another's Arms. And I (reply'd the gallant *Loque Yupanqui*, interrupting his dearest Princess at these last Words) have a fresh Scene of Woe to discover to you. I thank you, says he, O Invisible *Pacha-Camac*, and our Father the *Sun*! that you have made me compleatly wretched; now Fortune do your Worst – Then after some Pause, recollecting himself he imparted to the weeping Fair, the sorrowful Message he had receiv'd from her Royal Father, the *Inca*, by the Mouth of one of his chief *Curacas*, which enjoin'd him to leave the Court, and return into his own Province Northward, beyond the great River *Apurimac*.[1] That he had great Reason to suspect the *Curaca Robilda* was at the Bottom of it all, as well the Author of his Banishment, as the Projector of her Marriage with Prince *Atabalipa*; that if she could procure this Favourite[2] to be discarded, they might (if not obtain the Accomplishment of their Desires) get some further Respite to their Misfortunes: He likewise inform'd her, that almost all the *Curacas* and *Caciques* of the *Peruvian* Empire hated this *Curaca Robilda*, that the Voice of the whole Nation, and of the Imperial City of *Cusco* was against him, on Account of his perswading her Royal Grandfather and Father[3] to impose heavy Taxes on their Subjects in time of Peace; that even in a publick Convention of the *Curacas* and *Caciques* some of them had not spar'd him, and that altho', by his immense Treasures, he had secur'd the Majority of them

---

1 *Apurimac*: The Key identifies this as the River Tweed.
2 Favourite: Curaca Robilda. Sir Robert Walpole was a favourite of King George, but was favoured even more by Queen Caroline.
3 Royal Grandfather and Father: King George I (1714–27) and King George II (1727–60). The heavy taxes referred to are the exorbitant land taxes levied in order to support the expensive standing army in case of war against Spain and France.

to his Interest, yet he did not Fear, but the brave uncorrupted few that were left behind, would soon open the Eyes of those that were dazzl'd with the Splendor of his yellow Mettle.[1] You know, says he my dearest *Mama Oello*, that the *Curaca Posinki*[2] has always attack'd him, and I doubt not but will Second us (as far as lies in his Power) in procuring the Fall of his Enemy and ours. Besides, I know the *Curaca Robilda* is now projecting a Scheme[3] (which I believe must prove fatal to him) since the Convention of States, now assembled, have been petition'd against it by the Provinces of *Caranca Ullaca*, *Lipi*, *Chicha*, *Ampara*, and most of the rest. You know, moreover, adds the disconsolate *Cacique*, that the *Curaca Robilda* is but an Upstart, not one of them, or of their Family, who join'd with your illustrious Ancestors, the first *Incas*, in civilizing these Nations; in diverting them from their superstitious Idolatries; from Adoration of Tygers, Lakes, Rivers, and Serpents, to the true Worship of the Invisible *Pacha Camac*, and our Father the Sun; that altho' it is strongly reported, and by some believ'd, that the illustrious *Inca*, who immediately preceeded your Royal Father, distinguish'd him by some Marks of Honour[4] for his good Services towards him, yet the *Curaca* has never been pleas'd to own his Titles, or to have his Ears bor'd to hang Jewels in, or to cover his Head with a black Tress.[5] – That he, for his part, had given her the most sensible Proof of his Esteem, since now, even this Moment while he is speaking to her, he hazards his Life, if he is betray'd or discover'd – The fair Princess was going to answer, but both recollecting they had over stay'd their Time, were oblig'd, tho' with the utmost Reluctance, to part. Remember, dearest *Cacique*, says the languishing Princess, Remember your *Mama Oello*, when you get beyond the great River *Apurimac*, and I will let you know by a trusty Messenger, when the

---

1   yellow Mettle: Gold. This refers to the popular idea that Walpole was notorious for bribery.

2   *Curaca Posinki*: Unidentified in the Key; however, the sound of the name suggests that it may refer to William Pulteney, one of the leaders of the Opposition.

3   projecting a Scheme: The Excise on Tobacco.

4   some Marks of Honour: In 1725 Walpole accepted a Knighthood of the Bath; a year later, George I conferred on him the Garter. Walpole was the first commoner in generations to receive such an honour.

5   Titles, ... black Tress: Although entitled to a place in the House of Lords, Walpole chose to remain in the House of Commons.

Storm is a little blown over, how we may meet again; and as to Prince *Atabalipa*, you know my Heart. Can you be ever absent to your *Loque Yupanqui*, says the enamour'd *Cacique*? No; were I ten thousand Leagues from you, beyond the snowy Mountains of *Challampa*, yet would you be always present to me: Adieu, fairest *Mama Oella*! Charming Princess, Adieu! and sometimes bestow a Thought on your constant *Loque Yupanqui*.

Thus parted these two Lovers; the *Cacique* retir'd to order his Matters so that he might leave the Court and Imperial City of *Cusco* the next Day, which he accordingly did, and departed towards his own Province Northward, beyond the great River *Apurimac*, according to the *Inca*'s Mandate; the Princess to her Place of Rest: but alas! none of that was to be found; for ten thousand Thoughts distract her divided Mind. The Absence of her belov'd *Loque Yupanqui*, the Thoughts of her losing him for ever are not her only Affliction; a far greater Trouble wrecks her Spirit; there was Hopes of her *Cacique*'s returning, and that Time, which effects every thing, might cool her Father's Passion, and then the Legislature of *Peru* forbid their Marriage, yet she might be happy in the Sight of her dear *Cacique*, and sometimes in his Company. But how could she accomplish this, if she must be wedded to Prince *Atabalipa*, as her Father and the *Curaca* told her in positive Terms she must? She farther pursues her Reflections, and vents her Grief in this melancholy Soliloquy.

Atabalipa *may be a deserving Prince as far as I know, but not comparable to my beloved* Cacique; *but if all be as Fame says, the Beauties of his Mind far exceed those of his Body.*[1] *I might have been happy in his Arms, had I not before given my Heart to the charming* Cacique: *They tell me moreover, that if Birth, Titles and Honour had not distinguish'd* Atabalipa, *that Nature had. But stay, thoughtless Princess, 'tis ungenerous to censure natural Defects, which in a great Measure proceed only from the Almighty. Aid me then, all-powerful Love, 'tis in your Cause I engage, to find Fault with the Object that must undeservedly be my Aversion; did all the Wisdom of the past and present*

---

1 *Charms ... of his Body*: According to Lord Hervey, the Prince of Orange was grotesque in appearance being almost a dwarf, deformed with a rounded shoulder and a high back: from the back it looked "as if he had no head," and from the front it appeared "as if he had no neck and no legs." He also suffered from bad breath (Halsband, 170).

Age center in Atabalipa, *yet should I be insensible of all his perswasive Eloquence, since my* Cacique*'s Rhetorick must and does surpass it all. Prince*
Atabalipa *may be fam'd for his Parts, which to me seems something strange,
since those that instruct my Brothers in the Manners and Customs of the
different Nations who inhabit the known World, and in what they call Geography, informs us; that the Province of* Quito *is a low, barren Soil, productive
of nothing but Pasturage for Butter and Cheese; the Inhabitants not fam'd for
Arts and Sciences, or any thing else but an over-reaching Method in Trade and
Commerce;[1] that they were esteem'd a few Centuries ago but a poor and beg-
garly People, and that they are indebted for their present Grandeur to one or
more of our Royal Ancestors. They tell me for Encouragement, that* Atabalipa
is Prince of Quito; *but then I hear from other Hands, that Part of his Principality is still in Dispute, that some of it is diminished; and if he was in real
Possession of the whole, yet many of our* Bobinquos, *or private Gentlemen,
in this mighty Empire of* Peru, *enjoy a larger Estate than all his Dominions
put together: Why then must I, who am Princess Royal of the mighty Empire
of* Peru, *leave my Country and Friends to be only Co-partner in the poor
Principality of* Quito?[2] *did I love indeed Prince* Atabilipa, *as I do my dearest* Cacique, *a Cottage with him would be a Palace, but to exchange better
for worse, to be confin'd to a Prince I can never like so well as* Loque Yupanqui, *must be very disagreeable. My Royal Mother, moreover, offers me her
Maiden-Plate and Jewels[3] (which to be sure must be of considerable Value) but
what is Plate or Jewels to me, or any Thing else, without the Man I love?*

Thus the fair Princess employ'd Part of the remaining Night, till
gentle Slumbers at last clos'd her Eyes; but too soon she awakes again
to Trouble and perplexing Thoughts; however she endeavours to stifle
them as much as possible, and puts on her wonted Gaity: All her
Thoughts now turn which Way she may divert the intended Match,
and re-establish her dearest *Cacique* in her Father's Favour. But in this
consisted the Difficulty; the Advice of her dear *Loque Yupanqui*, was to
attempt the Favourite *Curaca Robilda*'s Fall, which to her seemed
impracticable: the Hints which she had received from her Lover gave

---

1   *Quito ... Commerce*: Mamo Oello voices the usual stereotypes of the Dutch.
2   *Why then ... Quito?*: It was generally believed that the proposed marriage was not
    to Anne's advantage.
3   *Maiden-Plate and Jewels*: Dowry, the money and property a woman brings to a mar-
    riage. *Plate*: Silver coins, utensils, or ornaments.

her some glimmering Hope that it might be effected, but which way to attempt it she was at a Loss; she hated the *Curaca Robilda*, as the Author of her intended Nuptials to Prince *Atabalipa*, but yet believ'd him to be firmly attached to her, and her Family's Interest, even to the Prejudice of his own Country, as she had often observed. Moreover, she knew her Royal Father and Mother to be so wrapt up in him, that his Counsels were always followed, tho' he often abus'd his Trust, and shelter'd himself under the Royal Wing, when he had transacted any Thing base or offensive. That likewise her Royal Mother Queen *Coya Mama* had been particularly oblig'd to the *Curaca Robilda* in many things especially for an ample Revenue, and a spacious Palace[1] in the imperial City of *Cusco*, which he procured for her as a Royal Maintenance after the Decease of her dearly beloved *Inca*, and chiefly by his own Interest; a Maintenance which far surpassed any that the Dowager Empresses of *Peru* had ever possessed; she thought it therefore in vain to attempt a Matter clog'd with so many Difficulties, and chose rather prudently to leave it to Time and Providence (which accomplish every Thing) to extricate her out of these Troubles; and as she was not without Hopes that the Scheme which the famous *Curaca Robilda* was to bring on the Carpet, at the next Convention of the *Curacas* and *Caciques* of the *Peruvian* Empire, might prove his Ruin, she was resolved to wait patiently till a favourable Opportunity offer'd itself. Whereupon she put on all the outward Unconcern she was Mistress of, and seem'd to be entirely resign'd to her Royal Father's Will and Pleasure. Her Marriage with Prince *Atabalipa* was publickly declar'd at the imperial City of *Cusco*, and all over the *Peruvian* Empire, and likewise in the Principality of *Quito*, and in the seven Provinces of *Havisca*, *Tuna*, *Chuncuri*, *Pucana*, *Muyuncuyu*, *Charcas*, and *Collasuya* thereunto joining. Both received the Compliments of their *Curacas* and *Caciques*, on their intended Marriage, as well as of the foreign Ambassadors; and now Prince *Atabalipa* is daily expected from *Quito*, at the imperial City of *Cusco*, to espouse his charming Princess.

Whilst these Affairs were transacting at the imperial City of *Cusco*, the charming Princess was not unmindful of her dearest *Cacique*, and

---

1   Revenue, and ... Palace: "A Key" notes that in July 1727 a Bill was passed for set-
    tling £100,000 a year "together with Somerset house [and] Richmond old Park on
    the Q[ueen] for life" should Caroline survive the King.

although she seem'd to pay an implicit Obedience outwardly to her Father's Commands, yet in secret did she earnestly wait for the happy Minute that might restore the lovely *Loque Yupanqui* to her Father's Favour, and her longing Eyes, which some time after offer'd itself; for the *Inca* looking upon the Marriage of the Princess *Mama Oello* with *Atabalipa*, Prince of *Quito*, as good as consummated, gave the banish'd *Cacique* Leave to return to the City of *Cusco*, and restor'd him seemingly to his Favour, tho' not to his former Places of Honour.

As soon as the Rumour was noised abroad that the noble *Cacique Loque Yupanqui* had Leave to return from his Northern Retirement, beyond the great River *Apurimac*, the overjoy'd Princess was resolv'd he should receive the first News of it from her, and therefore dispatch'd away a trusty Messenger to inform her beloved *Cacique*, that his Doom was revers'd, and how Matters stood (for Prince *Atabalipa* was not yet arrived at the imperial City of *Cusco*, from his Principality of *Quito*, altho' he had been for some time contracted to the Princess, and daily expected, proving, it seems but a sluggish Lover) that he was to move in a little Time to the Palace of *Capuac*,[1] in the Province of *Capuany*, and therefore she advis'd him not to come to the imperial City of *Cusco*, but wait her Arrival at *Capuac*: The Messenger was likewise order'd to deliver the *Cacique* the following Letter, which we shall insert in this Translation, for the Satisfaction of the fair Part of our Readers, and to give a Specimen of the *American*[2] Gallantry in those Times.

The Princess Mama Oello, *Daughter of the* Inca Manco Capac, *and Queen* Coya Mama, *Son and Daughter of* Inca Huascar (*for the* Incas *of* Peru *commonly married their Sisters*) *of* Huana Capac, *of* Tupac Yupanqui, *of* Inca Palhacutec, *of* Inca Virachocha, *of* Vahuar Huacac, *of* Inca Roca, *of* Capac Yupanqui, *of* Mayta Capac, *of* Sinchi Roca *Child of the Sun.* (*See how fond the* Indians *are of tracing their Genealogy.*)

To the Noble Cacique Loque Yupanqui, *sendeth Greeting.*
Most Illustrious CACIQUE,

'Tis with no small Satisfaction I acquaint the Cacique Loque Yupanqui, *he may with Impunity repass the great River* Apurimac, *and without*

---

1   *Capuac:* Hampton Court.
2   *American:* South American, Peruvian; however, it refers to European manners.

Danger revisit the Princess Mama Oello: *Had I been less condescending to my Father's Commands, I had been the longer depriv'd of this happy Opportunity. You shall know what has been transacted in your Absence, when you come to the Palace of* Capuac, *according to the Bearer's Instructions. Believe me, noble* Cacique, *I am as highly pleas'd at this good-natur'd Action of my Royal Father, as it is proper for the Princess of* Peru *to declare; I don't doubt but your own Prudence will so time our next Meeting, that it shall receive no Interruption till that happy Minute arrives.*
I remain Yours,
MAMA OELLO.

Soon was the belov'd *Cacique* inform'd (in his Retirement, where he had now been for some time, diverting the melancholly Hours one while with the Thoughts of his dearest Princess, and at other times with Books and rural Sports) that a Messenger was arriv'd, in Post-haste from the imperial City of *Cusco*, at his Palace Gate: He steps with eager Strides to learn the Reasons of his Journey. But how agreeably was he surpris'd, when, to his great Joy, he found it to be the trusty *Sinchal*? What News, says he, faithful *Sinchal*? What News dost thou bring to me from my Princess, and the imperial City of *Cusco*? Does she live? Is she well, or is she for ever lost in the Arms of *Atabalipa*, Prince of *Quito*? Most illustrious *Cacique*, replies *Sinchal*, my Royal Mistress lives, and is well, is not yet in the Arms of Prince *Atabalipa*, but how soon she may I know not: But if you will give me Leave to enter your Palace, I will tell you more of the Matter. Dismount, honest *Sinchal*, says the impatient *Cacique* (ordering his Servant to take his Horse) for I long to be inform'd of all that concerns my charming *Mama Oello*, as well as the State of the Court, and of the imperial City of *Cusco*. The trusty Confidant then deliver'd the Letter. Go you, says the enamour'd *Cacique*, and refresh yourself with such a Collation[1] as my House affords, and in the mean time I will retire till that is over, and then will send for you into my Closet.[2] Having so said, he bid one of his Domesticks entertain the Messenger with the best he could procure, and himself hasted away to peruse the welcome Epistle.

---

1 Collation: A light meal or repast.
2 Closet: A room for privacy or retirement (*OED*).

And does my Princess, says the transported *Cacique*, condescend to acquaint her Slave that his Doom is revers'd? How prudently must she have acted, so soon to have wip'd off all Suspicion that she had ever cast a favourable Eye on her undeserving *Loque Yupanqui*? but she mentions nothing in her Letter of Prince *Atabalipa*, or the *Curaca Robilda*'s Disgrace; 'tis in vain for me to hope for any Success, whilst that *Curaca* continues in my Royal Master's Favour! he was, and always will be an Enemy to true Merit. But I will call for *Sinchal*, and inform myself from him of what has past since my Retirement; he us'd to be conversant in Court Affairs, and is a likely Person to acquaint me what Things of Moment have been transacted at the last Convention of the *Curacas* and *Caciques* of this glorious Empire, during my Absence; then shall I be better able to judge how I must behave in this critical Juncture, and to accomplish my Desires in seeing the Princess *Mama Oello* at the Palace of *Capuac*.

He rings the Bell, and commands his Servant in waiting to convey the trusty *Sinchal* to him. Well, says he, faithful Servant, now you have refresh'd yourself, let me hear a little of the present State of the *Peruvian* Empire; what Affairs of Importance have the Convention of the *Curacas* and *Caciques* been busied about, since I left the Imperial City of *Cusco*, the usual Place of their Resort when any National Affairs requires their Attention.

I will answer your Demands, (replies the trusty *Sinchal*) as far as lies in my Power. Know then, that immediately after your Departure, the Scheme which the *Curaca Robilda* had been so long projecting was brought on the Carpet; a Scheme entirely distasteful to the whole Empire of *Peru*, as you yourself must know full well by the many Petitions handed up against it from all the Provinces of the *Peruvian* Empire.

Yet notwithstanding this the *Curaca Robilda* was resolv'd to carry his Point, to effect which he employ'd all his Emissaries[1] to insure Notions among the Vulgar how advantageous it would be to the Empire of *Peru*, if this Scheme was once to take Place.

In Answer to that, the mercantile Part of the Nation, and especially those of the Imperial City of *Cusco*, plainly shew'd it would be

---

1 Emissaries: People sent on a mission to promote the interests of a cause. Used in a bad sense, implying something odious or underhanded (*OED*).

destructive and pernicious to all Trade in general, subjecting them to the Enquiry of every petty Officer; besides many other Inconveniences.[1]

It was particularly oppos'd by a Set of Men amongst whom were several *Caciques* of Note, who had formerly been *Curacas* in chief to some of our *Incas* headed by the *Curaca Posinki.*

Robilda's Party[2] stiled these Men Malecontents, and disaffected to the *Inca's* Person and Government, because their Arguments were unanswerable; but those of the Imperial City of *Cusco*, and the Generality of the People of the *Peruvian* Empire distinguish them by the honourable Appellation of Patriots,[3] being those who stand up for their Country's Good.

Indeed, if I may be allow'd to give my Opinion of what may be gather'd from the Writings of both Parties, these in Reality are as firmly attach'd to our *Inca's* true Interest as those of the *Curaca Robilda's* Clan.

Upon a Set-Day then the *Curaca Robilda* procured it to come before the Convention of States of the glorious Empire of *Peru*, and a Majority of Votes (after his usual Method)[4] for its being brought in: but when it came to be canvassed whether it shou'd pass or not, the Superiority inclin'd to the Patriots Side;[5] whereupon one of our waggish Wits compares the *Curaca Robilda's* mercenary *Bobinquos* to Men *drawn thro' a Horse-Pond befoul'd with Mire and Dirt, and all to no Purpose.*

But give me Leave, trusty *Sinchal,* how did the *Curaca Robilda* himself escape? Was he not entirely discarded the *Inca's* Service for his wild and ill-tim'd Projects? 'Tis the Belief of many, (answers *Sinchal*) most illustrious *Cacique*, that he is more firmly rivetted than ever in my Royal Master's Favour; which to the wise and considering Part of Mankind seems somewhat surprizing. But the exasperated Populace

---

1 pernicious to all Trade ...: A reference to Walpole's proposed Excise Scheme of 1734.
2 *Robilda's* Party: Whigs.
3 Appellation of Patriots: The popular name of the opposition headed by Bolingbroke, Pulteney, and Wyndham against Walpole and the Whig government.
4 usual Method: Bribery.
5 the Patriots Side: On April 11, 1733, Walpole withdrew the Excise Bill from the House of Commons rather than see it defeated.

dealt quite otherwise with him; as soon as the News spread that the *Curaca Robilda's* Scheme had miscarry'd, the Imperial City of *Cusco* was immediately illuminated, Bonfires and Bells ringing express'd the general Satisfaction of the Inhabitants: the *Curaca Robilda* was hang'd, and burn'd in Effigie[1] in several Parts of that great Town; and nothing prevented them from venting their Rage on his Person but the Respect and Duty they ow'd to their Sovereign the *Inca:* the other chief Cities and Towns following the Example of *Cusco*, express'd their happy Deliverance from this pernicious Contrivance by wonderful Demonstrations of Joy, have most of them in general return'd Thanks to their respective *Bobinquos* for their brave and strenuous Opposition of it.

Thus most noble *Loque Yupanqui*, I have endeavour'd to comply with your Request, as far as my shallow Memory will permit. You have indeed in part, (answer'd the attentive *Cacique*) but I have ten thousand Questions more to ask you concerning my Princess and *Atabalipa*, but will inform my self from her own dear Mouth concerning that Affair, having already trespassed on your Patience after so long a Fatigue.

I perceive you are tir'd, says he, and want Rest. Good Night to you, honest *Sinchal*; whatever you have Occasion of, call freely for it, and I will dispatch you away to-morrow on your Return homewards.

No sooner was *Sinchal* retir'd, but the *Cacique* muses on what he had heard. I was in Hopes (says he) to have receiv'd the News of *Curaca Robilda's* Fall; but if that did not accomplish it, sure nothing will. Unhappy *Peru!* How are you degenerated from what you were in good *Inca Virachocha's* Time! What a glorious Empire was you then! How formidable your Armies! How terrible your Canoes! How upright your *Curacas* and *Caciques!* You might justly then be esteem'd to hold the Balance of *America*; but how often lately have you shamefully purchas'd a Peace with Money from those who formerly you compell'd to sue for one? Your Trading Canoes are now taken Captive by the sluggish *Araucans*[2] without Recompence or Restitution; your

---

1 burned in *Effigie*: As the city riotously celebrated the withdrawal of the Excise Bill, Walpole and Queen Caroline were burned in effigy.
2 *Araucans*: Spaniards. The Opposition claimed that Walpole's Treaty of Seville (1729) had led to Spain's attacks on British shipping in the West Indies and to Spanish fortifications against Gibraltar.

Curacas consist only of *Robilda*'s Creatures, who consult nothing but to impoverish your People by insupportable Impositions: A man that would now arrive at Preferment must commit something deserving the greatest Punishment.

But why do I employ my Time in such useless Reflections, unless I could reform all the Abuses which so flagrantly dishonour my beloved Country; rather let me shift the Scene, and turn my Thoughts to Love and my dearest Princess, I must to-morrow dispatch away the trusty *Sinchal*, and answer the Charming *Mama Oello*'s Letter. It will be better for me, I believe, not to return immediately to the Imperial City of *Cusco*, but wait here till I receive News of the Court's Removal to the Palace of *Capuac*; then shall I find Means to see my Princess without Danger. It is now high Time for me to think of inditing her letter, that it may be in Readiness to give to *Sinchal* to-morrow Morning; the Contents of it were as follows:

The Cacique Loque Yupanqui *to the Princess of* Peru, *Daughter*, &c.
Most High and Mighty Princess,
How happy must the Cacique Loque Yupanqui *be, since the charming* Mama Oello *expresses her Satisfaction at his Return, which, without her Approbation, would have been entirely useless to him: Yes, my dearest Princess, since you graciously permit, I will fly on the Wings of soft Desire, but shall take Care to pay an implicite Obedience to your Directions, both as to Time and Place. But how uneasy shall I be till that bright Day appears which shall give the lovely* Mama Oello *to the longing Eyes of her humble Adorer,*
LOQUE YUPANQUI.

Early the next Morning the happy *Cacique* deliver'd his Answer to *Sinchal* with Orders that he should hasten back as fast as possible to his Princess: he himself thought it advisable to stay behind till he shou'd hear of the Court's Removal to the Palace of *Capuac*, which he in a little time was advertised of it by means of his fair *Mama Oello*.

Now he prepares with all Diligence for his Return to the glorious Empire of *Peru*, and *incog.*[1] enters the Province of *Capuany*. He is inform'd by the host where he stopt to refresh himself, that Prince

---

1 *incog.*: Incognito; in disguise.

Atabalipa was not yet come, that it was strongly rumour'd abroad, his intended Journey to *Peru* was entirely laid aside; that, nevertheless the Princess *Mama Oello* was to espouse him by Proxy,[1] and so to be sent to the Province of *Quito*: That in order to which her Royal Highness had but few Days before made Choice of *Yaya Napa*,[2] a near Relation of the Noble *Cacique Loque Yupanqui*, (who was sometime ago forbid the Court) to accompany her to the Prince of *Quito*.

The *Cacique* thank'd his Landlord for his courteous Information, thinking it most advisable to send to his Sister *Yaya Napa* first, that he might consult with her the proper Means of seeing his dearest Princess; he therefore dispatch'd away an hir'd Servant of his Host's to the Palace of *Capuac*, with a Letter to his Sister desiring her Company. The Messenger soon arriv'd at the Palace of *Capuac*, and deliver'd his Letter to the Lady *Yaya Napa*, who immediately comply'd with her dearest Brother's Desires.

After a Meeting full of Brotherly Love and Affection, they began to consult about the main Affair, how the *Cacique* might safely see his Princess. I am acquainted with a *Bobinquo* who lives near this place, (says the compassionate *Yaya Napa*) in whose Gardens my Royal Mistress often diverts herself in an Evening: I have Interest enough with this *Bobinquo*, if you like my Contrivance, to get you admitted into his House as his Gardener; and under that Disguise you may securely converse with the Princess *Mama Oello*.

I thank you, my dearest *Yaya Napa* (says the passionate *Cacique*) for this lucky Thought, which will succeed, I hope, according to my Wishes: let us hasten then, and put our Designs in Execution; for I burn to throw myself at the Feet of the Charming *Mama Oello*. Accordingly the impatient *Cacique* discharged his Host, and was conducted by his Sister to the *Bobinquo*'s House, to whom she introduced her Brother, and unravell'd the whole Secret. The *Bobinquo* receiv'd the *Cacique* in a very kind Manner, and told him he was ready to serve him to the utmost Stretch of his Capacity, although he should thereby incur the *Inca*'s Displeasure.

---

1 espouse him by Proxy: Mama Oello would wed the Prince through a substitute, a person appointed to act in his place for the ceremony in Peru. This is another example of Atabalipa's disinterestedness in marrying the Princess except for political purposes.
2 *Yaya Napa*: Unidentified in the Key.

The over-joy'd *Cacique* thank'd him for his great Civility, and accordingly put on his Gardener's Habit. In the mean Time *Yaya Napa* hastens away to the Palace of *Capuac*, to acquaint her Royal Mistress of all that had pass'd, as well of her dearest *Cacique's* Arrival, as the Stratagem made Use of to procure an Interview between them.

. In a lucky Hour, says the fair Princess (overjoy'd at this agreeable News) did I chuse you, charming *Yaya Napa*, from the midst of the bright Circle of Ladies that adorn this illustrious Court; O dearer to me than Sister, tho' I dare not make thee so: They shall never tare thee from this Breast, tho' they do thy Noble Brother. You shall always remain with me, the only Comfort I shall have left to calm the Sea of Troubles that now hastens to overwhelm me: But To-morrow-Night I will see my dearest *Cacique*, and till then endeavour to compose myself. Accordingly she bids *Yaya Napa* send her Brother Intelligence that she would take an Airing in the *Bobinquo's* Gardens the next Evening.

How restless these impatient Lovers passed that Night may be easily guess'd at; at last the long desir'd Minute comes, when the Princess enter'd the Garden, as usual, dismissing all her Attendants but the fair *Yaya Napa*, seating herself in a Cypress-Grove, there expecting her dearest *Cacique*. The transported Swain, in a Gardener's Dress to prevent all Suspicion, now trembling draws near, and presents her with a curious Nosegay of Roses and Carnations. The fair *Mama Oello*, lost in Thought, lifts up her Eyes gently, and seeing her dearest *Cacique* so near, being overpower'd at the Sight, closes 'em again in a fainting Fit. The distracted *Cacique* could not forbear taking her in his Arms, altho' had he been overseen, it must have prov'd his utter Ruin; whilst the officious *Yaya Napa*, who was the only Person present, hasten'd to the nearest Fountain for Water, and after a second or third sprinkling, the swooning Fair began to revive, and finding her self in the Arms of her beloved *Cacique*; Oh! Ye Gods! says she, *what do I see! here let me die, and never enter the Palace of Capuac more: With what Pleasure could I end my Miseries and Life in these dear Arms! But, what have I let drop?* (somewhat recovering herself) *Expressions, I fear, too unguarded for the Princess of Peru to utter. And art thou not contented, most illustrious Cacique, to bring me all the Fragrance the World contains center'd in thyself, but must you give me also the selected Sweets,* (says she smelling to the Nosegay) *that this Garden affords?*

'Tis in Yourself, your own incomparable Self, (replies the trans-ported *Loque Yupanqui* interrupting her) that not only the Sweets of this delicious Place but of the whole Universe are compriz'd. Talk not of dying, my Princess, 'tis your unfortunate *Cacique* that must die: You shall live long, and be happy in the Embraces of *Atabalipa*, Prince of *Quito*, while the miserable *Loque Yupanqui*, not able to endure that hateful Consummation, will soon put an End to his wretched Life.

Why those killing Words to me? (answers the fair *Mama Oello*) why any Talk of *Atabalipa*? You know my Heart is as true to you as the Needle to the Pole; every Thing conspires to compleat my Sorrows, and there is no Redress, nor any Hopes on which my ship-wreck'd Love may anchor: But till that fatal Day that will force me from this dear Retreat, and those dearer Arms to the ungrateful *Atabalipa*'s, will I repeat this Evening's Delights, and after that bid a long Farewel to every Thing that's pleasant.

I know you must be ever lost to me, answer'd the amorous *Cacique*, and therefore have been long arming myself with all the Philosophy I am Master of against that fatal Time; but in vain, I can never survive it. I have heard, since my Arrival in this Province of *Capuany*, tho' you, my fairest Princess, have been cautious in discovering the dis-tasteful News; that your Marriage with *Attabalipa*[1] is irrevocable, and that an extravagant Character of him has been industriously spread up and down this glorious Empire in the publick Prints: One tells us, COURTESY *and* AFFABILITY *are a part of his Constitution.* But how is this consistent, when you, my Princess, on whom, and only whom it ought to have been bestow'd, have been entirely insensible of it? Had I been Prince *Atabalipa*, had I been that happy *Cacique*, swift as Light-ning would I have flown to have paid my Devoirs[2] to you; no Com-pliments of the *Amanta*'s or *Vimo*'s should have stopt me. His Complaisance,[3] his ingenious Advocate tells us, costs his Highness no Pains; and I believe that indeed to be the only true Part of the Description.

'Tis true, illustrious *Cacique*, answers the disconsolate *Mama Oello*, what you say is too true; but alas! how can I help it? Who amongst us

---

1 *Attabalipa:* The spelling of his name changes occasionally from one "t" to two.
2 Devoirs: Dutiful respects, courteous attentions (*OED*).
3 Complaisance: Desire and care to please; courtesy, politeness (*OED*).

all can resist Fate? O invisible PACHACHAMAC,[1] and our Father the SUN! How can you be said to be just, when you are thus partial? How deplorable is my Condition? Under what an unfortunate Planet was I born? But yet, says she, this present Moment will I enjoy, in Spite of you, O invisible PACHACHAMAC, or our Father the SUN.

Thus did this faithful Couple pass the Hours away in soft Complaint and amorous Converse, till the good-natur'd and beautiful *Yaya Napa* returning from a Walk of Orange-Trees, where she had retreated to favour the Lovers in their Converse, told 'em the Clock had struck One, and it was Time to part. They were oblig'd to submit to pressing Necessity, and after mutual Promises of seeing each other every Evening, whilst the Court remain'd at the Palace of *Capuac*, retir'd, the *Cacique* to his Bed, and the Princess to the Palace of *Capuac*; where musing on her past Evening's Conversation, and admiring the Composure of her beloved *Cacique*'s Present, she observ'd in the middle of it a Paper artfully wrought up: when unfolding it, she found the following Copy of Verses; which we insert, as they are found in the Original, only with this Alteration, that we have changed the *Indian* Names which are rough, and not sonorous in Verse, for some made Use of by the ancient Heathen Poets.

On a NOSEGAY presented to the Princess MAMA OELLO.

I.

For once, my Princess, learn to prize
  Thy Beauty by a Flower;
And think how both may charm the Sense,
  Yet neither live an Hour.

II.

Think that Thyself art planted here,
  But to be pluck'd by Man;
And think how short is Beauty's Date;
  If Life is but a Span.

---

1 *PACHACHAMAC:* Appeared earlier in the text as *Pacha Camac*.

III.

Then MAMA, *seize the flying Bliss,*
  Nor foolishly rely
On charms that for a Moment's Bloom;
  But ev'n in blooming die.

IV.

Such Roses wanton on thy Cheeks,
  And put such Beauties on;
This Blushes with a stronger Red,
  To see itself outdone.

V.

While on thy Breasts the Lillies smile,
  They mourn in secret there,
To see those fragrant Rivals rise
  More soft, and sweet, and fair.

VI.

Think on their Doom, fair Nymph, to thine;
  Then be the Thought apply'd:
And the same Cause at once must raise,
  And mortify thy Pride.

VII.

Oh! Could those Flowers, that once were Boys,[1]
  To know their Bliss attain;
How would they wish to be transform'd
  From Flowers to Boys again.

VIII.

Had e'er Narcissus[2] *view'd that Face;*
  He had renounc'd his Pride:

---

1 *once were Boys*: Refers to the following stanzas in which are described boys transformed to flowers.
2 Narcissus: In *Ovid's Metamorphoses*, a beautiful youth who fell in love with his own
   reflection and, realizing he could never possess the vision, died. He was transformed
   into a flower with white petals and a yellow centre (III.353ff).

Nor for his own, but Mama's *Charms,*
The blooming Youth had dy'd.

IX.

Or, could fair Hyacinth[1] *revive,*
And all his Charms renew,
The Boy had scorn'd Celestial Joys,
And left his God for You.

And is it possible, says she, that Prince *Atabalipa*, with all the Accomplishments they say he is Master of, can produce such a Proof of his Wit and Gallantry as this; when, as my *Cacique* well observes, he has never given himself the Trouble of coming or writing? Unhappy Princess! Unfortunate *Mama Oello*! Why was I not the Daughter of one who sues for the Scraps of the well-fed Rich from Door to Door? Then might I have singled out the Man I lov'd; then might I have shar'd the pleasant Toil of the Day with him, and at Night sate down under the green Turf to what the invisible PACHACHAMAC, and our Father the SUN had granted to our Prayers *with Content*. O miserable Restraint! O free, yet captive Princess! What availeth thy wide and far stretched Greatness, if you must be a *State-Slave?* I am, indeed, somewhat like the gaudy Vegetable;[2] my charming *Cacique* resembles me too: but the Emblem would have been more exact had it been of the *sensitive* Plant; for, like that, shall I shrink and withdraw myself from the Hand that is to pluck me.

In such melancholy Reflections as these did the disconsolate *Mama Oello* waste away a great Part of the Night, till the God of Sleep with his Leaden Wand lock'd up her Eyes and Sorrows together for some short Interval of Time: but *Phoebus*[3] being now almost half advanc'd to his middle Station, too soon awakens both. The Peerless

---

1   *Hyacinth:* Hyacinthus, beloved of the god Apollo, was struck and killed by a discus. From his blood sprung up a crimson flower on which Apollo inscribed "Ai, Ai," Greek for "Alas!" (Ovid's *Met*.X.164ff).

2   gaudy: Highly ornate, showy, brilliantly fine. Vegetable: living and growing as a plant or organism endowed with the lowest form of life. Mamo Oello may be picking up on the flower imagery of Cacique's verses, comparing herself to an attractive plant that is used and consumed to benefit others.

3   *Phoebus:* The sun.

Fair knocks for her favourite *Yaya Napa*; and rising, adds new Lustre to the Day.

How does lazy Time, says she, my faithful *Yaya Napa*, seem to flag his Wings whilst I am absent from my *Loque Yupanqui*? I thank you, however, drowsy God of Sleep, that I have been some few Hours lost to Thought and Woe: The heavy Gloom, that constantly hangs o'er my Soul, has for this short Space quitted Possession; but, I fear, will soon return: yet must I dissemble, put on the Vizor,[1] gay Looks and pleasant Mirth; very unsuitable to the present Tenour of my Soul! So speaking she bends her Steps with her Favourite to the publick Room of State, with a feigned, but becoming Cheerfulness.

The natural Sympathy that is between Lovers produced almost the same Thoughts in the Breast of the restless *Cacique*; he could not build any Hopes on the Continuance of this Interview with his Princess, knowing *Atabalipa*, Prince of *Quito*, would shortly, either in Person, or by Proxy, espouse the fair *Mama Oello*; both which were confidently reported, and both alike fatal to him: He resolves, therefore, to inform himself, if possible, from the courteous *Bobinquo*, whether the Marriage was to be perform'd personally or not: to put that Question to his Princess, he thought would be ungrateful: and besides, she was kept in so much Ignorance, tho' the principal Person concern'd, that it was to be doubted whether she could resolve him when or how she was to be dispos'd of.

He therefore after Dinner asks his kind Entertainer, if it would be agreeable to him to pass an Hour or two away in the Garden? Upon the *Bobinquo's* compliance, the disguis'd *Cacique* intices him to the same Cypress-Shade, in which he had been so happy the Evening before, and hoped shortly to be so again. Well, says he, my Friend; for I must, and will call you by that Name, since the uncommon Civility you have shewn me highly deserves the title: what News does the *Peruvian* Court afford? For, tho' I am so near it, which you know has not been long; yet do I wander as much in the Dark, in that Affair, as if my own Province now detain'd me beyond the great River *Apurimac*.

The Eyes and Tongues of this mighty Empire, reply'd the good-natur'd *Bobinquo*, are all now wholly employ'd on this intended

---

1   Vizor: Mask.

Marriage betwixt the *Princess Royal* and *Atabalipa*, Prince of *Quito*; but how, or when, where, or in what Manner it is to be solemniz'd, I don't find that any Dependance can be form'd. Self-Contradiction, in this Case, reigns; our publick Intelligence one while affirming, and at other Times denying what before it asserted: However, this is certain, that it is to be; accordingly, Badges, and Marks of the highest Distinction and Honour[1] have been transmitted to him; tho' it would seem not worth his Acceptance, since not worth coming after: He has been presented with Jewels to hang in his Ears, after they are bored; and the black Tress to tye round his Head: Verses and Orations on his illustrious Self and Family have deduced his Original from the invisible PACHACHAMAC, and our Father the SUN: By them he is already deify'd, and inscrib'd amongst the Number of the Gods.

But you know full well, most illustrious *Cacique*, says he, all these Arts to render him dazling bright and glaring, serve only to darken him in the Esteem of the disconsolate Princess *Mama Oello*: how your Presence may dry up her Tears I cannot tell; but 'tis reported, and that not without some Foundation of Belief, that they incessantly flow from Morning to Night: that Prince *Atabalipa*'s Absence will be no Disappointment to her, tho' it may to several others, where Interest makes his Presence needful: Nay, even Numbers of People, as well *Curacas*, *Caciques*, as *Bobinquos*, have been so fantastical as to imitate *Atabalipa*'s favourite Colour in their Garbs and Dress; the Colour of *Quito* being now all the Mode.

I must not, however, forget one remarkable Story related in this Affair, which, notwithstanding all your present Gravity, I hope will make you smile; The disconsolate *Mama Oello* being found some time ago by her Sisters the other Princesses in Tears; Why all this Grief, happy Princess, say the young Ladies? Mirth and Gladness should be your Portion now, for you are sure of an illustrious Prince to your Husband. But no one, except the invisible PACHACHAMAC, and our Father the SUN, can certify wherever we shall have one.

What fresh Materials for News the Court may have furnish'd out since I was there I cannot tell, neither is it in my Power to acquaint

---

1 Marks of Honour: "On the 15th July 1733 the P[rince] of Or[ange] was invested with the Order of the Garter at the Hague" [Key].

you with any thing else worthy your Notice, unless 'tis the Removal of the wise and learned *Curaca Sinchi*, and the valiant and couragious *Cacique Cobinqui*:[1] But you'll excuse my entering upon the particular Causes of this our great Loss; (for I call it so, it being universal to the whole *Peruvian* Empire) being engaged to meet some Friends this Afternoon at a neighbouring *Bobinquo*'s. I will not make you the Compliment of going with me, because I know you are at present indispos'd to all Company; but beg, illustrious *Cacique*, you will pardon my Absence. So saying he departed, and left the *Cacique* to himself.

A strange Account I think, says the pondering *Loque Yupanqui*, I have heard, which leaves me as much in the Dark as I was before: It is to be, he says, but when, where, or in what Manner he knows not, and thereupon forms a Certainty out of an Uncertainty; yet this I am secure of, as may be easily gather'd from his Discourse, my Princess's Love: So far am I happy, but what is Love, if not enjoy'd? The Impossibility of this renders me again miserable. As to the Prince of *Quito*'s Honours, Titles, Dignities, I envy him not the Possession of them, or any earthly Grandeur the giddy World can heap on him, but that of my Princess: Let Orators and Bards make a God of him, I shall not envy him Heaven itself, if he will but leave my Princess here below. But to what Purpose do I dwell on this melancholy Subject, cherish Woe, and contemplate my own Misfortunes? I find I am not the only Man or *Cacique*, that is at present singled out by the invisible PACHACHAMAC and our Father the SUN, to be the Sport of Fortune; the sage *Curaca Sinchi*, and the brave *Cacique Cobinqui* bear a Part with me: But say what could occasion such a Change, ungrateful I am sure to the *Peruvian* Empire, as well as prejudicial to my once Royal Master? All this must come from the *Curaca Robilda*, that cunning old Fox; for, can *Peru* produce any pernicious Alteration that was not first contriv'd by him? Who, now the Rudder's gone, can steer the Helm? Who can supply the judicious *Curaca Sinchi*'s Place? 'Tis a Weight too heavy for common Shoulders to sustain, and therefore adapted to no one but *Curacas* of uncommon Ingenuity and Penetration, such as

---

1 *Curaca Sinchi, Cacique Cobinqui*: The Earl of Chesterfield was dismissed by the King on April 13, 1733, and Viscount Cobham lost his place and his regiment for opposing Walpole's Excise Bill.

Sinchi is; but where shall we find such another now he is gone? How long did the ingenious Artist, as History reports, keep his Enemy without the Walls, and maintain a perfect Union within by his prudent Councels and Advice? So long has this *Curaca* diverted our Foes from Abroad by his wise Negotiations, and heal'd our private Differences by a well-temper'd and prudent Moderation, just to his royal Master, our most sacred *Inca*, true to his Country, indefatigable in serving both; his Affability, Courtesy, Complaisance, and his Capacity in publick Affairs, let the Provinces of *Havisca*, *Tuna*, *Chuncuri*, *Pucana*, *Muyun Cuyu*, *Charcas*, and *Collasuyu* confess, as dear and agreeable did *Sinchi's* blameless Conduct render him to them as his matchless Deportment deserv'd.

Again, who shall essay to enumerate the brave Actions of the valiant *Cacique Cobinqui*? What Nation has been able to withstand his victorious Sword? For thirty tedious Winters, and as many sultry Summers, has *Peru* seen him head Part of her Armies, and in all her Wars (since he has been a Commander) given Proofs of an undaunted Courage. Must then the Wise and Brave truckle[1] to the capricious Humour of this *Curaca Robilda*? Cannot Wisdom secure, nor Valour save? No; I find that the wise Man, who will not come into his Measures, must be discarded; and the couragious Man, that will not run his Lengths, must quit his glorious Profession: But, sure, it wo'n't[2] be always so. Look down, O invisible PACHACHAMAC, and our Father the SUN, and behold Extortion, Bribery, and Corruption, triumphantly lording it over your Favourite Empire; whilst Virtue, Probity, and true Merit skulk about from Place to Place entirely disregarded: But, soft! Methinks, an unusual Fragrance strikes my ravish'd Senses far sweeter than any that this delightful Place can afford. So saying, he leaves at once his Arbour and Meditations, and advancing sees his Princess, who was just enter'd the Garden with the fair *Yaya Napa*, coming towards him.

With the greatest Restraint upon his Passion, for Fear of being overseen, the lovesick *Loque Yupanqui* retires again into the Cypress-Shade, and there expects his charming *Mama Oello*.

---

1   truckle: To take a subordinate or inferior position; to be subservient, to submit, to give precedence (*OED*).
2   wo'n't: Contraction of "would not."

For many tedious Minutes and Hours, which to me seem Months and Days, says the enamour'd *Cacique* to his dearest Princess upon her entering the Arbour, have these longing Eyes waited for the Sunshine of your Presence? 'Tis that dispels all my Cares, sooths all my Misfortunes; and for the Time it lasts, renders me entirely happy.

Illustrious *Cacique*, answer'd the Princess, I take as much Satisfaction in your dear Company, as 'tis possible for you to enjoy in mine; tho' I can't express myself in such gallant Terms as you: But (added she, letting fall some pearly Tears) how long this Pleasure may last I can't determine. I perceive (says she looking in a languishing Manner upon him) you would be better pleas'd to hear your Destiny and mine from me than any one else, could I but inform you: but alas! my *Cacique*, I am kept so much in the Dark myself, as to that Affair, that I know but very little of it; yet that very little is by far too much.

With less Regret, reply'd the Gallant *Loque Yupanqui*, most adorable Princess, could I hear you pronounce my Doom than any other, because I could for ever dwell with Attention on the soft Musick of your Voice: which in one Respect, tho' it would be piercing and killing; yet in another it would be medecinal and healing.

If I could unravel the whole Secret concerning myself, which lyes so close conceal'd in my Royal Father's and the *Curaca Robilda's* Breast, yet would the Task be too ungrateful, and my faithful Tongue unwilling to perform so distasteful an Office, would soon faulter in my Mouth. But let us shift this Talk, and from so melancholy a Subject think of somewhat more entertaining. I did not know, illustrious *Cacique*, says the Princess, till very lately that you were a Favourite of the Muses: I thank you for the present you conceal'd in your Nosegay last Night; the Sight of some more of your Performances would oblige me very much, as well as divert our Melancholly a little.

Charming *Mama Oello*, dearest Princess, answers the enamour'd *Cacique*, I never pretended to Poetry in my Life: but if ever any thing worth Notice dropp'd from my Pen, 'twas when the Thoughts of my Princess inspir'd me. I am glad, replies the fair *Mama Oello*, I have so much Influence over you; and therefore will exert it, by commanding you to repeat, or shew me some more of your Works: (for more you must have I am certain) those you favour'd me with seem not to be the Flights of a young Beginner, but to flow from a Pen well vers'd in that harmonious Art.

Can I any Ways disobey my Princess? says the brave *Loque Yupanqui*, (putting his Hand in his Pocket) I should have a Copy of Verses, which I compos'd on your own dear Self, when I was in my Northern Confinement beyond the great River *Apurimac*; after (proceeds he, pulling out a Paper) I had ransack'd Heaven and Earth, the Sea and Air, to find out amongst the cœlestial Inhabitants above, or the terrestrial below, or the Goddesses of the liquid Deep, one that was comparable to my far surpassing Princess; and finding it all to no Purpose, that the four Regions could not produce your Likeness, the following Thoughts presented themselves to me, which I now offer to my dearest Charmer: So saying, he gave her the Paper; I am afraid, if that be the Subject-Matter, answers the Princess, that your good Opinion of me has transported you too far; and, instead of making a *Simile*, you seem by your own Discourse to have soar'd beyond an *Hyperbole*, if that is possible: but pray (returning him the Verses) let me hear you read them, and then I shall be a better Judge. The *Cacique* taking the Paper, and kissing the fair Hand that restor'd it, read as follows. We observe the same Method here as in the preceding Verses.

MAMA OELLO, a SIMILE.

The antient Bards who felt Love's piercing Fires,
And by Enjoyment eas'd their fierce Desires;
Those Charms they tasted, and the sweet Delights
Of Vows by Days, and Ecstacies by Night.
Each form'd his Muse, as she inspir'd, repaid;
Each form'd his Goddess of some mortal Maid,
Liken'd her beauteous Charms as was his Love,
To all that e're was great and good above.
Thus fair Corinna *in Love's softest Strain*
Brightens as Venus *rising from the Main.*[1]
Thus we find Delia *by* Tibullus *drawn,*
Like silver Phoebe[2] *tripping o'er the Lawn.*
Lycoris *too, as* Gallus *sweetly sung,*

---

1   *Venus … Main*: Goddess of beauty and sensual love. The reference to her rising from the ocean alludes to Botticelli's famous painting "The Birth of Venus."
2   Phoebe: Goddess of the moon, Diana or Artemis.

With all the easy Softness of his Tongue,
Had Majesty superior in her Face,
And awful Juno[1] *heighten'd every Grace.*
Feign would I thus my Charming Princess paint,
But why? alas! those Images are faint;
Those heavenly Beauties are compriz'd in one,
And every goddess meets in her alone.
In her shines forth the lovely Cyprian Dame,[2]
Youth, Beauty, Vigour, all but the lascivious Flame:
She seems Diana[3] *with her silver Hair,*
As greatly virtuous, and divinely fair.
Saturnia's[4] *State in all the Nymph is seen,*
She moves a Goddess, and she speaks a Queen:
Then who a proper Simile *can find,*
Since Heaven collected scarce can paint her Mind:
Her own Antithesis[5] *must match the Fair,*
And none but MAMA *with her Self compare.*

Very great Encomiums[6] indeed, says the Princess, and not only superior to my Deserts, I believe, but to those of any Mortal living. She had scarce utter'd these Words but the fair and faithful *Yaya Napa* hurry'd into the Arbour with Advice that the Empress of *Peru* was just entering the Garden. The affrighted *Cacique* retir'd in Haste by a Back-door into the *Bobinquo*'s House, and the Princess advanc'd out of the Arbour into a walk to meet her Royal Mother.

You have had a long Airing, Princess Royal, says the Empress; sure this Garden is very tempting, that it engrosses so much of your Time; Night after Night you constantly frequent it, and this Spot of Ground seems to be your sole Delight.

---

1   Juno: Goddess, wife of Jupiter.
2   Cyprian *Dame:* Venus, in ancient times worshipped in Cyprus, an island in the eastern Mediterranean.
3   Diana: Goddess of the moon; patroness of virginity and of hunting.
4   *Saturnia:* A combination of Saturnalia, a period of unrestrained licence and revelry, and the astrological sign of Saturn, symbolic of remoteness, slowness of movement, causing coldness or gloominess.
5   Antithesis: In rhetoric, an opposition or contrast of ideas.
6   Encomiums: Formal or high-flown expressions of praise (*OED*).

Retirement, please your Majesty, answers the Princess, is sometimes grateful; and indeed, with your Royal Leave, to me more pleasing than the Noise, Hurry and Pomp of Courts. You must talk now, reply'd the Empress, contrary to your own Sentiments; Splendor and glorious Appearances, such as the *Peruvian* Court affords, captivates the Hearts of all young Persons in general, how happy would the Majority of the Universe, that are of our Sex, think themselves, were they but in your Condition; to be Princess Royal of the mighty Empire of *Peru*, to possess every thing that your Heart can wish for or desire, to be happy in the Arms of a young and powerful Prince, as *Atabalipa* Prince of *Quito* is, are Blessings which the invisible PACHACHAMAC, and our Father the SUN, has reserv'd in Store only to bestow on the Princess Royal of *Peru*. The Blessings your Majesty mentions are too valuable for any one Mortal to possess, or even hope for: my Expectations, tho' towering enough, soar not so high as what your Majesty represents. I am, indeed, in the first place, indebted to the invisible PACHACHAMAC, and our Father the SUN, for my illustrious Descent; and next to my royal Father the *Inca*, and Yourself, for that tender Regard Ye have always shewn; but who I may thank (says she sighing) for matching me to *Atabalipa* Prince of *Quito* I can't tell: It could never be ordain'd by the invisible PACHACHAMAC, or our Father the SUN, it could never be contriv'd by the Royal *Inca* my Father, or Yourself, because all Ye, I am perswaded, firmly interest Yourselves in my Welfare and Happiness. From whence then must it proceed, or who can be the Author but the *Curaca Robilda*, or *Quatzultoult* the God of the Air, and an Enemy to this mighty Empire. I seem, added the Princess weeping, to be *Atabalipa's* Aversion, since, tho' I have been contracted to him so many Moons, yet have I never receiv'd the least Mark of his Esteem, either in Person or by Proxy; how then can I be said to be happy in his Arms, whilst they seem to be as it were shut against me; and I alas! am constrain'd to force them open much against my own Will, and I believe against his?

No, Princess, says the Royal Empress, he loves you, he's enamour'd with you, altho' he never saw you; your Picture has charm'd his Eyes already, and what must the Original do? The Fame of Beauty flies swift, very swift, and often wounds before the Object is seen. I might add here important Reasons which, were the Prince of *Quito* less agreeable, would be able to outweigh any Consideration. But I think the Air is somewhat cool, 'tis now Time for us to return to the Palace of *Capuac.*

The Princess was obliged to leave her beloved Garden, and much more beloved *Cacique*, without seeing him any more that Night; she wip'd her Eyes, and put on her usual, tho' now feign'd Smiles, she accompany'd the Empress into the Drawing-Room: but how insipid did all the Company appear to her! She was present and absent at the same time. She play'd indeed at *Noveda*, an *Indian* Game, to oblige the Princesses her Sisters, and the other Ladies, but hardly knew what she did, or what she said.

At last the wish'd for Hour of Repose came, and as soon as the faithful *Yaya Napa* and she were retir'd into her own Apartment her Thoughts immediately arrest the dear Bower, and her dearer *Cacique*. Why, says she, O invisible PACHACHAMAC, and our Father the SUN! did you permit the Empress to interrupt me and my lovely *Loque Yupanqui*? Have we drawn down the Envy of the Gods upon us as well as Men? Then is our Fate irreversible. My Royal Mother mentions nothing but Happiness and Blessings, but I fear Misery and Discontent will be my Portion. Tell me, faithful *Yaya Napa*, tell me, my sole Comfort, now thy Brother's absent, can you find nothing to sooth my Affliction? No Remedy for my Disease? If to act always by Constraint, to speak, and be obliged almost to think contrary to my Inclinations? If to know nothing at present hardly but Woe, and to expect nothing for the future but Uneasiness? If these are Blessings, then are they plentifully bestow'd on me. 'Tis the Part of a desponding Mind to be so very much dejected, answers the good-natur'd *Yaya Napa*, Things may fall out, my royal Mistress, beyond our Expectation; you see *Attabalipa* is not yet come, and perhaps, may not come at all. What if he is not, or what if he shou'dn't? reply'd the Princess hastily, yet shall I be sent over to him like a Victim to the Altar. It may be so, says the soothing *Yaya Napa*, but then you know there are strong Dissentions Abroad now at *Policany*,[1] occasion'd by their electing a new

---

1 Dissentions ... at *Policany*: Under the influence of France, Polish nobles elected Stanislas Lesczynski, father-in-law of Louis XV, king, a second time. Russia and Austria induced a minority to choose Augustus III, Elector of Saxony, and supported the election by the presence of troops in Poland. France, Spain, and Sardinia

King, in which all the Powers of *America* seem to be concern'd. Should a lucky War now break out, it might be, perhaps, of some Service to you, by diverting *Atabalipa* from the inglorious Pursuits of Love (as he terms it, to be sure) to the more glorious Profession of Arms. What the Fate of War may produce, no one (except the invisible PACHACHAMAC, and our Father the SUN) can foresee: *Atabalipa* may fall in Battle, or *Atabalipa* may return victorious; if the former, it eases you of the heaviest part of your Misfortunes at once: if the latter, whatever Trophies he brings home will be thrown at your Feet, and add a brighter Lustre to the intended Nuptials.

You talk extravagantly, answer'd the Princess, I ha'n't Patience to hear you any longer; *Atabalipa* has nothing to do in the Affairs of *Policany*: that will do us no Good. Death! nothing but Death, either mine or his, can put an End to my Misfortunes. O ye Sea-gods, if he does prepare for *Peru*, whilst he is on your Element bury him in the Deep.

But stay, wicked Princess, as well as unfortunate, why do you imprecate an undeserved Fate on an innocent Prince, rather let the ravenous Billows swallow me up in my Passage, if I must be sent to him, or drive me to some unknown part of the World, where I may never see *Quito* or *Peru*. Thus did the disconsolate *Mama Oello* vent her Complaint to the faithful *Yaya Napa*, till Nature at last prevail'd, and she fell into a Doze.

In the mean Time the most melancholy Thoughts exercis'd the now half distracted *Cacique*; he foreboded some extraordinary Misfortune attending for which he could give no Reason. To be thus interrupted in his Happiness was almost Death to him; but alas! a far greater Tryal of his Patience was immediately to ensue.

The next Morning he receiv'd a Note from his Sister *Yaya Napa*, which express'd that Prince *Atabalipa* would certainly be at the Imperial City of *Cusco* in less than the Space of a Moon,[1] in Order person-

---

took up arms for Stanislas (1733-35). The 1731 Treaty of Vienna stipulated that Britain should support Austria with troops; however, Walpole convinced the King to put off war at least until after the 1734 general election. The Dutch had signed a treaty of neutrality with France. The marriage between the British Princess Royal, Anne, and the Prince of Orange, was, in part, to allow Britain to extricate itself from the demands of the Treaty of Vienna and offer itself, with Holland, as a mediator between the warring powers.

1 Space of a Moon: The Prince of Orange arrived in London on November 7, 1733.

ally to espouse his dearest Princess; that the Empress entertain'd some Suspicion of her Daughter on his Account, because she had of late so often frequented that *Bobinquo*'s Garden, who was a particular Acquaintance of the fair *Yaya Napa*. Surpriz'd, astonish'd, and confounded, he first curs'd his Fate, and then the *Curaca Robilda*, as Author of his Misfortunes. ★ ★ ★ ★ ★ ★ ★

Here the Original breaks off, but to be continued as soon as the Remainder comes to Hand,

FINIS.

Appendix D:
[*George Lyttelton*],[1] Letters from a Persian in England, to his Friend at Ispahan.
4th ed., Corrected (London, 1735).

To the Bookseller.

SIR,

I NEED not acquaint you by what Accident these Letters were put into my Hands, and what Pains I have taken in translating them; I will only say, that having been long a Scholar to the late most learned Mr. *Dadichy,* Interpreter of the Oriental Languages, I have acquir'd Skill enough in the *Persian* Tongue, to be able to give the Sense of them pretty justly; though I must acknowledge my Translation far inferior to the *Eastern Sublimity* of the Original, which no *English* Expression can come up to, and which no *English* Reader wou'd admire.

I am aware that some People may suspect that the Character of a *Persian* is *Fictitious,* as many such Counterfeits have appear'd both in *France* and *England.* But whoever reads them with Attention, will be convinc'd, that they are certainly the Work of a perfect Stranger. The Observations are so *Foreign* and *out of the Way,* such *remote Hints* and *imperfect Notions* are taken up, *our present happy Condition* is in all Respects *so ill understood,* that it is hardly possible any *Englishman* shou'd be the *Author.*

Yet as there is a Pleasure in knowing how Things *Here* affect a Foreigner, though his Conceptions of them be ever so extravagant, I

---

1 George Lyttelton: 1709-73. He joined the opposition to Walpole in 1731, authored several articles for the *Craftsman,* and was elected to the House of Commons in 1735. He was described as "an amiable, absent-minded man, of unimpeachable integrity and benevolent character, with strong religious connections and respectable talents." Unfortunately, "his ignorance of the world and his unreadiness in debate made him a poor practical politician" (Barker, *DNB* 12:371). His *Letters from a Persian in England,* based on Montesquieu's *Persian Letters* (1721), went through four editions in 1735. Lyttelton is perhaps best known for his active support of the arts, for which Henry Fielding dedicated *Tom Jones* to him in 1749.

think you may venture to expose them to the Eyes of the World, the rather because it is plain the Man who wrote them is a Lover of Liberty; and must be suppos'd more impartial than our own Country-men when they speak of their own admir'd Customs, and favourite Opinions.

I have nothing further to add, but that it is a *great Pity* they are not recommended to the Publick by a Dedication to *some Great Man about the Court*,[1] who wou'd have Patroniz'd them *for the Freedom of their Stile*; but the Publisher not having the Honour to be acquainted with any Body *There*, they must want that inestimable Advantage, and trust entirely to the Candour of the Reader.

I am,

Sir,

Your most humble Servant.

Letters from a Persian in England

LETTER I
SELIM *TO* MIRZA *at* Ispahan.
From *London*.

Thou knowest, my dearest *MIRZA*, the Reasons that moved me to leave my Country, and visit *England*; thou wast thyself, in a great Measure, the Cause of it. The Relations we receiv'd from our Friend *Usbec*[2] of those Parts of *Europe* which he had seen rais'd in us an ardent Desire to know the rest, and particularly *this famous Island*, of which, not having been there himself, he cou'd give us but imperfect Accounts.

By his Persuasion we determin'd to travel *thither*, but when we

---

1 *some Great Man about the Court*: Sir Robert Walpole was often referred to as the "Great Man" for his wealth and power rather than his moral greatness. Walpole, who was notorious for his suspicion of the arts, would not patronize writers "*for the Freedom of their Stile*," but would attempt to censor or imprison them for any condemnation of his ministry.

2 *Usbec*: The hero of Montesquieu's *Persian Letters* (1721), Usbec writes from France to his wives in his harem, his eunuchs, and his friends, with his observations on French society, politics, and religion.

were just ready to set out, the sublime Orders of the Sophi our Master,[1] detain'd thee at the Feet of his sacred Throne.

Unwilling as I was to go alone, I yielded to thy Importunities, and was content to live single among Strangers and Enemies to the Faith, that I might be able to gratify thy Thirst for Knowledge.

My Voyage was Prosperous, and I find this Country well worthy our Curiosity. The Recommendations given me by *Usbec* to some *English* he knew at *Paris*, are a great Advantage to me; and I have taken such Pains to learn the Language, that I am already more capable of Conversation than a great many Foreigners I meet with here, who have resided much longer in this Country.

I shall apply myself principally to study *the English Government*, so different from that of *Persia*, and of which *Usbec* has conceiv'd at a Distance so great an Idea.

Whatever in the Manners of this People appears to me to be *singular* and *fantastical*, I will also give thee some Account of; and if I may judge by what I have seen already, this is a Subject which will not easily be exhausted.

Communicate my Letters to *Usbec*, and he will explain such Difficulties to thee as may happen to occur; but if any thing shou'd seem to you both to be unaccountable, do not therefore immediately conclude it *false*; for the *Habits* and *Reasonings* of Men are so very different, that what appears the Excess of *Folly* in one Country, may in another be esteemed the highest *Wisdom*.

LETTER IX
SELIM *TO* MIRZA *at* Ispahan.
From *London*.

I have receiv'd thy Answers to my Letters with Pleasure, which the Distance I am at from my Friends and Country, render'd greater than thou would'st believe, I find thee very impatient to be inform'd of the Government and Policy of this Country, which I promis'd to send thee some Account of; but though I have been diligent in my Enquiries, and lost no Time since my Arrival here, I am unable to

---

1   Sophi our Master: Sultan, a Mohammedan sovereign.

answer the Questions thou demandest of me, otherwise than by acknowledging my Ignorance.

Thou askest if the *English* are as free as heretofore: The Courtiers assure me confidently that they are; but the Men who have least Relation to the Court, are daily alarming themselves and others, with the Apprehension of Danger to their Liberty. – I have been told that the Parliament is the Curb to the King's Authority; and yet I am well inform'd that the only way to Advancement in the Court is to gain a Seat in Parliament.

The House of Commons is the Representative of the Nation, nevertheless there are many great *Towns* which send *no* Deputies thither, and many Hamlets[1] almost uninhabited, that have a Right of sending *Two*. Several Members have never seen their Electors, and several are elected by the *Parliament*, who were rejected by the *People*. All the Electors swear not to *sell* their Voices, yet many of the Candidates are undone by the Expence of *buying them*. This whole Affair is involv'd in deep Mystery, and inexplicable Difficulties.

Thou askest if *Commerce* be as flourishing as formerly: Some whom I have consulted on that Head say, it is now in its Meridian; and there is really an Appearance of its being so; for *Luxury* is prodigiously encreas'd, and it is hard to imagine how it can be supported without an inexhaustible Trade: But *others* pretend, that *this very Luxury* is a Proof of its Decline; and they add, that the *Frauds* and *Vilanies* in all the *trading* Companies are so many inward Poisons, which, if not speedily expell'd, will destroy it intirely in a little time.

Thou would'st know if *Property* be so safely guarded as is generally believ'd: It is certain that the whole Power of a King of *England* cannot force an Acre of Land from the weakest of his Subjects; but a *knavish Attorney* will take away his whole Estate by those very *Laws* which were design'd for its Security: The *Judges* are uncorrupt, *Appeals* are free, and notwithstanding all these Advantages it is usually better for a Man to lose his Right than to sue for it.

These, *Mirza*, are the *Contradictions* that perplex me. My Judgment is bewilder'd in Uncertainty; I doubt my own Observations, and distrust the Relations of others: More Time, and better Information,

---

1   Hamlets: Small villages

may, perhaps, clear them up to me; till then, Modesty forbids me to impose my Conjectures upon thee, after the manner of Christian *Travellers*, whose prompt Decisions are the Effect rather of Folly than Penetration.

LETTER XXI
SELIM *to* MIRZA *at* Ispahan.

[In Letter XII, Selim began relating a thirteen part History of the Troglodites,[1] a continuation of a history that Usbec began in his *Persian Letters* from Paris, Letters XI to XIV. Selim tells Mirza in Letter XII that he is continuing the history "to shew ... by what Steps, and through what Changes, the original Good of Society is overturn'd, and Mankind becomes wickeder and more miserable in a State of Government, than they were when left in a State of Nature."]

Among the various Speculations that this modern Fashion of Philosophizing produced, there were two more pernicious than the rest, and which greatly contributed to the Corruption and Ruin of the People. One was, that Vice and Virtue were in themselves indifferent Things, and depended only on the Laws of every Country; the other, That there was neither Reward nor Punishment after this Life. – It has already been observ'd how many Defects the *Troglodites* found in their *Laws*, and how many Quibbles were invented to elude them.[2] But still there was some Restraint upon their Actions, while a Sense of Guilt was attended with Remorse, and the Apprehension of suffering in another State. But by these two Doctrines Men were left at perfect Liberty to sin out of the Reach of the Law; and Virtue was deprived of Glory here, or the Hopes of Recompence hereafter. There was a

---

1   Troglodites: In his *Persian Letters*, Usbec mentions this small nation of people who live in Arabia and "were so wicked and ferocious that there were no principles of equity or justice among them" (Montesquieu, Letter 11, 53).

2   Defects ... in their *Laws*: In Letter XIV, Selim states that "The Institution of Laws among the *Troglodites*, was attended with this inevitable ill Effect, that they begun to think every thing was right, which was not legally declared to be a Crime. It seemed, as if the natural Obligations to Virtue were destroyed, by the foreign Influence of human Authority, and Vice was not shun'd as a real Evil, but grew to be thought a forbidden Good."

third Notion, less impious indeed, but of very ill Consequences to Society, which placed all Goodness and Religion in a *Recluse and Contemplative Way of Life*.[1]

The Effect of this was, to draw off many of the best and worthiest Men from the Service of the Publick, and Administration of the Commonwealth, at a Time when their Labours were most wanted to put a Stop to the general Corruption – It is hard to say which was most destructive, an Opinion that, like the former, embolden'd Vice, or such a one as render'd Virtue impotent and useless to Mankind. –

LETTER XXII
SELIM *to* MIRZA *at* Ispahan.

While the Principles of the People were thus depraved, and their Understanding taken off from their proper Objects, the Court became the Center of Immorality and every Kind of Folly. Though Flattery had been always busy there, yet the former Kings, who were frequently at War, had been us'd to a certain military Freedom, and there were not wanting Men about them who had Courage to tell them Truth; but the Effeminacy of the present Set of Courtiers took from them all Spirit as well as Virtue, and they were as ready to suffer the basest Things, as to act the most unjust. The King,[2] wholly devoted to his Pleasures, and seldom seen out of the Walls of his Seraglio,[3] thought it sufficient for him to wear the Crown, without troubling himself with any of the Cares and Duties belonging to it: the whole Exercise and Power of the Government was lodged in the Hands of a Grand Vizir,[4] the first of that Title which the *Troglodites* had ever known. It seem'd very strange to them at the Beginning, to see the Royalty transfer'd to their Fellow Subject, and many thought it was debasing it too much. The Priests themselves were at a Loss how to make out that this Sort of Monarchy was divine; however, they found

---

1 *Recluse and Contemplative Way of Life*: This refers to Bolingbroke, his Patriots, and the Country independents who were out of power at the Court and opposed Walpole's ministry of "general Corruption" and "Vice."
2 The King: George II.
3 Seraglio: Palace, especially the part where the women are kept, the harem.
4 Grand Vizir: Sir Robert Walpole; the Grand Vizir is equated with "a Prime Minister" at the end of the paragraph.

at last, that the Grand Vizir was a God by Office, though not by Birth. If this Distinction did not satisfy the People, the Court nor the Priests were not much concern'd about it. – But a Prime Minister was not the only Novelty these Times produced.

The *Troglodites* had always been remarkable for the Manner in which they used their Women: They had a greater Esteem for them than any other of the Eastern Nations. They admitted them to a constant Share in their Conversation, and even trusted them with their private Affairs: But they never suspected that they had a Genius for publick Business, and that not only their own Families, but the State it self, might be govern'd by their Direction. They are now convinc'd of their Mistake. Several Ladies appear'd together at the Helm: The King's Mistress, the Mistress of the Vizir, two or three Mistresses of the Vizir's Favourite Officers, join'd in a political Confederacy, and manag'd all Matters as they pleas'd.[1] Their Lovers gave nothing, and acted nothing but by their Recommendation and Advice. Some times indeed they differ'd among themselves, which occasion'd great Confusion in the State; but by the pacifick Labours of good Subjects such unhappy Divisions were compos'd, and every thing went quietly on again. If there was any Defect in the Politicks of these Female Rulers, it was, that they could never comprehend any other Point or Purpose in the Art of Government but so much *Profit to themselves.*[2] The History of the *Troglodites* has recorded some of their wise and witty Sayings.

One of them was told, that by the great Decay of Trade the princi-

---

1 Several Ladies ... political Confederacy: This statement is a slight to the ministry, suggesting that the king and his ministers are governed by the whims of their women. George II's reputed mistress was Mrs. Henrietta Howard; Walpole's mistress was Maria (Molly) Skerrett; however, in order to avoid the libel laws, Lyttelton is probably making reference to the German mistresses of King George I (Ehrengard Melusina von Schulenburg, the Duchess of Kendal, and Charlotte Sophia Kielmannsegge, Countess of Darlington) who were very influential in his Court due to their taking of bribes. When their greedy involvement in the South Sea Company made them targets in 1720 for the nation's desire for revenge against the South Sea Bubble, Walpole's interventions indebted the King to him and served, in part, Walpole's meteoric rise to power after 1721.

2 *Profit to themselves*: This was an accusation levelled at Walpole and his ministry, not their mistresses. The author is ridiculing the government here by feminizing it and equating it with selfish, materialistic women.

pal Bank of the City wou'd be broke. What care I, said she, I have lain my Money out in Land.

Another was warn'd, that if better Measures were not taken, the *Troglodites* threaten'd to revolt; I am glad to hear it, replied she, for if we beat them there will be some rich Confiscations fall to me.

LETTER XXIII
SELIM *to* MIRZA.

Painful Experience had, by this Time, taught the Troglodites what their Fathers were too happy to suspect, that human Nature was not perfect enough to be trusted with excessive Power: They saw an evident Necessity of restraining that which had been given to their Kings, as well for the Dignity of the Crown itself, as for the Good of the Commonwealth.

The whole Nation unanimously concur'd in this Resolution, and that Unanimity cou'd not be resisted: They therefore consider'd by what Means to reform their Government, and did it with equal Vigour and Moderation. It was decreed that the Crown should be preserv'd to the Prince then reigning, out of respect to the Family he was of; but that he shou'd wear it under certain Limitations which divided his Authority with the Senate.[1]

To prevent the Mischiefs that might arise from evil Ministers, and the too great Power of any Favourite, they declared, that the Ministers of the King were the Servants of the People, and could not be protected by the Court, if they were found disloyal to the Nation.

Under these wise Regulations the shatter'd State recover'd itself again: Their Affairs were managed with more Discretion, and many Publick Grievances were redress'd. They thought that in limiting their Monarchy they had cut the Root of all their Evils, and flatter'd themselves with a permanent Felicity. But they quickly discover'd that this new System was not without its Inconveniencies. Very favourable Opportunities were sometimes lost by the unavoidable Slowness of their Councils, and it was often necessary to trust more People with

---

1   divided his Authority with the Senate: The idea of the limited, or mixed monarchy which guarded the liberties of the people by dividing power among the King, Lords, and Commons.

the Secret of Publick Business, than could be relied on with Security. There were many Evils which the Nature of their Government oblig-ed them to connive at, and which grew, as it were, out of the very Root of it. The Abuse of Liberty was inseparable, in many Points, from Liberty itself, and degenerated into a shameless Licentiousness. But the principal Mischief attending on this Change, was the Divi-sion of the Senate into Parties.[1] Different Judgments, different Inter-ests and Passions, were perpetually clashing with one another, and by the unequal Motion of its Wheels, the whole Machine went but heavily along.

Yet one Advantage arose from this Disorder, that the People were kept alert, and upon their Guard. The Animosities and Emulation of Particulars, secur'd the Commonwealth, as in a Seraglio; the Honour of the Husband is preserv'd by the Malice of the Eunuchs and mutual Jealousies of the Women.

Upon the Whole, the *Troglodites* might have been happy in the Liberty they had gain'd, if the same publick Spirit which establish'd, cou'd have continu'd to maintain it.

LETTER XXIV
SELIM *to* MIRZA *at* Ispahan.

There was in the Senate a certain Man of great natural Cunning, and Penetration, factious, enterprizing, vers'd in Business, and above all, very knowing in the Disposition of the Times in which he lived.[2] This Man came secretly to the King, and entertain'd him with the following Discourse.

'I perceive, Sir, you are very much cast down with the Bounds that have been set to your Authority: But perhaps you have not lost so much as you imagine. – The People are very proud of their own Work, and look with great Satisfaction on the Outside of their new-erected Government;[3] but those who can see the Inside too, find every thing too rotten and superficial to last very long.

---

1   Parties: Whig and Tory; Court and Country.
2   a certain Man ...: Sir Robert Walpole.
3   new-erected Government: The mixed, constitutional government of monarch, Lords, and Commons as ratified by the Revolution Settlement of 1701.

'The two Things in Nature the most repugnant and inconstant with each other, are the Love of Liberty, and the Love of Money: The last is so strong among your Subjects, that it is impossible the former can subsist. I say, Sir, they are not HONEST enough to be FREE – Look round the Nation, and see whether their Manners agree with their Constitution. Is there a Virtue which Want does not disgrace, or a Vice which Riches cannot dignify? Has not Luxury infected all Degrees of Men amongst them? Which way is that Luxury to be supported? It must necessarily create a Dependance which will soon put an End to this Dream of Liberty. Have you a Mind to fix your Power on a sure and lasting Basis? Fix it on the Vices of Mankind: Set up private Interest against publick; apply to the Wants and Vanities of Particulars; shew those who lead the People, that they may better find their Account in betraying than defending them: This, Sir, is a short Plan of such a Conduct as wou'd make you really superior to all Restraint, without breaking in upon those *nominal Securities*, which the *Troglodites* are more attach'd to a great deal than they are to the Things themselves. If you please to trust the Management to me, I shall not be afraid of being obnoxious to the *Spirit of Liberty*; for in a little while I will extinguish every Spark of it; nor of being liable to the *Justice* of the Nation, for my *Crime* itself shall be my *Protection*.

LETTER XXXVII
SELIM to MIRZA at *Ispahan*.
From *London*.

I had, last Night, so extraordinary a Dream, and it made such an Impression on my Mind, that I cannot forbear writing thee an Account of it.

I thought I was transported, on a sudden, to the Palace of *Ispahan*. Our mighty Lord was sitting on a Throne, the Splendour of which my Eyes cou'd hardly bear: At the Foot of it were his *Emirs*,[1] and Great Officers, all prostrate on the Ground in Adoration, and expecting their Fate from his Commands. Around him stood a Multitude of his Guards, ready to execute any Orders he shou'd give, and striking

---

1   *Emirs*: Princes and dignitaries.

Terror into the Hearts of all his Subjects. – My Soul was aw'd with the Majesty of the Scene, and I said to my self, Can a King of *England* compare himself to this? Can he, whose Authority is confin'd within the narrow Bounds of Law, pretend to an Equality with a Monarch, whose Power has no Limits but his Will?

I had scarce made this Reflection, when, turning my Eyes a second time towards the Throne, instead of the *Sophi*, I saw an *Eunuch*[1] seated there, who seem'd to govern more despotically than he. The *Eunuch* was soon changed into a Woman, who also took the *Tiara* and the Sword; to her succeeded another, and then a Third: But, before she was well establish'd in her Seat, the Captain of the Guards that stood around us march'd up to the Throne, and seiz'd upon it: In that Moment I look'd and beheld the *Sophi* lying strangled on the Floor, with his *Vizir*, and three of his *Sultanas*.[2] Struck with Horror at the Spectacle, I left the Palace, and going out into the City, saw it abandon'd to the Fury of the Soldiers, who pillaged all its Riches, and cut the Throats of the defenceless Inhabitants. From thence I made my Escape into the Country, which was a waste uncultivated Desert, where I found nothing but Idleness and Want.

O, said I, how much happier is *England*, and how much greater are its Kings! Their Throne is establish'd upon Justice, and therefore cannot be overturn'd. They are guarded by the Affections of their People, and have no military Violence to fear. They are the most to be honour'd of all Princes, because their Government is best fram'd to make their Subjects rich, happy, and secure. –

LETTER XLV
SELIM to MIRZA at *Ispahan*.
From *London*.

I lately fell into Discourse with an *Englishman*, who has well examin'd the Constitution of his Country: I begg'd him to tell me what he thought of the present State of it. Two principal Evils, answer'd he, are making way for arbitrary Power, if the Court shou'd ever be inclin'd to take Advantage of them, *viz. Corruption* and *Eloquence*: The last is,

---

1   *Eunuch*: A castrated man, usually a guard of the harem as he would not have any temptation to trifle with the Sophi's wives.
2   *Sultanas*: A female Turkish or Persian sovereign; wives of the Sophi.

if possible, more mischievous than the first; for it seduces those whom Money cou'd not tempt. It is the most pernicious of all our Refinements, and the most to be dreaded in a free Country. To speak Truth is the Privilege of a Freeman; to do it roundly and plainly, is his Glory: Thus it was, that the ancient *Romans* debated every Thing that concern'd the Common-wealth, at a Time when they best knew how to govern, before *Greece* had infected them with Rhetorick: As nothing was propounded to them with Disguise, they easily judg'd what was most for their Honour and Interest. But the Thing call'd Eloquence is of another Kind: It is less the Talent of enforcing Truth, than of imposing Falshood; it does not depend on a true Knowledge of the Matter in debate, for generally it aims at nothing more than a specious Appearance; nor is Wisdom a necessary Quality in the Composition of an Orator; he can do without it very well, provided he has the happy Facility of discoursing smoothly, and asserting boldly. I own to thee, *Mirza*, this Account surpriz'd me; we have no Knowledge in the *East* of such an Eloquence as this Man describ'd: It is our Custom to speak naturally and pertinently, without ever imagining that there was an Art in it, or that it was possible to talk finely upon a Subject which we do not understand.

Pray Sir, said I, when these Orators you tell me of have been caught two or three times *in a Lie*, don't you treat them with the utmost Contempt? Quite the contrary, answer'd he, the whole Merit and Pride of their Profession is to *deceive*: They are to lay false Colours upon every thing, and the greater the Imposition is, the greater their Reputation: The Orator who can only persuade us to act against some of our lesser Interests, is *but a Genius of the second Rate*; but he who can compel us by his Eloquence to violate the most essential, is *an able Man indeed*, and will certainly *rise very high*. I suppose, it may be your custom in *Persia* to bestow Employments on such Persons as have particularly qualified themselves for them; you put the Care of the Army and the Marine into the Hands of Soldiers and Seamen; you make one Man Secretary of State, because he has been bred in foreign Courts, and understands the Interests of your neighbouring Princes; to another you trust the Revenue, because he is skilful in Oeconomy, and has prov'd himself above the Temptation of embezzilling what passes through his Hands. Yes, replied I, this is surely the right Method, and I conclude it must be yours. No, said he, we are above those vulgar Prejudices; such Qualifications are not requisite among us; to be fit for all or any of these Posts, one must be *a good Speaker in Parliament*. How! said I, because I make a fine Harangue upon a Treaty of Peace, am I therefore fit to superintend an Army? We think so, answer'd he: And if I can plausibly defend a Minister of State from a reasonable Charge brought against him, have I thereby a Title to be taken into the Administration? Beyond Dispute, in this Country, answer'd he. Why then, by *Mahomet*, said I, your Government may well be Sick: What a distemper'd Body must that be, whose Members are so monstrously out of Joint, that there is no one Part in its proper Place! If my Tongue shou'd undertake to do the Office of my Head and Arms, the Absurdity and the Impotency wou'd be just the same.

Yet thus, said he, we go on, lamely enough, I must confess, but still admiring our own wise Policy, and laughing at the rest of the World.

You may laugh, replied I, as you think fit: But if the *Sultan*, my Master, had among his Counsellors such an *Orator* as you describe, a Fellow that wou'd prate away Truth, Equity, and common Sense; by the Tomb of our holy Prophet, he wou'd make a *Mute* of him, and set him to watch over the *Seraglio*, instead of the *State*.

At these Words, I was oblig'd to take my Leave, and our Discourse was broke off till another Meeting.

LETTER LXXIX
SELIM to MIRZA at *Ispahan*.
From *London*.

I felicitate Thee, *Mirza*, on thy new Dignity; I bow myself reverently before thee, not with the Heart of a Flatterer, but a Friend: The Favour of thy Master shines upon thee; he has rais'd thee to the right Hand of his Throne; the Treasures of *Persia* are committed to thy Custody:[1] If thou behavest thyself honestly and wisely, I shall think thee much *Greater* from thy *Advancement*; if otherwise, much *Lower* than before. Thou hast undertaken a Charge very important to thy Prince, and to his People; both are equally concern'd in thy Administration, both have equally a Right to thy Fidelity. If ever thou shalt separate

---

1   Treasures of *Persia* ... thy Custody: Mirza has been made the the Persian equivalent of Walpole's position: the First Lord of the Treasury. Selim's advice to Mirza is also Lyttelton's to Walpole.

their Interests, if those shalt set up the one against the other, know, it will end in the Ruin of *Both*. Do not imagine, that thy Master will be richer by draining his Subjects of their Wealth: Such *Gains* are *irreparable Losses*; they may serve a present sordid Purpose; but dry up the Sources of Opulence for Futurity. I wou'd recommend to thy Attention and Remembrance, the Saying of a famous *English Treasurer* in the happy Reign of Queen *Elizabeth*.[1] *I don't love*, said that truly able Minister, *to see the Treasury swell like a distemper'd Spleen, when the other Parts of the State are in a Consumption.* – Be it thy Care to prevent such a Decay; and, to that End, not only save the Publick all unnecessary Expence, but so *digest* and order what is needful, that *Perplexity* may not serve to cover *Fraud*, nor *Incapacity* lurk behind *Confusion*. Rather submit to any Difficulty and Distress in the Conduct of thy Ministry, than *Anticipate* the Revenues of the Government without an absolute Necessity; for such Expedients are a *temporary Ease*, but a *permanent Destruction*.

In relieving the People from their Taxes, let it also by thy Glory to relieve them from the infinite Number of *Tax Gatherers*, which, far worse than the *Turkish* or *Russian* Armies, have *harrast* and *plunder'd* our poor Country.

As thou art the Distributor of the Bounties of the Crown, make them the Reward of Service and of Merit; not the Hire of Parasites and Flatterers to thy Master, or *thyself*. But above all, as thou art now a *publick Person*, elevate thy Mind beyond any *private View*; try to enrich the Publick before thyself; and think less of establishing thy Family at the Head of thy Country, than of setting thy Country at the Head of *Asia*.

If thou can'st steadily persevere in such a Conduct, thy Prince will want *Thee* more than Thou dost *Him*: If thy buildest thy Fortune on *any other Basis*, how high soever it may rise, it will be tottering from the *Weakness of its Foundation*.

He alone is a *Minister of State*, whose Services are *necessary to the Publick*; the rest are *the Creatures of Caprice*, and feel their Slavery even *in their Power*.

---

1 famous *English Treasurer.* William Cecil, Baron Burghley (1520–98). He was Elizabeth I's principal advisor for forty years, serving as her Secretary of State (1558–72) and then as her Lord High Treasurer (1572–98). Elizabeth's reign was held up by Bolingbroke as the paragon of monarchies.

LETTER LXXXII
SELIM to MIRZA at *Ispahan*.
From *London*.

My Ship waits for me in the Mouth of the River *Thames*, and thou may'st expect e'er long to see thy Friend, with a *Mind* a good deal alter'd by his Travels, but a *Heart* which to thee is still *the same*.

It would be unjust and ungrateful in me to quit *this Island*, without expressing a very high Esteem of the good *Sense*, *Sincerity*, and *good Nature* I have found among *the English*: To these Qualities I might also add *Politeness*; which certainly they have as good a Title to as *any of their Neighbours*; but I am afraid that this Accomplishment has been acquir'd too much at the Expence of other Virtues more solid and essential. Of their *Industry*, their Commerce is a Proof; and for their *Valour*, let their *Enemies* declare it. Of their *Faults* I will at present say no more, but that *many* of them are *newly introduced*, and so contrary to the Genius of the People, that one wou'd hope they might be easily rooted out. They are undoubtedly, all Circumstances consider'd, a very *Great*, a very *Powerful*, and Happy Nation: but how long they shall *continue so* depends entirely on the *Preservation of their Liberty*. To the *Constitution* of their Government alone are attach'd all these Blessings and Advantages: Shou'd That ever be *corrupted* or *depraved*, they must expect to become the most *contemptible*, and most *unhappy* of Mankind. For what can so much aggravate the Wretchedness of an Oppress'd and Ruin'd People, as the Remembrance of former Freedom and Prosperity? All the Images and Traces of their Liberty, which, it is probable, no Change will quite destroy, must be a perpetual Reproach and Torment to them, for having so degenerately parted with *their Birth-right*. And if Slavery is to be endured, where is the Man that wou'd not rather choose it, under the warm Sun of *Agra* or *Ispahan*, than in the Northern Climate and barren Soil of *England*?

I therefore take my Leave of my Friends here, with this affectionate, and well-design'd Advice, That they shou'd vigilantly *watch over their Constitution*, and guard it by those Bulwarks which alone are able to secure *it, Justice, Vigour, Perseverance*, and *Frugality*.

FINIS.

Bibliography

[This list includes items consulted for the historical and literary background of the *Adventures of Eovaai* as well as works cited in the Introduction and used or mentioned in the explanatory notes to the novel and the Appendices.]

Armstrong, Nancy. *Desire and Domestic Fiction: A Political History of the Novel.* New York: Oxford University Press, 1987.

Aristotle. *The Politics.* Trans. T.A. Sinclair. Revised and re-presented by Trevor J. Saunders. Markham: Penguin Books Canada, Ltd., 1962. Rev. 1981.

Barker, George Fisher Russell. "George Lyttelton." *Dictionary of National Biography.* Eds. Sir Leslie Stephen and Sir Sidney Lee. 22 vols. London: Oxford University Press, 1917, rpt. 1973. 12:369-74.

Battestin, Martin C., and Fredson Bowers, eds. *The History of Tom Jones, A Foundling.* By Henry Fielding. 2 vols. Oxford: Clarendon Press, 1974.

Black, Jeremy, and Roy Porter, eds. *The Penguin Dictionary of Eighteenth-Century History.* Harmondsworth, Middlesex: Penguin Books Ltd., 1996.

Bolingbroke, Henry St. John, Viscount. *The Works of Lord Bolingbroke.* 4 vols. London: Frank Cass & Company Limited, 1844, rpt. 1967.

Butler, Iris. *Rule of Three: Sarah, Duchess of Marlborough, and her Companions in Power.* London: Hodder and Stoughton, 1967.

Dickinson, H. T. *Liberty and Property: Political Ideology in Eighteenth-Century Britain.* New York: Holmes and Meier Publishers, Inc., 1977.

Fielding, Henry. *Jonathan Wild.* Ed. David Nokes. Markham: Penguin Books Canada Ltd., 1987.

Gallagher, Catherine. "Political Crimes and Fictional Alibis: The Case of Delarivier Manley." *Eighteenth Century Studies* 23 (Summer, 1990): 502-21.

Gay, John. *The Beggar's Opera. Eighteenth-Century Plays.* Intro. Ricardo Quintana. New York: Random House, Inc., 1952. 179-237.

Goldgar, Bertrand A. *Walpole and the Wits: The Relation of Politics to Literature, 1722-1742.* Lincoln & London: University of Nebraska Press, 1976.

Halifax, George Savile (Marquis of). "The Lady's New Year Gift; or, Advice to a Daughter." *Complete Works.* Ed. J.P. Kenyon. Middlesex: Penguin Books, 1969. 270-313.

Halsband, Robert. *Lord Hervey: Eighteenth-Century Courtier.* New York and

Oxford: Oxford University Press, 1974.

Haywood, Eliza. *Memoirs of a Certain Island Adjacent to the Kingdom of Utopia*. 2 vols. 2nd ed. London: 1726.

——. *The Secret History of the Present Intrigues of the Court of Caramania* (1727). Intro. Josephine Grieder. New York & London: Garland Publishing, Inc., 1972.

Hervey, John, Lord. *Lord Hervey's Memoirs*. Ed. Romney Sedgwick. London: William Kimber & Co., 1952.

Hill, Brian W. *Sir Robert Walpole: "Sole and Prime Minister."* London: The Penguin Group. Hamish Hamilton Ltd., 1989.

Kramnick, Isaac. *Bolingbroke and his Circle: The Politics of Nostalgia in the Age of Walpole*. Cambridge, Mass.: Harvard University Press, 1968.

Locke, John. *Of Civil Government: Second Treatise*. Intro. Russell Kirk. Chicago: Henry Regnery Company, 1955.

Lyttelton, George. *Letters from a Persian in England to his Friend at Ispahan*. 4th ed. London: 1735.

Mack, Maynard. *The Garden and the City: Retirement and Politics in the Later Poetry of Pope 1731-1743*. Toronto: University of Toronto Press, 1969.

Mandeville, Bernard. *The Fable of the Bees*. Ed. Phillip Harth. Harmondsworth, Middlesex: Penguin Books Ltd., 1970.

Montesquieu, Charles-Louis de Secondat. *Persian Letters*. Trans. C.J. Betts. Markham: Penguin Books Canada Ltd., 1973, rpt. 1987.

Ovid. *Metamorphoses*. Trans. Rolfe Humphries. Bloomington & London: Indiana University Press, 1955.

Plumb, J. H. *The First Four Georges*. London: B.T. Batsford Ltd., 1956.

——. *Sir Robert Walpole: The Making of a Statesman*. London: The Cresset Press, 1956.

——. *Sir Robert Walpole: The King's Minister*. London: The Cresset Press, 1960.

Pocock, J.G.A. "Machiavelli, Harrington and English Political Ideologies in the Eighteenth Century." *Politics, Language and Time: Essays in Political Thought and History*. Ed. J.G.A. Pocock. London: Methuen & Co. Ltd., 1971.104-147.

——. *The Machiavellian Moment: Florentine Political Thought and the Atlantic Republican Tradition*. Princeton: Princeton University Press, 1975.

Pope, Alexander. *The Dunciad. The Twickenham Edition of the Poems of Alexander Pope*. Ed. James Sutherland. 6 vols. London: Methuen & Co. Ltd., 1943. Rev. 1953. Vol. 5.

———. "Epistle II: To a Lady: Of the Characters of Women." *The Twickenham Edition of the Poems of Alexander Pope.* Ed. F.W. Bateson. 6 vols. London: Methuen & Co. Ltd., 1951. 3.ii: 44-71.

———. *The Rape of the Lock. The Twickenham Edition of the Poems of Alexander Pope.* Ed. John Butt. 6 vols. London: Methuen & Co. Ltd., 1940. Rev. 1954. Vol. 2.

Savage, Richard. *An Author to be Lett* (1729). Ed. James Sutherland. Augustan Reprint Society 84. Los Angeles: William Andrews Clark Memorial Library, University of California, 1960.

Secombe, Thomas. "Charles Seymour, 6th Duke of Somerset." *Dictionary of National Biography.* Eds. Sir Leslie Stephen and Sir Sidney Lee. 22 vols. London: Oxford University Press, 1917. Rpt. 1973. 17:1235-37.

Speck, W.A. *Stability and Strife: England, 1714-1760.* Cambridge, Mass.: Harvard University Press, 1977.

Staal, Julius D.W. *The New Patterns in the Sky: Myths and Legends of the Stars.* Blacksburg, VA: McDonald and Woodward Publishing Company, 1988.

Swift, Jonathan. *Gulliver's Travels.* Ed. Paul Turner. Oxford & New York: Oxford University Press, 1986.

Varey, Simon. *Henry St. John, Viscount Bolingbroke.* Twayne's English Authors Series 362. Boston: Twayne Publishers, 1984.

Selected Secondary Sources on Eliza Haywood, *Eovaai*, and other Works:

Ballaster, Rosalind. *Seductive Forms: Women's Amatory Fiction from 1684-1740.* Oxford: Clarendon, 1992.

Beasley, Jerry. "Politics and Moral Idealism: The Achievement of Some Early Women Novelists." *Fetter'd or Free? British Women Novelists, 1670-1815.* Eds. Mary Anne Schofield and Cecelia Macheski. Athens, Ohio: Ohio University Press, 1986. 216-36.

———. "Portraits of a Monster: Robert Walpole and Early English Prose Fiction." *Eighteenth-Century Studies* 14 (1981): 406-431.

Blouch, Christine. "Eliza Haywood and the Romance of Obscurity." *Studies in English Literature 1500-1900* 31.3 (Summer 1991): 535-51.

Craft-Fairchild, Catherine. *Masquerade and Gender: Disguise and Female Identity in Eighteenth-Century Fictions by Women.* University Park, PA.: Pennsylvania State University Press, 1993.

Firmager, Gabrielle M. "Eliza Haywood: Some Further Light on Her Background?" *N&Q* 38 (1991): 181-83.

Gibson, Suzanne Byrl. "The Eighteenth Century Oriental Tales of Eliza Haywood, Frances Sheridan and Ellis Cornelia Knight." Diss. McMaster University, 1996.

Grieder, Josephine. "Introduction." *Adventures of Eovaai, Princess of Ijaveo*. New York & London: Garland Publishing, Inc., 1972.

Lockwood, Thomas. "Eliza Haywood in 1749: *Dalinda*, and Her Pamphlet on the Pretender." *N&Q* 36 (1989): 475-77.

London, April. "Placing the Female: The Metonymic Garden in Amatory and Pious Narrative, 1700-1740." *Fetter'd or Free? British Women Novelists 1670-1815*. Eds. Mary Anne Schofield and Cecilia Macheski. Athens, Ohio: Ohio University Press, 1986.

McBurney, William H. "Mrs. Penelope Aubin and the Early Eighteenth-Century English Novel." *Huntington Library Quarterly* 20 (1957): 245-67.

Merritt, Juliette. "'That Devil Curiosity, which too much haunts the Minds of Women': Eliza Haywood's *Female Spectators*." *Lumen* 16 (forthcoming, 1998).

Nestor, Deborah J. "Virtue Rarely Rewarded: Ideological Subversion and Narrative Form in Haywood's Later Fiction." *Studies in English Literature 1500-1900* 34.3 (Summer 1994): 579-98.

Oakleaf, David, ed. "Introduction." *Love in Excess*. Peterborough: Broadview Press, 1994.

Richetti, John J. *Popular Fiction before Richardson: Narrative Patterns 1700-1739*. Oxford: Clarendon, 1969.

Schofield, Mary Anne. *Eliza Haywood*. Twayne's English Authors Series 411. Boston: Twayne Publishers, 1985.

——. *Masking and Unmasking the Female Mind: Disguising Romances in Feminine Fiction, 1713-1799*. Newark: University of Delaware Press, 1990.

——. *Quiet Rebellion: The Fictional Heroines of Eliza Haywood*. Washington: University Press of America, 1981.

Spencer, Jane. *The Rise of the Woman Novelist from Aphra Behn to Jane Austen*. Oxford: Basil Blackwell, 1986.

Todd, Janet. *The Sign of Angellica: Women, Writing and Fiction, 1660-1800*. London: Virago Press, 1989.

Whicher, George Frisbie. *The Life and Romances of Mrs. Eliza Haywood*. New York: Columbia University Press, 1915.

Wilputte, Earla A. "The Textual Architecture of Eliza Haywood's *Adventures of Eovaai.*" *Essays in Literature* 22, 1 (1995): 31-44.

——. "Gender Inversions in Haywood's *The Distress'd Orphan, or, Love in a Mad-house.*" *Lumen* 14 (1995): 109-117.

——. "Wife-Pandering in Three Eighteenth-Century Plays." *Studies in English Literature 1500-1900* 38.3 (Summer 1998): 447-464 [includes Haywood's *A Wife to be Lett*].

broadview literary texts

"This is a series in which the editing is something of an art form."
The Washington Post

"Broadview's format is inviting. Clearly printed on good paper, with distinctive photographs on the covers, the books provide the physical pleasure that is so often a component of enticing one to pick up a book in the first place.... And, by providing a broad context, the editors have done us a great service."
Eighteenth-Century Fiction

"These editions *[Frankenstein, Hard Times, Heart of Darkness]* are top-notch—far better than anything else in the market today."
Craig Keating, Langara College

The Broadview Literary Texts series represents an important effort to see the ever-changing canon of English literature from new angles. The series brings together texts that have long been regarded as classics with lesser-known texts that offer a fresh light—and that in many cases may also claim to be of real importance in our literary tradition.

Each volume in the series presents the text together with a variety of documents from the period, enabling readers to get a fuller, richer sense of the world out of which it emerged. Samples of the science available for Mary Shelley to draw on in writing *Frankenstein,* stark reports from the Congo in the late nineteenth century that help to illuminate Conrad's *Heart of Darkness;* late eighteenth-century statements on the proper roles for women and men that help contextualize the feminist themes of the late eighteenth-century novels *Millenium Hall* and *Something New*—these are the sorts of fascinating background materials that round out each Broadview Literary Texts edition.

Each volume also includes a full introduction, chronology, bibliography, and explanatory notes. Newly typeset and produced on high-quality paper in an attractive Trade paperback format, Broadview Literary Texts are a delight to handle as well as to read.

The distinctive cover images for the series are also designed (like the duotone process itself) to combine two slightly different perspectives. Early photographs inevitably evoke a sense of pastness, yet the images for most volumes in the series involve a conscious use of anachronism. The covers are thus designed to draw attention to social and temporal context, while suggesting that the works themselves may also relate to periods other than that from which they emerged—including our own era.